RACE

A BLACK LIVES MATTER THRILLER

SLMN

Kingston Imperial

Race Copyright © 2021 by Kingston Imperial, LLC

Printed in the USA

Rights Department, 144 North 7th Street, #255 Brooklyn N.Y. 11249

First Edition:

Book and Jacket Design: Damion Scott & PiXiLL Designs

Cataloging in Publication data is on file with the library of Congress

Trade Paperback: ISBN 9781954220140

EBook: ISBN 9781954220157

1

If you'd asked me that August morning if I was surprised, I'd have looked you square in the eye, shook my head, and told you, "*Why the fuck would I be surprised? Look around you, we live in a nation that always chooses hate.*" Thing is, as much as I'd like to pretend, I've become inured to the subtle racism as much as the not-so-subtle shit, truth is I didn't really have a clue. But I was going to learn, real fast.

Maybe it was down to the heat. It had been unbearable for the better part of two weeks. Humid, sticky heat. The kind of heat that gets under your skin and into your brain and makes you do stupid shit because your brain's fried. Around the office we called it short circuit heat. The amount of brains that melted during these short circuit weeks was frankly frightening. And it didn't help the tension that had been building all summer long. That stuff has been on the simmer for a long time, pressure building and building until something had to blow. It was always going to be a mess when it did, the only question was what sort of mess. Looking back, we call it the inciting incident. That's a fancy way of saying when the story of the cops shooting a kid and his dog broke there was no going back for this place. And I hold my hand up, I must shoulder some of the blame. The piece I wrote for the paper the next day didn't help diffuse things. My only defense, that's not my job. I'm a watcher. I watch. I tell you what I see. I don't put myself into the story.

Or I didn't before now.

The boy and his dog changed the way I thought about myself and my place in this world—and more importantly my responsibility as a voice.

"You got something for me, Caleb?"

"Still working on it, Phil. I want to get this right. It's important."

Phil leaned in over my shoulder. That was his management style—hot breath on the back of the neck. He was doing his rounds, which usually meant barking out at anyone running things close to the wire. He was a born worrier. He wanted everything in place well ahead of print deadlines. The closer drop-dead came, the more stressed he became about every square inch of white space that needed to be filled.

The truth is I was done, and had been for half an hour, but I was second guessing myself. It wasn't like I hadn't done this a thousand times before, but this one felt different.

I felt Phil nodding along behind me, then stop cold.

I knew what he was going to say before he said it.

"What the fuck's that?" He jabbed a fat finger at the third paragraph.

"It's about the boy's dog."

"I can see it's about the fucking dog. Lose it. We don't do dead pets."

"But it's important."

"Really? You've got a dead kid. What flavor does a dead dog add? It's just a fucking dog. The cops shot it because it threatened their safety. Animals are unpredictable. They're all instinct. In a situation like that, they want to protect their masters. They might as well be rabid junkyard dogs."

"It was a Bichon Frise," I said, pointing out the obvious flaw in his reasoning.

"A what?" he snapped, like thin ice cracking under my feet. But there's a time to retreat and a time when you just have to put your full weight on the ice and trust it will hold you.

Maybe I should have hit delete on the paragraph and left it at that, the tragedy of the boy and his dog cut down to the tragedy of the boy. That was enough.

But—and ain't that one of the most powerful words in the language? —it wasn't right. And it was important to say exactly what I knew, not some watered down, more palatable version of it. Because the truth has to mean something if we're ever going to escape this Post-Truth world.

"The dog that three armed cops were so fucking frightened of?" I shook my head. "Small enough to fit in Stacy's purse."

Stacy paused at the sound of her name and looked over at us. She had a bag slung over her shoulder. Phil's eyes went to the bag, running whatever mental calculations he needed to realize that we weren't talking Cujo here. The moment dragged out, surrounded by the sound of keys and the low-level hum of computer fans. Phil had no words. I couldn't remember the last time he'd been struck dumb?

Even so, part of me thought he was still going to insist that I still cut the paragraph, that we couldn't afford to upset the local cops. That's the small-town trade-off. We feed off each other, pilot fish and shark. One can't exist without the other. Well, it can, but life is worse. We needed each other to keep the peace, that was the usual argument. Hell, it wouldn't have been the first time he'd backed down. but not this time. He nodded, and just said, "Good job. Run it and be damned. A fucking toy dog. Bastards."

He headed back into his glass-doored office. Maybe he still had his doubts. Maybe he still feared the consequences. But he'd made his decision and he was going to stick to it and be damned. He was a genuine News Man.

3

I sent the file to print and leaned back in my chair, hands behind my head.

It was done.

A couple of the others looked my way, then the first of them got up and went over to the subs desk to read about the boy and his dog. One by one, they followed, the sickness they felt plain on their faces.

Within an hour of the paper hitting the newsstands the whole world had gone mad.

2

Less than 24 hours after the kid had taken that bullet, the world had started to change.

At first it had been a handful of people gathered outside the police station, but within an hour it was thirty easily, within two it was sixty and growing, with spreading. I figured it would be upwards of four or five hundred come dawn, and then more, with a righteous anger sustaining them. I had my orders, get down there and get whatever I could. Phil wasn't big on the specifics, and it really didn't matter what the something was, if it made good copy. He'd have done it himself a few years ago, but he'd grown lazy, and liked to chase stories about runaway dogs being found and hero fire fighters. This sort of stuff, not so much. Plus, and he wasn't about to say it out loud, there was the other thing... the color of my skin.

I'm not an idiot, he wanted to get something out of the police, and they'd clam up facing a black reporter, closing ranks. They wouldn't see me as an ally. They'd see me as the enemy. It was racial profiling, but this whole world was constructed around racial profiling. But Phil was smart, I was only the first line of attack, after my story, he'd send Stacy in for the kill. A pretty white woman was going to look like the ally they needed, they'd talk to her differently than they would to me, especially when racial tensions were running high. Like I said, I'm not an idiot. I know how the game works, and luckily for me, so did she. That's what made us the dream team.

I arrived to see four officers standing outside, shotguns at the ready.

It wasn't exactly a picture of peace and contentment, let's put it that way.

There was an edge to the atmosphere that went beyond tension. This was cut it with a knife shit. Pent up violence almost desperate to explode.

The protesters gathered around the stone steps that rose to the station door, some crushed up on the sidewalk, most spilled out into the road making sure no traffic came or went. But, for now, they weren't trying to crush in closer. They chanted the kid's name. They issued cries for justice. There were some hastily made placards, some with misspelled words but bang-on sentiments, and that was what mattered most.

I looked around the crowd in search of familiar faces and saw a few I kind of recognized, but none of the names leapt to mind. That was the problem with living and working in a place like this; you met plenty of people but knew hardly any of them. Cities, like it or not, are some of the most crowded, and at the same time loneliest places in the world. It wasn't about being alone, it was about being cut off, isolated, made to feel like you didn't belong. The loneliness inflicted by a city was cruel and unusual punishment, end of conversation.

While I was busy being philosophical, a battered old bus with rust eating into its sides pulled up a block away and at least another couple of dozen people spilled out, already chanting for justice, for the value of a life to mean something. They punched their placards into the air. It didn't take much for the volume to escalate, these newcomers adding anger and threat. I imagined myself in the place of those four cops on the steps with their rifles, and through their eyes saw a baying mob. It was intimidating, even this close to their home turf, or maybe especially because it was this close to their home turf. Put it this way, it didn't take long for reinforcements to join them, front of the line, a man that pretty much everyone in the crowd would have recognized.

Chief of Police Able Dwyer had no problem with being seen. He was that kind of man. He enjoyed publicity. Hell, he milked every ounce of it. There was the inevitable talk of him running for mayor down the line. This was a man going places. Destined. I'm a cynical sort, goes with the territory, but I couldn't help but wonder if he'd been holding out for a camera crew to catch a glimpse of him in action. That would be his style. I saw at least a dozen camera phones pointed his way. No TV cameras. Yet. But they would come.

He raised his hands, calling for silence.

The gesture had zero effect.

The babble of voices grew louder, angrier. It was virtually impossible to make out what anyone was saying, and I mean anyone, even the guy standing next to me. So many voices had all become one, but their words had lost shape.

Dwyer remained calm.

He just stood there, waiting, motionless.

Behind him the glass doors opened, and a dozen more officers came out.

These ones were in full riot gear, with plastic shields creating a barrier. Nothing about the move was deescalating the situation, it was inflammatory, surely, he could see that? Right now, it was peaceful, bar the shouting. But deploying riot cops, even if only to hold the line, it projected an expectation of violence. They expected the crowd to turn ugly. Thing is, from where I was standing, any ugliness wasn't going to come from the protesters.

On cue another van arrived, this one with broadcast antenna and a huge station logo on the side.

Dwyer waited for the cameraman, and the on-camera talent, a young woman, to emerge, then raised his hands again, making a show of calling for calm. I'd seen the woman a few times, but never on anything I would have considered high profile. It took me a second to drag her name up from the depths of my memory. Alicia White. Dwyer waited for her to get into position before he launched into his big speech. The whole thing was a set-up.

"Folks, please," More placating gestures. "I know you're all upset, believe me, I get it," he began, raising his voice to be sure it carried above the rabble. "You've lost one of your own, and it is a tragedy. It truly is. When this community hurts, I hurt. When this community bleeds, I bleed," someone heckled loudly enough that I could hear his bullshit from the other side of the crowd. The mics wouldn't have missed it, but they'd mute it out in the editorial suite later. "There will be a full investigation into what happened. No whitewash. A full and transparent investigation, and if it turns out there is wrongdoing involved, there will be repercussions. Every officer with me is dedicated to the safety of this city and its citizens. They are one of you. We all are, and this is not an easy time for any of us..."

He almost had me believing his polished spiel, but there's this old saying, if you can fake sincerity, you can fake anything, and Dwyer was faking it like Sally meeting Harry in that diner scene. The only thing he wasn't doing was banging the table.

The noise began to abate.

People tried to listen to what he had to say. They wanted to hear it. I had no idea if they believed a word of it, but that's a whole different thing.

I turned my attention to Alicia White and her cameraman, more out of professional interest than genuine curiosity. I knew how this worked. She had the camera, she was the one going to blessed with an audience with Dwyer when this was all over, and it was going to be her questions going out on the hour every hour as the studio ate this news story up for the masses. If I was lucky, I might get close enough to listen, meaning I might even get my story in before hers went out, meaning I'd get to look good with Phil.

Someone pushed me from behind. I caught my balance and turned, realizing the size of the crowd had grown by another couple of hundred protestors in the time I'd been here. No surprise in that. What jarred was the sight of more than a few white faces in the crowd. Allies. They looked like ordinary working Joes, not media representatives, and their voices were just as loud as the brothers and sisters demanding justice.

It was good to see.

Together we are strong. It's a simple creed.

I half-thought I recognized one of them; he was the kind of guy who'd look more at home in a bar room brawl breaking skulls than a peaceful protest demanding justice be done, but I have to admit, right at that second, I thought little of it. I couldn't remember where I had seen him before, or what his name was. Jed? Jez? Something like that.

"But and I can't stress this enough, what is really important is that you give me the time and space to investigate this properly... I can't do my job—" Dwyer stopped abruptly, mid-thought process, as something was hurled from within in the crowd. It missed him by maybe a foot but hit one of the officers standing behind him.

I hadn't seen who'd thrown it, only the general direction it had come from. However, I didn't miss the backs of two white guys slinking away from the crowd, neither one of them looking back even for a moment. They'd done what they set out to do, and like the gunshot heard around the world, that glass bottle hurled from the middle of the crowd ensured all hell was let loose.

Cries went up. Voices raw.

Another dozen officers emerged from inside the station house, all of them in riot gear. Some carried night sticks, banging them on their plastic shields, others appeared to be wielding tasers.

There was this horrible feeling that the bottle gave them permission to do what they'd wanted to do from minute one, crack a few black skulls without the risk of comeback.

The woman in front of me screamed at the swing of the first baton, and by the time the taser was unleashed, its electrified heads anchoring onto the chest of an old guy who'd been foolish enough to dare climb the first steps, still not even close to Dwyer, she was hysterical.

The man jerked and thrashed as he fell to the ground, the current charging through him making him dance with guilty feet —no rhythm—but I couldn't tell if he screamed or not, for the rage of the crowd drowned out everything else. He fell backwards. The crowd behind him stepped back, flinching away from the brutal surge of electricity, none of them saving him from the fall. I knew without being able to see or hear that his head had hit the concrete with a sickening thud. I knew there'd be blood, too.

"Caleb!"

I heard a woman's voice calling my name as the wall of riot shields pushed into the crowd. Some of them pushed back but others desperately tried to get out of the crush. The problem was there were too many there, and the crowd behind them wasn't moving.

"Caleb!"

I turned to try to see who was calling my name, and saw a hand raised in the air. It might have been meant for me. It might not. The swell pushed me this way and that. And, I'll be honest, it was getting frightening in there. So many bodies. The crushing weight, the panic. I have no idea how many hundreds were there now, enough to cause some damage if hysteria kicked in.

The woman in front of me screamed again. I twisted sideways, trying to let her squeeze past me.

I don't know if she made it out before the real trouble started. I didn't see her again after that day, but then there were plenty of others I didn't see again either.

What struck me was the fact that none of the police had tried to get the man out of the melee, they'd tased him, then gone after the first people who tried to help him, with a nightstick. Protect and Serve.

Hand to God, there were so many people in the crush just trying to get out while everything around them spiraled out of control.

The baying of the crowd rose, the chants angrier, more frightened. I didn't hear my name called again.

The police line pushed back.

The ever-growing crowd didn't want to surrender ground. More nightsticks lashed out, delivering a beating. It was ugly. I saw the guy who'd taken the taser to the chest being pulled behind the row of riot shields. He offered no resistance. Hell, he didn't so much as twitch. That didn't matter to the two uniforms who bundled him inside the building. They handled him like he was some dangerous banger rather than an old man barely able to get to his feet, with piss stains around his groin where the taser had done its worst. Poor bastard. It's hard to explain why, but the sight of that humiliation pissed me off almost as much as them gunning down a kid who'd posed no threat to them. They operated in a different worldthan the rest of us. And I was here as an observer, meant to watch and report back to our world.

But that was the moment I stopped being good at my job. I stopped watching. I became the story.

The shouting, the noise, it was deafening. Worse than a concert, the hammering of the nightsticks the driving bassline. But none of it touched me.

I know I shouted. We all did. But I have no clue what words if any came out of my mouth. I'm not even sure they were noises. All I know is that I was part of the chorus, adding my voice to the horror at the way they'd treated that old man, the shooting of the boy and his dog. But that wasn't all of it, not by a stretch. The face of every man and woman in front of the police station was white. That line was in stark juxtaposition to the fact that almost everyone in the street was black. I'll admit, that took a moment to register, but when it did, I glanced around, very deliberately, making an effort to count the number of white faces in the crowd. Six. And that included Alicia White and her cameraman.

That was our America in one stark image.

More pushing, more shoving.

All the time the camera lens pointed at the crowd, not at Dwyer.

He was making a show of asking for calm. But words and manner weren't one and the same. I could feel it. His men were eyeing the line of black skin looking for an excuse to wade into the thick of it, batons swinging. And make no bones about it, the men hiding behind their riot shields were more than capable of inflicting pain. It didn't matter if they weren't some Olympian ideal of fitness, but rather looked like frightened Elmer Fudd's, they were itching to hurt someone. Anyone. Dwyer kept his hands raised, placating the crowd, urging everyone to disperse in a calm and orderly manner. The threat was that it would turn violent if they didn't. That was when I realized all of this was for the camera lens, not for the people here. He was acting a part, playing a role. We weren't seeing so much as a glimpse of the real Dwyer in all of this. That was a revelation.

The sun was a bastard.

The linen of my shirt stuck to my skin. Sweat puddled at the base of my back. The longer we stayed out there, the worse it became.

It was brutal; the hammer of the sun beating down against the anvil of the blacktop, us poor bastards stuck in between.

More pushing. Some shoving. Less gentle.

I stumbled but kept my footing. It would have been easy to get swept away in it all, but I

I saw a couple of people being helped out of the crowd. The protestors did their best to create a passage to allow them through, but as the crowd swelled it became harder and harder.

It was only when a young father tried to get his panicked girl out of the press of bodies that I heard voices yelling behind me— they were different to the chants and cries of protest. These were warnings.

Twisting, I saw—looking across the tops of the heads—that beyond the TV van two police cars had blocked the street. Their lights flashed. Behind them, using them for cover, I marked more cops, weapons drawn.

Not good.

So far, from not good, we were moving into the realm of clusterfuck.

"Shit," I grunted, not that anyone could hear me.

I forced my way between a couple of people, angling to the side to squeeze through a gap that wasn't really there. The change of perspective offered up two more squad cars that had moved into mirror positions of the others. I didn't like it. Even an idiot knew that it meant no one was going to be allowed to walk away, even if they wanted to. They were being contained. Which set another alarm bell ringing in my hindbrain; it was all about the spectacle. Dwyer had tipped off the network that something was going to go down, not just to highlight his little show of asking for calm.

I closed my eyes, hoping against hope that Alicia White and her cameras might just save some bloodshed. But all it would take was one trigger happy idiot.

"Caleb!" I heard my name called again. This time I saw who had said it.

"Stacey? What the hell are you doing here?"

"Boss man sent me," she said, struggling to make herself heard as she pushed her way towards me.

"Big Phil doesn't think I'm up to the job, eh?" I said as I managed to get a little closer to her.

"It's not that," she said, shaking her head as we tried to make it through the press of bodies to somewhere nearer the back. Again, and again, my eyes darted towards the cops with their weapons drawn, keeping a watchful eye from behind the safety of their cars.

"Then what is it?"

"He's worried it's going to blow up."

"Under their fucking eye."

"We need to get out of here."

"How can I write the piece if I don't *see* this play out?"

"Here, as in the thick of it. Let's just get behind the cordon." More barriers were being erected. The entire crowd, as much as it had swollen, was being penned in like cattle.

"You think they'll just let us walk out of here?"

"Follow my lead, I know a couple of the guys over this side, they'll let us through."

I stood my ground for a moment, looking back at the protestors. I could feel their anger rising. I saw Alicia White doing another segment to camera, smiles gone. Somber now, beneath the weight of the protest and the city's pain. I couldn't tell if she was going out live, or just compiling footage for the evening news. It didn't matter. The story was taking on a life of its own. It would be heard.

"Now or never, Jimmy Olsen," Stacey said.

That was when the first shot was fired.

3

I t started with a single shot.

I couldn't tell which direction the shot had come from; either behind us or from the steps with Dwyer. The acoustics of gunfire are weird. The shot was so fast, the walls so close, that the sound folded back on itself before it had a chance to boom. Shit, any one of the cops at the end of the street could have pulled the trigger, or someone in the press of the crowd.

I didn't immediately see a head explode with a blood red rose flowering in its forehead. But I didn't want to be stuck in this side of the cordon if the shit hit the fan from here.

The ricochet of sound made me stop in my tracks and turn, trying to source it, but Stacey wasn't about to get sucked up in the crowd again. She dragged me. Even as the cops parted to usher us through, I knew a black truth—if I'd been a black man on my own, there was no fucking prayer they'd have let me through. It was only the white woman clutching my hand that kept me safe.

We were two steps through when the screaming started again.

People scattered in every direction, desperate to get out of there, without caring where they were trying to get to, as long as it was safe.

I didn't hear a single shot in response.

That had been bone-deep instinctive fear. One shot starts a war. The difference was no one out of uniform had come here today to shoot anyone, they'd come to make their voices heard. There was a kind of willful innocence to that way of thinking. That somehow being right would shield them from the bullets when they flew.

When the second shot came, I heard something else in the echo, every bit as brutal as the shot, but so much more human, the sound of laughter. Harsh. Cruel. And there was no mistaking that it had come from the ranks of the cops.

People ran toward us. Others ran away from us. No one knew which way was safe if any way truly offered safety.

A couple of men threw themselves at the newly erected barrier, trying to scale it. The sight of the black eyes of the guns leveled at them was enough to see them give up. They weren't getting to the other side.

I saw a handful of civilians amongst the officers along the barricade. It was a fat boy militia—those supposedly well-regulated fucks with overhanging guts so ample and dicks so small they hadn't seen them in years. The assault rifles in their hands were way beyond anything the cops carried. It was a chilling sight. This America...

It was in their faces.

This was some kind of sport.

They had hard-ons at the thought of putting rounds into the crowd.

In that heartbeat, frozen in the blistering heat and the horror, I had a vision of bodies sprawled across the street, their blood staining the blacktop.

It was the purest definition of hell I had ever imagined.

More men and women ran towards us, desperately crying to be allowed out, one of the officers raised his shotgun and fired over their heads—not that I realized it had gone over their heads at first. It stopped them in their tracks for one more heartbeat, but that was it. They couldn't withstand the weight of the crowd behind them, in full panic now.

I saw at least two women fall, trampled in the chaos.

I felt sick to my gut.

Safe where I was, only a few feet away from them, I felt their panic as primal as if it was my own, my heart hammering as rapidly as any of theirs.

And there was *nothing* I could do about it.

"Christ, I hope Alicia is getting this," I said.

Stacey's head whipped round, viper fast. "Shut the fuck up, idiot, unless you want to get thrown back in there?"

I didn't say anything, and my silence was as bad as anything happening in front of me. It made me complicit. Another man might have stayed and fought. Not me. I let the white woman drag me away to where her car was parked. The closest I came to protesting was to glance back towards the crowds, trying to read the crush and press, and the relentless crash of black flesh on the thin blue line. All I could hear were frightened and angry voices.

But that was a blessing because it wasn't more shots fired.

Stacy relinquished her hold on my arm when we reached her little red Ford.

I didn't turn around and start walking back towards the mayhem, but I didn't clamber into the car, either. She didn't seem too concerned. We were a distance from the crowd. Safe.

We leaned against the trunk of the car and watched, tailgating it like it was a spectator sport.

"You ever see anything like this before?" she asked.

I knew how to read between the unspoken lines. There was no real surprise in her voice, no real shock that ordinary decent people could be treated like animals.

I shook my head. I was black, but not in the hood black. Not that way. More blackish. I lived in a white man's world and did OK for myself. "You?"

She shrugged her shoulders and tilted her head to one side. "Nothing like this. Not here. I mean, sure I've seen it on TV, but that's different somehow. You just accept that what you see on TV is happening in some far and distant reality that you're separated from. But it's not. It's here. Right here. On your own doorstep. And it's on her doorstep and his, and every doorstep up and down this damned country and the worst of it is that nothing gets done. They can show a gallery of faces, of black men gunned down by cops, they can tell stories about how a cop is off her tits and goes into the wrong apartment building and shoots her black neighbor and you know what? Nothing changes. Choke the life out of someone with your knee, and that one cop might lose their job, they might even go to jail if they're unlucky enough that someone caught it on their cellphone and shared the fuck out of the murder. But otherwise, it'd just go down as misadventure, another death in custody, and they'll find themselves shuffling along into another department. It's always the victim's fault. There's always something out there, some shit to smear, to prove that they were bad and deserved what came to them."

I don't think I had ever heard Stacey give such an impassioned speech. Hell, not so black and white. My surprise wasn't so much what she'd said, I've felt the same often enough it's become some sort of existential despair. The black condition. But it felt strange hearing it from the mouth of a white woman.

"You're stealing my lines," I said.

"Guess you're rubbing off on me." There was no trace of a smile on her lips. She wasn't mocking me. She was saying she was an ally. I appreciated it. Sometimes it felt like I was the token black guy, tolerated rather than liked. And in a world of positive discrimination, sometimes it was hard to shake the feeling that I'd got the job because of my skin color, not despite it. But maybe Stacey was different?

Back up the street a car started up. I saw one of the police cars back up a few feet and a slow trickle of people come through from behind the cordon. They moved slowly, warily. It was immediately obvious they didn't trust the cops, even when they were a good few steps beyond the cars, because instinct had them running before the cops could sucker punch them somehow. Every single one of them was understandably desperate to get as far away from there as possible, as quickly as they could. Maybe I'd been wrong, even after the gunshots. Maybe the situation wasn't going to escalate. And, even if there was no great crescendo to my story, no denouement that would have nailed the chief's lies or the department's cruelty, the inhumanity of killing a boy and his dog, I could live without it. I'm not sure what sort of reporter that made me? Hopefully an honest one. Better that everyone walked away from here fit and healthy than me getting a cool paragraph to hammer home my point.

I looked to see if Alicia White was still in place, mic in hand, recording these final moments of climb down as everything just petered out. But I guess she'd read the situation the same way I had; there was no sign of the mobile tv van she'd arrived in.

They were slow to disperse, but by the time the cops had moved their vehicles and broken the lines, there were only maybe a couple of dozen people left to vacate the area. Some leaned on each other as they walked, worse for their time in the crush. They were in no hurry to move out.

Cops stood around chatting, tension diffused. They were laughing and joking with the handful of good old boys who'd bolstered their ranks.

I caught sight of one face and shuddered, a sudden realization hitting me hard.

I knew that face.

"Let's get out of here," I said.

LESS THAN AN HOUR later I'd finished writing.

I'd sat myself down at the terminal as soon as I'd walked through the door, ignoring the questions. Everyone wanted to know what had happened out there, or more accurately hadn't happened, and why. I shut them all out. I needed to get this down on paper exactly; I wanted readers to feel what I'd felt trapped in amongst those people; I wanted them to know how terrified I'd been, and by extension everyone else in that protest had been, and how the police had only made the situation worse.

When I finished, I sat back, linked my fingers behind the back of my head, and let out this huge sigh of pent-up relief, the catharsis of words cleansing my system. I'm a man of words. I process the world through them. It's the only way I make sense of it. I read back through the piece, satisfied I'd nailed it, and hit key combo to send it to Phil at his desk. I saw him mimicking my own pose as he watched the big flatscreen on the wall.

When my piece hit his computer, he leaned forward and started to read.

I watched him, trying to read his expression. He gave nothing away. I was nervous. My heart actually tripped. It was like I was suddenly desperate for his approval, for validation, that what I'd felt was right and I was right to feel it, and my words made him feel it. I got no such satisfaction from watching him.

Eventually he got to his feet and moved to stand in the doorway to his office.

"Caleb," he called. "A word."

He didn't actually beckon me inside with his finger, but he might as well have.

He was back in his chair before I got there.

"You might want to close the door," he said, and I knew I was in for the polar opposite of validation, and Big Phil was going to bottle it, killing the piece as it stood.

"That bad?"

"No. But you'll get a better view of the TV."

He touched the remote and I was confronted by Alicia White talking straight at me. I could barely hear what she was saying. A knot tied in my gut. TV media was faster than print, that was the curse of the whole rush to publish and the 24hr news cycle, but that didn't devalue what we did. We took time. We got it right, not first. Right was more important.

"So, she beat us to the scoop, doesn't mean we don't cover it. We just do it better."

"Watch," Phil said.

Alicia's face disappeared. The focus shifted to the crowd I'd been part of. There was Dwyer giving his speech, appealing for calm, then some pushing and shoving, some shouting, but when the angle panned back before the brick was thrown the crowd was nowhere near what it had been. They'd spliced in footage from before the real protest had mounted to diminish it, toning down the outage. I was sickened, not only because I knew what was going to follow the brick, but so much more so because it didn't happen on screen. The reality they portrayed on the evening news bore no resemblance to the crush, the fear and panic I'd experienced. There was no old man being tasered, no gunshot fired, and none of those screams of panic. This was sanitized. Instead, they offered up a wide angled shot from further down the street, showing people emerging from between police cars while the cops watched, laughing, all amicable.

"Chief of Police Dwyer diffused what could have otherwise proved to be an unpleasant situation with strong leadership and calm authority. His men were a credit to the department, remaining calm in the face of hostility, allowing the protesters to have their say without resorting to any sort of heavy-handed crowd control techniques. There was a single arrest, a local man who attacked a police officer. His name has not yet been released."

Alicia's face returned to the screen. Phil hit pause on the

remote, but he didn't say anything. He just looked at me and waited, knowing I'd fill the silence.

"That isn't what happened," I said, like that mattered in our post truth world.

"Doesn't matter," Phil echoed. "These bastards told the story first and with pictures, so that's the one people will want to believe. Not yours. Look, I'm not an idiot, I know this has been edited to within an inch of its life, but Joe Shithead out there won't. They'll think this is the god's honest truth. And it doesn't matter how loudly we cry 'fake news' they'll want to believe her over our story. You know how they're going to counter this, the angry young black man, they'll say you couldn't have been there because your story doesn't tally with what they saw with their own eyes. Sorry Caleb, we've missed the boat on this one."

"So, we're not going to run anything? We aren't going to even keep the truth alive? I saw what happened, so did Stacy. That's two of us. Corroboration. There are witnesses out there, that crowd was huge. And it was terrifying when the gunshots went off. People will back us up."

Phil tilted his head, like he was listening to voices. "You got any pictures? Anything to prove that what you say happened happened? Something that contradicts what they've shown on the TV?"

I shook my head. "But all those people... what happened... their voice... This is important."

"I'm not arguing that it isn't. But without serious concrete proof we're fucked. You know that. Think of it as a life lesson: *if you're hellbent on becoming some crusading truth seeker, maybe our little rag isn't the place for you.* You're not going to win a Pulitzer here. You want that kind of influence, you're better off with somewhere like WaPo. You want to make a difference? Be a different kind of voice for the people, join Jordan Thomas and his team. I know he's looking for someone to beef up his communications team. You'd be good. Fuck it, I'm not telling you anything you don't know, if you want things to change, you have to look at all the angles, you can't just run at things head on and hope to batter it down. The only thing that happens that way is your skull breaks."

My first instinct was that Big Phil was fucking with me. Jordan Thomas was standing for mayor; the first black guy to even try for the office let alone have a shot at taking it. It was going to be a Sisyphus-like struggle just avoiding humiliation. But he was a believer. He wanted to do good. To help. So, in all likelihood, the system would chew him up and spit him out and put some prick in his place like Grandpa Munster.

"I can feel your frustration from here, Caleb. I get it. I live in a permanent state of disappointment these days. Best advice I can give you, take a couple of days, think about what you *really* want to do."

"That sounds like an ultimatum. Toe the line or fuck off."

"Maybe it is, but it'd be self-imposed. Hand on heart, I don't want to lose you, but that doesn't mean this newspaper isn't its own living breathing thing, with its own needs, and there's plenty of shit it doesn't need if it is going to survive in this new age of consumption. We're fighting a losing battle here. Ads are down. Readership is down. Our entire purpose is down."

"Which makes this all the more important."

"It really doesn't. What it makes it is a noose. I cut you some slack on the first story because you were right, killing a toy dog is beyond outrageous, claiming they felt threatened is a joke. You had an angle that others had missed or, and let's be honest about this, chose to ignore."

"And are still choosing to ignore," I leveled a finger at the TV in a whole *J'Accuse...!* moment while Alicia White was all fake tits and faker smile.

"Think of it another way, working for Thomas could be good for you, Caleb. You wouldn't even need to get him into office to show what you're capable of. You've got good instincts and ideals.

The best advice I can give you is to choose your battles. Remember, that you don't always have to win to make a difference."

It was a point. There were plenty of losers who'd gone on to rewrite history. Off the top of my head, the crucifixion of Jesus and the Alamo sprung to mind, though that offered up a pretty weird, juxtaposed image. "You think Thomas would want to talk to me?"

"Want to? Sunshine, he'd bite your hand off." He barked out a laugh at that. "You are exactly what he's looking for. And I mean exactly. So, take a couple of days, and if you decide you want to speak to Jordan, I'll make the call for you."

"Christ, you really are trying to get rid of me."

He shook his head. "Hardly. Look, here's an offer. If you decide it's a job you need to do, I'd keep your position here open until after the election. Best of both worlds. Go be a hands on special correspondent. Change the world."

"Sounds like you've already given this some thought."

His smile was rueful. "Confession time," he said. "Jordan came to me last week. We had a good talk. He asked if I knew anyone I thought could be the man he needed, and even as the words came out of his mouth, I knew you were the perfect fit...."

And then the penny dropped. "Fuck me, Phil I've never been offered a job *because* of the color of my skin before."

"Want another piece of advice? Before you speak to Jordan, go get the police's side of the story? Once you're in bed with Jordan you won't get the chance."

"There is no their side. I was there. There's the truth. That's it."

"Trust me, it's a good chance to get the measure of what you're going up against. Know your enemies. After all, it's a family business you're fucking with. It's generational. These people think it's their god given right to power, the Dwyers."

Richard Dwyer, chief of police, Able Dwyer, incumbent mayor.

It's that kind of town.

Incestuous.

They're father and son, Dwyer senior had been in post for the better part of a decade, which certainly hadn't hurt his boy's prospects when he'd coveted his own little piece of the pie.

4

—————

"I really appreciate you taking the time out of your day to see me, Chief Dwyer," I said, all conciliation and smiles.

It was a day after.

There was no sign of any protests when I'd arrived.

People have short attention spans for outrage these days and move on to the next thing to be angry about without so much as batting an eye. I blame social media. It's brilliant for mobilizing outrage, and for stoking anger, but with so much out there to be outraged over one tragedy barely gets its fifteen minutes of fame before another one topples it from the trending top spots.

There was no sign of the rapidly constructed steel barrier that had blocked the street. It was as if nothing had happened. Despite having agreed to the sit down, Dwyer seemed a little surprised to see me. Maybe it was just the color of my skin that caught him off guard? I wouldn't like to make any assumptions or accusations of racism on his part without solid proof, but I didn't see another black face in this inner sanctum that wasn't behind the cell bars.

The man looked relaxed, and close up, younger than he did

on the steps as he faced the crowd. But this was home field; out there he'd been the visitor.

"Think nothing of it, we live to serve, Mr...." he paused to check the hastily scribbled entry in the desk diary in front of him, "...Moon. So, what is it I can do for you? I'm more than happy to talk to our friends in the press."

"I was hoping you could give me your thoughts on yesterday's protest."

"Protest? I think that's a colorful way of describing what we saw, don't you? That was just a bunch of your people out to make mischief."

I couldn't quite believe what I'd just heard. "My people?" I tried to keep the edge of incredulity from my voice, but I'm not sure how well I succeeded.

"You know what I mean," he said, not about to apologize for his poor word choice. I thought about making a thing of it but thought better of it. Not the place to stir things up. Not the time. Yet. "They wanted to blow off some steam, we let them get it out of their system. No harm no foul. Only one person got hurt, an officer of mine, who was hit by a projectile thrown by one of your *protesters*."

Again, I resisted the temptation to correct his version of eventBut that would have been overplaying my hand. He had no idea I'd see the manifestation firsthand, and frankly the phrase, 'you all look the same to me' had been made for this guy.

"I assume you understand and appreciate why these people were so angry?"

He looked at me like I was mad. "Of course, I do, of course, but what you have to understand, Mr. Moon, is that my officers are faced with dangerous situations like that on a daily basis. These aren't some yokels with a gun, they are highly trained individuals who respond with a mixture of instinct tempered by experience. They can read a situation like no one else, and if they believe their lives are in danger, they are going to protect themselves. They must. The sad truth is that sometimes people get things wrong."

Which offered me a nice way into a difficult question I couldn't see him answering truthfully. "Which begs the question, do you think these officers were in the wrong?"

A suck of breath. A slight incline of the head. "Well, we won't know that until a full investigation has been carried out, of course. Anything I said to you now, one way or another would only prejudice that, wouldn't it? So, let's wait for the facts."

"OK. Let me ask this, have any of the officers involved been suspended from duty pending that investigation?"

"Why would we waste your tax dollars like that, young man? Unless, of course, you are suggesting it might be wise to keep them out of the public eye for their own safety, until this is resolved in which case, rest assured, I've got them as full-time desk jockeys for the foreseeable. They both probably think that's punishment enough given the weather we've been having."

This guy was unbelievable. He had such a punchable face. "I'm not sure that the poor boy's mother would see it quite the same way." I winced. I hadn't meant my own feelings to filter through, but sometimes it's hard to stay neutral when you're listening to so much bullcrap.

"We all have our own ideas of justice," Dwyer said, smoothly. "Trust me, there will be due process. Justice will be done. You have my word on that."

I wanted to believe him, and maybe there was a small part of me that believed the truth *would* come out and whoever was responsible *would* feel the full weight of the law, but it was a small part, let's be honest. Nothing I'd seen gave me cause for hope.

"And the old man who was injured in the demonstration? Can I ask how he is doing?"

"He's just fine and dandy," he said, though there was nothing sincere about the smile plastered over his face. "He was a little bit shaken up, got carried away. One of my officers reacted quickly and disabled him. No harm no foul."

"Did *you* think he was a threat?"

"Me? Personally? To be honest, I didn't really see him. I was too busy concentrating on the crowd. I'm a big picture guy. That's what my men were on the steps with me for. To make sure things didn't turn ugly."

"Ah, of course. So, would you say your officers believed the old man posed a threat in that moment?"

"They did, but thanks to their training they were able to react quickly enough to neutralize it without things escalating."

"We should be grateful for small mercies."

He ignored the comment. "The officer in question used appropriate force, I can assure you. Let me try and paint a picture for you. We see a man coming at the stage. We don't know if he's armed. We don't know what his intentions are. Our priority in that moment is public safety. My men took appropriate measures to defuse the situation."

"Wouldn't it have been good if the same judgment could have been applied with that poor kid and his dog?"

Then suddenly the mask slipped. Just like that. One second it was there. The next it was gone and the real man beneath was exposed for all to see.

Dwyer leaned forward and jabbed a fat finger at me. "Now just you listen to me, boy. I'm doing you a big favor letting your sorry black ass in here to talk to me, I'm treating you with respect," he pronounced it ree-spect, heavily laboring over the front end. "And all you do is disrespect me? Come into my house making out like I'm some evil man. Me. Well, I don't mind saying I'm starting to think you might be in need of a lesson in manners, son."

I tried to stay calm.

But it was hard.

I began to worry he was going to summon one of his guards

and have them escort me out, making sure I accidentally fell on the way down to the street.

I'd come across people like this before; men who thought they were better than me for no other reason than the color of my skin. Give them a bit of authority and they were dangerous.

"One last question," I said, pushing my luck.

"I think we're done here," Dwyer said, and started to rise for his feet.

I wanted to see his reaction, unguarded, so I asked my question anyway.

"What do you think of your father's chances of being re-elected?"

It was enough to make him smile, and this time I was sure it was genuine.

"I know my city. I trust the people. They can see that he has their best interests at heart."

"So, you think he'll win easily?"

Dwyer laughed this time; a deep belly laughed that was almost a roar. "You can't honestly believe that a place like *this* would ever give its vote to the likes of Jordan Thomas? Don't get me wrong, I'm sure he's a perfectly good and decent man, but that doesn't mean that he's capable of doing the job. And let's be brutally honest here, what's to say the good people of this city would even do what he said if he ever made it as far as the hot seat?"

"Why do you say that?"

"OK, kid, I ain't going to spell it out for you," he said. "You got lines, read between them. You know he's damned lucky to have a vote never mind stand for mayor. That's fifty years of progress for you, but it's slow progress round these parts. But there will be an election, and Jordan Thomas is free to stand if that's what he wants to do, that's the law of this fine land, but when the song and dance is over, he can crawl back into whatever tar pit he crawled out of."

Dwyer walked to the door and held it open without saying another word.

The interview was over.

Big Phil had been right, the face to face had sure as shit helped me make up my mind about certain things.

5

———

We met up in a dive bar after I'd finished work.

I'm a fan of those downbeat places, more spit and sawdust than glass and aluminum dazzle. Give me the kind of bar alcoholics go to die.

I'd written up my notes on the meeting with Dwyer, which felt like a pointless exercise because I was never going to do anything with them. There wasn't a story in a racist police chief, even in the 2020s. And that was a damnation of everything about our society right there.

Even before I was out the office door I'd made up my mind. It wasn't exactly a Road to Damascus moment, but it was a revelation. For the first time in a long while I knew exactly who I was, and that person was going to do everything in his power to get Jordan Thomas elected. Which is kinda funny when you remember I've got about as much power as a 40-watt bulb.

Things needed to change. The truth was as simple and as hard as that. Change here and change in the country as a whole. And not just some clever poster either, real change needed to be affected. When you live in a place, where giving 20% of your salary to insurances makes you a smart capitalist and proves you have good money sense, and the thought of giving 4% of your salary to Medicaid turns you in to a raving commie you know you've been indoctrinated by a fucked-up system that's chewing itself up. And who does that hurt? The poor. Always the poor. I couldn't change that. Christ, even Obama had struggled to make any sort of dent into that twisted logic and he was the president, I'm just a lowly journalist. But here I could have some influence. I needed to believe that. I needed to believe that I could do something to aid Jordan's campaign and help him deliver his message —but only if he wanted me to be part of his team.

It wasn't that I doubted Big Phil, but it was one thing him saying the job was mine if I wanted it, and quite another hearing it from the candidate himself. And look, I'm an idealist. I needed to know that I was backing the right man. Not just the only black man running. Even though that was important. It's all about personal chemistry, knowing you fit. So, the next hour or so was going to be fundamental in the direction of my life from here on out.

Jordan wasn't hard to find.

He was the smartest dressed guy in there, black, or white. He sat alone, running his fingers across the glass screen of an iPad. He had a half-drunk beer on the table in front of him, which told me two things about Jordan, one, that he'd been here a while, meaning he was the kind of person who got to a meeting twenty minutes early just to ensure he wouldn't be two minutes late, and the other, that he wasn't out of place with the workers who gathered here. A glass of wine would have looked wrong, and a couple of fingers of single malt would have been the equivalent of that song, *meet the new boss, same as the old boss*. I approved of the messaging, even if it was subliminal.

First impressions, he was comfortable with who he was.

This wasn't some guy who'd never done the hard work, getting his hands dirty pushing a broom in the local high school, or packing groceries in the supermarket to work his way through college as he picked up his degrees in economics and social planning.

He was the new breed, upwardly mobile, smart, educated, and charismatic. When he spoke, he had the kind of voice that was smooth as honey and twice as sweet.

He rose to his feet and held out a hand. "You must be Caleb," he said. "Jordan Thomas."

"Mr. Thomas," I said, taking his hand. It was a firm shake, but not aggressively so, like some power play pulling you in as he crushed your hand. His smile was easy, natural.

"Jordan," he said. "Please. If we're going to be working together, we need to be on first name terms, so why don't we start off that way? Can I get you a drink?"

Already it was a sharp contrast with my meeting with Dwyer. The only thing I had gotten from the chief was a condescending smile, and the only time he'd made it as far as his feet was to signal that our interview was over. There had been no hand-shake. He was probably frightened he'd catch something.

"Whatever you're having sounds good."

He glanced at the barmaid, offered her a flash of perfect teeth in a powerful smile and gave her a two-finger signal to request two more of whatever he'd been drinking. The smile she gave him in return was as every bit as broad as the one he'd given him. This was a good sign. He was easy to be liked. That would make my job so much easier than trying to sell a skeevy candidate that got under people's skin. I wasn't going to read too much into it. Maybe he was just a good tipper.

"So, Caleb, tell me, what's it like working for Phil?" he asked after the waitress had put the glasses of beer down in front of us.

"Never less than interesting," I said. "Let's just say that I've learned a lot."

That earned a low-throated chuckle from the other man. "And yet you're thinking about leaving him?"

"I wasn't," I admitted. "He was the one who suggested I talk to you," I took a sip of the beer. It was the first one I'd had in more than a week, not for any ethical reason. I hated drinking alone, and I'd been alone for a while, so while everyone else was keen to get home to their own lives I did the same, though mine was more Hungry Man dinners and instant coffee, than rug rats getting under feet and beautiful partners to share that home life with. Which makes me sound pitiful, but I was content with my lot.

"Well, he speaks very highly of you," Jordan told me. "And I've seen some of the things you've written for the paper..."

I nodded. Of course, he'd done his due diligence. He'd have been a fool not to. "There have been other stories, too. Things that Phil couldn't, or *wouldn't*, print."

"Can I ask how that makes you feel? Knowing that the truth isn't worth as much today as we like to believe it was a generation ago, before things got so complicated with all of these paid for news channels peddling their versions of reality?"

"Angry. Disappointed. Depressed. I mean, I get why he must make those decisions. We're puppets dancing to our paymaster's whims as they pull the strings or pull the finances but knowing that and then facing the reality of it doesn't stop it sticking in my craw when we back down over something important. Because the truth must matter. Doesn't it? The reality of our lives must matter. The inequality of being a black man in America must matter. Call me an idealist, but I *need* to believe that. Otherwise, we become a population of George Floyds with knees making damned sure we can't breathe."

"And you're not afraid of being labeled an angry black man?"

I shook my head. "I am angry. I am black. Those two things are not mutually exclusive. But they do not define who I am."

"Good. Being angry is good. You should be. Hell, you'd have to be blind not to see something to be angry about in the world outside this bar. So, yes, being angry is good. It shows that you care. I'm angry too. But I'm smart enough to know I can't rail against every injustice. Sometimes it's smart to keep your powder dry. Are you smart Caleb?"

"Smart enough to know I don't know everything."

"Good answer. I like that. It's the kind of answer that I want my people to give. So, the million-dollar question, I need someone like you on my team, but do you want to be part of this or shall we shake hands and agree it was nice to meet each other and never see each other again?"

"And if I was to ask you if the color of my skin makes a difference to your offer?"

He laughed then, a proper booming belly laugh. "You mean would I hire you if you were white? Yes. Because I want the right man for the job. Simple as that. And you'll see it the second you walk through the door of the campaign office. We are a diverse bunch. I'm all about walking the walk."

"I'm interested," I said. "In theory."

We chatted for another hour, making our way through another beer.

He told me about his ambitions for the office, about the changes he wanted to see happen, and underneath it all I sensed a deep-seated desire to help the poorest in the community. Jordan Thomas was an old-fashioned good man. He grilled me on my personal beliefs, getting a feel for my instinctive reaction to issues and hot button topics, and getting a good read on me. What was interesting was how much we agreed on, what was good was where we disagreed, he listened to my own thoughts, taking on board my arguments, some of which he agreed with as being valid concerns, other times he found compromises between our ideas that worked. There was a lot to like about Jordan Thomas.

By the time we had finished, it was obvious he was looking for someone to work with him, actively contributing to the campaign and beyond, not just help him spin his ideas into a palatable message.

"So, how soon could you start working with me? Assuming it's a yes?"

"I've got to work the month out, but seeing as it's already the 27th, I guess I'd be good to start on Monday."

He nodded. "Now to the economics. We're running a political campaign on a poverty level budget. I've not courted the big money donors. The benefit with that is that, should I win, is that I'm not beholden to some old money intent on maintaining the status quo. The problem with that is I can't offer you anywhere near what you're getting at the paper. That's the ugly truth. There's no money in politics. At least not if you're honest. That changes if we win. Then I can offer you a permanent place on staff, on the county's dime. But that's a big if. No promises."

"None needed, or expected," I assured him. I didn't need to explain that Phil had promised to keep my job open in case I wanted to go back. One thing I'd realized over the last few minutes when I should have been evaluating the offer was that I'd already decided I was going to take this job before I set foot in the bar. What I hadn't expected was to be having doubts about returning to the paper even if we lost. Jordan Thomas was a comet blazing a trail, and that was exciting.

He slipped his iPad into the case I hadn't even noticed on the booth seat beside him, then held his hand out to me. "I'm going to take that as a yes. Welcome aboard, Caleb. I think this is going to be the beginning of a beautiful friendship."

6

Jordan had already sent me the official welcome to the team email before I made it home, including the salary confirmation for the next month along with the repeated apology that it wasn't as much and he wished it could be more.

What surprised me wasn't the money, it was the fact that I probably would have done it for nothing. There was something very different about seeing a campaign from the inside, and maybe there was a book in it? Big Phil might have joked about the Pulitzer, but in every joke there's an element of truth lurking somewhere, deep beneath the surface. This kind of veracity couldn't be bought. That would make me a better writer for it, even if I didn't change the world. If I had a hand in improving the lot of some of the people suffering in the place, I called home, then that was all the win I needed.

I put a call through to Phil before I put the coffee on.

I'd promised to let him know how the meeting had gone. It wasn't about heading off any difficult conversation, right now I figured he was my biggest cheerleader, and I got the impression that he and Jordan went back a way. This was more like sharing the good news.

"That's brilliant, Caleb," he promised me. "I had a feeling you two would get along like a house on fire. I've got a sixth sense when it comes to these things. Now, enjoy your month taking on the ugly face of racism that is the Establishment, capital E, in this place, and don't worry about your job. It's safe for you. At the very least I'm expecting an insider story on the election, right?"

"I can do that," I promised him in return, not that I truthfully expected to write another piece for the paper.

"You get a start date?"

"Monday. I'll be in tomorrow to get a few things off my desk. Can I ask you something Phil, a BS answer, why are you so happy to see me go? I'm leaving you a man down, no notice. That can't be ideal."

"I can dust off the old notepad and pen if needs be, son, don't you worry about that. As to why? I'm pretty sure that the press releases you'll be drafting for Jordan will be a lot more coherent than the crapola Dwyer's people put out. So, you're helping Jordan, but I like to think of it as helping me too, less work wading through the shit to make sense of it. And hey, you'll be filling plenty of column inches without me having to pay you. That, my friend, is capitalism at its finest," he joked, but I knew none of that was the truth. Not the real unvarnished truth. He wanted to make a difference just as much as I did.

A boy and his dog.

It mattered.

We chatted for a couple of minutes more, which was mainly him assuring me everyone was onboard with the opportunity and wished me well for the next month raging against the machine. And no-one had complained about the extra workload that me being gone meant for them. Which sounded like so much bull-crap I burst out laughing. I knew these people.

Later, I made a couple of calls, checking in with friends and family around the country; some thought it as a great idea and could see me fighting the good fight, others, like my long-suffering mother, were less enamored with me throwing away a perfectly good job and ruining my career. It didn't matter how many times I told her I could go back, she just kept saying, *but you won't.*

She knew me so well.

————

THE FOLLOWING DAY WAS SUBDUED.

The staff wished me well, but there was no talk about going for a drink after work, and no send-off gift. No one really thought that I was leaving. I guess Phil had sold it more as a month-long assignment. Several times I was made to promise that I'd drop into the office now and again over the next few weeks, with mock threats that if I didn't, they wouldn't run a story for me.

I left it until the last minute to clear a few things from my desk and cardboard box them.

I took one last look around before I headed home.

It was rare to experience silence in this place.

"You ready to start your new life then?" The voice caught me by surprise. I turned to see Phil standing in the door of his office. "A more observant man, a journalist for instance, might look at this moment, cardboard box in hand, and think you're not coming back."

"You know how it is... Just in case," I said, and it was almost true. "I hate goodbyes." Which was true.

"Fair enough," he said and held out a hand to shake mine. "Do I need to check your box to make sure you're not making off with the office stapler?"

We both laughed. "Curses foiled again. That stapler had been my grand plan... an excuse to return in case I ever start missing you lot."

"You don't need an excuse. And if you need anything, you know where I am," Phil said. "Now go, do some good."

"I'll do my best," I said.

A few minutes later I was standing outside the building with my back to the door. It felt like a chapter of my life hand ended and a new one was about to begin.

It was raining.

That should have been a sign.

7

I spent that weekend reading through the masses of information Jordan had sent through. It was akin to getting to know him; his thoughts on the way that the vote was being taken away from the people he saw as his natural supporters and integral to our campaign, some of the ways he intended to correct the voter suppression, there were copies of older press releases, cuttings from newspapers along the campaign trial, and along his life too, some of which I had already seen. There was also a wealth of opposition research.

There was a real difference in the language the two sides employed, the language of fear against the language of hope. That was only to be expected when the incumbent had been in power for so long. They got complacent and believed themselves indestructible. Dwyer was playing to his fan base. They'd served well in the last election, and he'd served them well since. What was interesting was how little he promised to do for those outside of his voter base. There were promises to people who were unlikely to vote for him, but they were at best nebulous and at worst empty. He didn't care about new votes, but why would he, he'd won by a landslide every other time it's gone to the ballot box.

I decided to do some work of my own, digging further back along older campaign trails.

It didn't take long to realize Dwyer's literature was recycled, in most cases word for word. The promises he made were always the same, to keep doing things the way he had done before. There were watch words like prosperity and commitments to bring blue collar jobs to the area. I haven't been here long enough to know if he's ever lived up to those promises, but there was no getting away from the fact that the glossy brochures made it look like he had.

His commitments to the poorer communities were still the same; to improve living conditions, sanitation, and power, but I'd seen zero evidence of that.

If anything, living conditions in some of these places had deteriorated rapidly. There was no pressure on slum landlords to bring their buildings up to code, and yet they increased their rents to cover the cost of non-existent repairs and improvements. It was the poverty trap laid bare, the piece of cheese in the middle waiting to lure the desperate in before the snap came down and broke their back.

I didn't need to look up any statistics to know that the vast majority of the poor were black or Hispanic. That was a pattern repeated across the country. I'd read something once about how expensive it was to be poor, which sounds stupid, but it was put perfectly. A poor person might spend thirty bucks on a pair of shoes that last them four months, while a rich guy can afford to pay for quality merchandise, his shoes imported, highest quality leather, incredible craftsmanship, made to last a lifetime, and pay three hundred bucks for them. The poor guy goes through three pairs a year, at ninety bucks, and in three and a half years paid more to keep the cheap shoes on his feet, than the rich guy did importing his fancy ones that would easily last another five or six years while still looking good. It was expensive living from day to day. It was just the way the system was set up to make sure those at the bottom couldn't rise to the top, even as they sold them the American Dream and convinced them not to vote for higher taxes on the rich just in case one day, they got to be one of those same rich. It was such a lot of bullshit, but people ate it up, because people wanted to believe. They looked at self-made men and said yeah, that could be me one day, I just need to work harder. I need an extra job to pay for the childcare so I can do my first job, to cover my mortgage and food, and a third job if I want anything approaching quality of life—which I won't be able to experience because I'll be too busy working three jobs.

It was a fucked-up system, and people bought into it.

And these were the same people who had been so badly let down by Dwyer.

Which meant they were the voters that Jordan needed to reach out to.

The problem was getting them out to vote, and getting their votes to count, given the voting stations were deliberately few and far between in the county, and new demands for photo IDs were in place to ensure that people who didn't drive couldn't get there to make their voices count. And who didn't drive? The poor. It was a deliberately vicious cycle.

When Monday morning came around, I had a wealth of material saved to my own iPad, annotated with notes I'd made highlighting how I thought we might do things better.

That included getting our message out, which meant press releases, which meant treading on the toes of whoever had been writing them up 'til now. They needed to know how to persuade as well as inform, and to inspire as well as persuade, so that together the message was enough to bring people out. We wanted a movement. And we weren't going to get that with the current PR stuff.

I sat down with Jordan, the candidate listening patiently as I told him what I'd been looking at, the lines of action and inaction I'd identified over the weekend, and where I saw our weaknesses from the outside looking in. After fifteen minutes I had no clue what he was thinking.

He'd barely said a word from the moment I started working through my stuff.

I kept going a little longer then stopped mid-sentence, shaking my head. I was an idiot. A well-meaning one, sure, but an idiot all the same. "You already know all this, don't you?"

He nodded, but he was smiling.

"Most of it," he confirmed. "But it's good to hear it from you. It's good to see that you get it. And I like the way you've rewritten a few of those press releases to better get the message across. That stuff is golden."

This time it was my turn to nod. "I didn't want to say anything in front of the others. Last I want to do as the new kid is piss someone off who's been working their ass off for you," I said, looking out through the glass window in the direction of a group of volunteers busy making calls at the far end of the campaign floor. Jordan had introduced me around when I'd arrived. It was going to take me a day or two to get everyone's names down and appreciate their roles. Jordan had mentioned there was another raft of volunteers who could only help in the evenings or at weekends. It didn't surprise me that there were only a couple of faces on the floor. "Especially if one of them had written those press releases." I offered a wry grin.

Jordan leaned back in his chair and released a roar of a laugh, so loud that all the volunteers turned to look in our direction.

"You wrote them didn't you?"

"I did. And believe me, Caleb, I am aware of my shortcomings. I may be many things, but I am no James Baldwin or Langston Hughes. That's just one of the reasons I wanted you on board." He reached behind him to pull a ring binder off a shelf and placed it on the desk. "I've been working on this for the last two years. I think it covers most of your concerns, and a whole lot more besides. Read. Digest. Get back to me." He pushed the binder across the desk to me.

I felt more than a little chastened.

"Don't beat yourself up. I've spent two years on this. You've had a weekend. Frankly, I'm impressed with how much you've worked out from a few bits of paper I sent through."

"I guess I was being naïve, thinking I could come up with things you hadn't considered. I wanted to blow you away with my insight."

Again, the smile, again the laugh, not booming this time, just warm. "Caleb, listen to me when I tell you this, because I'm only going to say it once. You did good. You impressed me enough to know I've got the right guy in my corner. So, based on your weekend of extensive research, what do you think we need to do to win this election?"

It was my turn to laugh this time.

"Get more votes than Dwyer," I said, quirking out a wry smile. "Voting here goes on ethnic lines. Dwyer owns the white vote, though a few liberals might see him for what he is and vote against him. The problem is that swing is counteracted by the black businessmen who are doing well out of the system and don't want to change things."

"Ah the illusive black unicorns. Believe me, there aren't many of those around these parts," Jordan said. "Go on."

"Your natural base not ethnic though, it's economic. The poor white, the black and Hispanic communities. The thing is, that's a bigger core demographic, if you can reach them. Mobilize that voter base and you're tapping into a seam that's richer than the number of votes Dwyer took last time around. You win."

"You're right. The thing is, with everything that is happening here the situation *should* be getting worse for Dwyer, but it's not."

"Walk me through it?"

"The ethnic population is increasing. The rich are getting

richer, while the poor keep getting poorer, and the fastest growing demographic we've got here is mixed race. They *should* all be voting for whoever stands against Dwyer."

"But they're not."

"They're not. And for lots of reasons, but primary among them, is that too many of them aren't able to vote. And of those that can maybe just aren't willing to vote. You know why Florida is such a mess voting wise? Identity. So many Hispanic voters are Cuban refugees and live-in absolute dread of returning to any sort of communist rule, so vote against their better interests because they can't face voting for anything even resembling socialism. That's life."

"How many people are we talking about?" I wasn't surprised to hear that both factions existed here, even if on a smaller scale than existed across the land. That was politics in a nutshell. A place like this was a microcosm. It shone a light on the bigger reality of the country. It was a bellwether.

"Enough to make a difference," he said. "I can't do much about those who can't vote, at least not without getting into office voice. I just don't have that kind of power. The reality is it's not just local elections, it's the whole State. It's whole chunks of the country. People are being denied a voice because they might speak out against the McConnells of the world. Remember the phrase, no taxation without representation?"

"Civil war," I said, knowing full well the way his mind was drifting.

"The difference now is that The British have been replaced by wealthy white men, by political lobbies, by pacts and super-pacts and the big businesses that back them. It's their interests to keep certain people in power, to make sure that the policies that serve them are followed. There's no great mystery here. The system is broken. And you know what cements their place at the top, keeping their money nice and safe? Making sure only the right people get to vote." He didn't need to say right colored skin, I got it. "They'd rather have uneducated poor white people whose prime concern is not having their guns taken away from them. They're easy to manipulate with promises of the return of factory jobs despite the fact the world has moved on and those jobs are never coming back—because back is backwards, and the world only marches forwards. Poor white folks might complain about the cost of health care, but they'd rather not have any, than have it if it comes with a black guy's name attached. They might protest pipelines and polluted drinking water, but at the end of the day they value the right to bear arms more than the right of their neighbors to drink clean water and eat chemical free food."

"It can't be as simple as that," I said, even though I knew the argument could be condensed into pretty much exactly what he'd just said. I wanted to believe we were more than that. Better. Black and white. Just better.

"It isn't. There are complexities of course. Shades of gray. Undocumented workers, not declaring, not paying tax, but they're jobs the good old boys can't bring themselves to do. There's the three-strike system that disproportionately punishes black kids because the private prison system has found a new way of exploiting slavery without ever calling it that, keeping a constant inmate count high as they're a source of free labor. It's a good thing for those wealthy people who don't have to see it. Out of sight, out of mind."

"You make it sound so... hopeless."

"But it isn't. There must be hope, even if it is hard to bring about change when the system doesn't want to change. The trick is making the rich guys to think they want the system to change for their benefit, and in that transition, encourage them to finance improvements to the infrastructure and living conditions that benefit those who otherwise couldn't afford it. It's a juggling act."

There was more, much more. And it all made sense. It wasn't basic stuff, hell half of it sounded like sleight of hand, look over here at what my right hand's doing while my left goes about fixing the stuff, I don't want you to see.

My first impression had been spot on, he was a good man.

I listened as he recounted policy after policy that needed to change because, on the face of it, they all sounded like reasonable ideas, but in practice served only to widen the gulf between the poor and the rest of society. By the time he'd finished I felt like that guy in the movie where they kept telling him to open his eyes until he could finally see the world for what it was. I saw. And I didn't like what I saw. I mean, I'd seen all this stuff to one degree or another, I'm not blind, and I like to think that most of the time I'm not an idiot, but this time I saw how the dots joined, and how one thing impacted on a dozen other and how each was designed to make it progressively harder for Americans to escape the poverty trap. It just so happened that it disproportionately affected people who looked like me.

I fell silent.

Jordan didn't say a word. He didn't fidget or fiddle. He simply watched and waited.

"Having second thoughts about taking the job?" He asked eventually.

"I think this is exactly where I need to be."

"So do I."

8

The first week felt like I was rushing to catch up. There was always something to do, and a dozen things crammed in behind that still needed doing. There was barely a minute to catch a breath in between. I was in the office by 7:30 most mornings, Jordan already in before me. I wouldn't be home before nine, leaving the office around eight, and he was still at his desk. This was a man who believed in leading by example. He wouldn't ask others to do what he wasn't prepared to do himself. That, or he was homeless. Lunch was often a grilled sandwich at my desk.

The only full-time member of staff was Carrie Marlow, who was best described as efficient. She handled scheduling, mapping out the candidate's days to the minute, and dealing with the small donations that regularly arrived in the office. Her most important task by far was marshaling the flow of volunteers and making sure everyone had something to do that best suited their own talents.

She was the dictionary definition of organized. Even so, I always managed to get through everything she'd blocked out for my day before leaving. I wish I had a fraction of her skills when it came to time management, but the only way that was happening was some sort of Faustian pact. What intrigued me more was the fact that Carrie was very much a white wasp making her the odd one out in the office. I was curious about her story. Something had made her hitch her trailer to Jordan, but there was rarely a moment when we weren't both buried in our work for small talk.

And then, on the fourth day, she came up to my desk with two mugs of coffee and put one down in front of me. It was a little act of humanity, but it was very much appreciated. I'd been on the phone for most of the morning, talking myself hoarse.

"Looks like you could do with one of these."

"You are a messenger from the gods," I said, took a sip, savored it, and leaned back in my chair.

"Sorry I haven't had chance to check on you this week," she said. "I guess it's been a bit of a baptism of fire for you."

"Trial by," I joked earning a chuckle.

"I can't imagine that it was quite this frantic at the paper."

"You'd be surprised, but yeah, this is a different kind of crazy."

She paused for a moment, and I knew she was trying to decide whether to ask what was on her mind. I could have told her to spit it out, because we didn't want anything festering in the office, even if I was only officially going to be around for a month, I had a feeling that we'd be working closely together, each of us standing at Jordan's right and left shoulder—though I'm not sure which of us was the angel and which was the devil.

I opted for tact. "I hope you don't think I'm coming in and treading on anyone's toes, that's the last thing I want, believe me," I said eventually, trying to preempt whatever might have been bothering her.

"Oh no, not at all. You've taken so much of the weight off Jordan's shoulders, it's been a genuine godsend. I've been telling him for ages that he needed to find someone he could trust. He did well by finding you."

"Ha, well, I have the feeling my editor's ink-stained fingers are all over that."

"Phil?" she laughed. It was a good sound. Not forced. Genuine. There was warmth and affection in it. "When has he ever been known to resist meddling?"

"You know him?"

"I do indeed. Not for as long as Jordan, but long enough that we were both a lot younger and more idealistic. Phil was a little less Big Phil and more Medium Phil."

And now it was my turn to laugh picturing a slimline Phil.

"They've known each other that long?"

"He didn't tell you. They were at college together, what nearly twenty years ago? Probably more like twenty-five now. Time doesn't exactly stand still when you're trying to change the world, does it? Jordan moved away. He only came back a few years ago and they rekindled the bromance."

"Nice. What made him come back? Family?"

"It's a good place to make a difference."

There was that wistful faraway look in her eyes and the beginnings of a smile on her lips that made me wonder if she had a thing for Jordan. A glance at her left hand confirmed she wasn't wearing a ring.

"So, were they close back then?"

"I don't think they were friends or anything, at least not to begin with. Though Jordan tells this story about how Phil got himself a broken nose by putting himself in front of a racist shit heel looking to hurt our boy. Let's just say that a white man sticking up for a black guy didn't go down too well in this sleepy little town."

"Some things never change," I said, appreciating my ex-boss just a little bit more for walking the walk. I raised the mug of coffee to my lips. "Here's hoping that whoever threw the punch got what was coming to him in the end."

"Not really. Unless you consider becoming chief of police punishment."

"Chief Dwyer?"

———

I LAY awake for hours that night, watching the blades of the ceiling fan slowly roll around. They wobbled slightly. I wouldn't have been able to sleep with the suffocating heat anyway, but my mind was wrapped up in trying to wrangle thoughts about Jordan's motivations. Was it simply personal? Was revenge just a bonus that came with trying to change the world and be a force for good? Sure, he was all about doing good, but there had to be an element of something else, didn't there? Going up against the father of his tormentor?

It was all guesswork and assigning motivations from my imagination, but that was all I could do. It was hardly Pulitzer level investigative journalism. More like painting by numbers. Did some buried revenge plot make Jordan a lesser man or prove he was the better man once and for all? Did it even matter what his reasons were? Noble or not, Jordan had it in him to change things for the better.

At some point I found sleep of sorts, thrashing about in a tangle of sweat-stained sheets, and woke to dawn's light creeping in through my bedroom window, the top sheet wrapped around my knees. A new dawn, a new day, and I felt... drained. I was ready to force myself out of bed and go through it all over again when I realized that it was Saturday.

The campaign had a stand in the town square that morning, but there were more than enough volunteers to set everything up and to man the stand, meaning for once I wasn't rushing. It seems it's easier to get people to give up a couple of hours on a Saturday than any other day of the week. I'd put in an appearance but give them an hour or so to find their feet.

The market was already busy when I wandered down there a little after nine.

The air was warm and sticky, a fair indication of how bad it was going to be later. It was filled with the chatter of voices. Stall holders were doing a steady trade already, peddling fruit and vegetables, flowers, and other farmer's market stuff that showed the ingenuity or maybe the boredom of the new generation. Their smiles were wide as they gushed over the various virtues of their wares. Happy people handed over money.

After a couple of minutes of wandering up and down the rows of stalls, I was beginning to wish I'd asked Carrie where the campaign's booth was going to be, but in the end, I found them a little offset from the main traders.

"How's it going?" I called, wandering over. Carrie saw me.

She didn't look very happy.

"Not great," she said. "We've already had a friendly visit from the cops, making sure we know they're taking an interest in us."

"We're not doing anything wrong," I said, knowing we'd have all licenses and permits in place. Our only crimes were running against the chief's dad and having the temerity to be black.

"Too many people crowding around us, supposedly. We caused an obstruction. They made us move the table by six inches to make sure the thoroughfare was clear. It's all bs. Shit about straying beyond the set boundaries. There are no boundaries," she said, gesturing to the ground. "It's just stuff to make our lives more difficult. I'm just glad I was here."

The cops would have behaved differently if the only people setting up had been the volunteers, but what she really meant was having a middle-class white woman in charge of things took the wind out of their sails. She knew this town better than I did. But I got it.

"You think they'll be back?"

"For sure. First sign of us getting too much interest they'll be looking for any excuse to get us packed away and off home."

"You need me to do anything?"

"Take the weekend off. I've got people doing two-hour shifts. We can't have more than four of us manning the booth at any one time. But if you fancy dropping by around lunch so I can grab a bite, that would be much appreciated."

"Better, place your order with me and I'll play delivery boy," I offered.

"Perfect." She gave me a not too complicated sandwich order.

I was about to leave when a couple of uniforms came around the corner stall, heading in our direction.

They glanced at me as they walked past, and although neither of them spoke I was pretty sure that I recognized one of them from the protest.

I waited until they were out of sight and left Carrie to it.

9

I called back just after noon bearing sandwiches. Carrie disappeared for maybe half an hour. I figured she deserved the break, so I manned the fort. I was surprised to see that there were so many leaflets still on the table, and more surprised that in the time I was there I could have counted the number of people who came close enough to see what we had on display on one hand.

"Has it been like this all morning?" I asked one of volunteers. Her name was Lola, but I didn't ask her if she was a showgirl. She'd been in the office a couple of times in the week. Most of the volunteers had other commitments that they worked around.

"We were busier for the first hour," she said. "Then it started to die off. Only a little at first. More so as we got closer to lunch. It will pick up again a little later."

I admired her optimism but couldn't see where it was coming from.

I took a minute to look at the people buying things from the nearest stalls, which were still doing a brisk trade. I was starting to see what was going on.

"When I called earlier there were hardly any white folks

about," I said. I was thinking out loud, but the woman nodded along, her smile just a little wider, like I'd just cracked the enigma code.

"You come to the market often?" Lola asked.

"Sometimes."

"And what time do you come?"

I had to think about it for a moment, but then said, "Mid-morning, I guess."

"And I suppose there's as many black faces as white ones?"

"I guess," I said. "I haven't really paid attention before."

"It's not just color of the skin, it's money. Poorer people come in the morning, hoping to grab any bargains, or come by right at the end, hoping to get any stuff that would otherwise be wasted. Folks with more money wait to avoid the crowds; they're in no hurry. It's just the way it is."

And while she said it wasn't about color, there were more poor black people than white; we both knew that.

A young white couple looked as if they were about to head our way, the young woman tugging the man's arm. Lola still had her smile ready, but I saw it drop a fraction when the couple turned back at the sight of the two uniformed officers coming around the corner again.

And the other shoe dropped.

"Have they been doing that all morning?"

"Yup. And their little patrols are just enough to scare some folks off. I guess they don't want the cops to see them fraternizing with us. Joys of running against the chief's old man. Some of them come over once the officers gone, but most of them don't."

"And let me guess, the patrols are a new thing, just for today."

That laugh again, accompanied by the shake of her head. "You're wasted in politics, you should be a reporter. This is the first time I've seen them here in months. Surprise surprise."

"I think I'm beginning to understand how this town works," I said.

"Not just this town. This kind of subtle intimidation happens everywhere, believe me. My sister lives thirty miles away over the State line, and the same thing happens there. The laws might be slightly different, but the end results are just the same."

It was depressing as fuck.

The two cops were set to make another pass, and now I was sure I'd seen one of them in the thick of it at the protest. "Do you know who the officer on the left is? The fair-haired guy, walks like he's got a baton stuck up his butt?"

"Jake Twomey," she said, no grin at what I thought was my colorful description of his strut. "Came close to giving him a clip around the ear when he was a young un. Stealing cakes from a stall. He had the money in his pocket to pay for it, but you know what it's like with some, the sense of entitlement, they take what they want, like it's theirs to take. I grabbed the little shit and made him pay for it. He ran home crying to his daddy, who came back all piss and thunder cussing me out, like I was the villain for daring to treat his boy like that."

"Sounds like a right charmer," I said.

"Like father, like son. Why the interest?"

I told her. "Thing is, he wasn't in uniform."

"You think he was there to cause trouble? I wouldn't put it past him. He's big on old school justice. Want my advice, don't go making an enemy of him."

I saw Carrie heading back in our direction.

"How's it been going while I've been away?"

"Quiet," I said. "Our friendly neighborhood cops seem to be coming around more and more frequently, I've noticed. Funny how that just manages to keep our numbers down."

"Hmm. Wonder how much longer they'll keep it up. I'll bet the lure of fresh donuts will call them away before too long." Which reminded me of a story I'd heard from a kid in LA once, how he'd been arrested for bribing a cop. His crime? He'd been pulled over for a traffic violation and without thinking offered the officer one of the donuts from a box on the backseat. He'd been high as fuck at the time, of course, which had nothing to do with his arrest.

The two cops appeared again, like clockwork.

This time they were grinning in our direction as they walked closer.

"I'm going to scoot," I said, not wanting to get so close that the other cop recognized me the way I did him.

10

I was still trying to place Jake Twomey's role in the protest when I reached my apartment.

The place felt empty after the constant noise of the farmer's market.

I must admit, I usually enjoyed the peace and quiet of my own company, but I could get itchy when there was something in my head that I couldn't quite scratch.

Twomey was that itch.

The more I thought about it, the surer I was he wasn't one of the officers on duty at the event. I'd thought for a while he might have been in riot gear, and that was why I might not have seen his face fully. But that didn't feel right. He wasn't in uniform. He'd been in amongst the protestors, I was more and more sure of that.

I grabbed a carton of juice and sat down at my laptop, more to satisfy my curiosity, than with any expectation of finding an answer. Plus, I had a couple of press releases I wanted to get out of the way. Weekend off? Hah. Who needed it? It wasn't as though I had a life anyway.

It didn't take long to find a picture of Twomey in his uniform, looking younger and considerably more fresh-faced than he had done today. What a difference five years could make. This one had been taken when he'd joined the force.

I checked the newspaper's on-line archive, one of the perks of Phil keeping my position open, my login was still active. Twomey's name returned a handful of hits. Most of them were little more than a name check, him being listed as one of the officers attending a crime scene, or a road traffic accident. There was one though, which had him photographed with his father, also in uniform, who was retiring from the force. I guess police work was the family business.

There was still something about him that felt wrong.

I couldn't nail it down.

A vibe.

Call it instinct of you want.

I'm not sure why I did it, but I put his father's name in the system, and was rewarded with a whole slew of responses; hardly any of them good.

It made for grim reading. Twomey's father, Walter, had been involved in four fatal shootings over the course of a 20-year career. Four. The mathematics of that went horribly beyond chance. I'm sure some algorithm somewhere must have flagged him, even though he was exonerated from any wrongdoing on every occasion. There was even a photograph of him receiving some kind of award for bravery. I felt sick to my stomach as I scrolled through the stories, reading the accounts of the petty crimes turned ugly, and how every victim had been black.

I tried to rationalize it; tried for a moment to convince myself that I was reading too much into this. I hadn't been here back then. Maybe there had been a period when the town suffered from a disproportionately high rate of violent crimes, maybe some sort of meth or oxy problem driving it, and that it was all just coincidental and not systematic. But that only made things worse, because I was trying to justify his actions; I was coming at it from a place of educated privilege. I couldn't read this stuff anymore. Instead, I turned to social media, wanting to find out more about the son. It was him, after all, who'd drawn me down this rabbit hole.

It didn't take long to find him. And none of what I found was good. Photos of him draped in the Confederate flag, or wielding a gun, often more than a few historic photographs of black people hanging from trees.

It was a grotesque mixture of images and one that any smart man would steer well clear of.

I closed the laptop and leaned back in my chair.

I really didn't want to go following him down that rabbit hole. It was enough that I knew him, even if I couldn't place him exactly within the crowd. It would come to me, or it wouldn't. The afternoon was almost over, and I had wasted too much of it. I'd downloaded a bunch of material when I was in the office, and I really need to read it. Jordan had asked me to look at it, though I'm not sure what he intended me to do with it.

I set my laptop aside to clear a space on my desk then fished the iPad out of the shoulder bag I used for work. I set a fresh yellow legal pad on the table, placed my favorite pen on top and did the one thing that I knew was going to make it just a little easier: I made a pot of strong coffee.

By the time I'd tapped my way over the last page my back was on fire.

I got up to walk around.

Outside the night was black and wet streets shone with the reflection of streetlights.

I hadn't even realized it had been raining. It was already past 11PM. At some point I had made a sandwich and a second pot of coffee. Then a third. My eyes were tired, but my mind was wired. I'd filled 20 pages of the legal pad with notes I thought that might prove to be useful, but I had no clue how we were meant to find the time to make half-decent use of it.

There were a million little inequalities that came about

directly and indirectly by the color of someone's skin, and the nature of white privilege. Things that most people wouldn't even register, but they were there to be lived by those without the luxury of being white.

One of the last things I read was a story about a seventy-six-year-old woman being sent back to prison for parole violations. She'd failed to answer a call from her probation officer. The take-away was, because they couldn't tell if she was robbing a bank at the time, they were going to treat her as though she was robbing a bank. It was bullshit. She'd been in a computer class, training and couldn't pick up the phone. But even that was bullshit. She was seventy-six years old and being forced to train, when her peers had been retired for a decade or more. It's a system meant to facilitate failure, not success. It wants her to fail and end up back inside. It's not a system designed for justice. Reading through countless stories like hers I was left with one logical conclusion, as sick as it was to even contemplate: with private prisons in existence, were probation officers getting kickbacks for how many parolees they could feed back into the machine?

It's easy to say that I wanted to do whatever I could to help Jordan win, but it was more than that, I wanted to make a difference. I was as naïve and willful at that. I wanted to change the world.

I should have known that violence is behind most real radical change.

I should have known that there was real pain behind any change.

———

I'M NOT sure what time I finally stumbled to bed, but I hadn't been asleep long when my phone rang.

By the time I finished flailing around blindly and found it, the caller had rung off.

I rubbed the sleep from my eyes and struggled to focus, the Caller ID a blur that slowly solidified into the name Phil. And for a moment, I thought I was late for work, my old and new reality fused in my sleep deprived head.

I wandered into the bathroom and splashed a few handfuls of ice-cold water onto my face before I went to the kitchen. I turned on the radio and started making coffee before I called him back.

He answered straight away.

"Hey, Phil."

"Have you heard?" he said.

"Heard what?"

"Sorry," he said. "I've been trying to get hold of Jordan, but his phone is off."

"OK," I said, not sure what was going on here, and it wasn't just sleep deprivation causing the problems.

"You met Lola? Lola Brown?"

Lola. There couldn't be that many in town, and certainly not that many Lola's linked to Jordan's campaign.

"Sure, I know Lola," I said. "We worked the stand in the farmer's market together."

Silence.

No not silence.

I could hear was Phil's breathing.

"What's happened, Phil?"

"She was attacked last night," he said. "The story just landed at the paper. I thought Jordan would want to know straight away."

"Of course. What happened? How's she doing? I should go see her."

There was another silence. I felt a hollowness in the pit of my stomach long before Phil said, "She's dead, son."

Three words. They didn't make sense. They couldn't. Because she couldn't be dead. She was so full of life.

"What happened, do you know?"

"The preliminary police report says that her house was

broken into. The place was turned over. I've seen the photos. It was a mess."

I didn't want to ask the next question, but I needed to hear the answer. "How did she die."

"There are no good deaths, Caleb," Phil said. "You should leave it at that."

"I need to know, Phil. I need to make sense of this."

"She was beaten, dragged out of her home and..." He couldn't say it. He couldn't say the last word. "They lynched her, Caleb... they fucking lynched her in her own yard."

11

I have never been in a room filled with so much sadness.
I'd tried to get hold of Jordan after Phil had rung off but
had no more success than he'd had. I tried Carrie next, and
she answered before the first ring had begun.

"Caleb," she said. "I was expecting Jordan."

"Do you know where he is? Phil's been trying to get hold of
him, and I can't get an answer."

"He's been at the hospital most of the night," she said.

And for a heartbeat I thought that he'd been hurt somehow,
but she quickly added, "Have you heard about Lola?"

She told me what she knew.

They'd found her, cut her down and Jordan had performed
CPR, trying to keep her alive until the medics could get to her,
but it was a lost cause. He'd known it. Even so, he'd followed to
the hospital and waited while the doctors and nurses did what
they could to save her life, even if there had been no real hope.
Carrie let it spill out in a rush, the horror of it too much for her.
She ended the call abruptly, saying that Jordan was trying to get
through.

There was no getting away from the fact there was a message in her death.

It left me feeling utterly sick to my core.

Jordan called me later to say that he and Carrie were calling around as many of the volunteers as they could. He wanted them to hear the news from one of them, not from the news bulletin that would be going out on the hour. I offered to call around but, and I'm not ashamed to admit it, I was relieved when he declined the offer. I knew my place. I was still a stranger to most of the team even if I saw myself as integral to Jordan's success. That was just the nature of being the new kid.

"I'm trying to get as many of us together this afternoon as I can," he said. "It would be good if you were able to call into the office around four?"

"Of course."

He sounded exhausted. Unsurprising. I doubted he'd slept more than a few minutes.

He looked worse when we convened at the campaign head-quarters that afternoon.

"Thanks for coming in," he said to the group. There were more people gathered in the main room than I'd seen in there at one time before. Most were familiar faces now, even if I'd barely shared a few words and a nod with them. There were a handful I'd never seen before. Carrie came out of the office and threw her arms around me. It was her grief, so of course she imagined we all felt it just as powerfully. I was disconnected from it in a lot of ways. Shocked. But I had barely known the poor woman. It was more the vicinity of death that rattled me, and the nature of it, rather than the victim, if that makes sense?

From the atmosphere in the room, it was obvious they'd heard the news.

Most of them were chatting in little clusters, expressing their disbelief and sorrow, saying her name again and again as though it could bring Lola back. There were others who stood alone, silent and lost.

I assumed I'd been brought in for the logistics—in the crudest terms, what we were going to do going forward, and what effect a death in the close-knit family would have on the campaign?

But seeing everyone, I couldn't help but wonder if he had something else in mind.

And then it hit me. He was thinking the unthinkable. He was going to pull out of the race.

The door opened a few more times as people came in. There were more welcomes and condolences. More hugs and tears.

Jordan called the room to order.

His voice had lost much of its richness, reduced to rasping.

"Thank you all for coming," he said. "I know that Sunday is a special day for many of you, and I cannot adequately express how deeply I regret the circumstances that have brought us here."

There was something about the way he spoke, the way he held himself, that reminded me of a minister talking to his congregation. But that's what we were, wasn't it? His flock of disciples at best.

"As I'm sure that you all know, we lost one of our own last night. Lola Brown was one of us. She's been with us since before most of you joined the campaign; she was even helping before I'd filed the paperwork to enter the race. That's how committed she was to the cause. She was the first, and it's impossible to comprehend that we've lost her." He looked around the room, at the faces, but it was in his eyes. He was lost. He was looking for something, a glimmer of hope, being reflected at him. It wasn't forthcoming. "She'll leave a hole in this world... in all of our lives... I don't know what else to say except that she will be missed."

There were murmurs of agreement and nods of head.

He wasn't telling them what they didn't already know.

"They're saying it's because of the campaign... that she was killed because she was working for you," a voice said from the huddle, loud enough for everyone to hear.

The room fell silent.

I looked at Jordan and saw his head drop. I'd considered that possibility. How could I not? She might have been *just* a volunteer, but she was a direct line to the candidate. It might not be Jordan lying on the mortuary slab but the effect on him was written all over his face.

Jordan took a breath and looked up. "I've heard the rumor too. I wish I could say it wasn't true. We all know there are people in this town who are desperate to stop what we are doing here. We always say things like we're prepared to do whatever it takes, but then we confront something like this, and you must wonder if that is the definition of what it takes, that fanaticism, or if it's coincidence. I don't want to believe it's true. But I won't lie, the chance that it might be terrifies me. Not for me, but for you."

Another voice called out. "We have families, children who are relying on us. My wife has already lost her job because we've been helping you. We were prepared for that because we believe in what we're trying to do here. But how long before someone else gets hurt because of this? How long before we're gathering again to say what a tragedy it is we've lost someone? I'm frightened, Jordan, and I don't mind admitting it."

Some of the voices were murmuring in agreement with the speaker.

Everyone in the room was frightened. There was no escaping it.

"I understand," Jordan said. "I do. I get it. And I don't blame any of you who are beginning to doubt what we're doing here... those of you who are thinking about your families, your safety, I won't try to stop you if you want to walk away, you'll do it with my blessing and my love and my gratitude. I won't try to talk you into anything. We must do what our hearts tell us. I hope I can still rely on your vote."

I listened to him, but I was trying to watch the reaction of his people.

The easiest thing to do in the face of Lola's murder was to pack their things and leave. He was giving them permission. Better than that, he was giving them his blessing. Guilt free.

"What about you? Are you going to walk away now?" one young female volunteer asked. Ruby. She'd brought me coffee a couple of times in the last week and we'd chatted a bit. She had a righteous fire in her. She was exactly the kind of volunteer we needed.

"In all honesty? I've thought about it. I lay awake most of the night thinking about it. I spent most of the morning thinking about it. I thought about it over lunch and on the drive here. I thought about Lola. And I thought about you. And I realized that as much as I want to, as easy as it would be to, I can't. Not now. That would be betraying Lola. I know it will sound stupid, but if she did give her life for us... for this... how could I let that be for nothing? Her life and her death must mean something. So no, I'm not going to walk away. And I'm hoping some of you will stand with me, because we don't have much time left and there's still much to do if we're going to change things here."

I watched them still.

Some couldn't take their eyes off Jordan.

I knew that they would stay.

They were enthralled by the man, the cause, or both, and wouldn't walk away from the fight. It had just become more important to them. It had become about Lola's sacrifice. Some looked at the walls, the floor, their neighbors, anywhere but into Jordan's eyes, and I knew they were gone. And I couldn't blame them.

Carrie though, was looking directly at me.

I didn't know if she expected me to say something, or if she was trying to figure out which side I was going to fall on. Stay or leave? I held her stare and nodded.

I wasn't about to walk away.

———

WE ONLY LOST three of the volunteers, and there were doubts about a handful of others who hadn't shown their faces at the meeting. They were a loss, but good to their word no one blamed them, and Jordan and Carrie were clearly relieved it hadn't been worse.

We were the last three there, with tasks assigned to everyone else for the coming days. A few volunteered to do more, to pick up the extra burden of those we'd lost.

No one said anything about replacing Lola.

"The police wouldn't let me enter the house," Jordan said, "But I got a look in through the window. The place was a mess. I mean it looked like a bomb hit. Whoever did this to her was determined to cause as much damage as they could. Like they were enjoying it."

He fell silent for a moment, then said what we were all thinking.

"It could have been any of us."

"You're sure it had to do with the campaign then?" I asked.

He grimaced and nodded and that was all he needed to do.

"She's lived in that house for more than twenty years. It's a quiet neighborhood; poor but quiet, and she's well liked. It's not the kind of place you break into looking for a fast score. But the police are convinced that's what it was, an opportunistic burglary. Some junkie looking for enough cash to get his next fix, which stinks like so much shit. What junkie has ever dragged a woman out of her home and hung her from a tree in the yard for fix money? It's a fucking joke..."

"You should get something to eat," Carrie said, placing a hand on Jordan's arm. It was an intimate gesture. Full of compassion and concern. "Then try to get some sleep. Actual sleep. You look dead on your feet."

"Too much to do before that," he said, but they were empty words. There wasn't much fight left in him now that the audience was gone. No need for the unbroken rhetoric. He could look every bit as battered as he really was.

It didn't take long to make a list of things that needed to be done before Monday morning, which was thankfully short. Carrie and I divided up the tasks, taking no argument from Jordan. This was the way it was going to be. We were a team.

"I'll drive you to your place, pick up a few things, and you can come back to mine. The spare room is already made up. I'll fix you something to eat while you grab a shower."

"People will talk," he said, and I couldn't really take it in. The words sounded like a joke, but they didn't, too. And this kind of thing, death, brought out a primal side, a need for physical contact, to affirm that you were alive.

"People are already talking," she said. "Let them. You need the ratings boost of a hottie like me." She burst out laughing at that. "Now let me look after you."

———

BY THE TIME I was back in my apartment it was already past seven.

It had been a long day.

Brutally so, on an emotional level.

I'd grabbed a burger and fries from the drive through because I couldn't face cooking. I managed to eat on the drive back.

I'm a workaholic. It's something I've noticed about myself over the last few months. I escape into work. Tonight, I needed somewhere to hide. The last thing I wanted to do was bump into social media posts about Lola. I opened the lid on the laptop, which woke on Jake Twomey's page.

I shouldn't have looked.

I wish I hadn't.

But if wishes were fishes and all that shit.

I felt sick when I saw he'd posted a photograph of the exterior of what had to be Lola's home, with the accompanying horror story. *'One less black bitch to vote.'*

It wasn't just the ugliness of it, it was the fact that the post had been liked almost 50 times and there was a slew of comments beneath it, all very similar to what he'd said.

I wanted to write something, to rage at him, but what good would that have done? But I couldn't just ignore it. That way lay madness. No, I needed to talk to someone who would understand. Jordan was in no fit state to deal with it and Carrie had a big enough burden of her own.

I rang Phil.

"I wish I could say it's a surprise," Phil said after I'd filled him. "Does Jordan know?"

"I haven't told him," I said. "I have to admit I'm feeling a little out of my depth here, boss."

"Don't," he said. "You've got this. You know what to do. Stay calm. Use your head. Think. No lashing out."

"Are you covering Lola's murder?" I asked. Of course, they were. It's not as if a murder in a small town had become so common place that it didn't bear reporting.

"Of course," he said, "We're not allowed inside the house, so I can only go on what the police have told us, plus whatever we can glean from the neighbors."

"Are you going to say she was lynched in her own yard?"

"What are you saying?"

"That's what Jordan told me... that he cut her down."

"Fuck..."

"Yeah... fuck."

"I don't know... I mean... I want to say yes..."

"But."

"Yeah. But."

"What about her murder being linked to the campaign?"

"Ah, son, you know that's pure speculation, until the cops say otherwise."

"OK. But you know it and I know it. And more to the point Jordan knows it. Everyone out there is talking about it. What if I wrote a piece about her, from the campaign side, saying how valuable her work has been, how deeply she will be missed, and that we are a family in mourning. Let people link it in their minds."

"Sure," he said. "Just don't come out and say it that bluntly. And make sure that you get Jordan to approve the copy before you send it over."

"Will you run it on the same page as the report of her death?"

"You know I will," he said. "And you know I'll be eating shit for a long time because of it. But it is the right thing to do."

It was a juggling act, truth vs sponsors, truth vs cops, truth vs public interest, truth vs fear and lies. We agreed on a word count and deadline to make sure it ran, and promised a proper sit down to catch up. But not today. Or tomorrow.

I gave Carrie a call. After all, she knew Lola better than any of us. I needed her to help me paint a real portrait, not just a children's sketch of the woman she had been. I wanted people to know who Lola Brown really was.

12

I was working until the small hours of the morning chalking things off my list, but the only one that really mattered was the piece about Lola.

It was also the hardest.

Carrie had thought it was great idea and was one hundred percent behind it, but Jordan had already been asleep so he couldn't give his OK. I emailed the completed article to him at around 1 AM, knowing I wouldn't hear back from him until the morning.

I hoped he'd be happy with it, first as a concept, then as a piece of work. It needed to be good enough, the problem was how could anything like that ever be good enough?

The last things on my list were a couple of phone calls to set up meetings over the next few days, none of which could be made until morning, so I crashed out on the couch. I know there was a comfortable bed only a few feet away, but it was so much easier to just lift my feet up and roll sideways than it was to get up and walk even a couple of steps to the other room. Besides, the couch was probably the most comfortable piece of furniture in the apartment.

I know I slept. I'm not sure how well or how long, with the light streaming into the lounge, and onto my face from dawn. It was only stubbornness that kept me lying there as long as I did.

Finally, I got up again, and went to the kitchen to brew up a fresh pot of coffee and grab a couple of pieces of toast before I went back to check my email and make sure I was still ahead of the game.

I was surprised to find a response from Jordan already waiting in my in-box.

His response was short and not particularly sweet. *'Hold fire until we've had the chance to talk. J.'*

He was one of those people who, after a couple of emails dropped into a very familiar pattern of signing off with an initial, or not signing off at all, like the conversation was still on-going.

I checked the clock on the wall. It was barely six. So, I'd probably managed about four and a half hours of actual sleep. I still had a few hours before I needed to file the copy to meet Phil's deadline if he was going to run it beside the murder story.

I drank my coffee and ate my toast, leaving crumbs on the carpet in front of the couch, then went to the bathroom to freshen up. The boiler wasn't up to much, and the water pressure was worse, so the shower was far from invigorating, but at least I wouldn't smell like a man who had fallen asleep in his clothes.

The mood in the office was somber when I arrived. It was a little after eight. There were only a handful of volunteers in, and they'd already been assigned their jobs for the day. There was an element of calm efficiency about it all. What there wasn't was a lot of talking.

Jordon and Carrie were tucked away in his office, the door closed.

I'd only seen it closed a couple of times in the time I'd been here. Jordan was an open-door kind of leader, always available to his people, welcoming.

But not today.

Seeing me through the glass, I was summoned in to join them. Judging from their manner there was something wrong—and I mean more wrong than there had been yesterday, which rattled me.

"Everything OK?"

"Not really," Jordan said. "You'd better sit down."

I did as I was told, taking one of the leather armchairs against the wall, and waited for one of them to explain.

"We've lost three more," Jordan said, and for that long-sliding silence between one heartbeat and the next I thought he meant lost like Lola lost. "All three work at the mill and they've been told, in no uncertain terms, that if they continue to work with us here, they can start looking for new jobs."

"They can't do that," I said.

Jordan shrugged. "But that's the thing, they can, or at least they can try for long enough to effectively mean they can. You ever read a contract of employment?"

"One or two," I said, though in truth I'd probably never done more than glance at them, even when I was signing.

"Right, so, the morality clause, the one about not bringing the employer into disrepute. That's their argument."

I couldn't believe what I was hearing. "What sort of fucked up moral crusade is it when you're not allowed to work on a legitimate political campaign? This town..."

"I know Dale Anders," Carrie interrupted, speaking up for the first time since I'd entered the room. "All he cares about is the almighty dollar. He's afraid that his business will take a hit if people associate it with us, and that's what happens when people who work for him are handing out our fliers and pins. It's a small town. People don't differentiate. It's not this and that, and both stay separate, it's all just blurred together in the minds of the townsfolk. You're his people, you're their people, it doesn't really matter normally as long as you're good people..."

"You think someone has leaned on him? Made threats? I mean the timing of it..."

She shrugged. "I have my suspicions, but it doesn't really matter in practical terms. It is what it is. And I doubt that Dale would admit someone's been threatening him, even if they have."

"Bullshit," I said, "You know it wouldn't happen if Jordan was some middle-class white guy." Jordan raised a hand to silence me mid-flow.

"That's not fair, Caleb. Dale Anders is a good man and a fair employer. Look at his roster, he has almost as many blacks on his payroll as white, and there's no pay disparity. They all receive the same money for the same work. He treats his workers equally. Trust me, I wish there were more men like Dale Anders around here. I can't blame him for protecting his business. And more than that, I won't because what he's doing is protecting his workers, the people who rely on him for that paycheck to eat. His hands are tied. What really matters is what happens next. If other businesses, and other good men like Dale, are forced into making the same choice we're in trouble."

"This is intimidation," I objected. "It's not about making choices, it's about interfering with the electoral process. Someone on Dwyer's side, maybe even Dwyer himself, is behind this."

"Then think of it another way. They must be afraid of us," Jordan said.

"We should include it in the piece going out today. There's a way to spin this." My mind was already thinking about how I could work it into the piece without mentioning any names, without pointing fingers but still getting the point across loud and clear.

"That's the other thing I wanted to talk to you about," Jordan said. "I appreciate what you did there, but we can't use it."

I couldn't quite believe what I was hearing. There was an edge of defeatism to his tone that I hadn't heard before. "What do you mean we can't use it? We *have* to."

Jordan shook his head. "You're good at what you do, but it's obvious, it's confrontational, you're not coming out and saying it, but only an idiot reads that and doesn't think you're linking Lola's death to the campaign and laying the blame at Dwyer's feet even if he wasn't the one who strung her up. It's going to do more harm than good, Caleb, especially when we have no proof that her murder was politically motivated."

"They lynched her, Jordan. They didn't beat her or stab her or shoot her. They dragged her out into her yard and lynched her. That's all about the color of her skin. That's all about the deep fucking shame of this State... You can't get much more political than that."

"We've written an alternative piece about Lola," Jordan said, ignoring me. That was worse than if he'd slapped me down. It reminded me where my place was. He nodded to Carrie, and she handed me a printout. I started to read it and couldn't help myself. I pulled out my pen to make some minor changes, striking through things, punching up a few turns of phrase. It painted a touching picture of a hardworking woman who loved her community. There was a single mention of the campaign and how, as with everything else she did in her life, she had given so much of herself to it. As an obituary, it was much better than the piece I had written.

"I get where you are coming from in this, Caleb. I really do. But I refuse to use Lola's death to incite more anger," Jordan said. "That's a dark path to walk, and if you ask me, she deserves better than that."

I nodded and handed him the piece of paper with my notes on. In truth I had done little more than change the order of the things he was trying to say about her and question a few verb choices. He glanced at it then nodded and handed it back to Carrie.

"I'm glad you understand, Caleb. Believe me, sometimes I hate the world we're living in, but I like to think that I've learned how it works well enough to survive in it." I nodded. I didn't say whether I thought that kind of survival was a good or bad thing. "I have a radio interview later, and rest assured they'll want to ask about it, so I need everyone on the same page. Can I count on you not to go rogue here?"

Before I had the chance to answer there was a knock on the glass door.

Jordan gestured for the young volunteer to come in.

"Sorry to bother you," she said, from around the door frame. "But there's a couple of police officers here."

Jordan sighed. "OK, I suppose I'd better talk to them. We'll come back to this later, Caleb."

"Oh, sorry, it's not you they want to talk to, Jordan. They're looking for Caleb."

13

They didn't just want to *talk* to me, they wanted me to accompany them to the station for a formal interview, which, I don't mind admitting, set my Spidey senses tingling.

It was worse when I realized Jake Twomey was one of them.

"What's this about?" I asked, and when that didn't work, "What do you think I'm supposed to have done?"

"If you don't mind, we'll talk about it down at the station, shall we," Twomey said.

"I do mind, I'd rather talk about it here."

"Ah, well, in that case tough shit. Now, are you going to come peacefully or are we going to be required to force you to comply?"

Forcefully comply felt like a euphemism for beat seven shades of shit out of me for supposedly resisting arrest, which would be hard, given I wasn't under arrest. And I knew I wasn't under arrest because neither of them had offered a charge, and there'd been no Miranda.

I saw Jordan had already picked up his phone and was making a call.

I wasn't the only one.

"Who the fuck do you think you're calling?" Twomey barked.

"His lawyer," Jordan replied, "That's the way it works in this country." He held the phone to his ear without breaking eye contact with the cop.

Carrie fumbled in her bag for her own phone. She'd done this dance often enough to know there needed to be video evidence. None of us were naïve enough to think justice had been behind Derek Chauvin's 22-year sentence for killing George Floyd. It was a shaky iPhone video that had convicted him. Without it, he would have been just another officer doing his duty against a subject resisting arrest.

Twomey held up both hands as if trying to reassure everyone, that whole keep calm and let's not let things get out of hand here thing, like we were all good friends here, no need to overreact. It's all good, man.

But he wasn't doing a good job of reassuring me.

Maybe that was because I'd seen his social media, and knew he'd been gloating over Lola's death. Maybe I'd got a glimpse of the real man, the one he kept hidden most of the time...

His partner pulled a pair of cuffs from his belt.

I felt the temperature of the room rising.

I'm a black man in modern America. I've had my share of encounters with the police and very few of them had been particularly pleasant, even when the cops were just doing their job. There's an element of guilty of being black in a place you don't belong, or at least that's the way it feels. I mean, its training, and that makes it worse. Profiling. The few of the times I'd stopped while walking in predominantly white neighborhoods, or well-to-do suburbs, it felt like they looked at me and saw the potential for crime, like they were Thought Police, even though the thought never crossed my mind. There's only one time I was stopped, and the cop apologized for holding me up. But I've been lucky. None of them, as unpleasant as they may have felt at the time, turned ugly. I've never had a gun aimed at me.

Twomey struck me as the kind of cop looking for an excuse to do just that.

"Are you going to come with us voluntarily, *sir*?" The word must have stuck in his throat, but Carrie was catching every moment of the exchange now. He flashed her a smile filled with shark's teeth. "Or do I have to arrest you? If I arrest you, and you still refuse to come, I urge you to consider the fact that I am allowed to use reasonable force in your apprehension, and I'm sure none of us would want that, would we?" Another smile.

I knew that I didn't have a lot of choice.

"Just for the record," Carrie said. "Could you just confirm what it is you would like to interview Caleb about?"

Twomey let out a sigh. "Caleb Moon, I am arresting you on suspicion of involvement in a civil disturbance on the 25th August this year..." He went on to read me my rights, but by then I had stopped listening—or at least hearing. Twomey's lips moved but I wasn't really hearing a word he said.

"You'd better go with them," Jordan said. "The only word you say before your lawyer gets there is lawyer, understand?"

I started to tell him that I didn't have a lawyer... I mean, why would I need one?

"Don't worry," he said. "It's all in hand."

I got to my feet and Twomey pulled one hand behind my back, a little rougher than he needed to be, and cuffed me.

"Is there really any need for that?" Carrie asked.

"There wouldn't be any need at all if he'd come along voluntarily," Twomey said, enjoying himself. He nodded to his colleague and motioned for him to lead the way. "No rush with the lawyer, there could be a bit of a wait. We're rounding up a whole bunch of folks this morning."

Twomey's grabbed my arm, fingers sinking in hard, and hauled me towards the door. I did my best to keep up with him, my thigh hitting the corner of a desk as he pushed and pulled me along. He was doing it deliberately.

I had this desperate urge to protest my innocence, to insist it was a mistake, I hadn't done anything wrong, but I knew Jordan was right. Not a word until the lawyer showed up. Nothing that could be twisted or used against me. Twomey didn't seem all that interested in talking either. The volunteers watched me being taken through the main office and out into the street. I couldn't help but wonder what they were thinking, because they hadn't been close enough to hear the supposed charges... and in a moment of sinking dread it occurred to me that maybe, just maybe, they thought this was about Lola.

A couple of minutes later and I was in the back of a squad car and heading to the station house with heads turning as we drove past.

I didn't think that many of them knew who I was, but that didn't matter. And it didn't matter for one reason and one reason alone. Perception.

What they saw was another black guy being taken away by the police, proof their prejudices were well founded.

————

THERE WERE at least twenty people waiting to be booked in when we arrived at the station. They'd rounded us up like cattle. It was deliberately degrading.

There was anger and confusion amongst those of us who had been at the protest, but worse was the element of smug amusement amongst the police. I didn't want to believe in the kind of institutional racism that would have them thinking of today as a fun day out, but it was hard to deny the evidence of your own eyes. Not a single person out of uniform was white. I recognized a couple of faces from the protest, and they'd been every bit as frightened as I had when things went to hell.

I was pushed onto a wooden bench and told not to move until I was called to the desk. Every man in uniform was armed with handguns and tasers. It gave me a very uneasy feeling. There was a dichotomy of power here, and absolutely no sense of presumed innocence. They looked at us like we were vermin.

Half an hour later, the number of bodies in the room had doubled. I'd given up my place on the bench to an elderly woman and sat on the floor next to it, arms wrapped around my knees, back pressed up against the cold wall.

My lawyer arrived as my name was called; his linen suit was crumpled, with what I assumed were sweat stains, his hair was unbrushed and he walked with a limp, favoring his right foot. I saw he wore sandals and no socks, and that there was some sort of eczema rash up around his ankles. He didn't inspire confidence.

I struggled to my feet, which wasn't easy with my hands still cuffed.

"Full name?" the desk sergeant asked.

"Caleb Daniel Moon," I said, then gave him a load of information that he already had on the form in front of him.

"I'd like a word with my client in private before we proceed to the interview," my lawyer said. It wasn't a request, no matter how politely he phrased it.

The desk sergeant let out a theatrical sigh, shrugged as if to say knock yourself out, and opened the door at the side of his counter to allow us through.

My lawyer made sure that the door clicked shut behind us as we went inside the interview room. "Someone will be along in a few minutes to talk you through what's going to happen next."

The lawyer introduced himself as John Havers. "Take a seat," he said, taking up a chair on the same side of the battered steel table as I was on. He opened a very full briefcase and pulled out a legal pad.

"Have you any idea what's going on?" I asked.

I didn't want to sit. I'd been sitting out there for too long already. I wanted to stand. To walk around. Pace. But most of all, I wanted to get out of there.

"Only what Jordan told me on the phone, which, let's be honest about this for a second, wasn't more than they came and took you away. I made a few calls on the way here, and in the interests of more of that honesty, no one has been particularly forthcoming. However, by the looks of the booking room outside, I'd wager that a number of people from that protest a couple of weeks back, about the boy and his dog, are being rounded up for some sort of civil disturbance charge."

"It was a peaceful protest until the brick was thrown, then it was frightened people trying to get out of the press of bodies. Nothing happened, not really. I sat down with Chief Dwyer the day after, he told me that he wasn't looking to take further action. He wanted calm restored."

"Well, what you've just described is hardly nothing, and, prima facia, it looks like he's changed his mind."

"But why? I mean why wait so long. What's changed?"

"To all of those questions I have the same rather unhelpful answer. I have no idea. But I will admit to suspicions, but then, you see, I am something of a cynic and know how the cogs in this town grind. Now, when the officer comes in, you are to remain silent. You say nothing unless I tell you to. Do you understand?" I nodded. "Good, let me do as much of the talking as I can, and we'll see about getting you out of here and back to the campaign office before lunch."

I admired his optimism.

There was a knock on the door, enough of a warning for us to stop talking before it opened. The arrival of a young officer prevented me from asking the one question that I wanted to. The cop looked like a strong wind would snap him in two. But he wasn't the one leading this little crusade. Twomey came in behind him. He didn't say a word. The young cop sat down on the other side of the table, across from my lawyer. Twomey took up a position behind him and leaned against the wall. It was all very deliberately staged. It reeked of too many bad cop shows on TV.

"Would you be so kind as to explain what this is about, officer?" Havers said, again with that slow Southern style. "I'm sure that you can appreciate, my client is a busy man at the moment, what with the campaign and everything. He's been waiting for some time and still has no idea why he is here, which, as you can imagine, is quite distressing."

The younger officer grimaced but didn't look to Twomey for instruction. He opened the manila folder he'd put down in front of him.

There were only a few sheets of paper in there.

He confirmed my name, address, and all the pertinent details again before he went on. I had the distinct impression he'd drawn the short straw with the grunt work while Twomey was going to get to play bad cop and have all the fun. He turned the page.

"I understand that you failed to come to the station voluntarily—"

Havers cut him off. "That is neither here nor there. Can we cut to the chase?"

"You don't want to drag it out, Havers? Thought your type were paid by the hour," Twomey mocked from the sidelines.

He might as well have not been there, no one in the room acknowledged his comment.

The young officer did his best not to be rattled by Havers, and went on, "You were made aware of your rights?"

"I'd like to see him deny that one," said Twomey, "given we've got it all on film, haven't we?"

The younger officer turned the arrest sheet over to reveal and eight by ten photograph which he turned towards me.

It was an image of the crowd from the demonstration with a circle around my face.

"Can you please confirm that's you?"

I glanced at my lawyer before saying anything in case he had any words of wisdom, but I could hardly deny that it was me. The image was perfectly clear. He nodded. I didn't like which way this was going.

"Mr. Moon?"

I nodded. "Yes, that's me."

"In that case, I can confirm that you are being charged with a number of public order offenses and will appear before a judge this afternoon to enter a plea. I'm sure that your lawyer can explain the process."

"But," I started to say but my lawyer stopped me.

"Officer, we both know how this works. Just because my client was present at a lawful protest does not mean he committed a crime. You'll note the term lawful protest."

"Frankly, that's for the judge to decide, not me," the officer said. "There were a number of missiles thrown at public officials, including a brick amongst other things, and shots were fired. We are treating this as an incredibly serious matter."

He returned the photograph to the folder and got to his feet.

He didn't say another word.

Twomey smirked at me as they left.

The other shoe dropped. I knew exactly where I'd seen him in that crowd. And what he'd been doing.

14

"You can't be serious," Havers said after digesting my explanations of the events surrounding the day of the protest. And of Twomey's role in it.

"Yeah, it struck me as off at the time, or at least if not off exactly, it raised my hackles. There were a couple of them who joined at the back and pushed their way through. I'm not sure anyone even noticed them, I mean it was right as Chief Dwyer was giving his grand speech for the camera."

"Understood, but let's be blunt about things, yes it was a predominantly black protest, but white guys can be allies. A voice is a voice, isn't that what we want, a unified voice?"

"It is," I said, "But that's not why they were there. I didn't see it clearly, but when that brick was thrown at the steps, they were right in the heart of it. I mean if they didn't do it, then someone close to them must have."

"And if they didn't do it, they may have seen who did," he suggested.

"Which makes perfect sense, but for one thing. Their silence. If they'd seen the guy who started the chaos with that brick they'd have spoken up by now. They're cops that drape themselves in Confederate flags. They'd have him nailed to the wall if it was some black guy."

"Assuming they could find the perpetrator."

"It's a small town. They're the law. Their influence is pretty much unchecked. They can do whatever they want. They'd make people talk to get the conviction they want. And the fact that Twomey was in the thick of it, watching me with that shit-eating grin on his face... this isn't good."

He leaned back in his chair and let out a sigh, then leaned down to scratch at the crusts of skin around his ankles. "That's a tough sell. A cop planted in the crowd to incite violence? You'd need something, a photo, film footage, something that places him in the heart of it, otherwise it's his word against yours."

"And he's the law."

"Worse than that, he's the one sweating other protestors right now, people with families and jobs and stuff to lose. People who didn't see him in that crowd."

"People who will say whatever they want him to say."

"You see the problem here?"

"I see it," I said, but I needed to cling to the idea that there was still justice in this country. The problem with that was the naiveté of it. We lived in a country where a white GOP rep in Ohio can get three days in jail for voting on behalf of his dead father and a black woman in Texas on supervised release from prison can get five years for voting when she didn't realize she was ineligible. That's black and white. That's justice in America. I couldn't believe I was about to say, "But we can tell the judge," like there was any hope he wasn't prejudiced in all of this.

I could tell Havers was of a similar mind, and it was more damning because he knew the man. "Unsubstantiated claims, wild accusations, it doesn't matter how true they are, the truth doesn't even matter, what matters is what you can prove. And if you can't prove your innocence—or Twomey's guilt—you're out of luck. Worse, I fear, it will only serve to make matters worse by getting the judge's back up."

The problem for me was that I couldn't see how things could get worse than they already were. But that was down to my lack of imagination. A trait the people railroading me didn't suffer from.

"So, what do you think is going to happen?"

"You'll appear in front of the judge this afternoon, and you'll be asked to be plead guilty, or not guilty. If you plead guilty—"

"No ifs, I didn't do anything. I'm not pleading guilty to something I didn't do."

"Like I said, if you plead guilty, you may get a sentence immediately. If you plead not guilty, a date will be set for your trial."

I couldn't believe what I was hearing. There was just this sense of inevitability about it. He'd said it himself, the truth didn't matter. Again, I was struck by the thought that Derek Chauvin would be a free man if it wasn't for that iPhone video. It didn't matter that I hadn't done anything. It didn't matter that nothing had really happened there, despite the size of the protest. It wasn't like we'd stormed the Capitol building.

"And what happens then?" I didn't waste my breath repeating my not guilty plea.

"We apply for bail."

———

I WAS CHARGED and put into a holding cell designed to cage no more than six people. There were twelve of us in there. We heard voices down the corridor coming from another cell just like ours, with the same crush of bodies. It wasn't like they could corral everyone who had protested, but they were hellbent on making an example out of enough of us to send a message. The judge had ignored my press credentials. As far as he was concerned that was a matter for the trial, and it would be up to me to prove I was there to report and observe and not participate. I noted that several of the people in the cells knew each other. They talked quietly amongst themselves. I kept to myself.

"You're that new guy, from the campaign, aren't you?" Someone said to me, and all heads turned in my direction.

I nodded. "Not that that's going to do me a lot of good."

"Could even do you worse," someone else said.

That had crossed my mind, too.

But now they knew who I was, they assumed I knew more than they did, and that I might have insight into what was going on. They had a barrage of questions I couldn't answer. Why we were there, what was going on, what happened next?

I repeated what my lawyer had told me, but that wasn't enough to satisfy them. They were sure I was holding out. And still they kept up the questions, most of them the same just phrased in a different way.

The questions only ended when an officer appeared to take us to the courthouse.

———

THE COURTHOUSE WAS HALF a block away. A decision had been made to forego the transport to take us there. Instead, we would walk, chained together in leg irons, our hands cuffed, reinforcing the image of our guilt in the minds of anyone watching. I tried to pick up my feet and walk tall, but the chains made it hard to do anything but shuffle and drag them.

The traffic had been stopped. The twelve of us were escorted by four officers, two at the rear who walked with their shotguns locked and loaded.

It was hard to see what kind of danger we might have posed, and harder still to imagine engineering some sort of breakout when we were basically chain-ganged. Again, it felt like it was for show. Being played for the cameras—or the half of the town that had turned out to watch the spectacle. Most jeered, plenty threw insults, some spat. A couple lobbed fruit at us. It wasn't pretty. I couldn't shake the feeling that most of the onlookers enjoyed the spectacle of a bunch of black men in chains, like it was the natural order. That was another thing about this country, in the backlash against a black man who'd had the temerity to rise to the highest office in the land, everything now was about putting those dreamers back in their place.

They removed the leg irons when we were ushered into the holding pen at the rear of the courthouse, but the handcuffs stayed in place. Again, it felt like it was about perception. A man in cuffs looks guilty. It's like the defendant who is forced to testify already dressed in the prison orange. It just serves to reinforce preconceptions of guilt.

The holding pen was even more cramped that it had been in the police station. The difference here though was that the mood was fraught. That tension was putting everyone on edge, making them turn on each other and snap, and chipping away at any sense of solidarity. There was psychology at play here. A manipulation. And it was working.

We were caged up in there for a good thirty minutes before the door opened. A name was called and the first of us was led out.

The door was about to be slammed closed when my lawyer appeared. He beckoned me over, and I was allowed out of the cell for a few moments to speak with him in the corridor. There was no privacy this time. A court officer stood a few feet away.

"I have some news," the way he said it, I wasn't sure I wanted to hear it.

"Good news?"

"I would suggest that rather depends on your point of view. I've had a chat the with District Attorney. I wanted to get a feel for what they were looking for in terms of charges and concessions, and what we might be able to plea down to, and really to get a handle on what would happen if you plead guilty."

I started to protest but he held a hand up.

"Yes, yes," he said. "I know what you are going to say, I know all your objections, but this is pragmatism. I wouldn't be doing my job if I didn't present you with all the alternatives. You need to know the facts before you go into the courtroom."

"Fine"

"Plead guilty and you get fourteen days."

"Fourteen days? For the grand crime of attending a protest. You have to know that's insane."

"It's not for attending a protest though, it is for conspiracy to commit violent conduct," he corrected. "And fourteen days in the face of that? Honestly, that sounds pretty light to me."

Fourteen days would take me out of the election campaign. Was that a coincidence or was I seeing conspiracies in every damned shadow?

"It's still trumped-up bullshit," I said.

"So, I am assuming you still intend to plead not guilty?"

"You assume right."

"And you will remember that I said I was a cynic? Now, ask yourself this, what's the point of sending someone to prison for a couple of weeks? What do they stand to gain?"

"The point? To prevent a repeat performance. To discourage protest. To send a message to others who might dare challenge the system. Plenty of reasons."

"There are indeed, but don't accept your first answer, it's invariably wrong. Dig deeper. Why not longer? Why not give you six months, but make it suspended? You're a first-time offender. It's a minor crime, all things considered, and you have good standing in the community. That six-month probationary period would send out the same message, wouldn't it? But without the added burden to the taxpayers to feed you."

Which fed in to my first instinct that this was about the

campaign and everyone else in the holding cell behind me was collateral damage for my making a stand against Dwyer and his good old boys. It was just another form of voter suppression. I mean, what was I to the campaign, really? The voice. And if the voice helps get the message to even a handful of the community who otherwise might not have turned out, and those could be enough to tilt the balance, then what am I? I'm the malignant cancer in their bloated white corpse.

Before I could answer any of that stuff a cough from the guard interrupted us.

"Time's up," he said and ushered me back inside, calling out the next name before he closed the door.

I found a spot to lean against the wall and wait.

"They're getting through us quickly," one of my fellow condemned remarked.

"Doesn't take long to admit that your guilty," another said with the kind of resignation that caused my soul to ache.

"My lawyer told me if I plead guilty there'll be a fine, which will hurt, we ain't got money to be throwing around, but I'll be home by supper," a third said.

Maybe he was right, and my lawyer had got it wrong, or maybe I was right, and it was one justice for them, and another for me?

———

THERE WERE ONLY four of us left in the cell by the time my turn came.

I'd covered a handful of court cases when I first started working as a journalist. They were never that compelling to be honest. Most of my energy was spent desperately trying to stay awake. I'd never seen a courtroom as empty as it was today.

There was me, and the guard who had taken me to the dock. The judge, a clerk, someone from the D. A.'s office and my lawyer.

That was it.

No one from the press, no interested parties up in the gallery.

I stood as the charges were read out by the clerk and I was asked to enter my plea.

"Not guilty," I said in as clear a voice as I could muster.

The judge looked up from whatever he was writing on his pad, clearly surprised.

"Has your client been informed of the offer that has been made by the prosecution?" He said, looking at my layer, not at me. It was a curious moment, as though I was utterly irrelevant in the fate of my own life.

"He has, your honor," Havers said, quickly getting to his feet. I saw flakes of dead skin on the carpet around his sandals.

The judge sighed. "Very well."

He took a moment and after consultation with the clerk came up with a date for trial that was two weeks away.

"As to the matter of bail, your honor, I would like to assure the court that my client is a man of good standing in the community, with full time employment, and with no history of violence, he does not pose a threat to either himself or the general public, and it is my considered opinion that Mr. Moon does not in any way present a flight risk."

The judge turned his attention from the lawyer to me, slowly looking me up and down as though assessing a cut of meat.

"Sadly, I cannot agree with your assessment, counselor. While I have not yet been presented with the evidence of either Mr. Moon's guilt or innocence, I must assess the weight of the prosecutions brought before me this day—and it has been a long day. I know the District Attorney well enough to know they would not have countenanced bringing so many charges before the court without the surety of securing a conviction. Indeed, the number of guilty pleas entered only serves to reinforce that assessment. And while it is currently true that Mr. Moon has gainful employment with the political campaign being run by Jordan Thomas, that is a position that will come to an end before I will be able to hear this case, meaning upon hearing he will in fact be unemployed. There is, I fear, something of an irony to be found in the fact that he will most likely spend more time on remand protesting his innocence than he would have if he had simply accepted the D.A.'s offer, but that is your client's right. On that basis, Mr. Moon's request for bail is denied."

The judge then banged his gavel and called, "Next."

15

I managed to get another five minutes alone with Havers before I was ushered towards the transporter ready to take me to the prison where I'd be held awaiting trial.

My head was gone. It was chaos in there. My body felt numb. I'd steeled myself to the idea of having to come back to fight my case, to argue for what was right and clear my name from this BS charge, but for some stupid reason, I hadn't even begun to consider I'd be playing into their hands and be held in custody until the trial. I was lucky the judge had found a date a few weeks away, it could just have easily been six months or worse with the prosecution requesting time to get their case in order. I felt like screaming.

Havers was as shocked at the denial as I was but had no real answers for me.

He promised to visit in the morning, to see I was being treated right, and to plan our case out. He'd let Jordan know what was happening. I didn't know what more I could ask from him, and he had nothing to say that could possibly make the few weeks easier to stomach.

It turned out that everyone else had pleaded guilty, but even so, we were all on the same bus heading to the same place. Word was that none of the women had received a custodial sentence. Maybe the judge had taken notice of their need to provide children care? The men in the van with me had accepted the grim inevitability of their punishment, and for a few of them this wasn't their first time in prison.

As the prisoner transport made its way out of town, following the dustbowl road towards the penitentiary, I was plagued with this sense of guilt. I'd let Jordan down. But more, I'd let everyone down who needed to hear his message. And all of this on the back of Lola and losing the other volunteers. If I was a superstitious kind of man, I'd say the stars were aligning against him.

"First time?" the man sitting next to me asked. One of the others had called him Levon. I hadn't heard him say a word until that moment. He was a big man; well over six feet, weighing in at 250 pounds, none of it fat.

"How can you tell?" It came out sounding more sarcastic than I'd intended it to.

"Because I got eyes. You're the only one arrested wearing a suit, see, I'm a better detective than any of those cops back there," he laughed, delighted with himself.

"I've seen plenty of well-dressed criminals," I said. "A suit does not make you innocent."

"Too true," Levon laughed. A big, deep laugh. "And one of those tubby fuckers became president!"

Everyone could hear our conversation. They laughed. Grim gallows humor. I was the last to laugh, not that I'd be laughing longest.

"What about you?" I asked when the noise subsided.

I didn't think he was going to answer at first, but then he nodded.

"Not my first rodeo. I did six months a couple of years back. Should have been a year but they let me out early on account of me getting sick. It was more convenient if I died outside, I guess. I don't know."

"What did you do?" I asked.

"You mean, why was I in there?"

The bus fell silent. I got the feeling I'd asked some unaskable question. It was an uncomfortable moment. Some of the men looked in our direction, others deliberately looked the other way, making a point that whatever Levon had to say, it was none of their business.

The guard who'd ushered us onto the bus hadn't said a word since we'd pulled away.

"Let me drop some wisdom on you, blood," the man beside me said, a touch of menace creeping into his voice. "Because I like you, and I know you don't know no better, but once we get off this bus, don't go asking no one that question, it ain't the done thing. And ain't no saying you'd like any answer, either. Why complicate life?"

"OK," I nodded.

"My story, I hit a man. I hit him so hard that I broke his jaw. That time, I deserved it. Lucky punch, but you wanna know the truth? I'd do it all over again if I was given my time over, even knowing I'd lose six months of my life inside. He deserved it. And more."

I wanted to ask why, but I'd learned my lesson.

He would tell me if he wanted to.

"Just keep your head down," he opined. "Stay out of trouble. Do whatever work you're told to do. It will make the time pass quicker. Ain't no point fighting the system, 'coz the system won't break. You feel me?"

I nodded. I felt him. I had these images of the kind of work prisoners were made to do in the movies, but that was all Hollywood BS. These places were an endless supply of free labor to keep the American economy competitive with Chinese sweatshops. That was another reason blue collar jobs weren't out there anymore, they were all inside, being done for free.

"I do, and I'll keep myself clean until my trial date," I told him.

There was a moment when he didn't seem to get it, then he shook his head and furrowed his brow, as word by word the meaning of what I said sank in. "You pleaded not guilty? They drop you on your head when you came out, boy? They show you a picture of your face in the crowd, they tell you they know that's you, and what, you gonna claim you got one of those evil twins? They got you, man. They got us all, and there ain't nothing we can do about it."

"I didn't *do* anything."

"None of us did anything. You were there. You need to know the system. You can't afford to take the risk that you'll be inside longer if we plead not guilty and lose. Suddenly you're looking at years of your life. That's some serious bullshit right there. I don't know where you come from, but it ain't around here if you don't already know the mayor, the police, the courts, the prison they're all in it up to their fucking necks in this shit... it is what it is. Fucked up. And there's nothing we can do about it."

I fell silent. There was no point arguing. And his one bit of advice had been to keep my head down. It felt like a good time to start with that.

It was only a couple of weeks after all.

I was going in there as an innocent man. I had to assume I'd be treated better than those who were going there as guilty men.'

It didn't take long for me to see the error in my thinking.

16

I don't know why, but I'd imagined there would be a separate part of the prison for those awaiting trial. It was naiveté, obviously, to think anything resembling innocent until proven guilty would exist. Of course not, we were thrown in with the murderer and rapists, the thieves, the con men, and gang-bangers and thugs like we were all one and the same.

I got lucky. I was put in a cell with Levon.

Not exactly a friendly face, but as close as I was ever likely to find in a place like this. And, I know it sounds dumb, but after the transporter ride, he felt like my protector. I needed someone looking out for me in here.

Another misconception quickly put to rest was the idea we'd get some kind of private interview with the prison governor, maybe not a greeting so much as a laying down of the law, but that idea died on the vine. We had our personal possessions taken away. We were lined up against a white wall, told to strip, searched, and as the guards walked the line, subjected to a high-pressure disinfectant shower that was so cold it burned, scouring the skin from our bodies. It was utterly dehumanizing, but that was the point. At the end of the humiliation, we were given our prison oranges and told to dress.

Then we were taken to our new homes, stood outside them, and told to wait until the rest of the new inmates arrived. Reality was biting hard by now. We weren't in Kansas anymore, put it that way.

"Must be pretty full at the moment," Levon said after the door slammed shut behind us. I heard the electronic bolt lock engage.

He dropped his bedding on the top bunk and tested the mattress.

The place was fairly modern but was already showing signs of wear.

"What makes you say that?" I asked, looking around to try and see whatever it was he'd seen.

"These luxurious surroundings of ours, they're usually single cells. Instead, they're packing us in. That's a good thing, 'specially for you. Means we should be able to avoid a lot of the shit that goes down in this place. Less chance of getting singled out and ending up with more time added to our sentences."

"Why especially for me?" I wasn't sure I wanted to know the answer.

Levon laughed, but there was no malice in it. "You ever hear the saying any hole's a good hole? Pretty boy like you could be in demand," he said. "But don't worry, I got your back. Now, wanna make tonight interesting, little wager on which of the new arrivals is the first to cry themselves to sleep?"

———

BY THE TIME the door was unlocked again we'd got to know each other. It wasn't like we were best buddies, but it was good to have a friend in here. And, following his advice, I didn't ask about the fight that had put him in here, and instead concentrated on what life out there was like. He worked construction. And the good news for his peace of mind, his boss had sent word through his lawyer that his job would be waiting for him when he got out. That, more than anything, convinced me Levon was a good man.

"He would probably have been here himself if he hadn't been tied up at the bank," he laughed. "Then we would have been in the shit. There wouldn't be any work for either of us when we got out if he'd been here too."

"What sort of construction work do you do?"

"Oh, we turn our hands to most things where there's money to be made. There's only four of us, but as long as it's not more than a couple of stories high, we're good. We ain't got no head for heights." He chuckled. "Why? You looking to have some work done?"

"Hah! Sorry, no. I live in a fifth-floor walk-up I share with the rats in the walls. Don't think my landlord would be too pleased if I let the rats out."

"So, you plan on sticking around once the campaign's done? I did hear right? You work for that Thomas guy wasting his time trying to become mayor?"

"Yeah. I do. I did, I guess. Won't be around to see it to the bitter end."

"Less pain that way. Poor bastard doesn't stand a chance," Levon said.

"There's always a chance. It's a free vote. Maybe people think it's time for a change?"

"Maybe they do, but they're the wrong people, put it that way."

———

THE BOLT SLAMMED BACK, an eerie sound that echoed all through the building at once. Orders were barked out, chased by the echo. Stand on the landing and wait until the guards were ready to escort us to a meeting with the governor. For all the similarities, it did not feel like orientation at camp.

There were grumbles and grunts from some of the others as we shuffled down the iron steps, all of them about food. We hadn't eaten all day. I'd had a couple of slices of toast before going into work, that was it. The unwashed plate was still in the sink and would be there waiting for me when I was finally allowed home. Whenever that would be. But, with all the stress of the day, I hadn't felt that hunger all day though.

"You'll get fed soon enough," the guard at the front of the line said. "And the fewer stupid questions you ask, the sooner you'll get fed. So, think about that when you're in front of the governor."

That was enough to quieten most of the complaints.

We completed our journey in relative silence, our path ending in a huge mess hall where we were greeted by the overpowering smell of overcooked cabbage.

"Pick a seat, any seat, doesn't matter where you end up. And keep the noise down while you're doing it," the same guard said. Levon and I found a place with our backs to the wall with metal shutters set into it.

He leaned in conspiratorially and said, "It's a good spot. We'll be the first in line for food." But I wasn't sure that was why he'd chosen it. I think the wall was more important. This was the kind of place where you didn't want to leave your back exposed, even with a half-decent wingman looking out for you.

A couple of the others who had been on the bus with us joined us at the table.

I took the chance to look around, really drinking in the dose of hard reality today had offered up. I counted more than sixty men, all dressed in the same prison oranges: all grim faced. The first thing I noticed, and it was hard to miss, was that you could count the white folks on a single hand. The rest of us were black or Hispanic. I realized there was a sixth white guy I'd missed in my first count because he had so many tattoos on his face it was hard to tell what his ethnicity was. The guy looked like an anorexic, he was that skinny. Those six were sitting together staring daggers at the one black guy who dared sit on their table.

I didn't recognize *them* from the protest. Even letting that rogue thought stray into my head nearly made me laugh, which would have been about the worst thing I could do under the circumstances.

A tenth of the new intake was white. What did that say about the racial mix of Gen Pop as a whole, or was this just down to the protest stuffing the numbers?

"On your feet!" barked one of the guards over by the main doors, and the room was filled with the sounds of chair legs being scraped against the floor. We were already conditioned to obey.

The governor nodded to the guard, who then motioned for everyone to sit.

More scraping of chair legs that seemed to go for longer than it needed to this time.

The governor waited patiently. I got the distinct impression this little act of defiance was such a regular occurrence he was inured to it. Eventually the room fell quiet again.

"Thank you, gentlemen," the governor said, his voice was reedy and raspy, a forty a day smoking habit behind it. "My name is Governor Morris, though to you I am and will always be The Governor, plain and simple. It's my responsibility to ensure this place runs smoothly and that you are all safe during your time here. I recognize a few faces as return visitors, a few more of you will have no doubt spent time somewhere like this before. But for those who haven't let me explain a few things. We work on a strict set of rules that are there to protect both the guards and the prisoners. And while we appreciate that men coming here for the first time might misunderstand a rule or forget they are no longer at liberty to act as they would outside, believe me, while we will make allowances, we will not tolerate our good nature being abused. Once is forgivable, perhaps, twice is not."

"A meal will be served in here when this orientation is over. You'll then have the opportunity to make a selection from the prison library if you so wish, before being returned to your cells where you will remain until the morning. There will be no exercise time today as we have a considerably larger intake than we would usually receive."

From where I was sitting, I saw a few of the new arrivals looking around at the faces of the others, whether for guidance or simply to gauge if this turn of events was expected. No doubt, they were like me, and had never been inside before.

Levon just looked at the tabletop.

"Tomorrow you'll each be spoken to in order to determine whether you have any specific skills which might best be used as part of the work program during your time here. Most, I understand, are only with us for a very short time, so it's unlikely that we will be able to teach you any useful skills to take with you back into the outside world, but for those of you who will be with us longer, more than six months that is, you will be offered that opportunity. Might I suggest, if that is the case, that it would be wise to avail yourself of that offer. The skills you learn in here could make all the difference when you are back outside in the real world and help ensure you don't return to us.

"Some of you will also receive a visit from your lawyer. This will be the last time for at least a week that you will be able to speak with them. Make the most of this meeting. Visitors will not be allowed until next week. And there will be no conjugal visits before that time."

This brought a little more disquiet, but the murmur didn't rise above a low grumble. It didn't bother me so much; there was no one out there who was likely to want to see me, and I'd forgotten the last time I had sex.

"Although the state pays for your food and accommodation here, certain luxuries can be bought from the commissary, paid for by credits you earn for the work you are assigned. It is a simple system. Work hard, be rewarded. Any credits remaining at the end of your sentence will be paid to you in the form of money to help you return to the outside world."

Levon snorted at that. I glanced in his direction, but he shook his head. I assumed it was the exchange rate that amused him. I looked away again.

"We keep a clean house here. There will be a series of escalating fines should you fail to keep your cells in good order."

He rambled on about Sunday Services for those who thought they might find God in here, and how access to proper medical attention worked, should the need arise. Then, seemingly done, the Governor asked if there were any questions.

I was about to ask one, about the difference between those of us found guilty of a crime and those of us bound over awaiting our trial, but Levon placed a ham hock sized hand on my arm and applied a little tension through his grip. He'd read my mind. He shook his head again, this time the warning was evident. Don't be seen. Don't make yourself someone these people know.

Someone asked about special diets and another about exercise before the Governor announced that orientation was over and left us to enjoy our meal with the promise that the food in here was surprisingly good.

The chatter started again as if a pressure valve had been released.

One of the guards hit a metal table with the flats of his hands, and the sound boomed out ensuring everyone fell silent again.

"Line up," he called out and a moment later the metal grills started to rise, and the smell of food filled the room.

17

_____

Later, with my belly full of mystery meat stew and root vegetables that was so bland as to be tasteless—apart from a peculiarly sour aftertaste—I lay on my bunk, looking at the book I'd chosen from the library trolley. There were stains on it that I didn't want to think about. I'd been promised a wider selection in the library itself, but the older inmates who ran it had loaded a trolley with what they figured most folks would enjoy so we didn't get to leave the dining room until the guards took us back to our cells. It was all about exerting control, I guess, removing the illusion of choice. Our lives were reduced to this new order. It was military in its nature, no room for remonstrations or complaints, just head down, follow orders, and make it out the other side in one piece. Ideally.

I'd picked up a well-thumbed copy of *The Big Sleep*. I'd never read any Chandler before, but it was one of those names I knew. The godfather of modern crime. I was surprised to find a crime novel in this place, all things considered, even a classic.

"You were about to ask if you were going to be treated differently, weren't you? Like not being guilty yet should set you apart?" Levon asked, leaning over the edge of his bunk, and looking down at me.

"That obvious?"

"Everyone does it. They come in here hoping there's a reason why they'll be treated better than the others, because in their minds they don't deserve to be treated the same way as all the rest. It's only human nature, and the guards expect it, but see, it's not the kind of question you ask in front of others. Not unless you want your life to be miserable in here. You act like you're better than other folk, they'll look to bring you down. It's human nature, too. Same goes for the guards. And if you get to ask the Governor privately, who knows, you might get an answer, though it'll only be one word. No. Most likely you'll just be laughed at."

"OK, that makes sense. What if I asked you the same question? Laughter or humbling?"

"Nah, I'd just give it to you real, you'll be treated just like everyone else, and that's like a piece of shit. You just need get used to it. Helps you survive this place. Besides, if you lose your trial, reality is you'll likely wind up in here a hell of a lot longer than the rest of us. The new blood will be coming to you for advice how to survive their first weeks and you'll be droppin' wisdom." He lifted his head, nostrils flaring, and I realized it was a silent laugh. It was an eerie thing to see.

I tried to laugh myself, wanting to argue the impossibility of that, but how was that more impossible than me ending up in here in the first place?

Nah, I had to believe that I'd be out of here in a couple of weeks.

I still had that job Phil was holding for me at the paper, regardless of the election night results. I'd promised him a write up of my experiences on the campaign trail. I'm not sure he'd be able to print them as things stood. But I was in here, and whatever else I was, I was a journalist at heart. I decided then and there, lying on my bunk, stained crime novel in hand, to see this time as a learning experience, something to feed my writing and enhance my understanding of the country and the prison system from the inside. I needed to see it as a chance to boldly go, and all that.

"What kind of work do you think we'll be assigned?"

"Tomorrow will be odd jobs, mainly. Grunt work meant to make you too tired to get into trouble on day one. Stuff like deep cleaning the shower blocks, or sanitizing the kitchens. Most days they're regular jobs on the schedule. Who knows, maybe there'll be some more mindless stuff, like painting that needs doing. Whatever they find, it'll be a job that can be started and finished in a day."

"After that?"

"Depends? You got any skills that might be useful?"

"Probably not. I've only had office jobs, basically, no hands-on skills." It wasn't exactly lying, but it was definitely into shades of gray territory as far as the truth was concerned. I figured there was little to be gained by telling people in here I was a reporter. They'd all want their stories told on the outside, after all no one in here had actually committed the crimes they were accused of. At least that was what they'd tell you if you asked. Prisoners get good at being economical with the truth and even better with flat out lying.

"Then you'll probably end up working on the farm. Must be getting' on for harvest time. It's hard work if you ain't used to it. Back breaking work."

"What about you?"

"Oh, there's always plenty of work for someone like me. A farm building that needs work, a wall that's falling down, or maybe the Governor is having his house extended. There's always something, even if it's just workin' in the shop on the lines."

"The Governor's house? What like painting and decorating? That's a joke, right?"

"Ain't no joke," Levon laughed then, confusing the issue in my mind, and swung his legs over the side of his bunk. He slid down so he could see me. "If he, or one of his cronies needs work doing, it gets done. Free. Governor gets a team together, prisoners with little time left to serve, then it ain't worth us dreaming of running away instead of putting up that drywall."

"What about the guys who are in here for longer?"

"The lifers, you mean? No different. They're still put to work; some of them made to work even harder, coz they're expendable."

I was lost in my thoughts and found myself wishing I had a notebook so I could jot some of this stuff down. Of course, it wasn't like I could exactly ask for paper, and if I did, well, how likely was it I'd get to keep the stuff private from the guards.

"At least we get paid in dollars, eh?" I said, and this time his laughter was a proper roar that shook the plastic chair he'd collapsed into.

There were tears streaming down his face.

"What's so funny," I asked when he started to dry his eyes with the heels of his hands.

"You really wanna know? OK, take a guess how much we get paid for a day's work? Go on, ballpark."

I blew out my lips. "No idea," I said. I'd already made a fool of myself and had no intention of giving him ammunition for more derision, even though I was sure that he meant no harm by it. I shot low. But not low enough.

"Five bucks," he said. "But hey, we might have had a pay hike since I was inside."

"Five bucks an hour," I made a face. It wouldn't exactly help these guys get back on their feet when they came out. But it was better than nothing. "That's not bad, I guess. Better than nothing."

There was the threat of more laughter, but Levon just shook his head, wry amused at the assumption I'd leapt to, and just how wrong it was. "Not five buck an *hour*, Caleb. Five bucks a *day*. And you can bet you'll lose a nice chunk of that courtesy of those fines the Governor mentioned."

And here's the madness of it; in my head I was trying to justify it. Five bucks a day. The State was covering the costs of keeping us in this place, including food and health benefits. There were going to be people out there in poorly paid jobs who didn't have five dollars a day left over from their paychecks. But it was vile. One of the most basic tenets of life must be a fair day's wage for a fair day's work. I hated the idea. I could hear some smug-faced politician defending the exploitation of people with no rights using these basic human rights as their defense.

"You should talk to Patrick if you get the chance. He's the fountain of all knowledge. He knows these places inside and out, far more wired in than I am. He's figured out there's a scam here, he's smart like that, can see what's going on beneath the surface where the duck's paddling away frantically while we're all just admiring how smooth it all looks up top."

"Patrick?"

"Yeah. Patrick. Little guy, white hair. He was in the transport with us. His old man was the blackest Irishman I've ever seen. We'll make sure that you're sitting next to him at breakfast. Get you acquainted."

18

I didn't sleep much that night.

It wasn't just the strange bed—which was a cruel and unusual punishment in and of itself—or the fact it was the first time I'd shared a room with someone in years, and the vulnerability that came with that, letting yourself fall asleep in the presence of someone else, being completely vulnerable. So easy to kill. In part, it was down to these kinds of thoughts that I couldn't shake loose from my head. In part it was the sounds of other prisoners.

It was a hard place to be for a lot of people. Their distress wasn't helped by the barracking of others, some shouting for them to shut the fuck up, others calling out bets on which of them would kill themselves, who'd be first and how they'd do it. It was ugly. It was well into the early hours before the noise started to die down. Sometime after that I drifted off into what I'll generously describe as a fitful sleep. I don't think I had managed more than an hour before the wake-up call came and we were marched to the showers. It was barely six o'clock. I'm not a morning person at the best of times, and this was far from the best of times. And my mood wasn't improved by the fact that the water was ice cold.

At 7:30 AM we were led down to the mess hall again, though led really meant the guards stood at various points along the walk down the hallways, including a double switchback metal stairway, and kept telling us to hurry it up while we shuffled along in single file. Levon managed to pull Patrick into the line with us. Now that I saw him, I remembered seeing him before, both on the bus and at the demonstration.

Likewise, he seemed to recognize me.

"You're the guy from the opposition campaign, aren't you? Backing Jordan Thomas against Dwyer?" It wasn't really a question. What was interesting was that less than a fortnight on the job, after nearly two years serving the community through the paper, this was all people knew me for, when before the miracle would have been if they knew me at all.

"Well, if folks have been noticing me instead of Jordan, I guess I've been doing a bad job," I said, only half joking.

"I wouldn't say that," Patrick said. "We're all men of the world. We know there's only so much you can do when you're fighting a losing battle."

Again, with the predestined defeat. People in this town really had given up fighting long before the final bell. "I'm curious, why does everyone keep saying that we're beaten before election day? I'd say we're in with a decent shout."

"And just how close do you imagine it might be?"

We bandied a few numbers around and I conceded that for us to win we needed black and Hispanic voters to put a cross in the right box, and probably a good few white voters to either back us or, just as helpful, not bother to turn out on election day.

Patrick was about to tell me why that was never going to happen, but we reached the front of the line and, trays in hand, collected our breakfast; a bowl of oatmeal, a slice of buttered toast, a small plastic glass of juice, and a mug of instant coffee that was more useful as a weapon than it was as a drink.

We settled at a table where we were joined by a couple of others. They nodded to each of us in turn but said nothing as they dove into their food. One of them, a younger man, barely out of his teens had dark rings around his eyes which looked painfully raw. He was one of the night criers.

"So, you were about to tell me what makes you so sure we can't win?" I said, reopening the conversation, much to Patrick's amusement.

"What do you know about voting laws in the State?"

"Every man and woman over the age of 18 has a vote," I said. Nice and simple.

"And like you said, the number of white votes versus the non-white voters are pretty much the same so if you can lure enough of the white vote to come over to your side, or just as effectively, not vote at all, you could win. That's your argument, right?"

"Pretty much," I said.

"OK. And you're right, in a fair and equitable society that *might* work. It'd be a stretch, lots of variables would have to line up. But here's the kicker, we don't live in a fair and equitable country, never mind State. Look around you, look at the racial make-up of this place, then ask yourself about the voting rights we're afforded in here."

He was right, of course, the racial balance was disproportionately black and Hispanic. I knew where he was going with this.

"They don't get one. Simple as that, and it isn't just us in here, it's all of us out there, too, on parole. Unspent sentence, no vote."

"What about people bound over awaiting trial?"

"That's him," said Levon, jabbing a finger at me. He was grinning when he said it.

"Strictly speaking you are entitled to one, but you'd have to take it up with the Governor. It's too late to arrange a postal vote, even if you are allowed one. Of course, if you were out on bail, that would be fine. But you're not. You're in here with the rest of us, the place where human rights go to die."

I couldn't believe what I was hearing, but it shouldn't have surprised me.

"You have any idea of what kind of numbers we're talking about in real terms?"

This time I could only shake my head.

And take a mouthful of coffee. It was bitter and already cold enough it could barely be called a warm drink.

"Then let your education begin. In the US, around 40% of the population is non-white, but it makes up more than 60% of the prison population. In this State it's closer to 50 percent of the population, like you say, but it accounts for more than 70% of those in prison. That's a big old chunk of people who won't be voting for your man even if they wanted to. And that's not factoring in those out on parole."

"How do you know all this stuff?" I asked.

"Because I read, son. Blessed with an inquiring mind."

I noticed that most of the people around us had already finished most if not all their breakfast and I'd barely touched mine. Looking up, I saw one of the guards doing the rounds, hurrying people up, and got the distinct impression that if I wanted to eat it, I needed to get it down my neck. The room was fuller than it had been the evening before. Inmates were being hurried through. There was a pattern to it. The newcomers were being integrated with the long-term residents.

Somehow Patrick had managed to eat all his while he'd been speaking, which was a skill all of its own.

The guard was almost at our table by the time I swallowed down the last mouthful of toast and washed it down with the cold sludge.

I had been in this place for less than twenty-four hours and I was already changing my behavior. I didn't like it, but it wasn't like I had a choice. Bend or break.

"Last to finish up, out of the first sitting," the guard said. "Looks like you boys have won the lottery. Washing up duty, the lot of you, chop chop." I hadn't even realized that the others who 'd joined us at the table had slipped away and were already in the line to leave.

―――――

THE JOB WAS NEVER ENDING, but we kept at it, it was a drudge job, but it needed doing. There were plenty of calls to talk less and work faster, even when we hadn't said anything for a few minutes. It didn't take long to figure out the metal trays with their separate serving compartments where in short supply, so the same ones were used at every mealtime, meaning the ones we were washing up were being used by the next inmates coming down the line for breakfast as fast as we could clean them.

Two hours of washing and drying until the last of them had been fed, and the silver trays were all washed, dried, and stacked ready for the next mealtime.

You can learn a lot about someone in two hours if you are prepared to listen rather than talk. Patrick had been a teacher at some point in his life. He hadn't exactly Broken Bad, but a complaint by a parent had eventually led him to lose his job. I didn't ask what the complaint had been about, as curious as I was to know. I had learned Levon's lesson well. If Patrick wanted me to know he'd tell me. Losing that job had made him pretty much unemployable in his chosen profession. So, he'd looked for work outside of it, only to be turned down by job after job because he was overqualified. It was a vicious cycle, if the feedback was truth, and not just a more pleasant fabrication. He seemed quite at home now. Such was the system, I guess. Take a good man and reduce him to this.

Eventually he'd found a job as a school custodian. It came with a small house in the grounds of the school, and he was pretty content with it.

"Of course," he said. "That was then. I ain't so sure I'll even have a job when I get out of here, and if I lose that, I'll lose my home too."

Considering what was at stake, he seemed remarkably sanguine about it all.

I didn't get the impression that he had any family, or if he did, they didn't live with him.

Strangely, his circumstances were not all that different from my own, even if it didn't feel like I was looking in the mirror.

When we'd finished, we were sent back to the communal area, where a few of the other men were playing pool on a table that had barely any cloth on it. Not for the first time, I was struck by the potential weapons within easy reach; pool balls in a sock to make a cosh that could easily brain someone; cues that could be snapped and turned into jagged spears. Four others gathered around a table playing cards. I saw another pair hunched over a small chessboard. It was all just variants of passing time and wasting life.

"You'll be called for your interview soon, then you'll be able to go back to your cell if you want to, the doors are open now 'til lights out."

"Is that all the work we're doing today?"

"Hard to say. There still time for more shit to drop in our laps," Levon said. "But it wouldn't surprise me if we were on washing up duty for rest of the day." That was a lot of silver trays, but it was better than scrubbing out the washrooms that were serving several hundred people with digestive issues.

Levon was the first to be called.

Ten minutes later Patrick was summoned.

Levon returned ten minutes later.

"Your turn," he said.

I was the last to be interviewed.

The familial resemblance between the guy on the other side of the desk and the weasel cop who'd interviewed me at the station did not go unnoticed.

19

I returned to the communal room after spending fifteen minutes answering the same questions, I'd answered dozens of times since this nightmare began.

My lack of usable skills, according to the questions the clerk asked, meant that I was likely to end up doing manual work for however long I was in here. There's something incredibly dispiriting about hearing how your college degrees and years of good employment aren't worth a crap, but then I guess my skills aren't transferable for a life of crime.

And, of course, I asked the question I kept asking, with me not having been found guilty of any crime, why was I being treated like I was, but the guy on the other side of the desk made it clear we were all treated the same. They didn't have a maybe your innocent part of the prison where they treated you like a human being, put it that way.

I'm not sure whether it was a deliberate choice, but most of the staff didn't know what we were in for. I guess that helped with the treating us all equally badly. The only real indicator of our crimes or potential crimes was the level of security assigned to each of us.

There was no sign of Levon or Patrick when I came out of the office. The guys who'd been playing pool had left, too. The table had been taken over by the three white guys I had seen in the dining room before. Close up, I saw a tattoo that could only be Aryan Brotherhood. That gave me the fucking chills.

"Where's everyone gone?" I asked.

"What the fuck? It talks," tattooed face said, setting his cue down on the worn-out cloth. "But what I want to know is who said it could talk to *us*?"

I tried to take a leaf out of the warder's voice. "You're not better than me, I'm not better than you, in here we're all equal," I said, and it was probably the dumbest thing I'd said in forever. I regretted it the moment the words left my mouth.

"Equal? Who the fuck do you think you are?"

I held his gaze, and in it, I saw a kind of madness I didn't want to taste. I was out of my depth here and sinking deeper.

I looked around the rec area, hoping to see a friendly face, someone who might stop this shit from turning ugly. I saw the backs of four men retreating from the room, no one else.

"Smart niggers don't want to get involved, Ziggy. That's evolution right there. They learned to fear the real threat when they see it."

"Shut it," Ziggy said, and the other man fell silent from his philosophizing, his gaze lowered to the floor. Humbled and humiliated in two words. It was obvious who had the power here. Ziggy.

Ziggy moved towards me. I couldn't help but look at the whorls and shapes of the lines tattooed across his face. They made up a tribal war mask. I tried but couldn't imagine him without them. I'd been close to dangerous men before, they all had this certain look in their eyes. This guy had the look. The two with him didn't; they were associates. They savored the power his nearness gave them. He didn't need them beyond serving as his audience.

"You're the fuckstain who thinks he's better than everyone else?"

He took another step closer, close enough that I could smell his rancid breath.

I said nothing.

"You think you special? You think you owed some respect? Better treatment?"

"I didn't do anything," I protested.

"Bitch, please. That's what everyone says. But see, the smart ones admit it to themselves at least, we all know, deep down, when we've been caught. And I'm meaning even if we didn't do what they've locked us up for, we all know there's something else we've gotten away with. We're all guilty of something, and you, you are just a piece of shit."

"Sorry," I said, not sure what I was apologizing for. "Look, you and me, I think we've got off the wrong foot. What say we start again, like men. Clean." I held out a hand, intending to diffuse the situation before it could spiral. "Caleb Moon."

Ziggy looked at my hand like it was a snake. He reached out to take it. And stupidly, I thought a truce had been reached, that we'd shake and agree to stay out of each other's faces. No need to worry about being friends. But as he wrapped his grip around mine, and really tightened his hold, he tugged me toward him, yanking me off balance, and as I stumbled, he stomped on one of my feet with the heel of his shoe. The pain was nothing like what followed. I lost my balance, only for his head to butt the bridge of my nose. Hard.

And now the explosion of pain was excruciating.

I didn't see stars. I saw blood.

My knees buckled and I thought I was going over. I had absolutely no control of my body.

"Everything all right in here?" I heard a voice behind me say. It sounded a million miles away.

"All good," Ziggy said, still gripping my hand tight to make sure I didn't collapse at his feet. He was calm. In control. No anger. No fear. It had simply been a power move. He'd done it because he could.

"You're up next," the guard said, and even without seeing him, I knew he'd turned to leave. It was like a barometric change to the air. A pressure drop.

Ziggy released his grip.

I reached out for the edge of the pool table to stop myself from falling.

Ziggy barged passed me, making sure that his shoulder bounced mine.

He didn't say another word.

One of his sidekicks laughed as they followed him out of the rec area.

I just wanted to sink into one of the chairs, but there was no way I was going to be sitting here when Ziggy returned. I didn't need warning twice.

I was out of there, not caring if it looked like I was running scared.

20

"Shit man! You look like you've seen a ghost," Levon remarked.

I'd found him in our cell, stretched out on his bunk.

He laid down his book and swung his legs over the side. "You doin' OK?"

"Been better. Remind me not to try and make friends again," I said, trying to make light of it.

"Don't tell me," Levon said. "Our Aryan Brother with the painted face?"

"The one and the same. Name's Ziggy, like the Stardust. Where'd you and Patrick go?"

"We had our own excitement. Your friend Ziggy took a dislike to our boy Patrick. We were playin' pool, doin' no harm. They seemed to think they had a divine right to kick us off the table. Patrick told 'em they were welcome to the table when we'd finished our game. They ain't the patient kind, put it that way. Could have gotten real nasty, but I got him out of there."

"And Patrick? He OK?"

"He's cooled down some. He liked the odds. He's a bit of a fighter. Or was."

"Maybe thirty years ago," I said.

"More like forty, and even then..."

I tipped my head back a couple of inches, acknowledging the likelihood of a beat down occurring even if Patrick acquired a time machine. "Where is he now?"

"Back in his cell. Safest place in here."

"You know anything about him?"

"Who, Ziggy?" Levon shrugged. "I've seen plenty *like* him. The swastika and confederate flag hanging over the bed at home. He ain't a unique individual. You want to stay out of his way," Levon said. "Don't be tempting fate."

"Anyway, the good news is we're on washing duty again this lunch time. Guess they wanna keep those dainty lil hands of yours soft." He cracked a smile. "We have to be down in the kitchens at eleven thirty. We get to eat first. One of the perks of the job."

A glance out through the open door of our cell showed the clock that would rule my life with an iron fist, and that was more than a match for any Ziggy's of the world.

We had less than an hour to kill before making our way down.

My first goal of prison life; avoid Ziggy for the rest of the day. Manage that and I'd call it a good day.

I tried to read my book for a while.

Levon seemed strangely quiet.

"You did the right thing," I said.

He knew what I was talking about.

"What would *you* have done?" he hung over his bunk again, his face looking down at me.

"The same," I said. "It was the only smart play."

"Patrick didn't want to leave. He wanted to stay there until you came out."

"And what would that have achieved? It would have been a throw down. You know that. You saved him from a beating. Nah, it's my fault for not walking straight out of there as soon as I saw you'd gone. I'm older and wiser now." And then, almost as an afterthought, I thought to ask, "Were there any guards around?"

"One, but he wasn't interested," Levon replied.

"Isn't it his job to be interested?"

"You really don't get it do you? Caleb Moon, you need to open your eyes and see what's going on."

Levon slid off his bunk and I knew this was going to take more than a couple of words.

I set my book aside and sat up, perching on the edge of my bed.

"When you look around, what do you notice that's different from the outside?"

"Apart from the bars, the lack of windows, and the doors that get locked at night?"

"Yeah, apart from those. You'd expect all those things, wouldn't you? That, and the bad food, and the smells, and the noises. That's what you think of when you think of prison. What else do you see?"

I thought about it for a moment but whatever it was, I was missing it.

He tried again.

"What did you see yesterday when we had that welcome to your new home thing with the Governor talk?"

"You mean apart from loads of people who looked like they didn't belong in here?"

"And what kind of people belong in here?"

"Shocked and confused and sad people."

"Not bad guys? Not dangerous folk?"

"Now you're making fun," I said.

He laughed and flashed a wide, white smile. "OK, let's try and get there by an easier route. How many white guys were at that first little gathering?"

"Three," I said.

I didn't even have to think about it.

There was Ziggy and his two sidekicks. That was it.

"And the rest?"

I'd looked around and I knew what he was driving at. "Mainly black, a few Hispanics and an Asian guy."

"Jimmy Ho," Levon laughed. "He's Vietnamese. And for your final question, what about the guards?"

"They were all white."

"They were all white," he echoed.

21

Patrick thought it was the funniest thing he'd ever heard—or at least you'd have been forgiven for thinking that when you heard his laughter as Levon recounted our little conversation.

The stairs clanged as we trudged down from our gallery accommodation to report in for washing up duty.

"This will be your last taste of freedom while you're in here," Patrick said as we reached the bottom.

"What do you mean?" I asked, suddenly spooked.

"Haven't you realized how quiet it is?" He was right, it was considerably calmer than I'd expected if I was honest. In my mind I'd figured I'd be walking into a hideous crush of us all, packed in like rats. "Chances are the only folk in here right now are yesterday's arrivals, any soul unlucky enough to be in either the infirmary or solitary, and the guards, of course." I thought about it. And he was right, I couldn't remember seeing anyone who hadn't been on the transport. "No open doors from tomorrow on, you can take that to the bank. Least not while we're in. We'll be lucky if we get an hour a day out of our cells apart from mealtimes. The rest, we'll be working, or caged. So, I gotta say, I hope you brothers are getting on."

"Who's your cell mate?" I asked.

"All on my lonesome," he told me. "I guess there was an odd number of us sent down. Luxury accommodation. I'm supposed to be getting a cellmate later today. Such joy."

I was the one yet to be found guilty of anything, he was the one given the single cell. All equals indeed.

"Hey, you might get lucky and get a deviated septum and irritable bowel," Levon laughed.

It was good for me, this, seeing them taking it in their stride. It was a good reminder that the smart play was this, keep our heads down and not draw any attention to ourselves, and we'd be out on the other side of this mess soon enough.

Them sooner than me, I reminded myself.

The guard waited for us at the bottom of the stairs. He grunted and gestured towards the kitchens.

We were early.

Lunch was another healthy portion of stewed grisly gray meat. There were a few barely identifiable vegetables in a thin gravy. The slice of bread was the tastiest thing on the tray. The strew just tasted of salt. The meal was rounded off with a bruised and woolly tasting apple.

"They'll have bought a load of those in cheap, for the pigs," Patrick said. "It's cheaper than wasting good food on us. Wouldn't want to eat into the bottom line."

He took a bite then spat it out onto his tray.

The inside was brown and wet and I'm pretty sure there was something twitching in the mush.

"How the fuck do they get away with this?" I said, not expecting an answer. I looked around, realizing that I'd said it aloud. I needn't have worried. The only other people in the canteen were the other inmates on catering duty. The single guard sitting near the door was utterly disinterested.

The cooks had already finished their meal. I'd assume they'd got the choice of the slim pickings for themselves before they'd dolled the rest out to the other poor unfortunates.

"Don't go getting ideas above your station, Moonchild," Patrick said. "No chance of the likes of us getting lucky with the kitchen, Michelin stars or not." I saw why. Ziggy and his crew would have a better shot.

I was starting to see what Levon had been trying to tell me.

There was a logic to it. The guards had the power. The guards were white. The prime jobs went to the white inmates, and the rest of us were left with the shit to shovel. A brother could get an inferiority complex in a place like this.

The others got up to leave, taking their trays with them. One turned in our direction. "Finish that shit off and get to the sink. If the trays back up and we don't get everyone fed nice and smooth, we'll have a riot on our hands."

It was something about the way the guy said it that made me wonder if he hadn't picked out the worst of the meat and fruit for us. To put us in our place. The guard made no move to hurry us up. Patrick started to get up, but I stopped him.

"I've got a dumb question for you."

"My favorite kind."

"How many black guards are there in here?" I pitched my voice low.

"When you say black...?"

"I don't need full census. Black, Hispanic, Asian, mixed race, whatever. What I'm asking is how many of them *aren't* white?"

"Ballpark? Including the guards, management, and clerical staff? Well, that's a tougher question than you'd think... but best guess there are maybe two hundred folks that work here, so..."

"How many?"

"One," he said, eventually.

"One? A single guard in the whole place?"

"Not a guard," he said. "A secretary or PA, I guess you'd call it now."

It took me a moment to realize that I was sitting there with my mouth open.

One black person on the other side of the bars.

One.

Patrick nudged me. I realized that the guard was on his feet. "OK, those pots ain't gonna wash themselves."

For the next three back-breaking hours, we washed and scrubbed and scrubbed and washed, the searing hot water scalding our hands until it was anything but hot and the grease got harder and harder to wash away.

We were still washing up long after the cooks had cleared away their knives, under strict supervision, and left us in the kitchen.

The guard sank back into his chair and spent his time reading a paper.

One black person wasn't a prisoner.

One.

22

We only had a couple of hours before we needed to get back down to the kitchen again.

The cooks would have done most of the prep for the evening meal before we waltzed in. But for now, the three of us wanted nothing more than to kick back for a while. The problem with that was it meant going back to our cells, and that meant the bolts slamming on us. The new arrivals would be landing in Hell soon.

But that wasn't the real problem, not that I'd have admitted it even under cross; going back to our cells meant passing the recreation room, where Ziggy and his cronies had taken up residence. They'd been joined by a couple of the cooks.

"Well, well, well, if it ain't the three little niggers," Ziggy mocked, squealing, and oinking like a frightened pig as we walked past.

The guard following us didn't react.

"You fancy shooting some pool, Sanders? Or do you gotta take these lil niggers to their cages?"

"They need their nap time," the guard grunted. "I'll swing by later, see if I can win some of your commissary credits off you.

Here, all yours, I'm done with it." He dropped the newspaper onto the pool table and led us way out.

All things being unequal, it wasn't a pleasant exchange.

"Make sure they're wrapped up nice and tight," Ziggy called after us.

I could still hear their laughter when we'd reached the end of the corridor and Sanders tapped the four-digit number into the keypad that opened the gate to let us though. I didn't bother trying to get the number. I assumed there was some sort of biometric aspect, too. His prints and his code. Something like that.

The gate clanged shut behind us.

Sanders followed us up the stairs to our landing, unlocking three more gates on the way. I saw a space in the ceiling for what I assumed was some sort of portcullis or blast door that would slam down if the alarms were triggered, and we went into lockdown.

A few minutes later, Levon and I were on our bunks.

The relief was palpable. To be honest, washing up was tougher than I'd expected. I could have fallen asleep as soon as my head it the flat pillow if Levon hadn't struck up a conversation with a wry observation.

"Not used to manual work?"

"Not particularly," I confessed. "Unless carrying a couple of bags of groceries up the stairs when the elevator isn't working counts?"

"It doesn't."

I didn't try telling him I'd done a hell of a lot more when I was younger. That was a long time ago, a different life.

"At least we don't have to do it again later," he said.

"The cooks told us we'd have to be down there again to take care of their mess."

"Did you hear the guard say that?"

"No—"

"There you go. If the words don't come out of a guard's mouth, they ain't worth shit in this place. Besides, you heard Patrick earlier, he said that there are more prisoners coming in today, so whoever is the slowest of them to finish their meal will have the honor, just like we did. Hakuna Matata and all that shit."

In that moment, the intense swell of relief that washed over me was sweeter than the one I'd felt as I'd collapsed onto my bunk.

I wasn't gonna take that promise to the bank, though. Life has a way of kicking you in the gonads when you get carried away thinking good shit.

But, for now, the idea that apart from going back down for our meal later, there was nothing else to do, was sweet soul music to my ears. And better still, no chance of getting caught up with Ziggy and his crew.

I closed my eyes, determined to enjoy the moment of peace.

That lasted about seventeen seconds.

A bang on the cell door a moment before it swung open.

The guard, unimpressed with having to hike all the way up to the dizzy heights of our gallery, said, "Your lawyer's here, Moon. Don't make him wait. Time is money, money, money."

Ten minutes later I was back in the same room where I'd been interviewed that morning.

"Good afternoon, Caleb," Havers said. "I trust you are keeping as well as can be expected?" He held out a hand. I shook it readily. And in that simple gesture, it was like the outside world reached into me, reminding me it was there.

"I'm not sure life as a prisoner suits me," I tried to laugh but it felt hollow.

He nodded. "Of course, and it shouldn't. But more importantly, they're treating you OK?"

"I'm being fed and haven't been beaten if that's what you're asking. What's happening out there? Please tell me you've got some good news?"

"I have news, I am not sure you would call it good, but it is what it is."

He opened the slim folder he had on the table in front of him. I wondered where his overstuffed briefcase was, but assumed he wasn't allowed to bring it into the room. I don't know why my mind wandered so willingly. It was almost like I didn't want to worry about the serious stuff.

"As you know, there's been a date set for your trial..."

"I do. But there shouldn't be a trial. I didn't do anything. I was there as a member of the press. I had a legitimate right to be there, to cover the story as it developed."

"And that's the purpose of the trial, to set the record straight. So far, all the judge is aware of is that you were at a protest that turned violent..."

"One brick was thrown, and dollars to donuts, that was a cop deliberately trying to incite violence."

"That's a mighty serious allegation, Caleb. Can you back it up with proof?" Havers was a lawyer first and foremost. He liked his ducks lined up in a row before they got to quack. He looked at me, his pen poised over the pad. He hadn't written anything down. "Were there any other witnesses?"

"Hard to say. I mean, Dwyer was grandstanding. Everyone was looking towards him on the steps of the police station. It was pure luck I looked their way."

"I don't suppose you've got a name for this officer?"

I told him and he wrote the name down.

"Are you going to speak to him?" I asked, curious as to what he'd do with the name now he had it. All the crime shows I'd ever seen on TV needed something like this to be the big break to crack the case wide open. Something like this brought justice.

But I wasn't living in a Netflix world.

"We may call him to the stand if it goes that far. Ideally, we'll get the whole thing to be thrown out before them."

"You think that's likely?" It was hard not to get my hopes up, but I was ready and primed for some good old straw grasping.

"This morning I spoke to Phil, your editor at the newspaper..." He flicked through his papers. "He confirmed that you were attending the demonstration in your capacity as a reporter, which is good. He's provided a written statement attesting to this fact." Again, a shuffle through his documents before he found the right piece of paper. Phil's statement. It confirmed the assignment and covered the time I had left the office and that I had written up a piece on it that we hadn't run. He listed the names of others who'd been there."

"This is good, right?" I said. "The judge has to throw it all out when he reads this? Freedom of the press, right there, in black and white."

"Perhaps."

"Why only perhaps?"

"The prosecutor will no doubt argue that you were not merely an observer but an active participant."

"You have got to be shittin' me. I didn't do anything."

"As you keep saying. And I have no reason to doubt you. If they can't prove active involvement, that still doesn't mean we'll get the case tossed. We're in a process now. And the wheels, they grind slow I'm afraid."

"This is fucking ridiculous."

"It is, but it's still the law."

"So, what happens next? Worst and best cases?"

"I'm seeing the judge first thing in the morning. I'll put the sworn statement in front of him and try to convince him to reconsider your bail conditions. Best case, you go home tomorrow, worst case you don't."

That didn't give me a lot of hope.

L evon read my face.

"Not good news I take it?" He said from his bunk.

I slumped into the chair and let out a sigh that could have deflated Snoopy in the Macy's Thanksgiving Day Parade.

"Could have been worse, I guess, but not so much," I said. "I'll know more in the morning hopefully."

"You can't let it get to you, Moonchild," he said, and I realized I'd picked up a prison nickname along the way.

It wasn't a touching moment.

I ran through what Havers had told me. He was more enthusiastic about my chances than I was. Me, I expected this life right up until the trial, and maybe even after, if the cops produced a bent witness to attest, they'd seen me in the thick of it. Favors traded, me sold out.

"So, is he coming back in to see you tomorrow?"

I shook my head. "Nah. I have to call him when I can. It's been cleared with the governor for me to make a call in the afternoon."

"You need to know how these people work. They think you want something, they'll go out of their way to make sure you don't get it. Like exact opposite. Don't let on how much is riding on this stuff. I mean, they can guess, but they don't need you confirming it for 'em. Anyway, the new blood's arrived," he said, twitching a wry smile. "I guess Patrick's got himself a cell mate. Let's hope for his sake they get along. We just counting the hours until we're out. You know the saying, one day at a time, like for alcoholics. Shame we'll miss the election. It'd be nice to put my x against your boy's name."

I'd lain awake thinking about that last night, or rather the fact that *I* wouldn't be around. I felt like shit for letting Jordan down, but maybe Havers could pull off some kind of miracle in the morning. And when that thought crept into my brain, hope stole in with it. And hope is a bastard.

Levon said something then that made perfect sense. "Who you reckon decided that we should be charged for what went down after the boy 'n his dog got shot?"

He wasn't really asking me. He was leading me to a point, an understanding. And in doing so was making damned sure I knew just how corrupt the system was. But how could I have escaped that? I mean, there was a black woman serving five years for picking up the wrong bag and a white woman who got three days for stealing a laptop and trying to sell it to the Russians in some weird Spygate thing. It's so disproportionate it stinks.

"Chief Dwyer, I guess," I said. "I'm assuming that he could have let it go. That's what he told me the day after when we had a sit down. That he didn't intend to take matters further."

"Then that begs the question, what changed? If he was gonna charge everyone, why not do it straight away? Why wait and then drag us all in so dramatically? It's like he's trying to feed a story, Mr. Reporter Man." Levon said, and it hit me.

"He didn't want to do it in front of the cameras."

Cameras. The TV cameras would have caught *everything*.

They were my salvation.

Even if they didn't have the actual brick thrower, they'd have caught the white guys crashing the rally. A bit of luck and they'd confirm the direction the brick was thrown from and put me somewhere far away from it. I needed to get Havers onto that.

But that wasn't what was nagging away at me.

"He changed his mind because someone changed it for him," It was the only answer that made sense. "I can't imagine there are many people who'd be able to make the chief change his mind."

"Apart from his daddy," Levon said. "He's a good little boy. He'll still do whatever his old man tells him to, and ain't that just a fact."

And there it was.

That was exactly what I'd been thinking.

It was a stupid idea.

But...

"Weren't no people in that protest gonna be voting for daddy Dwyer."

"Only the ones in uniform," I agreed.

It's all connected.

"So, stands to reason rounding a load of us up and taking us off the streets until *after* the election serves a purpose, don't it? Fewer votes Jordan, bigger victory for daddy Dwyer."

"But, I mean, they only bagged what, forty, fifty of us? That ain't be enough to make a real difference unless the count was gonna be *real* tight. And it isn't. You keep telling me that."

Levon laughed. "You still don't see it, Moonchild? It ain't about keeping *us* away from the ballot box."

"No? Then what is it about?"

"Forgive me while I shatter your innocence, Caleb Moon. It's all about the example. That's what keeps *other* people in their place. And their place is away from anywhere they might exercise the right to vote. You feel me?"

"I feel you," I said.

The people at the protest weren't there to support Jordan, but Jordan had spoken out about the cop killing of a boy and his dog. A vote for Jordan was a vote against the police.

I remembered seeing the way that people reacted at the market when the cops were milling around; they didn't dare go and see what the stand had been all about. They didn't want that mental association, their face, the opposition message, in the cops' minds.

"It's dictatorship tactics. Freedom? Liberty? What the fuck is that?"

"That, Moonchild, is the way it is here. We're fighting a war and we ain't winning when they come out with shit like this, there's good folks on both sides, and somehow, they paint this idea that being anti-fascist is some bad shit right there. The greatest trick the devil ever pulled was convincing white men they're supreme, the master race. And things ain't in no hurry to change, least not while Dwyer senior is in power. And maybe not even after. Junior probably sees it as his by divine right."

Money, power, and influence. It was a heady cocktail. You could see how someone could get a taste for it, and when they'd gotten that taste, want to hang onto it for longer than they had any right. But then, this was a place they still had their confederate statues on proud display alongside their flags, their guns and their yeehaws.

24

At the end of dinner word came that we'd be working off-site in the morning. There wasn't much else to it, no word of what or where.

As soon as we'd eaten, we were ushered out of the dining hall and taken back to the gallery and our cells.

Patrick had been in a foul mood all meal but hadn't been sitting with us.

I assumed it was a new cellmate issue.

We'd hear about it in the morning.

That night the galleries were filled with the sound of sobbing again.

It was a wretched sound.

Another new arrival breaking. The same voices called for him to be shut up or get on with killing himself because they needed to sleep. Eventually the sobs subsided. With new inmates arriving every day, I figured it'd be the same every night, and worse. I didn't pity them. There but for the grace of... well, I was getting to where I didn't think there was a god, and there sure wasn't a lot of grace to go around.

After breakfast we gathered in the yard. Some of the guys had gone to prayer, but they joined us, filling the lines. It was a revelation. I mean, statistics are abstract, when you find yourself looking at hundreds of faces, all of them like your own, then you *know*. The only white faces were the guards.

We were loaded, fifty men at a time, into run down buses that would take us to wherever we were going. Two guards traveled with us, each with some serious weaponry. I didn't doubt for a second they'd be delighted to have an excuse to use it. I didn't see Ziggy or his two sidekicks.

Probably lined himself up a day shooting pool with the guards.

Patrick was the last to board the bus. He sank into a two-seater across the aisle from us. He didn't sit with us for breakfast either. Something was eating at him.

"You OK?" I asked when the bus finally pulled away.

I was looking at the guards as I asked.

He turned his head slowly to look at me.

I saw the swelling around his eye and the damage that had been down to his mouth.

"What the fuck, brother?"

He shook his head but then seemed to regret it.

He raised a finger to his lips and grimaced.

He wasn't going to talk about it. Not in here with everyone listening. My first thought was if they'd done that to his face, what was it like where you couldn't see? Had Ziggy caught up with him? That didn't make sense. He wouldn't have had the opportunity. That left the new cell mate which was not good.

We drove for half an hour or so in near silence. You've never seen poverty unless you've driven through the clapboard houses of the south, and the trailers with the rottweilers in the yard on chains, trees of rubber tires stacked high, and dirt where there should have been rich soil. It wasn't so much what was on the surface, it was what lay beneath. The idea that the world would make right the wrongs done to them, selling a lie of a dream.

There was no crawling out of this poverty, even if money was only a few miles away.

We left the built-up trailers behind, heading through industrial buildings next. I had images of us breaking rocks in the hot sun like we were in some old-time movie. Levon figured we'd be doing farm work.

"I want you to keep an eye on Patrick," he said. "Make sure he gets plenty to drink. It's going to be brutal out there in the heat all day."

"I will."

The bus slowed to a halt on a patch of dirt miles away from anywhere.

A second bus pulled up alongside us.

"Looks like I was right about farm work," Levon said.

I hadn't been on a farm since third grade. You never forget the smell. There was none of that permeating the air here.

"Here we are, boys," one of the guards said from the front of the bus. "This is where you've been handpicked to work for the day."

The other guard sniggered. This didn't feel good.

"Don't you be worrying none, you boys have all the right attributes for this work. Hell, you might say you were born into it."

The second guard laughed again, this time louder. The driver joined in. I didn't get the joke, but beside me Levon obviously did. "Fuck." He pressed a hand to his face.

"OK, up up up, time to make your grandparents proud," the guard said, this time struggling to hold back his own laughter. "Walk a day in their shoes, so to speak. Picking cotton. Make you appreciate how good you really got it."

I was lost for words.

I looked to Levon, I wanted to say something, but nothing came out. I felt completely numb. It was worse than a gut punch.

We started to file off the bus, chains rattling as they ran through the hasps bolted to the floor of the van.

There was mumbling, angry stares, and a sudden heat that had nothing to do with the sun. But none of them stood up to the guards as they stepped off the transport. They weren't stupid.

"No need for all the grim stares, boys. You've got this covered. It's in your blood. Anyway, we've all got our crosses to bear. You do you, and we'll be doing what our great grand pappies did. We'll be watching over you."

Someone said something. I didn't hear what. They were too far from me and too close to the guards to be heard. The guard took three steps across the hardpacked dirt and cracked him across the side of the skull with the butt of his rifle. It was like watching the light go out. He hit the ground a second later, body slamming off the side of the bus with a sickening thud.

"Shit!" said the other guard. "What the fuck you do that for?"

"He was going for my gun," the guard said, flatly. "No word of a lie."

Together, they lifted the downed man back into the bus, and manhandled him onto one of the seats. They left the poor bastard slumped against a window.

"You can't just leave him like that," I couldn't stop myself saying it loud enough to be heard, ignoring Levon's tugging at my sleeve. "He needs help."

"I wouldn't get involved, boy," said the driver, scuffing his feet in the dirt. He had taken a cheroot cigar from his shirt pocket and was lighting up. "Best you let them handle it. Best for you at least." That last bit was said around the butt of his cigar and followed by a lot of chewing.

The guards from our bus conferred with those from the other transport. It was a short conversation that ended with nods. The downed man needed to go back to the infirmary. Let them deal with his busted skull. There was no contrition or care in any of it.

They didn't think of him as human, not on the same level as them, at least. That much was plain to see.

My gut churned as I watched the transport drive away, the guy's head still pressed against the window. There was a blood red rose smearing the glass now.

There was plenty more muttering, but this time folks were smarter with their grievances. None of it loud enough to be heard by the guards.

Three men, three guns. A fuck of a lot more of us without them. And that was justice for you, a few men with guns.

This is not America, land of the free, home of the brave.

And yet, this is one hundred percent America.

Black America.

There's an old joke about gun control. How'd you get the NRA to support gun control? Give black men guns.

25

I t was back-breaking labor—a rush to gather the crop before the storm that was heading our way in a couple of days from now. They called it the storm of the century. I wasn't so sure they weren't just fucking with us to make us work harder when we were lagging. There wasn't much in the way of water either. Levon and I managed to keep Patrick between us most of the time. He didn't look good. Maybe they'd busted something inside when they gave him the beating?

I'd never picked cotton. I didn't know anyone who had ever picked cotton. I knew full well the choice of labor was deliberately degrading, but in that moment, I chose not to think about it that way. I didn't want to give these racist cocksuckers the pleasure of living inside my head. Normally the harvest would be brought in by some sort of mechanical picker operated by either one or two people. I saw a harvester abandoned in the field and assumed it had broken down with half the crop unharvested. Coincidence. Right? A farmer wouldn't jeopardize half of his crop simply to put some black prisoners to work reenacting slave days in his fields. Would he?

The work was easy enough if a drudge of repetition. We just

had to pluck the white balls of cotton from the plants and drop them into the hessian sack we were given. It wasn't heavy work, but the pain came from the constant bend, crouch, and stand, making sure that we picked every last piece of the crop from a plant. Nothing could be wasted. This was a pricklier problem because the casing that the cotton budded out from barbed.

My fingers were bloody long before we were done.

Between us, Patrick was slow. Every now and then Levon and I stopped filling our sacks and added our crop to his instead. The guards made it painfully obvious that there was no water without a full sack. The guards enjoyed their power over us. Their constant barbs got under my skin more effectively than the cotton casings. The guy on the bus didn't seem to bother them in the slightest. Who was going to call them on it?

And there was me, feeling guilty for not even knowing his name.

It was Levon who managed to get Patrick to open up, eventually. We'd guessed right. It was his new cell mate. Unsurprisingly, he was dreading going back. The cotton fields gave him a few hours peace. It was painful to see how this humiliation, a deliberate mockery of black America, could ever be peace, but I understood him. His new cell mate was that kind of man, taking offense to everything and looking to show his strength. It didn't matter than Patrick was a gentle man. The guy had pulled Patrick out of his bunk and dumped him on the floor, claiming it for his own, even though Patrick had been sleeping at the time. Then he'd lost his shit in the middle of the night because of Patrick's snoring. But it was the color of his skin that set him off in the end and brought out the worst.

"He lost his shit with one of the guards," Patrick said, head down, unable to look at us. "He wasn't about to share no cell with a nigger. They told him to shut the fuck up or they'd make me deep dick him. That was it. Soon as they were gone, he took all of his rage out on me. And the guards... they were watching on the security cameras, you just know they were. They primed like a bomb and walked off with him set to explode."

By midday, under the hammer of the sun, we were finally allowed out of the field, and gathered inside a barn. It wasn't much cooler inside, with the metal roof turning it into a cooker. There were bales of straw to sit on, but not enough for even half of us. But, even with all that taken into consideration it was still a damned sight better than being out there.

We were given a lunch of bread and cheese, some fruit, mostly apples, and as much lemonade as we could drink. The bread was good. The cheese was better. The lemonade might as well have been mana from heaven. Homemade stuff from the farmer's own kitchen.

"You're spoiling them," one of the guards said to the farmer, as a couple of his teenage boys brought the food down for us. I was close enough to catch most of the conversation that followed, with the farmer asking who he should pay for our help. He said he was so grateful, that we were saving his farm. He wanted to see us rewarded. "Don't worry, they'll get their share. We've got strict rules governing all that. Fair's fair." Yeah, five dollars a day fair. You can bet the farmer was paying a fuck of a lot more than that for us. I got the distinct impression the farmer thought he was doing a good thing here, helping provide for our reintegration into society once we'd completed our sentences. The bit that caught my attention though was the talk about why we weren't using the protective equipment that he'd provided. The guard just brushed that off. No need.

By four we were done. Exhausted but we'd reached the end of the field.

The second transport had returned and as we stood by the buses ready to be taken back, I looked back over the field. There were a few patches of white but not many. We'd done a good job. It was a peculiar thing, but I felt an element of pride looking out at the field. The two sons appeared again, this time wearing face masks and gloves. They took a couple of sacks.

By the time we were back on the bus and driving away they were working their way along the rows of plants, plucking the odd bits we'd missed.

Every inch of me ached and my hands burned.

I wasn't in a hurry to repeat the experience.

Across from us, Patrick slumped down in his seat and fell straight to sleep.

He looked as eerily as the man the driver had taken away.

We needed to do something to keep him safe, but what? I had zero faith we could turn to the guards for help. So, then, what? Gather a band of black defenders to stand watch over him? The thing is, of the group they'd arrested from the protest, we were clerks, office workers, postal workers, cashiers, and warehouse laborers, we weren't underworld figures, we weren't hardened criminals with organized crime backgrounds We were just ordinary decent folk who'd been outraged by police violence and wanted to be heard. We didn't make for a great protection detail, even if we could organize one.

And when the cell door closed Patrick was always going to be alone with him.

As the industrial buildings on the edge of town came back into view, I remembered that I needed to call Havers.

Somehow, I'd manage to forget about him all day—and in the process forget about my freedom...

26

The guards insisted that we showered and changed as soon as we got back to the prison. It was every bit as humiliating as the pressure hose had been. But we did it. They herded us like animals.

We showered in groups of ten and the water was little more than tepid with the first group. It'd be ice by the time the last of us were through. It seemed that those who had worked on the prison's own farm had already returned and showered and were taking it easy in their cells until mealtime. I managed to get in that first group so I could get that call. The guard didn't care which ten went first and no one seemed to object to me being one of them, so I joined the line, soap and a towel the size of my hand to dry myself with.

I hadn't showered with other men since college days and I wasn't a gym rat either. I felt uncomfortable being naked around other people, more so with a guard watching. I'm sure a shrink would say I had all sorts of repression issues.

Twenty minutes later I was dressed in a clean pair of oranges and a pair of plastic crocs. I was dog tired. The urge to just say fuck it and go back and lay on my bunk was strong. My future could wait. But that's not who I am. I say I'm gonna do something, it gets done if I can humanly do it. So, while the others headed down for the evening meal, I went looking for a guard.

All the doors on our landing were open. The others came and went to the showers at the far end of the gallery. One thing I haven't mentioned, the smell. You'd think it would be of sweat, a lot of men packed in together in shitty conditions, but it's not, it's this weird ammoniac reek. It took me a couple of days to work out what it was, a combination of cabbage and piss.

What I noticed, walking along the gallery was that the gates at the far end were barred. You've got to figure there was a rule about dropping that shield door down that breached fire regulations, or at least safety regulations with it blocking the only way to safety should something go horribly wrong.

But I'll be brutally frank, I had long since stopped believing these people gave a damn about our safety; we were a by the head profit scheme for them, and the less we cost, the more profit they made.

I found a guard who took me down to the small office where the telephone was. There was more privacy than I'd expected. It was a lot better than lining up for the payphone—not that I had my call card yet. That was next week's treat to look forward to. And it came at a cost of whatever we'd racked up so far in credits to be exchanged at the commissary.

Havers didn't have any good news.

"No dice, I'm afraid," he said, though he drawled those four words out, so they seemed to last an eternity. "Judge assured me he'd take it into consideration when your trial comes around, but not before. The aspect of the refusal that concerns me, I have to admit, is that he insists that nothing in that sworn statement materially changes the case."

He knew it was bullshit, I knew it was bullshit, but the way to handle this wasn't outrage and becoming an angry black man in their eyes. It was about fighting them with concrete proof. I told him about the television cameras, and how the footage they'd shown on TV was nothing remotely like the real protest, which they had on camera. We knew it wasn't a live relay, and odds were they had more footage that had ended up on the editing room floor. That could be my saving grace.

"I like a client who thinks rather than yells, Caleb. This is helpful. I did a background deep dive on that cop you mentioned. He was indeed off duty on the day of the protest. As far as I could ascertain he was requested but was supposedly out of town according to the duty reports. Which effectively rules him out as your brick thrower unless we can prove that he's lying. Which, of course, we both know he is. Seems there were a few others struck down by some mysterious illness that day, but of the entire force Twomey was the only one fit for duty who didn't report in."

"Well OK then, we just need his face to show up on the footage and we've got him, even if no one saw him throw that brick. Without him, things wouldn't have turned violent. It's as simple as that."

"True, and that might be enough to see him reprimanded by his superiors, but I'm not sure it will make a substantial difference to your case. And before you object, I know everything you're going to say. And I agree with you. But we are up against a system here. It's a tougher fight than it has any right being. That is just the way it is, I'm afraid. Justice isn't really for all. I will keep you appraised of the situation. Try not to let the bastards grind you down."

We ended the call with me resigned to the fact that I wasn't getting out of here before my trial. The biggest fear I had now was that the trial date would be postponed, and I'd end up serving months or even years instead of days, just so the system could be sure to break me down. There was talk of one guy who'd been in here for eleven years awaiting trial. When I'd heard that, a little piece of me had died, I swear.

The second I put the phone down the office door opened.

The guard nodded, "Ready to go back to your cell?"

I nodded. They'd been listening in, either to my voice, or to the call itself.

"All done," I said, glancing back at the phone.

"Bad news?" he said.

He'd unhooked a baton from his belt and was slapping his palm with it; the slap of meat sound filled the room.

My heart was under siege.

"Could have been better," I admitted.

"I bet you were hoping that some white knight was gonna come riding in and you'd be back home to your nice soft bed, didn't you, nigger?"

I shrugged, determined not to let him goad me. Nothing mattered. I repeated it over and over in my head. Nothing mattered. I wouldn't rise to it. The bastard wasn't getting a reaction out of me. Not with that baton in his hand. I wasn't giving him the excuse.

"See, we don't like people who think they're better than everyone else. College boys who act above their station. Outsiders. People who think they are too good to be in somewhere like this." This wasn't the first time he'd delivered a little speech like this. "Let me tell you, nigger, you fit right in. You know why? Stripped down, under the skin, you're just like the rest of them. You deserve to be here. Now, listen and listen good, this is the last time you get to come in here and make a call to your lawyer. If he wants to see you, he can come down in person, and he can do it at a time that suits us. You ain't on holiday here."

"I understand," I said, keeping my tone even, placatory.

I made a move towards the door, but he blocked my way.

He stared at me for a moment, and in that second, I thought he was going to swing that baton anyway, but he stepped aside. I didn't cross the threshold until he'd secured the baton back on his belt.

I walked out of the room.

I wasn't a full step out before I felt a sudden pain in my back and my knees buckled.

He grabbed me before I could fall to the floor and leaned in close, whispering in my ear, "That was a gift from my good friend, Jake Twomey. He's in a generous mood, it seems. If he's got any more gifts for you, I'll be more than happy to pass them on."

27

The guy who had been hit outside the bus was Daniel Rivers.

He was mid-thirties, married with a couple of kids, and in pretty much every way imaginable, a model citizen. Never been in trouble with the law. Never paid a bill late. He was related by marriage to the boy who'd been killed by the cops.

Rumors circulated about what had happened to him depending upon who you asked.

At first the word was he'd been taken to the infirmary. Problem with that was Patrick was tight with someone who cleaned in there. They hadn't seen any sign of him and none of the medical waste they disposed of, was consistent with the head wound stuff. Then there was a story that he'd been taken to hospital, and would be transferred to another prison when he came out, assuming that he was discharged before his sentence was complete. His personal possessions, what few things he had with him, were removed from his cell to be sent on to him.

The third story though, the one that most of us believed, was that he was dead and had been so before he hit the dirt beside the bus.

I'd seen him go down.

I swear I'd seen the life go out of his eyes.

What did that mean then? Did they have some pit somewhere they buried niggers who got uppity? Was it really back to the slave days with our lives being worth nothing once they were inside the machine?

The only good thing out of all of this was that Patrick was moved. But that had been a matter of necessity. The day after our cotton picking, Patrick ended up in the infirmary. Guards had found him in his bunk after his cell mate had gone down to breakfast. He'd been beaten so badly they were worried about brain damage for a while, but he pulled through, and when he did, they moved him to Daniel's bunk while his cell mate, a close friend of Ziggy in the real world, had earned himself a stint in solitary before he was moved on to a different wing of the prison. Out of sight, out of mind seemed to be the solution to every problem in here.

For the next couple days Levon and I were put with a small team on another farm. This time we were applying a coat of creosote to a barn. We were given gloves and face masks, but they had to last us for both days work. We'd barely finished when the rain came. For the fourth day running we went back to our cell, absolutely exhausted. My body wasn't made for this. But I kept focusing on the finish line. The election. That's why I was in here, I was sure of it. Silence me, silence Jordan Thomas, fuck with the electoral process, everyone's a winner, baby, that's no lie.

"So, question for you, Levon. How much do you reckon we'd have pocketed if we were getting paid a real wage for these jobs?" I dropped onto my bunk and closed my eyes. I was done in.

"Dunno, depends, I guess. Maybe a hundred bucks a day. Maybe less. You know the farmers are paying less though, discount labor, all about the free market economy, keep labor cheap and in plentiful supply. And we're both cheap and plentiful. We're pure profit for the company who owns the prison. We get maybe five bucks a day, even if we're being generous and reckon on the farmer's paying half the going rate, that's' fifty bucks a day per man, and that's serious money when you add it all together."

"Big business," I agreed. And that's exactly what it was, prison for profit. Big business. The government paid the company who built the prison to keep prisoners locked up, to feed them and provide a basic level of care, and if they could do that in a way that made a profit without breaching any human rights violations, that was a win.

But this was more than that.

It wasn't just about delivering a service at a lower cost than they were being paid for it, it was modern day slavery plain and simple and I said as much aloud.

"Man, you've lived a sheltered life haven't you, Moonchild?" Levon said. "I'd say you need to look at getting a refund for that fancy college education of yours. You need to spend more time with Patrick, he'll re-educate you. Have you even read the thirteenth amendment, or has it just got stuck in your head that it's what ended slavery?"

He didn't wait for me to respond.

He was dropping wisdom and truth bombs.

"Neither slavery nor involuntary servitude, except as a punishment for crime whereof the party shall have been duly convicted, shall exist within the United States, or any place subject to their jurisdiction.

"And that my young Moonchild, is word for word. Now I ain't no great reader like Patrick, but he's recited those few lines to me so many times that they're ingrained in my mind. And you know what, contrary to what you believe, even that didn't end slavery straight away. There were plenty of former slaves who ended up having to stay with their own masters for a time while they learned how to be free. But you got the important part of that amendment, right? We can be made to do this work as part of our punishment. It really is slavery. And it's always been about big business profiting. Like it or not, plenty of railway lines would never have been built without convict labor to call on, the chain gangs breaking rocks in the hot sun."

"I fought the law, guess who won?" I said, riffing the line from the song.

28

There was no work the following day.

There was a buzz around the place. Visiting day.
Neither Levon nor I were expecting anyone to come calling, so we stayed in our cell.

The alternative was an hour in the rec area watching Ziggy play pool or the old timers playing chess. We weren't that fussed about either, so we hung out in the room. The door was open. We could step out and shoot the shit with any of our neighbors along the gallery. I didn't want to admit it, but most of my being here was down to it feeling like a safe space, which was as much an illusion as anything Criss Angel pulled off.

One of the guards trudged up the metal stair, calling everyone down for their visitors. He stuck his head in our door and said, "You too, Moon."

"Me?" I said.

He doubled checked the list he carried. "That's what it says on the visitation list, Caleb Moon," he repeated. "Your lucky day."

"Who is it?"

"Do I look like a messenger service? Get downstairs and find out for yourself. You know, some people actually like surprises."

He grinned, but I could have sworn there was an edge to it, like he knew it was a nasty surprise waiting for me down there.

"OK. OK," I said, figuring it was likely to be Havers as anyone. Maybe Big Phil.

I flashed a glance at Levon who smiled and nodded before the cell door was closed and locked, keeping him out of mischief.

A couple of others from the gallery were led down with me.

I always wondered who in their right mind would want to bring family into a place like this.

The mess hall had been cleared and tables set out, well-spaced apart to give the illusion of privacy. There were already people sitting at most of them.

I glance around the room, trying to spot someone I recognized.

It took a moment before I saw her—and to be honest it could have been a while longer without the wave as she saw me.

Carrie.

I hadn't realized how much I'd missed normal people, but in that moment, walking towards someone from my old life, I felt this overwhelming sense of grief that almost undid me.

"Hi," she said as I sat down. Her lips twitched into a sweet smile. "How are you doing?"

I shrugged and blew out my cheeks. "Honestly? I feel like shit, but that's not what you want to hear."

"Sorry. Silly question."

"No," I said, and I really meant it. "I'm sorry. It's not your fault that I'm in here. And you came. No one else has. I appreciate it. I can't tell you how much."

She smiled and glanced around, scanning the faces.

Ziggy was a couple of tables away, the woman with him distraught. Tears and red eyes. She looked old enough to be his mother, but I wasn't going to jump to conclusions.

"So, tell me something fun. How's the campaign going?" I asked, looking for a distraction.

"Jordan would have come..."

"I know. Optics. He can't be seen visiting me," I stopped her. "I get it. We all know the other side will do anything stop him. Last thing I want is to hold him back. Besides, I'll be out soon enough. I'm just wish I was there to fight the good fight with you guys."

"Dwyer has made an offer," she said, cutting to the chase.

"What kind of offer?"

"One I'm not sure we can refuse."

"Go on," I said, not loving the way this was going.

"He'll see the charges against you are dropped if Jordan withdraws from the election. You could be home for dinner. Jordan's pretty sure he can get Dwyer to extend it to a pardon for all the others arrested from their involvement in the protest."

"No one did anything wrong."

"They all pled out in court. It's on their records, and it's going to screw with their job prospects. People aren't big on hiring felons."

Another twist of the knife in the gut.

"He can't be thinking about it. Seriously? Christ listen to what Dwyer's admitting here. He's rattled. There's no way he makes an offer like that otherwise."

"We're not so sure. Jordan thinks it's about the optics, Dwyer gets to play the big man, being magnanimous and benevolent and showing the entire town who has the real power here. In this place he's not just the law, he's as good as God. He gets to decide who has a future and who doesn't. And Jordan's worried you're on the no future pile."

"What does Havers think about it?"

There was a sudden change in her expression. It was a tough read. Something was troubling her, and it had come out the second I'd named Havers.

"That's the other thing I need to talk to you about, Caleb," she said, but fell silent again. There was something here she really didn't want to say.

"Let's hear it," I said, ripping the band aid off.

"He's had threats…"

"OK."

"The kind of threats you'd be wise to take very seriously."

"Because he's defending me?"

She nodded. "Yep. He's had it laid out pretty plainly; if he doesn't walk away, he's going to find himself in a world of hurt. They sent him a postmortem photograph of Lola. He got the message loud and clear."

"Shit!"

A different angle of intimidation, but every bit as brutally effective as any of the others these bastards had been working. I wanted to punch something.

Heads turned our way.

The guard standing nearest to me gave a cough loud enough to silence the room.

I said nothing for a moment.

I needed it to sink in.

It didn't take long for the conversations around us to pick up again. This time was too precious to be wasted wondering what had some other inmate riled up.

"He's not in a good place," Carrie said.

"I can imagine. If you talk to him, tell him I understand, no hard feelings if he feels he's got to walk away."

"He's got small children. Even so, he's more worried about what happens to you if he does. Any new counsel coming in is going to need time. And time means—"

"Longer in here for me."

"A new trial date. Even a court appointed brief will want time to read through whatever Havers has done so far, talk to any witnesses themselves and piece together your defense."

"How long?"

"No easy answer. It could be a week, it could be a month, it could be a lot longer depending upon what's on the judge's docket."

"This is just going from a shit day to a fucking shit day."

"I told you, Jordan's seriously thinking about taking the deal. You're their bargaining chip. They can do pretty much anything to you while you're in here. The last thing he wants is you getting hurt like Lola. And the longer you're in here and he holds out from making the deal, the more likely that is to happen."

"I'll survive," I said.

"Will you?" She said, dead serious. "Let's be honest, with Dwyer basically ruling the system here, there's nothing to stop the courts from finding endless reasons to delay your trial."

"But I didn't do anything."

Heads turned again, but this time I glared at them.

I was in no mood for staying quiet.

"I was doing my job."

It sounded hollow. The truth didn't matter in a post truth world.

This time the guard took a few steps towards our table. It looked like he was going to remove me from the visitor's room. I shrank a bit inside. Carrie flashed him an apologetic smile. He didn't come any closer.

"Take a breath," she said. "Getting angry isn't going to do you any good. Not in here."

"Easier said than done," I said, but I knew she was right.

"I'm sorry," she said. "I really am."

I let out a sigh. "It's not you. You didn't do this."

"No but I feel like shit. Is there anything I can do for you? Anyone I can call?"

I felt more hopeless now than I had when the judge had denied my bail. I didn't know what to do. It wasn't like I had many friends on the outside apart from Phil. But if I'd lost Havers, I needed someone working the angles on the outside, and he was my best shot.

"Can you call Phil for me?"

"What do you want me to tell him?"

I leaned in so I could keep my voice low and not be overheard. "Ask him to give Alicia White a call..."

"I know Alicia," Carrie said. "I can call her for you. What do you want me to ask her?"

"This could go very badly if she's in bed with the chief, but I'm not sure what other option I've got."

"Well," she said. "Why don't you tell me what you have in mind, and I'll tell you if you're asking too much."

And so, I did.

29

Carrie left me with a feeling of hope.

She'd do whatever she could, and who knows, maybe she'd have more luck trading on her personal relationship with Alicia White than Phil would have, for all his undoubted charms.

"So, fess up, who was your mystery visitor?" Levon asked as I appeared in the doorway. The door closed behind me and the lock engaged with that familiar heavy sliding bolt that sounded more and more like an animal being put out of its misery.

"Someone from the campaign," I said.

"Was it the white cougar?" he asked, grinning. "Please tell me it was."

I hadn't ever thought of her in that way, but I didn't think for a moment there was anyone else I could imagine he was thinking of. I nodded.

"I knew it. She got it bad for you, Moonchild? A taste for black meat."

"I've got no idea what you're talking about," I laughed, sliding onto my bunk and putting my hands behind my head. For all his joking, I hadn't really thought of Carrie that way before. She was basically my boss. But... once that genie's out of the bottle... there's no putting it back in. She was a good-looking woman.

"Why else would she come here to see you? You'll be out in no time. Nah, it's all about the sex, my man, trust me. I know the ways of the flesh."

Then I remembered, and my mood soured. "That's just it, it isn't going to be a few days, I could be in here a lot longer than any of us expected."

I heard the sudden groan of bedsprings a moment before his face appeared over the side of his bunk. "What are you talking about?"

"My trial's going to be pushed back. My lawyer's been getting threats, he's stepping off the case." I said and let the whole story come out, and as I recounted it, I was amazed at my own calm. Levon was more agitated than I was. But then, maybe he'd already worked out how all of this was going to play out? I was just the dumb Moonchild.

"Fuck, brother, that's some sick shit," he said when I'd finished telling him about the postmortem photos. He didn't ask what I was going to do about it, because we both knew that there was nothing I *could* do.

"I guess it means I'll be out of here before you," he said after a moment of silence.

I gave a bitter grunt of a laugh. "Looks like."

"That's just not right, man. You sure you can't get your man to stay on long enough to get you out of here?"

"He's got a wife and a couple of young kids. I can't ask him to take any risk. Not when they murdered Lola. Too big an ask."

"Then you're gonna have the same problem again and again, ain't you? It's a small town. Ain't no one gonna be keen to stare down death threats just so's you get your day in court."

"Jordan's making a couple of calls to firms out of the area."

"Well, let's hope your man comes through."

The longer I was in here, the more fiercely I was convinced we needed people like Jordan to make a difference.

And to make that difference they had to get into power.

Which meant not letting him take that deal, whatever that meant for my liberty.

Was that a price I was willing to pay?

Was I that much of a crusader?

"I'm starting to wish I'd just pled guilty," I said, earning a bark of laughter from my cellmate.

I picked up my books and pretended to read.

I had talked enough.

Levon didn't take offense. He climbed onto his bunk, and I did the same until the call to food rang out.

Patrick was a little more like himself, even if he still moved like a man who had been beaten badly. Ziggy and his crew barracked us as we made our way down the stairs. It was the usual racist homophobic bile. I wouldn't want to live inside his head. I can't imagine it was a pleasant place to be. The guards just let them spout their hate. But the moment Levon rose to it and heckled back he was chastised and told to fall in line by a guard who had his baton in hand. Levon fell silent. He was many things, but stupid was not one of them. He knew this wasn't the time to kick the hornet's nest, not when he was so close to going home. One fight now and he could be looking at an extra month for his pain, if not more. Which only served to empower Ziggy, who turned rabid, frothing at the mouth, flecks of white all around his hips from his posturing and snarling as we joined the food line.

The slop was ladled out. It looked about as appetizing as a dose of herpes.

When we had found a table, I ran through it all again with Patrick, looking for his take. It wasn't my choice; Levon broached it with all the subtlety of a drag queen parading through this place in warpaint and heels.

"Got to say, my friend, that pretty much bites the big one,"

Patrick said. "You thought about changing your plea? Admit the guilt, get time off the sentence in lieu of time served? Just make sure your lawyer speaks to the DA first. There are always deals to be made."

I reminded him that it was likely that I didn't have a lawyer thanks to the intimidation tactics of Dwyer and his people.

"Then call him yourself, find out where you stand. What could it hurt? It's in no one's interest to keep you in here, so get a deal in play for the plea change in return for the same deal that the rest of us were offered. Got to be worth a shot."

"You think they might try to fuck him?" Levon said, but I was already way ahead of him.

"Who knows? They might decide he's been wasting everyone's time."

"But I didn't do anything!"

Patrick shrugged. "Haven't you worked out that that really doesn't matter? No one at that protest did anything. What makes you so different? Your tie? Your education? Your job with your candidate?"

"I was reporting on the protest for the paper. I had every right to be there."

"So? Every single person had a right to be there, the right to peaceful protest is enshrined in who and what democracy is, but that didn't protect them, did it? So, you tell me, Caleb Moon, who's to say you didn't get swept away with the outrage of the mob and go from observer to active participant? Without evidence, it's just your word. Now, before you get heated, I'm merely playing devil's advocate, but you can bet your bottom dollar that's the kind of reasoning the prosecution will use against you. Truth is as dead as that boy and his dog."

Which was a grim though, but it was right. There was no guarantee that I'd get out at the same time as the others, and I'd still have a conviction on my record.

"Speak to your lawyer."

30

I've got to be honest, I'd expected resistance from the guards, given everything that had happened, but I traded my hours for a phone card which would buy me a few minutes with Havers. Not that he was duty bound to answer my call, let alone help, but I had nothing to lose.

"Hi," I said, grateful that he'd picked up. "This is Caleb Moon."

"I am aware, Mr. Moon, but you really shouldn't be calling me. We are not friends, I was your lawyer, I am no longer your lawyer. That was the sum of our relationship."

"I know. Please don't hang up. I have a question and I don't know how else to turn to."

I heard his heavy sigh down the line. "Jordan is looking for a new lawyer for you. They will be able to answer any questions you have."

"They'll request a continuance. That means I'm in here longer."

"Most likely," he said. "But be that as it may, I can't do anything for you." He paused for a moment then added. "If your new lawyer wants to talk with me and bring them up to speed, he is welcome. It could speed the process along for you...a little."

"You are a good man, Mr. Havers," I said. "And I know what they did to you... the threats..."

"What's your question Mr. Moon?"

I steeled myself for more bad news. "If I changed my plea to guilty, could I get the same sentence the others were offered?"

"It isn't unreasonable to hope so, but it rather depends on if the DA is feeling particularly vindictive, I'm afraid. There are no guarantees."

"I hate to ask this..." I said.

"You said you wanted to ask a question. You've already asked it," he said. "But you're going to ask another one, aren't you? You want me to call the DA and find out."

"I do," I admitted.

"I won't be able to do that until the morning."

"You are a lifesaver, Mr. Havers."

"Well, let's hope it doesn't go quite that far, eh? I'll be unlikely to have an answer for you until this time tomorrow, so I will expect your call then."

"Carrie is looking to something else that might make it unnecessary," I said.

"Times up," called a guard from down the corridor.

"I have to go," I said. "If you speak to Carrie, she'll tell you what it's all about and let you know if she's had any luck."

"I'm not your lawyer, Mr. Moon."

The guard's meaty hand reached past me and ended the call.

I didn't bother protesting. Compliance was king if I wanted to get access to the phone again tomorrow. It wasn't the same guard who'd agreed to the call.

"You shouldn't be making calls at this time."

"I'm sorry, I had no idea," I said. "The guard said it would be OK."

"Life lesson for you, I don't give a shit what anyone else says, can't you read? Or maybe your mammy didn't have time to make sure you learned your letters? Was she too busy on her back, nigger?"

The anger rose, black and ugly.

He knew nothing about me, and he had no fucking right to disparage my mother.

And even if I was fully cognizant of what he was doing, I was still rising to the bait. If it hadn't been for Levon calling, "You coming, Caleb?" from along the corridor, I fucked up. It was that easy. I was starting to understand how the fix was in.

The guard jabbed a finger at the notice on the wall. I looked at the cut-off. I'd run over by maybe a minute and a half. The punishment for my transgression was a fine of five bucks.

That would take a bite out of the little I had left in the ledger after paying for the phone card. I was about to protest the fine because the call had begun before the cut-off, when I saw the guard who'd told me it would be fine leaning against the wall with a shit-eating grin on his face.

He'd set me up.

They liked their little victories.

They were a constant reminder, kick by kick, of where the power lay.

They *wanted* us to step out of line.

"What did he say?" Levon asked when we were back in the relative privacy of our cell.

"He's going to give the DA a call in the morning. He made no promises. But it was more than I could have hoped, really."

"Well, let's just hope he works his magic and you're out of here in no time."

Hope. That word again. I was finding it hard to share his optimism. "I have to call him around the same time tomorrow."

"Maybe try for five minutes earlier if you want to have the big bucks to spend when you get out," he laughed, and I couldn't help but smile.

"You have any idea what's happening tomorrow?"

"I figured we'd take a trip to the ocean, always fancied learning how to surf," he said. "What do you think? Hire an open top car, cruise around, pick us up a couple hot mammas. You'll have to pay for the car though 'cos I've used all my cash on hookers and blow."

"You can drive," I said.

"That's mighty kind of you."

"I'm a very generous guy," I said. "Besides, I'll be drinking an ice-cold beer with the girls in the back seat. Best place to be."

And so, it went.

It wasn't the first time Levon had let loose his imagination, and it was so much better than contemplating the same four bare walls.

"Shame we have to work," he said, bringing me crashing back to reality. "Early start. No shower. That's the only thing they said."

"Sounds like fun," I said.

"We'll get to go to the ocean another day."

"Another day," I agreed, a solemn pledge.

31

I hadn't expected the early morning call to be quite so early. We were roused at five, and by five thirty were scoffing down to a plate of scrambled eggs that were a jaundiced yellow. They weren't real eggs, they were reconstituted. Even so, they were a marked improvement on the oatmeal.

Three buses waited for us.

We were loaded straight on them as soon as we'd finished eating.

The convoy of buses kept moving for the best part of an hour. We drew gazes, with other drivers gawking up at us like exhibits in a zoo.

Eventually, all three buses pulled in through an opening as a pair of wide, high steel gates parted to let us in. The entire property was surrounded by a high steel and mesh fence. And by high, I mean well over six feet high.

The security was every bit as tight as the prison.

That should have set alarm bells ringing.

"What do you think this place is?"

"Fuck knows," said another.

"Area 51," some smart ass at the back opined.

Levon had it figured otherwise, some kind of detention center for illegals. "Kids in cages. It's not right, man. 'Give me your tired, your poor, your huddled masses yearning to breathe free?' Bullshit. This ain't the land of opportunity if you don't look the part."

It would explain the security, but not our presence.

After disembarking, one of the guards fell into conversation with a man in red coveralls who'd walked up to meet us. There were nods, some pointing, and then we were ordered off.

The guard went around to the baggage hatch and pulled out a sack that he emptied out onto the hard-packed dirt.

"OK, grab yourself a pair of these coveralls. Everyone dressed, snap snap. It's going to be fucking hot in there so, you want my advice, strip down before you put these on. We got some covers for your shoes, and there's a bandana for anyone who wants to use one."

Which was a strange set of instructions, but we did as we were told, and most of us stripped down before we put the coveralls on. Most, but not all. The others made the wrong call. This was the only time I remember a guard showing us anything like consideration.

"We ready?" asked the employee in the red coveralls.

"They're all yours," the guard said.

"You're not coming in?"

"Not a fuckin' prayer," the guard grinned. "They're not going anywhere until they've done what they came here to do." He pulled out a pack of cigarettes. "They help with the smell, right?"

"Not so much," red coverall guy said. "This way."

We followed him towards the first of what looked like half a dozen giant metal barns. There was a strangely muffled background noise in the air that exploded when he opened the door. But it wasn't just that noise that felt overwhelming; it was the smell.

"Fucking chickens!" someone muttered. Levon, maybe, but I couldn't swear to it.

The light was dim inside the barn, but there must have been thousands, maybe even tens of thousands of birds in there.

The air was filled with the stench of ammonia and thick with dust that was agitated every time a bird tried to take to the wing. Not that they could fly.

"Fuck me, man. How many of these damned things are there in here?"

"A thousand," he said. "More or less."

Which was way below my guess, but still a daunting number. It was a mass of white feathers punctuated by beaks and touches of red. They were crammed in so tightly they could barely move. You couldn't walk through them without cracking a spine in the process. Some of these birds could be dead but they would still be standing, it was that crowded with them in there.

The light had agitated them.

Maybe they associated it with feeding time.

They started to shift and sway like water, each one trying to get closer to the feeding troughs.

We stood in a kind of lobby between the outside world and chicken town.

A few of the guys were already choking on the noxious fumes and dust.

The bandana made sense now.

I tied mine to cover my nose and mouth, the others soon did the same.

"OK folks, it's time for these ladies to be moved out of here." Red grabbed a metal cage from a stack of them in the corner of this lobby area and held it to show how the door at the top worked. It wasn't rocket science.

"You'll get twenty-five birds into one of these." The space that afforded was worse than the hell of the barn. "You might get more in, but to be honest, that just makes the cages heavier and they're harder to deal with at the other end. Get your twenty-five in a cage, bring it out here, grab another cage and do it all over again.

Rinse and repeat. It's easier if you work in pairs. There's a stack of gloves over there if you want 'em. Everything clear?"

"What you do wit' 'em after we've put 'em in the cages?" someone asked.

The man laughed. "Well, then they go off on their vacation, of course."

They were being caged ready for slaughter.

"And if we find any dead birds in there?" Levon asked.

"Throw them in the corner, it'll save time later when we hose this place down."

We were going to have to catch these damned birds, who obviously wouldn't want to be caught, toss any corpses aside, and spend who knew how long shoveling chicken shit.

For the next few hours, we were scratched, clawed, pecked and wing-slapped.

The barn grew hotter and hotter, cooking us.

Each time we tried to catch one of the hens it kicked up dust, feathers, and shit, making the air unbreathable. The poor bastards knew what was happening to them. There was some sort of metaphor going on here, they were in their cages, we were in our cages. We were all animals with no sense of freedom.

"Now, I know why that bastard guard laughed when we had eggs for breakfast," Levon grunted.

After a couple of hours, the door opened, and sunlight flooded in.

Red, the guy who had shown us in, had come to see how we were getting along. He seemed happy enough, apart from when he saw the pile of corpses in the corner, but his anger wasn't directed at any of us.

"All right, I'm assuming you've worked up a decent thirst. Go get a drink and some fresh air."

32

It took us another couple of hours to catch the remainder of the birds to send on their way to death.

The last few were ridiculously hard to catch, with them running round, like, well, frightened chickens. It was almost comical. We slipped and fell, sprawling face first into the shit and straw on the floor time and again.

But eventually, all of the birds had been caught.

The double doors that stretched half of the length of the barn slid open, and vents in the roof opened.

It didn't improve the smell but made clearing out the mess out faster than it would otherwise.

With the carcasses of dead fowl taken away for incineration, the shit and straw shoveled onto wheelbarrows and added to shit heaps that were to be supplied to farms as fertilizer, the bare concrete floors were disinfected, and pressure hosed. And by the end of that, we were dead beat.

We'd been worked like dogs.

Or slaves.

"Ok people, out of those overalls before you get back on the transport," the guard ordered, while we were taking on water and rinsing as much of the crap from our hands and face as we could.

We removed the covers from our shoes and slipped out of the shit caked coveralls.

Dust and debris had gotten inside. Everything underneath was a mess of filth and sweat.

We waited to get back on our bus.

Raised voices coming from one of the others.

"I said get those fuckin' clothes off!" one of the guards snarled.

The inmate on the other end of his temper? Ziggy. And the guard wasn't taking any shit from the man. He'd already stepped out of his overall, but as he'd kept his usual day clothes on underneath, they were plastered in chicken shit.

"You're not getting back on the bus like that," the guard yelled. "Now get out of those fuckin' clothes before I beat you, boy."

None of us had heard any of the guards giving a white guy shit in all the time we'd been inside. Maybe this one hadn't got the memo.

With no real choice in the matter, Ziggy caved. But he very deliberately chose to look in our direction just as Levon took it upon himself to laugh at the naked skinny white dude.

Ziggy was sent to the bowser to rinse some of the crap off his skin before he was allowed to join us on the bus, still naked, still stinking of shit. I have no idea why they put him on with us. Maybe he stank too much to ride with the white boys? It didn't matter, he was not happy to be naked with us all around him. There's a vulnerability in skin that even the toughest bastard feels. Like they've just been stripped of their armor.

He sat at the front on his own.

All the way home he kept turning and glaring at Levon, who just smiled back.

There was going to be payback. A bastard like Ziggy didn't

take losing face well. Levon was making himself an enemy here. But he didn't seem to care. I pulled him on it.

"Weren't you the one who warned me about making enemies?" I said.

"I did," the big man laughed, his smile almost stretching one ear to the other, "but you tell me this, can you take the guy seriously now you've seen his skinny white ass and that limp fucking twig dick? Coz I sure as hell can't."

Ziggy was still growling, but maybe Levon was right, maybe he was just a dog who'd been beat too much?

The transporter finally drove back through the prison gates.

The sun was already sinking low in the sky.

I'd almost forgotten that I needed to call Havers.

As we got off the bus, I tried to talk to one of the guards, but Ziggy started losing his shit about the humiliation. It was the perfect time to ask about my call, as it gave one of the guards an excuse not to have to deal with his shit. He nodded, but instead of leading me straight through to the phone, he told me to "Get yourself cleaned up. You can make your call after you've eaten."

I was about to protest the time without knowing what it was, but knowing I had to be close to cut-off, when he gave me this look and I knew not to push it. This was the deal, take it or leave it. I took it.

33

A lot of what happened next is still a blur.

    I went to my cell and grabbed my stuff, determined to be one of the first in the shower. There were a couple of guys in there already, but none of them had been at the chicken farm with us. They'd been working out in the fields somewhere and had burned red raw in the sun. We showered silently, each going about our business. I scrubbed my skin trying to get the ingrained chicken shit smell out.

It took me a second to realize what was wrong.

It was quiet.

There was the sound of the shower spray, but that was it.

No one else had come in to get cleaned up.

I reached for my towel.

I was not alone.

Ziggy.

"Chicken shit nigger, you still think you better than us? Well, fuck you."

"I don't," I said. I could have gone into a long defense about how we're all the same under the skin and this place is the great leveller, but he wasn't buying. Anything I said was only going to get his back further up. He was angry and humiliated and looking to make someone else hurt for that pain.

"But we ain't all the same, are we? Look at you. You're nuthin' like me. Fuck that. You *are* nuthin'."

Still wet, very naked, totally vulnerable, I tried to move past him, but he shifted his stance, making damned sure he blocked off any way out of the shower room.

"Where the fuck you think yer goin', *nigger*?" He stressed the final word, every bit as vile in his mouth as it had ever been as an insult up and down this land.

He meant know your place, beneath me in the evolutionary chain, remember where you belong.

I was burning up inside, but if I let it out... if I dared rage... it would only make things so much worse for me. It was a fight I couldn't win, even if I left the motherfucker in the infirmary. He was the kind of racist bastard that I'd joined Jordan's campaign to fight. He was every bit as bad as Twomey and the others, all that separated them was their uniforms. They had the law, and all this man had was the threat of violence.

But I wasn't going to take it anymore. I couldn't. Not if I wanted to walk the walk. Behave like an equal, not just bow my head, mutter 'massah' and take whatever was handed down.

Equals.

But how could I even believe in anything as remotely naive as equality after everything I'd seen in here? This country hadn't moved that far since slavery was abolished, the bastards just found subtler ways to wield their power.

And yet I was more afraid of this one man than I'd ever been afraid of anyone in my life.

Not because I thought he would kill me, though he might have, his rage was that unpredictable after his humiliation, and he'd bought the guards off long enough to ensure we were alone.

No, I was afraid because he had the power to keep me in here.

"I need to go dry off and make a call," I said.

"You ain't goin' nowhere," Ziggy said. It was tempting to pull him up on the double negative, ain't going nowhere meant I had to be going somewhere. "You 'n me, we got some business to take care of."

"No, we don't."

"Yeah we do."

"You don't need to do this, brother."

"I ain't your fuckin' brother. I ain't got no stinkin' black blood flowin' through ma veins," he snarled. "Fuck you, nigger. Fuck you."

He glanced over his shoulder, but there was no one there.

His crew were waiting outside, making sure that no one disturbed us.

I stood up against him, naked and afraid. I had no choice.

"You laughed at me. No one laughs at me."

"Everyone laughed," I said. "It was funny."

"Fuck you," he seethed.

I was done. I pushed past him. I didn't use any force, I just put my hand on his shoulder and turned him and kept walking like it was the most natural thing in the world. And that only served to enrage him more.

"Where the fuck d'you think yer goin, cocksucker?" he threw the word like it was the most offensive thing imaginable in his world, a guy taking a dick, but I just kept walking.

I felt him move up behind me.

I wasn't about to stop walking. I didn't even care that my cock was flapping in the wind, as long as I got out of there, this would be over.

For now, at least.

And then I felt the heat of his breath on my skin, the smell of chicken shit, and the sudden red fire of pain that stopped me mid-step.

I didn't know what he used for a shiv, or where he'd got it from. It could have been a filed down toothbrush for all I knew, the impact was the same. There was maybe a heartbeat when I still didn't understand that I'd been stabbed.

But then I felt the wetness in my side and saw the red pooling on the floor between my bare feet. He rammed the shiv in three more times, each one a fresh hell, before my legs buckled, and I pitched to the ground.

And then nothing which seemed to last forever.

34

I kept waking up only to find that I was dreaming or dreaming that I woke up. It was hard to know what was fever, and what was real, what was torment and my own demons, and what was memory. There were chickens and cotton, and voices that kept saying my name. They didn't seem to want me, or maybe they wanted to hurt me, or punish me? It felt like they wanted to do that, yeah, they wanted to see me suffer. And they had such agonies to show me.

They say hell is a place of our own making.

I believed that now.

Body and soul.

Eventually I opened my eyes for more than a fractured second, seeing beyond the blur and the light, and they stayed open. I didn't know where I was. I wasn't on the shower block floor. I was in a bed, not sprawled out on bloody tiles.

The only thing that made sense was someone had dragged me back to my cell...

But that didn't work, either. The mattress beneath me was too soft, and there were no wooden slats from Levon's bunk over me.

Hospital.

A proper hospital, and not the prison infirmary.

"Mr. Moon," a voice said. "Good to have you back with us. You gave us all quite a fright back there." I tried to find her, to look at her, but it hurt to move. "Easy, easy, young man. Don't go wrigglin' around like no lizard in a tin pulling the doc's fine needlepoint apart. Don't want you to spring another leak now, do we?"

"Where..." I couldn't really say much more. My throat was sandpaper dry, that one word grating over my tongue. I had so many questions. They came at me thick and fast; too fast for me to be able to ask them.

She rested a hand on my arm. "Shh," she said. "Just you give yourself a minute. Ain't no rush to prove you're Black Panther."

"Wakanda... forever." I said, my lips twitching.

She chuckled at that like it was the funniest thing.

"The doctor will answer whatever questions he can. You're a very lucky young man, believe me. You've been through the wars."

I didn't even know what day it was.

"OK." I said. I remembered it all now, up to a point. The shiv driving home, the sudden blossom of pain at the base of my spine, with Ziggy going for my kidneys to end my life...

The doctor, when he came, didn't seem much older than me. I could hear the ghost of my dear old mom telling me, see, here's a young man who ain't wasted his life, and smiled at that.

He seemed genuinely pleased to see that I was awake.

"How are you feeling?"

"Been better," I said. "Mainly sore. Tired." And I added "Thirsty," after a moment.

"Well, I'm sure we can sort out something for you to drink," he said, and I heard the soft shuffle of the nurse's shoes as she slipped out of the room. "I'm surprised you're feeling tired. You've been out of it for nearly three days."

"Three days?"

"Do you know what happened to you?"

"I was stabbed."

"You were. But that, as they say, barely scratches the surface. When you fell you must have hit your head, hard. There was swelling on the brain which meant we had to keep you sedated, giving it a chance to go down. Fortunately, the wounds in your back didn't do as much damage as they might have done. An inch either side, different story. All things considered, you've been very lucky."

Lucky.

I blew out a slow breath. In the last three weeks I don't think I'd had a single bit of luck that wasn't bad.

"So how long 'til I get out of here?"

"How long's a piece of string?"

"OK, I get it, no commitment to a time frame, but I mean, are we talking days or weeks?"

"Probably."

The nurse came back with a jug of water and the doctor left me to it. I drank the first glass like a man coming out of the desert, despite the nurse's warning to take it slow.

"You feel like you might be up to eating something? Maybe a pudding cup?"

Despite the growling in my stomach, I couldn't face the thought of food. "I'm good. I just want to sleep."

The next time I woke I felt considerably more human.

I knew even before I opened my eyes that there was someone in the room with me.

It's a weird sensation, knowing you should be alone and knowing there's someone in that space with you. I jokingly thought it was my prison sense finally kicking in, too late to stop me from getting shivved. I turned slightly, my head hurting as I moved, and saw Phil in the armchair. I'd been expecting one of the prison guards, making sure I didn't run.

"Welcome back, my friend," he said. "You want me to call the nurse?"

"It's all good," I lied, which brought a smile to his lips at least. I'm a terrible liar. We both knew that about me.

"I assume you want the gory details?" He said, and for a moment I didn't follow, then realized he knew stuff I didn't which would help put the pieces together.

"I want the gory details."

"Ever a newsman. Good for you. So, your friend Levon found you in the showers when you didn't show up at your cell. He saved your life, no two ways about it. He raised hell calling for help, and knelt over you, pressing your soaking towel to staunch the blood loss, and wouldn't be moved until the paramedics were on scene. And even then, he refused to take his hands away until he knew you were good, that they had you."

"Good old Levon."

"Good old Levon indeed. They've got the guy who did it to you. He's up on an attempted murder charge. I have to say, getting stabbed didn't do your cause any harm, my friend. You're a celebrity," He picked up a stack of newspapers from the floor next to him. "I thought you might like to read all about yourself."

"I lived through it once, not sure I can do it again. How about the edited highlights?"

"Well then, here's the fun stuff, Havers spoke to the DA's office who'd told him that they hadn't objected to you getting bail, point of fact they were surprised you were bound over. It was Chief of Police Dwyer who'd personally insisted on it. He'd also insisted they file charges. The DA wasn't looking to make an example of you. That was all Dwyer. And it was personal. By then, Carrie had spoken to Alicia White, who corroborated your story of the white guys agitating at the protest and managed to find some footage of them standing in the crowd. Which might not have been enough to save your bacon, save for the fact the lovely and fearless Alicia had something else cooking that has tipped the scales in your favor."

"Tell me, tell me," I said, eager to hear the fun stuff, and knowing full well Big Phil would drag it out for his own amusement.

"She's been working on a big story. And I mean B.I.G. Corruption. Mayor Dwyer and his boy slap bang in the middle of it, right along with the judge on your case. She'd wanted to run it already, but the Big Wigs at the station ordered her to stand down until the race was run. They figured the impact would hit harder then."

The election. I had almost forgotten about it. "How did it go?"

"All in good time, kiddo," he said, raising a hand. "Anyway, she put her head together with Stacey and they shared the byline under the promise we'd run it before the election, because she didn't want to wait and risk it getting buried. Now, I'll be honest, our corporate sponsors shit a brick, and not a metaphorical one, my friend. It could have cost all our jobs, but it was the right thing to do, and sometimes... well, you know that quote, right? All it takes for evil to flourish is for good men to do nothing? Sometimes you just have to stand up and be counted. Alicia's going to come out of it well, trust me, that woman, she can fall in the shit and come up smelling of roses, but you owe her.

"The nationals got hold of her story alongside another piece about a young reporter who'd been arrested and charged for reporting on a protest about a cop killing, a boy and his dog. The comparisons were drawn to the communist regime, which is always good ink. No one likes a commie," he grinned. "It made a splash. Not above the fold, but it was a front-page story in all the majors."

"No shit," I said, admiring her chutzpah. For all the teeth, tits and fake smiles for the camera, Alicia White was a real journalist.

She put me to shame.

"The joke is that it wasn't enough to swing the election. Dwyer still won, but he's in so much shit he'll need a digger to get out of it. Alicia dug it all up, prison stuffing for profit, excessive sentences for black defendants, kickbacks from the corporation behind the prison. And the nail in the coffin, one of his boy's deputies was paid off to cause a riot during that protest."

"Twomey."

"That's the rat bastard. He's up on co-conspiracy charges, including malicious threats against your lawyer, as those autopsy images came back to his computer. There's a growing belief he was behind the murder of your girl, Lola Brown. Hard to prove, given his DNA was all over the scene as he was the responding officer. But it's not looking good for your friend Jake. Not looking much better for the judge who presided over your case, either. Retirement on health grounds."

"So, I'm a free man?"

"Technically no, a new judge has already heard from both Havers and the DA's office and you've been released on bail immediately, hence the lack of stooges here keeping an eye on you. Let's just say the prison board couldn't get rid of you fast enough. Seems like they think you're more trouble than your worth."

I laughed at that. And like that old joke, it hurt.

"Bail? I'd have thought—"

"Don't worry, the judge is on it. He's a good man. Eyes are on this. He's got to play the optics. He's going through every single arrest, including those who took the deal and pled out. The whole thing's going to get tossed, but it's got to be done properly. So, tell me, how's it feel to be the story?"

"I wouldn't recommend it."

35

I was in the hospital for another nine days all told, before the doctors were happy to see the back of me and discharge me. I'd needed another minor procedure on the damage caused by the stab wounds, otherwise I might have been out of there sooner.

Levon and Patrick visited me, and it felt like a genuine reunion of old friends. We had bonds now, the three of us, forged in fire. We'd seen how this world really worked for people like us. We understood the system was stacked way against us, and that a few stories about disproportionate sentencing for black youths and stacked dockets looking to profit off the cheap labor they provided wouldn't change the world. But they didn't need to. They were a step. One step. The important thing was that there was another, and there would be another after that. BLM protests were a step. The protests for the boy and his dog, they were a step. The locking up of a corrupt cop was another. The weeding out of his white supremacist buddies from the force, that was another. Little steps. One little victory at a time.

I did my best to thank Levon for saving my life, but there really aren't the words.

He just said I would have done the same.

And he was right.

What neither of us were prepared to admit was that if it had been Ziggy bleeding out on the shower room floor we wouldn't. But that was a confession we didn't need to make. Because contrary to popular opinion, I like to think we've already established, sometimes confession isn't good for the soul.

Carrie visited too, with a fruit basket and a card signed by some of the volunteers from the campaign. I noticed Jordan's name but I knew his signature well enough to know he hadn't signed it himself.

I remembered what Levon had said, and found myself looking at her again, and really seeing her for the remarkable woman she was.

I was immeasurably glad she was there.

I don't know what that meant, only that I was.

"He's gone to Washington," Carrie said. "There's a job for him if he wants it. He's been making ripples. Ripples, he hopes, will eventually become waves."

"Of course, he has. That's who he is," I said.

"He told me to tell you to get in touch if you're interested in getting the band back together. Does that sound like something you'd be interested in?"

I thought about it for a second, but I didn't have to think much longer than that. I'm a communicator. I'm not backroom staff. I don't shape political agendas. And as much as I really do care, the only way I'm ever going to change the world is with my voice.

"I've been having a rethink about what I want to do with my life."

"Oh yes? Sounds intriguing. Do tell."

The truth is I'd spent a lot of the last few days reading the newspapers Phil had left me, as well as a second bundle he'd brought in a couple of days later.

I saw the difference that a story had been able to make. I tracked the way it had broken open the corruption, exposing the rotten core, and the fallout from it, and how words had changed people's lives.

I realized it was exactly the kind of thing that had made me want to go into journalism in the first place.

And that I missed it.

I also realized that I'd been wrong, in a Post Truth world the truth mattered more than ever.

I could make a difference here. My words could be powerful in a time when this place needed powerful words to see it right. The town was going to be undergoing some seismic shifts with the new regime, a new mayor and a new chief of police. Someone needed to hold their hand to the fire. I wanted that to be me.

Besides, I had friends here.

I reached out and took Carrie's hand from where it rested on the bed and gave it a gentle squeeze. "There's a life here I want to start living," I told her. "And who knows, I might even write a book."

THE END

KINGSTON IMPERIAL

Marvis Johnson — Publisher
Joshua Wirth — Designer
Kristin Clifford — Publicist, Finn Partners
Emilie Moran — Publicist, Finn Partners
Roby Marcondes — Marketing Manager

Contact:
Kingston Imperial
144 North 7th Street #255
Brooklyn, NY 11249
Email: Info@kingstonimperial.com
www.kingstonimperial.com

PRAISE FOR
THE PERFECTLY PROPER PARANORMAL MUSEUM MYSTERIES

Déjà Moo
"Weis many quirky ongoing characters add charm and humor …"
—*Kirkus Reviews*

"The third volume in this engaging series (following *Pressed to Death*) will appeal to fans of paranormal cozies by Sofie Kelly and Christy Fifield."
—*Library Journal*

Pressed to Death
"Well-drawn characters and tantalizing wine talk help balance the quirky aspects of this paranormal mystery."
—*Publishers Weekly*

The Perfectly Proper Paranormal Museum
"A delightful new series."
—*Library Journal* (starred review)

"A quirky murder mystery with plenty of small town charm."
—*ForeWord Reviews*

"Humor, hints of romance, and twists and turns galore elevate this cozy."
—*Publishers Weekly*

"A clever combination of characters."
—*Kirkus Reviews*

Chocolate à la MURDER

A Perfectly Proper Paranormal Museum Mystery

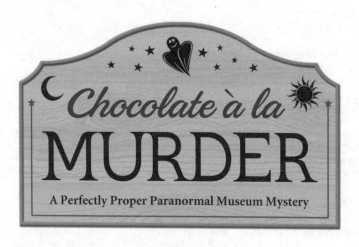

Chocolate à la MURDER

MURDER

A Perfectly Proper Paranormal Museum Mystery

by

KIRSTEN WEISS

MIDNIGHT INK
WOODBURY, MINNESOTA

FIRST EDITION
First Printing, 2019

Book format by Samantha Penn
Cover design by Kevin R. Brown
Cover illustration by Mary Ann Lasher-Dodge

Midnight Ink, an imprint of Llewellyn Worldwide Ltd.

Library of Congress Cataloging-in-Publication Data

Names: Weiss, Kirsten, author.
Title: Chocolate a la murder / Kirsten Weiss.
Description: First edition. | Woodbury, Minnesota : Midnight Ink, an imprint of Llewellyn Worldwide Ltd., 2019. | Series: A Perfectly Proper Paranormal Museum Mystery ; #4.
Identifiers: LCCN 2018049343 (print) | LCCN 2018051279 (ebook) | ISBN 9780738757353 (ebook) | ISBN 9780738757131 (alk. paper)
Subjects: | GSAFD: Mystery fiction.
Classification: LCC PS3623.E4555 (ebook) | LCC PS3623.E4555 C46 2019 (print) | DDC 813/.6—dc23
LC record available at https://lccn.loc.gov/2018049343

Midnight Ink
Llewellyn Worldwide Ltd.
2143 Wooddale Drive
Woodbury, MN 55125-2989
www.midnightinkbooks.com

Printed in the United States of America

To the Krolikowskis

ONE

I adjusted the Aztec priest and frowned.

Afternoon sunlight painted the black-and-white floor tiles. Black pedestals dotted the room. Displayed on each was a different aspect of *The Magic of Chocolate*.

I adjusted a gilded cocoa pod on the *Chocolate Alchemy* pedestal so it leaned against a dusty alchemical beaker.

Normally, the tiny Gallery room in my paranormal museum was filled with quirky local art. This weekend, the San Benedetto Wine and Visitors Bureau was kicking off Wine and Chocolate days. Since the local wineries had the wine side handled, I was going with a chocolate theme at the museum.

And I had no chocolate.

My stomach butterflied, that feeling of nerves and excitement common to the self-employed. This would be okay. I had an amazing if odd museum, with ever-changing exhibits that kept me on my toes. An amazing and definitely-not-odd boyfriend. Plus, amazing friends—Adele and Harper. The chocolate would arrive in time.

"I've got it!" Harper hurried into the room, her olive cheeks dusky-rose from exertion.

I wished sweat made me sexy like it did my friend, the Penelope Cruz clone. I could feel the grit clinging to my damp forehead.

Harper carried a picture frame beneath her arm, and my shoulders slumped. For one relieved moment, I'd thought she'd come bearing chocolate. But Harper was a financial planner, not a delivery girl.

"Sorry I'm late." Chest heaving, she adjusted the lapel of her pin-striped pantsuit. "Am I too late?"

"You're right on time. I was just finishing up." Knotting my brown hair into a ponytail, I motioned around the room.

She handed me the ornately framed poster. "You didn't get it from me," she said. On the hand-drawn poster was a modern witch's perspective on chocolate.

"Of course not," I said. "You were only doing me a favor and picking up a framed..." Spell? Meditation? Whatever it was, the poster looked spooky, written in Harper's elegant script and bordered by a cabernet-red mat and black frame.

Harper was a secret strega, a classical Italian witch. But she kept that aspect of her life firmly in the broom closet. It didn't fit her high-powered, financially savvy image.

She shivered, her expression becoming a careful blank.

"Harper?" I asked, suddenly alert.

Slowly, she turned and walked to the pedestal closest to the door to the museum proper. On it, a whisk from Mexico called a *molinillo* stood upright in a ceramic jar. Used for mixing Mexican hot chocolate, the molinillo was a thing of beauty. Decorative geometric shapes had been whittled into the pale wood and burned black for contrast. A feminine hand had been carved at the top of the spindle. Beside the display, a tent card read: *Haunted Molinillo—Rattles When a Lie Is Told*.

Circling, Harper bent toward the pedestal and slipped her hands into the pocket of her pinstriped blazer. "What have you got here?"

"A molinillo. I can't believe I found one that was haunted."

She glanced from me to the molinillo. "I'll say." Abruptly, she straightened. "My name is Adele Nakamoto," she deadpanned. She stared intently at the display. "Strange. It's not rattling."

"That's because it's not a very important lie." I pushed a wisp of hair behind my ear. Was my witchy friend sensing something I hadn't? "And besides, I know you're lying. The molinillo doesn't need to give me a warning."

Harper arched a brow.

"Okay," I admitted. "I don't know why it's not rattling, but that's the legend."

She tugged on her plump bottom lip. "What's its story?"

"It's a little vague. My collector—"

"Herb? You're trusting him after the cursed cowbell incident?"

"In fairness," I said, "the riot wasn't his fault." And Herb wasn't exactly *my* collector. He was *a* paranormal collector who occasionally dropped by the museum peddling his wares. "Anyway, I got lucky. He turned up with a haunted molinillo right when I needed something chocolate-themed." Which, on reflection, seemed somewhat suspicious. "I'll change the sign so it's clear only important lies set off the molinillo."

Harper pointed to a corner of the Gallery, where I'd arranged a red-velvet canopy above a round table covered in a star-spangled black cloth. "What's happening there?"

"A fortune-teller's coming in to do chocolate scrying for customers." I bounced on my toes. It was going to be awesome. I'd been promoting her all over town. Though it worried me a little that Harper hadn't seen my flyers and advertisements. I was also a little concerned about melted chocolate being used during the scrying process and the potential for burns. But the fortune-teller had assured me she had it handled. "She's also promised to read with the chocolate tarot cards," I said. I'd be giving everyone who bought a ticket to the museum a single chocolate tarot card-of-the-day as a free gift.

"Are the cards actually made of chocolate? Because that sounds sticky."

Sticky and delicious! "Sadly, no. They're paper and ink, just chocolate-themed." As a confirmed cacaophile, chocolate tarot cards were something I could get behind.

Harper turned to the shelves on the wall opposite the windows. Aside from one that was filled with the boxes of tarot and oracle cards, they were empty. "And the empty shelf space?"

I hung her framed offering over a small ebony table between the shelves. "Actual chocolate, if it ever gets here. The delivery man's late. He was supposed to arrive this morning."

"Where are you getting the chocolate?"

"From Reign."

Harper whistled. "That new place? Good stuff. I've been giving their chocolate away as thank-yous to my clients."

I nodded. Reign's chocolate was expensive and beautiful, but it tasted just okay to me. My favorite was still See's Candy, a West Coast institution. That *I Love Lucy* scene with Lucy and Ethel working the chocolate conveyer belt? Filmed at See's.

"Listen," Harper said, her expression turning serious. "I'm thinking of—"

"Where is it?" Our friend Adele Nakamoto, chic in a slim, ice-blue skirt and ivory blouse beneath her Fox and Fennel apron, bustled into the Gallery. She looked around wildly. "Is it here?"

Harper pointed to the black frame.

Adele tossed her head and a wisp of ebony hair floated free from her chignon. "That's not chocolate. Where's the chocolate?"

Uh oh. "It hasn't arrived yet," I said, fighting a reflexive cringe.

She planted her fists on her slim hips. "But I need it now. Twenty retirees are going to arrive in my tea room in fifteen minutes, and they expect Reign chocolate." Adele's tea room, the Fox and Fennel, was conveniently located right next door to the museum. "Plus, Allie is out sick, and our main oven stopped working this morning. I've already had to cancel my appointment with the caterer. This week has been a disaster. Even Pug has a cold."

"Oh no," I said, frowning. Adele's pug was sweet as a sugar cube—I cut a glance at GD—unlike some animals I knew. The black cat sneezed, turned, and sauntered into the main room.

"You've hired a caterer for your own tea room?" Harper asked.

"No, for the wedding!" Adele paced, her apron strings flying out behind her. "Dieter and I are getting married in three months," she wailed, "and we haven't even finalized the menu."

Easygoing Dieter Finkielkraut and uptight Adele Nakamoto seemed an unlikely couple at first glance. But I believed they had what it took. Unfortunately, Adele was caught in the iron grip of the bridal-industrial complex.

"Let me see what the holdup is." Hastily, I pulled my cell phone from the back pocket of my jeans and called the chocolate shop.

No one answered.

After the fifth ring, a machine picked up. I left a message and pocketed the phone. "I'm sure they'll call back." Preferably before Adele went nuclear.

"Will they? You don't know that." Adele's fingers dug into her ebony hair. "Twenty retirees!"

Ignoring my pleading look, Harper backed out of the Gallery. "I'd help you with your little chocolate problem—"

"Little!" Adele's eyes bulged.

"—but I've got a client meeting." Harper turned and sprinted into the museum's main room. The bell above the front door jangled.

I smiled tightly. "It's fine." *Jussst fine.* I brushed off my hands. "The delivery's probably on its way, but I'll go to Reign and pick up some chocolate in the meantime. Leo can run the museum without me." My assistant would have no trouble managing things. The place was depressingly empty this afternoon; Wednesdays are not boom times for paranormal museums.

"How much do you need?" I asked Adele as I walked past her into the main room. It smelled of old objects and furniture polish, and I inhaled a calming breath. I checked the black crown molding for spiderwebs and found none. Freestanding shelves displayed haunted objects and creepy dolls. On the opposite wall, a door disguised as a bookcase led to Adele's tea room. I loved that secret door, and not just because there were scones on the other side.

Leo, seated behind the glass counter, poured over a college textbook. His thin frame hunched in a comma shape beside the antique cash register. My assistant's black leather jacket hung over the back of his tall chair. He glanced at me and flashed a grin, and then his head dipped again to the book.

"I need the amount of chocolate I ordered," Adele said, waspish. "But if I can get seven of each of their bars, it will get me through the retirement party."

"No problem," I said lightly. "Leo, do you mind watching the museum while I'm away? I'll be gone for about thirty minutes."

"Yeah ... sure." His dyed-black hair fell forward, hiding his eyes. The heater whirred behind him.

"He's got an exam coming up," I said in a low voice to Adele.

"Education first," she chirped.

Leo attended the local community college, and he had bigger things in store than working at a paranormal museum. But I hoped I had a couple years left before my Goth assistant moved on to greener and less-haunted pastures.

The museum's ghost-detecting cat meowed from the haunted rocking chair in the opposite corner. He rolled, stretched, and yawned. The old wooden rocking chair swayed beneath him.

"Thank you, thank you, thank you." Adele pressed the spine of a book on the bookcase. The case pivoted outward, opening into her tea room.

I grabbed a handful of postcards off the counter. "Wait—"

But she'd already vanished through the secret door. It snicked shut behind her.

I sighed and returned the postcards for my *Magic of Chocolate* exhibit. Last night, after a few glasses of wine from her family's vineyard, Adele had agreed to stack them on the counter in the Fox and Fennel. I could give them to her later.

I glanced around the main room one last time. Everything was in order. Haunted photos of murderers stared down at me, their black frames gleaming. Rows of shelves containing haunted objects gleamed, dust free. From high atop a wall pedestal, a bronze skull seemed to wink.

"See you in thirty minutes," I said.

"Mmph," Leo grunted, not looking up.

I strolled through the bookcase and down the tea room's elegant, bamboo-plank hallway to the alley. Spring in San Benedetto could be iffy, and this was one of those days that couldn't decide what it was going to be. Fog hung low in the sky. But it was warm enough for me to shrug out of my Paranormal Museum hoodie, exposing my museum T-shirt beneath. When you're self-employed, fashion takes a back seat to advertising.

I drove down Main Street in my vintage red pickup. Yes, I could have walked, but there was a chance I'd be returning with a massive chocolate delivery, and for that I needed wheels.

I slowed in front of Reign. A burly, red-headed man in jeans and a slouchy blue T-shirt picketed in front of the chocolate shop's windows.

Huh. Was a strike the cause of the late delivery? The chocolate shop didn't seem like a big enough business to have organized labor.

Frowning, I turned the corner, looking for parking. I found a spot on the street beside the bank and walked back to Reign.

"Reign, unfair! Reign, unfair!" The man bobbed his sign, decorated with the single word: *UNFAIR!* He marched back and forth on the brick sidewalk.

Adele would kill me if I let a single picketer stop me. Averting my gaze, I scuttled past the man and through the glass door into the shop. The aroma of chocolate stopped me in my tracks. Tension dropped from my shoulders. Chocolate might not be magic, but it was great aromatherapy.

The shop's cinderblock walls were painted light gray and glistened with a dreamlike sheen. A long, polished wood counter the color of dark honey stretched across the back of the store. Driftwood displays showed off jars of sauces and bars of chocolate wrapped in simple brown paper. Colored crowns in varying colors decorated the top of each bar. Rows of chocolate-covered fruits and nuts and truffles infused with wine lined a glass case on the counter.

My mouth pinched, and not with delight. No sales person stood behind the chic counter. Was the guy on strike supposed to be manning the front of the store?

The heady scent of chocolate twined around me, and I told myself not to freak out. If I had to wait somewhere, this wasn't a bad spot. An artisanal chocolate shop beat a paranormal museum, hands down. Of course, if I owned a chocolate shop, I'd probably be fifty pounds overweight instead of my usual ten.

Ignoring the temptations along the way, I marched to the cash register and rang the bell.

No one responded.

"Hello?" I called, leaning across the counter.

Silence.

If I returned empty-handed, Adele would have an aneurysm. And I needed chocolate for the museum too. Settling in to wait, I picked up a brochure and scanned through it.

After years spent working with European chefs and chocolatiers, friends Atticus Reine and Orson Malke began making handcrafted, ethically sourced, single-origin chocolates in their San Francisco apartment. They opened their flagship branch in San Benedetto, close to the organically grown nuts and other ingredients that complement the subtle flavor of the cacao.

Their pledge? To forever change the way you look at choco-late bars. Because our craft chocolates are made in small batches from select beans, our chocolates are as complex as a fine wine. Sign up for our Chocolate of the Month Club and make sure you get the best of our chocolates when they're made.

Mouth watering, I flipped past the photos of the owners to the page with wine and chocolate pairings. It listed wines from local vineyards, as well as a logo that proclaimed Reign an associate member of the Wine and Visitors Bureau. Plot 42, owned by Adele's father, was on the winery list. No wonder my friend was hell-bent on including Reign chocolates at her tea room.

Something metallic clanked in another room, like a heavy door closing.

My head jerked up. "Hello?"

No reply.

My scalp prickled and I fisted my hands. I needed to get a grip. This was an innocent chocolate shop, for Pete's sake. The counter guy was on strike outside, and an owner would have to show up eventually. I needed to stop thinking like I was in a haunted mu-seum and lose the paranoia.

I returned to studying the brochure. I'd done a lot of research prepping my *Magic of Chocolate* exhibit, and the story of the cocoa bean and what people had done with it amazed me. How did the Mesoamericans figure out that the slimy cocoa bean could be fer-mented and turned into such a delicious drink? Casanova had drunk chocolate daily, believing it to be an aphrodisiac. The trypto-phan in chocolate is part of serotonin, a chemical in the brain con-nected to sexual arousal.

Not that I needed help in the romance department. I was still in the honeymoon stage of a relationship with the sexy Detective Jason Slate. No outside stimulants were necessary. But the honeymoon would end sometime. I hoped it wouldn't end with the sort of painful discovery my last relationship had.

Folding the brochure, I jammed it into the rear pocket of my jeans. *Where was everyone?* "Hello?"

Silence.

Oh, come on! I couldn't wait here all day. Not with Adele tapping her expensive shoes while waiting for my return.

I edged around the counter. A long, rectangular window in the gray cinderblock wall behind the register looked into the kitchen. I peered through the window and saw metal racks and metal counters and tall machines. Something in the kitchen whirred softly. But there was no one inside.

This was getting ridiculous. The store was open. The door was unlocked. The guy on strike couldn't be the only employee working today.

Fuming, I pushed open the swinging door to the kitchen area and leaned inside. Metal racks of cooling chocolates were stacked high on wheeled carts. "Helloooo?"

No response.

Suddenly uneasy, I sidled into the room. Gleaming metal countertops with massive metal bowls. Black rubber fatigue mats on the floor. At the back, beside a glass-fronted room, a well-lit hallway that cut along the left side of the room.

Promising-looking boxes sat stacked against the wall in the hallway, beside a closed office door. Were those our order? Maybe someone was in the office and couldn't hear me?

I probably shouldn't be in their kitchen, but Adele and I needed our order. I headed toward the open hallway.

The whirring sound grew louder behind me.

Hair prickling the back of my neck, I froze, then looked over my shoulder.

In the kitchen, a man lay supine on the floor beside two narrow metal vats. The vats angled downward, chocolate dripping onto his face and chest.

TWO

"Oh my god," I whispered. Dizzy, I stepped around the chocolate pooling on the floor and knelt beside the slender man. He wore a brown Reign apron, so he must work here, but I couldn't recognize him beneath the chocolate covering his face. His chocolate-coated beard looked obscene. "Sir? Are you all right?"

His arm was one of the few parts of his body that wasn't covered in chocolate. Not having any better ideas, I grabbed his wrist and felt for a pulse.

There wasn't one.

My breath came in quick gasps. "Dammit." I fumbled in my jean pocket for my cell phone and called for help.

"911, what is your emergency?"

"This is Maddie Kosloski," I stammered. "I'm at Reign Chocolate on Main Street. There's been an ..." Accident? Murder? "There's a man lying on the floor in the kitchen. I can't find a pulse. I'm alone here, and I don't know what happened."

"Is he breathing?"

"Um." I studied his unmoving form. "No. But … he's covered in chocolate." My gaze darted around the gleaming kitchen.

"Excuse me?"

"Melted chocolate. He fell beneath some vats, and the chocolate's all over him."

"Hold please." The dispatcher clicked off.

"Wait! What …?" Was there a special dispatcher for chocolate-related emergencies?

"Hello," a man said. "This is Emergency Medical Services. Can you tell me what's happening?"

I repeated my story.

"All right. Do you know CPR?"

"Yes, but—"

"Your friend may be choking, or even drowning. I need you to clear his air passage with your finger and turn his head sideways. Can you do that?"

"He's not my—" *Not important!* "Yes. Yes. I'm putting the phone on speaker." I set the phone on a dry spot on the thick black floor mat.

Steeling myself, I parted the man's jaw and reached inside. I felt more squeamish about the process than I wanted to admit, but I did it anyway. I didn't have much choice.

When I was done, I heaved the man onto his side. A glug of chocolate dribbled from his mouth.

"Okay," I said, relieved that was over. "I did it. His throat is clear." I wiped my hand on my jeans.

Far off, a siren wailed.

"Good work," the medical dispatcher said. "Now you're going to need to perform CPR."

I stared at the chocolate-smeared face. *Oh boy.*

"Fine." My voice cracked.

Unwrapping my Paranormal Museum hoodie from my hips, I wiped chocolate off the man's mouth with a sleeve. I winced and pressed my mouth to his, then breathed into his mouth.

His lips were warm and slippery beneath mine.

I turned my head and sucked air in. The damp bristles of his beard tickled my cheek. Involuntarily, I licked melted chocolate from my lips. My stomach made a quick, unpleasant bolt toward my throat. *Keep it together, Maddie.* Grimacing, I repeated the process, punctuated by bouts of chest compressions.

"What's happening?" the dispatcher barked, his voice thin over my cell phone's speaker.

"Nothing," I panted, tasting the bitter sweetness of dark chocolate. Oh, God, it was delicious. And that was so wrong for so many reasons. I shuddered.

"Keep at it," he said. "You never know."

The bell over the front door jingled.

"Police," a woman called out.

My shoulders crumpled inward but I kept up the CPR. I knew that voice.

"Back here," I shouted, my breathing ragged from the compressions. "In the kitchen."

Detective Laurel Hammer strode into the kitchen and stopped short. Tall, blond, and muscular, she stared down at me, her ice-blue eyes crackling with ... surprise? Annoyance? With my old high school bully, it was hard to tell. In her opinion, I'd never been an innocent. Over time, her attitude toward me hadn't relaxed. It had morphed into anger.

She gave herself a little shake, her short hair settling in place, then dropped to her knees on the other side of the fallen man. She grasped his wrist, pressed two fingers to his neck, and shook her head. "What have you done?"

Defensive, I sat back on my heels. "The dispatcher told me to—"

"Save it." Her neck muscles corded. "I'll take the chest compressions. You keep up the mouth-to-mouth."

I blinked, then bent my head to the fallen man's. We worked until the paramedics arrived a few minutes later, and let them take over. I backed away, my knees groaning.

"And for God's sake, wipe your face," Laurel snapped. "You look like a fat kid let loose on a hot fudge sundae."

"I'm not fat!" It was only an extra ten pounds. Roughly, I wiped my mouth with the back of one hand, but I couldn't escape the taste of chocolate. Dark, delicious chocolate. I fought a gag. *Wrong. Wrong!*

I turned, feeling sick, and raced down the hallway. There had to be a bathroom down here somewhere.

"Hey!" Laurel shouted. "Where are you going?"

I ducked into a unisex bathroom and splashed water on my face. The heady scent of chocolate turned my stomach. In the mirror over the utilitarian sink, chocolate streaked my mouth and chin. Brown streaked my bare arms, and I was willing to bet if I looked hard enough, I'd find it dotting my black T-shirt. I looked like Count Chocula after a particularly messy snack.

Grabbing a paper towel from the bin on the wall, I scrubbed my face.

"Thanks for disappearing on me." Laurel appeared in the open door and glared. "Getting rid of the evidence?"

"I don't feel so good."

"What happened to that guy's not catching. I doubt the victim was poisoned."

"Victim? Is he …" But of course he was dead. In my heart, I'd known he was gone.

"He's dead." The detective glanced down the hallway and nodded at someone beyond my vision. "What are you doing here, Kosloski?"

"Adele and I placed a big chocolate order last week. It was supposed to be delivered today, but it was late. When we tried calling Reign, no one answered. We thought the easiest solution was for me to drive here and collect whatever I could. No one was at the counter, so I walked into the kitchen and found … him." I imagined the body and angled my head. Something wasn't right.

No kidding, something wasn't right. A man was dead.

"Did you recognize him?" she asked.

I tasted a bit of chocolate behind my front tooth and my stomach rolled. "Are you serious? Under all that chocolate? I mean, he was wearing a Reign apron. It looked like one of the owners, Atticus or Orson. They both have beards like …" I swallowed, remembering the man's chocolate-covered bristles against my chin. "They look a lot alike."

Laurel's blue eyes narrowed. "You seem to know a lot about them."

"Their pictures are in the brochure." I waved vaguely toward the front of the shop, my sense of not-rightness growing.

"Did you see anyone?" she asked.

"Only the guy out front, picketing."

"What guy?"

I rubbed my forehead. My hand was sticky, and I dropped it to my side. "One of the employees, I think. He was red-haired and about my age, or maybe younger."

"Thirty-five?"

She *knew* I was a year younger than her. "Thirty-three. He was wearing jeans and a blue T-shirt." I squinted. "I think he might have been the cashier, but I'm not sure. I've only been here twice before."

"And yet you managed to find a dead body and mess up the crime scene. Again."

"I didn't know he was dead," I bleated, as if that made it any better. "And the dispatcher told me—"

"Use your head next time."

Laurel had been right there beside me giving him CPR! Or at least, we'd been together until I cut and ran. But if I'd stayed, I would have really messed up the scene.

I cleared my throat. "I did hear something when I was waiting by the counter. It sounded like a door closing in the back."

"When was this?"

Time had done weird, *Star Trek* dilations since I'd entered the chocolate shop. Had I been here an hour? Twenty minutes? "It was only a minute or two before I went into the kitchen, I think. And then I called the dispatcher right away. Does that help?"

Her nostrils flared. "Does it sound like it helps?"

Detective Jason Slate, tall, dark, and commanding, appeared in the bathroom doorway behind Laurel. He wore his detective uniform, a navy business suit he filled to perfection.

At the sight of my boyfriend, relief cascaded through me. I sagged against the bathroom's tiled wall.

"Laurel, what's …" His gaze met mine and he took a half-step back. His brown eyes, flecked with gold, widened. "Maddie?"

"I didn't know he was dead," I wailed. "I tried to fix it."

"Did you break it?" Laurel asked.

"I didn't mean that," I said. "I just found him there. What was I supposed to do? Ignore the dispatcher and let him die? I didn't know he was already dead." But what if he hadn't been dead when I'd found him? What if he was dead now because I'd done bad CPR? What if I hadn't cleared his throat properly? What if he could have been saved? Bile swam up my throat. I raced to the nearby toilet and made it just in time.

Someone gently pulled my hair back from my shoulders.

I fell sideways, half onto my butt on the cold bathroom tiles.

Jason knelt beside me and placed a gentle hand on my shoulder. Warmth seemed to flow through his broad palm. "Hey, you okay?"

"Yes," I said weakly.

"Because you're green," he said.

"I think it's the smell." Normally I adored the scent of chocolate. I'd even bought a cocoa-based perfume once. Now the smell clung to me like a nauseating miasma.

"Laurel, will you give us a minute?"

The detective's mouth twisted. She nodded and stepped from the bathroom.

"What happened?" Jason wrapped his hands around mine.

I ran him through everything. "I didn't mean to find a body again." I hiccuped. "What's wrong with me? Why does this keep happening? You don't think he was murdered, do you?"

Jason lifted me to my feet, his hand remaining on mine, firm and calming. It was all I could do not to lay my head on his chest. One of the best things about Jason was his even keel. He was a good man to have nearby in a crisis.

"It's too early to say, but I think it looks like an accident," he said. "He probably slipped, hit his head, and knocked over those vats on the way down."

I frowned. "But there are rubber mats beside them. They're non-slip."

"Maddie, we don't know what happened yet, and a good detective doesn't make assumptions. We don't have all the facts. In fact, we hardly have any facts."

But I wasn't a good detective. I wasn't a detective at all. I was a paranormal museum owner, and I had a very bad feeling.

THREE

THE NEXT MORNING, I sat behind the glass counter in my museum. Fog pressed against the windows, sinking the museum in gloom. I unfolded the local paper. The death of the chocolate maker, Atticus Reine, was front-page news.

PROMINENT BUSINESS OWNER DEAD
Atticus Reine, co-owner of Reign Chocolate, was found dead in his San Benedetto shop yesterday. Investigators believe foul play may have been involved. Authorities say he suffered a head wound caused by an unknown trauma. The body was found, covered in chocolate, by a hysterical customer.

"The investigation is still in its preliminary stages," said San Benedetto Detective Laurel Hammer. "Detectives and the medical examiner's office are still looking into it. We're asking anyone with information to come forward."

Colleagues, family, and friends were shocked by the choco-
late maker's death. Orson Malke described his business part-
ner as "a brilliant chocolate maker and good friend. We're all
devastated."

Atticus Reine and his partner were at the forefront of the
bean-to-bar chocolate movement. Reign Chocolate roasts ethi-
cally sourced raw beans to create "two-ingredient" chocolate—
cocoa and sugar. The company adds local organic ingredients
to create simple and elegant confections.

The exact cause of Mr. Reine's death is still being investigated.

"I'll bet not everyone's devastated," I muttered to the bronze
skull on the pedestal. I should have stopped to talk to that picketer.

The skull didn't reply.

But I had real sources, if I wanted information. Penny Beauvais
might have some useful gossip about the murder. As president of
the Wine and Visitors Bureau, she knew community members even
remotely connected to wine. And Reign Chocolate had been an associate member of the Bureau.

GD, sprawled beside the tip jar on the counter, rolled onto his
back and meowed.

"Nice try." I wasn't going to be fooled into a belly rub. The cat
hated them and was looking for an excuse to sink his teeth into his
favorite and only chew toy: me.

My cell phone rang, and I checked the screen. It was my mother.
"Hi, Mom."

"Madelyn, this is your mother."

"Yeah, I—" My mother would never understand caller ID. I
rolled my eyes. "Hi."

"Has Shane spoken with you recently?"

"No. Why?" Shane was my overachieving brother who worked for the State Department. He lived a charmed life, getting sent to all the posh posts. I'd be jealous, but I was happy staying put in California.

"Oh, nothing. I was just wondering. Melanie's seeing someone new. An Italian count."

And that was my wunderkind sister, the opera singer. "And you wanted to know if Shane had a new girlfriend?"

"Is it wrong to be interested in your children's love lives?"

"Um. Yeah." Wrong in so many embarrassing and uncomfortable ways.

"Now, about that detective you're seeing ..."

The bell over the front door jingled.

"Sorry, Mom," I said hurriedly. "Customer. I've got to go."

"Make lots of money, dear! Bye!"

Relieved at the interruption, I pocketed the phone and looked up.

Harper, natty in a sleek caramel-colored jacket and suede pants, strolled into the museum. She looked around. "Slow day?"

"It's Thursday morning," I said by way of explanation, folding the newspaper.

She nodded toward it. "Tell me you weren't the hysterical customer who discovered the body."

"I was not hysterical." I grimaced. "Until Laurel arrived."

"Ohhhh. No." Harper's brown eyes widened. "She didn't arrest you, did she?"

"No, but I could tell she wanted to." Laurel and I had a long and tangled and public history. Needless to say, I was one hundred percent innocent. Mostly.

Harper braced one hip against the counter. "What did Jason say?"

"Not much. He can't really talk about cases." And I hadn't spoken with him since we were at Reign yesterday. I was trying not to be bothered by that. We had a date scheduled for tonight—a surprise he'd been dangling in front of me for weeks—so maybe he figured he'd fill me in then. Besides, even if the police did now think foul play was involved, I couldn't be a suspect, could I?

"I knew Atticus," Harper said quietly. "He and his wife were clients."

"I'm sorry. I had no idea."

"They were a fun couple."

I rotated a pen between my fingers. "I don't suppose he had any life insurance?" I asked, fishing.

She shot me a look. "You know I can't talk about that."

My cheeks burned. Of course she couldn't. That sort of thing was confidential.

"But they didn't have any children," she said neutrally.

I straightened. Harper wouldn't have taken them as clients if they had kids and didn't have life insurance. Her own parents had died when she was young, and they'd had nothing in place. Her grandmother had raised her. Money had been tight, and Harper had never forgotten the worry and hardship.

"There are other kinds of insurance I recommend," she continued, bland. "In business partnership arrangements, I like to recommend buy-sell insurance. That way, if one partner dies, the other partner gets an insurance payment to buy out the deceased partner's spouse."

"That sort of thing would make lots of sense for business owners like Atticus and Orson," I said.

"Mmm," she said, neither confirming nor denying. "Was it true he was covered in chocolate?"

"He was lying beside two chocolate vats. Not huge vats—probably five gallons. They'd tipped over."

"Melangeurs," she said.

"Huh?"

"They grind the cocoa beans into a liquid. It takes hours. Maybe days. I can't remember. I got a tour of the kitchen when Reign opened. But the melangeurs tip so the chocolate can be poured out for the next stage in the process."

A chill crawled up my spine. Jason had seemed to think that the melangeurs were accidentally knocked over. But if it was murder, had someone dumped the chocolate onto Atticus intentionally?

"Could his murder have been random?" Harper asked. "A robbery?"

"I don't know," I said slowly. "The cash register was closed. Nothing looked disturbed, aside from, you know." *The chocolate-covered body*. But a robbery in San Benedetto, especially one that ended in a murder, would be a very bad thing.

"If someone were to get this buy-sell insurance," I said, "how would it work?"

"Well, you would have to have a business partner."

"Which I don't. I'm just curious. For my future paranormal museum empire."

"Financial education is important," my friend agreed. "If one were to get buy-sell insurance, one would have to value each partner's share of the business. The insurance would cover the other partner's share."

"So, if you and I were partners, and our paranormal museum was valued at a million dollars—"

She raised a brow.

"A hundred thousand dollars," I amended.

Harper stared.

"It *could* be worth that someday." I flipped my ponytail over one shoulder. "I need to pick a number."

"If the museum was worth a million, and we were equal part-ners, I'd have insurance on you for half a million. You'd insure me for the same. Then, if I died, you'd get the half million, so you could buy the business from my hypothetical husband. That way, you wouldn't have to worry about my imaginary husband trying to tell you how to run the museum, and he'd get a quick payout."

It was easy cash. And it would give Orson a motive for murder. Atticus's wife, too, since she'd ultimately get the money when Orson bought her out. Of course, the victim's spouse was always the prime suspect.

"Who has an imaginary husband?" The bookcase creaked open and Adele clacked into the museum on three-inch heels.

"No one," Harper said quickly.

Adele flushed. "Maddie, I hate to ask, but did you get any idea what happened to our chocolate delivery? My father didn't get his either, and he's supposed to start wine and chocolate tastings at Plot 42 tomorrow."

I hung my head. "Sorry. The only people I talked to were the police."

She blew out her breath. "This is a disaster. No one's answering the phone at Reign. I've been promoting our chocolate as part of Wine and Chocolate Days. Everyone's asking about it, especially after the M-U-R-D-E-R."

"Who are you spelling it out for?" I asked, bemused. "Harper? I'm pretty sure she can read."

"Since kindergarten," Harper agreed.

"For the C-A-T." Adele placed her hands over GD's ears.

"GD isn't exactly sensitive to death. God knows how many mice he's massacred." The cat left them for me and only me on my chair. Leo never got a dead mouse surprise. I knew it was intentional.

"But killing mice is a cat's job," Adele said.

GD's green eyes gazed up at me, and I swear they were filled with disappointment.

"The point is, customers have been understanding under the circumstances," Adele said. "But I feel like I've been engaged in false advertising."

"I know." I glanced toward the Gallery room at my right. It had everything for my *Magic of Chocolate* exhibit but the chocolate. "We may need to come up with an alternative plan."

Adele wrung her hands in her Fox and Fennel apron. "I suppose I can make some calls to other chocolate wholesalers."

"Look," I said, "Leo's going to work in the museum this afternoon. Why don't I swing by Reign again and see if they're open? Since no delivery man came by yesterday, I assume our chocolate is still at the shop." Besides, the museum got busy on Fridays and the weekends. If I didn't have premium-priced chocolate in the Gallery by tomorrow, I'd lose sales.

Adele smiled. "Thank you. I'm sure with everything that's happened, they're too busy to think about deliveries. Maybe you could just bring back the delivery yourself? It would take some pressure off them. And me."

"Sure. You know how I am," I said, marveling at her newfound Zen and waiting for the other stiletto to drop. "Always thinking of others." Plus, it was a great excuse to go back and snoop.

Harper narrowed her eyes at me.

"Now," Adele said, "about the wedding." She whipped a folded sheet of paper from her apron and spread it on the glass counter beside GD. "As you can see, we're here." She pointed to a spot on the timeline. "And we need to get all these things done before the big day."

GD sneezed and hopped from the counter. He ducked beneath the rocking chair. I thought he had the right idea.

Adele parceled out tasks, argued herself out of and then back into almond favors, and got our opinions on how to ensure people didn't give inappropriate toasts.

When she finally left through the bookcase, Harper gave a pained cry and fled the museum.

I sagged on my tall chair. Detail-oriented Adele was going to make sure her wedding was perfect, even if it killed us.

Shaking myself from my stupor, I grabbed the feather duster and walked into the Fortune Telling Room. This was my favorite part of the museum, filled with relics from America's nineteenth-century Spiritualist movement. I stopped in front of a tall piece of wooden furniture that looked like a wardrobe but was a spirit cabinet. Turn-of-the-century mediums would sit locked inside to perform their ghostly conjurations as "proof" they weren't cheating. Since no one could see what they were doing inside the cabinet, this made it even easier for these early ghost whisperers to cheat.

I dusted the framed vintage Houdini poster beside the cabinet, then opened the doors.

A narrow, bespectacled man in a bow tie sat on the bench inside. "Hello."

I shrieked, leaping backward and dropping the feather duster. "Herb!" I willed my heart to slow. "What ...? How did you get in there?" I'd been in the museum all morning, except for the few minutes when I'd slipped next door to sneak a blueberry scone from Adele. Had he been waiting here the whole time?

"I had to make sure the coast was clear," he whispered. His eyes bulged behind coke-bottle glasses. "We're alone, aren't we?"

Grinding my teeth, I scooped up the feather duster. The paranormal collector had supplied most of the exhibits in my museum. He was also freakishly paranoid about police, a stance I couldn't understand since as far as I could tell, he was on the up and up. "The coast is clear," I said. "No police."

"It's not the cops I'm worried about." Herb leaned forward and peered from the cabinet. "It's the public."

"Why? Is an angry mob on your tail?" Because it wouldn't be the first time. I crossed my arms, the feather duster sticking out behind me like a misplaced tail.

"It's the molinillo. I heard you were the one who found that dead chocolate maker at Reign."

"Ye-es," I said, baffled. What did that have to do with the molinillo?

"Last December—"

I brandished the feather duster like a duelist. "Don't say it."

"We have to consider the possibility—"

"No, we don't."

"It may be cursed."

"I told you not to say that!" Last December, one of the supposedly cursed objects in my museum had started a town-wide panic.

"It's a supernatural molinillo," he hissed. "For chocolate making. And now a chocolate maker is dead. Connect the dots."

"There are no dots. It's a coincidence. They do happen."

He adjusted his thick glasses. "In the world we work in, they don't," he said portentously.

We? Good God. I *was* in Herb's world now. "Right. Let's back this up. You told me the molinillo is haunted, not cursed, and it rattles when someone lies."

"Well, yes, that's what I told you."

My eyes narrowed. "What's that supposed to mean? Is there something you *didn't* tell me?"

"Well … What I told you is what was told to me, but I wasn't able to verify it from the original source. You know how stories can get distorted. And since the original owner in Mexico died, people might think it's—"

"If you tell anyone it's cursed—" I stepped closer.

Feathers brushed Herb's nose and he reared backward, bonking his head on the rear of the wooden cabinet. "Ow! I won't! What do you take me for? But I do think it's worth taking extra precautions. Now, that shaman friend of mine, Xavier, is back in California. For seven hundred dollars, he can perform a binding spell—"

"Seven hundred?! It was five hundred last time." And that had been way overpriced. I'd only paid because … long story.

"He *was* nearly killed."

"You can't blame me for that," I groused. "And *nearly killed* is an exaggeration."

"Be that as it may, he's got a right to be cautious."

"I will not hire Xavier for another exorcism." The last time I tried one, I'd turned it into a public event to get more publicity. It had gone badly. Understatement. "It's your duty to make sure your buyers have all the facts about the objects you sell and their haunted histories." Paranormal collectors had to have some code of ethics, didn't they? "If you really think it's cursed, I want to know why. I want details, Herb. Names. Dates. Contact numbers."

Herb's shoulders slumped. "Fine. I'll see what I can dig up on the molinillo. But if you want Xavier, let me know. A binding ritual wouldn't be a bad precaution."

"No to the exorcist."

"Shaman."

"Whatever." He shut the cabinet doors, barricading himself inside.

I blinked. Was Herb planning on apparating out of the spirit cabinet?

Leaving that mystery for another time, I returned to the main room, hoping for clients and a chocolate delivery.

Neither came.

FOUR

STILL TRYING TO THINK positive, I drove through a caul of fog to Reign. I parked my pickup on the street beside a plum tree. Its spring flowers had made way for small, burgundy-colored leaves. They hugged the silvery bark, dripping with moisture.

I shrugged off my museum hoodie and scanned the brick sidewalk.

The picketer wasn't there today. An *Open* sign hung in the chocolate shop's lit window.

Not bothering to lock my vintage truck's door, I strolled inside the shop. The heady scent of chocolate flooded the silvery room.

My stomach twisted. Had chocolate-tainted CPR ruined my love of the bean? I clamped my lips shut and hurried to the vacant wooden counter. Angry voices—male and female—drifted from the kitchen and echoed off the dove-colored cinderblock walls.

"Hello?" I called.

The voices fell silent.

A tall, willowy woman with hair like honey strode through the kitchen's swinging door. She didn't wear an apron over her skinny jeans and matching ivory sweater. And she wasn't wearing a hair net either, so she couldn't be an employee. She braced her slim hand on the cash register. "Yes?" She smiled warmly. "How can I help you?"

"Hi, I'm from the Paranormal Museum."

"Oh?" Frowning, she adjusted a pyramid of chocolate bars wrapped in brown paper with purple crowns. They were displayed beside a piece of driftwood, and she snapped a picture of the arrangement with her phone. "Sorry. Atticus usually…" She exhaled shakily. "I'm late with our social media promotion."

"Um, Adele Nakamoto from the Fox and Fennel and I put in a bulk order for chocolate," I continued. "It was supposed to arrive yesterday, but it never turned up…" I trailed off.

A broad-shouldered man in his mid-thirties emerged from the kitchen. He wore a baseball hat over his wavy brown hair, and a beard net over his chin. "The museum? You're Maddie Kosloski, aren't you? The one who found Atticus."

The blond woman gasped.

The man hurried around the counter, wiped his palms over his brown apron, and stuck out his hand. His brandy-colored eyes moistened. "Orson, Orson Malke. I heard you did everything you could to save him. Thank you."

His hand engulfed mine, his grip firm but not crushing. He stood close enough for me to smell his piney aftershave, to see that his eyes were red-rimmed and watery.

"Anybody would have done it," I said. "I'm sorry I was too late."

"What did you …? What happened?" He released my hand. "The police didn't tell us much."

"I stopped by to see about our chocolate delivery," I said. "No one seemed to be here, so I began to walk back to the office. That's when I saw Atticus. He was in the kitchen, beside the melangeurs."

The woman's face paled. "How awful. We could tell from the police tape where—" Her phone buzzed and she glanced at the screen. "Where the police had blocked off the kitchen."

"I'd gone to the Wine and Visitors Bureau," Orson said. "They wanted some specially decorated chocolate squares. Normally Atticus dealt with promotional issues like that. But he was flooded with marketing work, what with the Wine and Chocolate Days. As you can imagine, they're a big deal for Reign."

"Orson is the real chocolate maker." The woman walked from behind the counter and brushed against him possessively. "Atticus was the marketing genius behind our success." She stuck out her free hand. "Lola Emerson-Malke."

"My wife and media star," he said, smiling fondly.

And another possible suspect. She could have killed Atticus for the insurance money just as easily as Orson. As Orson's wife, she would benefit too. But did they need the money?

"Not quite a star." Lola's mouth trembled. "Atticus was determined to make my husband and me known on social media. He said it's all about building an online community." She flipped her longish hair over her shoulders. "So, you're the woman who runs the Paranormal Museum. I've heard so much about it."

I was afraid to ask what. "I've been focused on marketing and social media myself. In fact, this month I'm promoting a *Magic of Chocolate* display in my Gallery." I waited a beat. When the couple didn't respond, I said, "But I'm missing the chocolate?"

Orson winced. "Right. Your order. Sorry about that. It's ready in the back. I'll get it for you now."

"Thanks," I said. "If you haven't delivered the order for Plot 42 yet, I can take that off your hands as well. I'm headed out that way."

"Thanks," he said. "You're a lifesaver." He strode behind the counter and disappeared into the kitchen.

"Plot 42?" Gaze drifting to her phone, Lola shifted her weight, her thumbs skimming across the keypad.

"The Nakamoto family vineyard," I said. "Adele Nakamoto mentioned that her parents hadn't received their delivery yet. They start wine and chocolate tastings tomorrow."

"And you're connected to them how?" Her arms dropped to her sides.

I scraped my hair back. Did she think I was trying to steal their chocolate? But coming so soon after Atticus's death, I couldn't fault her suspicion. "Literally. There's a secret passage between my museum and Adele's tea room. We've been friends for years."

Her phone buzzed and she glanced at its screen. "Sorry, it's just—"

"It's okay," I said quickly.

The swinging door from the kitchen bumped open and Orson backed through. He rolled a dolly stacked with cardboard boxes. "Have you got a car?"

"A truck," I said. "It's out front."

"I'll help you load these." He followed me onto the sidewalk and hefted the boxes into my truck bed. "The boxes are labeled," he said. "A 42 for the winery, and the other is your joint order with the tea room." His brow creased. "Did you and Adele decide how you were going to split them up? I didn't see any notations in our files, or I would have packed them in separate boxes."

"Yeah, don't worry about it. We went in on the order together. We've got it figured out." I shut the truck bed with a clang. "If

Atticus was in charge of marketing, what was he doing in the kitchen yesterday?"

"I don't know. He was supposed to be manning the front counter while I was dealing with the Visitors Bureau. But there are all sorts of reasons he could have gone into the kitchen." Orson's face creased, and he blinked rapidly. "Atticus was ..." He cleared his throat and looked toward the kitchen.

Sympathy squeezed my chest. "I'm so sorry for your loss. Please let me know how I can help. I can't imagine what you're going through, losing a friend and partner and trying to keep a business going."

He looked down the wide street and adjusted his ball cap. A mail truck trundled past. "I don't know how I'm going to manage. I always did the chocolate-making myself, but I relied on Atticus for most everything else. He was a marketing genius. And one of our counter workers, Sam, has left and keeps picketing outside."

"Left? What happened?"

Orson's face tightened. "Not everyone's cut out for this business," he said shortly.

"I could put the word out if you need counter help," I offered. "My colleague may have friends at the local community college who could do the job. And Ladies Aid is a surprisingly good source. Someone always has a grandkid or niece who's looking for work."

The chocolate maker smiled crookedly, but I couldn't forget the flash of anger I'd just seen. "Counter help would be great," he said. "If you find anyone, tell them to call me at Reign." He extracted a card from the pocket of his brown apron and handed it to me.

Eyes glued to her phone, his wife stepped from the shop. "Orson? Would you mind helping me with something?" Her voice sharpened. "If I'm going to take over Atticus's job—"

"I'll be right there." He waved to her. "And thanks again, Maddie." He trotted into the store and the door closed slowly behind him.

I drove down Main and beneath the adobe arch that marked the exit from San Benedetto's downtown (such as it was). On the other side of the railroad tracks, the buildings turned industrial, and then I was in the vineyards. I whizzed past gnarled, bare vines sunk low in fog. Mustard flowers sprouted from the thick greenery between the rows.

My tires crunched on Plot 42's gravel drive. I parked between a picnic table and weeping willow. The door to the nearby barn/wine tasting room stood open, brown grapevines climbing the faded wood. Orange and yellow mums bloomed beside the brick path to the barn, spots of cheeriness in the fogbound gloom. A chalkboard sign leaned against the dull red wood. In elegant pink script, it proclaimed, *Yes, We're Open!*

I hefted a box labeled *42* from my truck bed and lugged it into the barn. A wall of barrels stacked in metal racks by the open door hid a storage area. Upright barrels formed makeshift tables at random intervals on the cement floor. A long, polished wooden bar ran along the right side of the room. Three thirty-something women leaned against the bar and sipped from fat wine goblets.

A fourth, behind the bar, glanced up and raised her chin. "Hi, can I help you?" Her smile was bleak. Two long brown braids dangled over her shoulders. She wore a blue denim shirt and rows and rows of tiny, multicolored beads around her neck.

I clunked the box onto the far end of the bar, away from the tasters. "Chocolate delivery for the Nakamotos."

She blinked, paled. "I should have picked that up myself."

"Sorry. I hope I didn't cause a mix-up. Adele asked me to collect the chocolate for her parents, and I thought—"

The woman shook her head, her braids swinging. "No. It's not … It's fine." She spun away, one hand gripping the edge of the bar, her knuckles whitening.

Mr. Nakamoto, slim and gray-haired, strolled into the barn and stopped short. "Maddie! What are you doing here?"

I glanced at the woman behind the counter. "Adele asked me to drop off your Reign chocolate."

His gaze tracked mine. "Uh, thanks. That will be fine. India, do you want to take a break?"

India's chin quivered, grief cracking her porcelain face. "No thanks. I'd rather keep working."

Had India known Atticus?

Mr. Nakamoto whisked behind the counter. Grabbing the box, he ducked, hiding it from view beneath the bar, and then he popped up.

I gestured with my thumb. "There's more in my truck."

"I'll get it." He strode outside, and I followed.

Peering into the bed of the vintage pickup, he said, "That's more than we ordered."

"Some of those are Adele's and mine. The ones labeled *42* are for the winery."

He stacked two boxes on top of each other. "India is—was—Atticus Reine's wife."

"Oh." Pity and guilt about the man I hadn't saved twined in my gut.

"She insisted on working today. Said it would keep her mind off things. I'm not sure it was a good idea, though."

"And then I brought in a box of chocolate from her husband's shop and reminded her of her loss." I wished one of the Malkes had mentioned that the widow worked here.

"It's not your fault. And she's tough. India will get through this."

"How long has she been working at the tasting room?" I asked.

"Three weeks. She said she needed to work or she'd go crazy, and she couldn't work with her husband because they'd kill each other." He winced. "She was joking."

"Of course," I said quickly.

He hefted the boxes and retreated into the barn.

Thoughtful, I shut the tailgate, which was slick with damp. The poor woman. India was too young to be a widow. Yet I couldn't help but wonder where she'd been when her husband had died. The newspaper article had said her husband was struck a blow to the head. With the proper implement, anyone could have used enough force. I hadn't noticed any bludgeoning instruments in the kitchen at Reign. But my attention had been elsewhere. Sickened, I swallowed, remembering.

India strode from the barn, her movements elegant and tense. Shielding her eyes from the watery sunlight, she beelined for me. "Maddie Kosloski?"

I walked to meet her beside the green-painted picnic table. "Yes?"

"You were the one who found Atticus. My husband."

"Yes." I glanced at my tennis shoes darkened by the thick, damp grass. "I'm very sorry for your loss."

She gulped. "Was anyone else there?"

"Anyone else?" Startled, I looked up. "No. I was surprised the shop was empty. Someone was picketing outside, though. A man named Sam, I think?"

Her expression darkened. "Sam Reynolds. It's because of him that my husband—" She snapped her jaw shut.

"Was working the counter that day?"

She nodded, blinking rapidly. "Sorry. I shouldn't … He probably had nothing to do with it," she said unconvincingly. "But did you notice anything strange?"

A vision of the dead man flashed into my mind, and I felt myself blanch. There had been something almost contemptuous in the scene, the way the chocolate had been splashed across Atticus's face. "Two of the melangeurs had tipped, so chocolate was everywhere. But aside from that, no. I assumed the melangeurs tilted when your husband fell."

"Maybe." She gazed over her shoulder at an outbuilding covered in grapevines. "You tried to revive him, they said."

"I tried." And failed. I stared harder at my darkening shoes.

"Thank you for that. At least someone was there, someone tried..." She blinked rapidly. "They're cruel, you know?"

"Who?"

"Everyone. The public. Reign was becoming known, thanks to Atticus. He and Orson had a name. And people thought that the success, the money, made us hard, impervious. People thought they could demand and push and criticize. But Atticus wasn't hard. He was a person, a good person, and he cared. He cared about so much."

I didn't know what to say, and so I said nothing.

"This wasn't random," she continued, her voice high and thin. "Someone killed my husband, someone who knew him. This was personal. And the chocolate..." She gasped and raced into the barren vineyard.

I wavered, wondering if I should go after her.

She squatted, head hanging, between the rows of gnarled vines and dug her bare hands into the earth.

I looked at my own hands, then got in my truck and drove off into the fog.

FIVE

GRAY, FOG-SOAKED TWILIGHT LEAKED through the Gallery windows. I stacked pyramids of Reign chocolate bars on the black-painted shelves, organized by nation of origin. The wrappers were a flat brown, the ink color of the crowns varying by country. A bag of Reign's chocolate-covered almonds slipped to the tile floor. I returned it to its shelf and adjusted another pyramid of chocolate-covered caramels in brown boxes. I didn't usually sell food; there was never a shortage of quirky art to fill the Gallery. But I was sure this would sell. Chocolate—even high-priced chocolate—was nigh irresistible.

Unfortunately, the thought of chocolate now made my stomach flip. I had to get over my squeamishness at some point, though. Right?

The bell over the front door jangled.

Half hopeful, half irritated by the interruption, I peered through the door to the main room. I had my date with Jason tonight, and a new customer would delay the closing time.

But it was my ex-boyfriend, Mason Hjelm, who ambled into the museum. Tall and muscular, with a mane of blond hair he kept in a ponytail, Mason wore his usual work uniform—jeans and a black Harley Davidson tee. He owned the motorcycle shop next door, so we couldn't avoid each other even if we wanted to. A small part of me wanted to. We'd ended things on good terms, but it was … complicated.

I straightened away from the boxes.

My ex said something to Leo, seated behind the counter. Leo angled his chin in my direction.

Mason strolled into the Gallery and jammed his hands in the front pockets of his jeans.

I fiddled with an arrangement of chocolate bars from Belize. "Hi, what's going on?"

He smiled, his Nordic eyes crinkling. "Why does something have to be going on?"

"It's a small town. Something's always going on."

He scanned the Gallery, the pedestal displays, the shelves filled with Reign chocolate. "What's all this?"

"For Wine and Chocolate days. It's our new *Magic of Chocolate* exhibit."

He quirked a blond brow.

"I *am* an associate member of the Wine and Visitors Bureau. I may as well take advantages of their promotions."

He peered at my haunted molinillo exhibit and quickly stepped away. "How's Adele?"

"In the throes of wedding planning," I said, curious. Usually Mason was better at getting to the point. And while he was always friendly, he also wasn't one for idle gossip.

"I suppose she's driving you and Harper crazy?"

"Driving herself crazy is more like it. Planning a wedding is a lot of work." Enough to make me consider eloping. I shifted my weight. "How's the bike shop?"

"Good." He looked out the square windows. A motorcycle roared past on the street outside. "Good."

"Well. That's good." I eyed him. "Was there something you wanted to tell me?"

His head snapped around. "What?"

"The reason you stopped by," I prompted.

He rubbed the back of his neck. "Oh. Right."

The bell over the front door jingled, and we both glanced toward the main room.

Jason, sexy in a blue business suit, walked into the museum. He looked around, spotted us, and strode into the Gallery. Touching my elbow, he kissed me on the cheek. "Hi, Maddie. Mason."

"Jason," he said.

I smothered a nervous laugh at the rhyme.

"Hi. What's going on?" Jason asked.

"Nothing," I said. "Mason just dropped by—"

"To see the new exhibit." My ex motioned toward the molinillo. His hip bumped the pedestal, and the molinillo rattled, rolling in its wooden bowl. "It looks great. I'll have to bring Belle by some day."

I frowned. "I thought she didn't like the paranormal."

Mason backed out of the Gallery. "It's chocolate. Who doesn't like chocolate?" Turning on his booted heel, he hurried from the museum.

43

Huh. That was weird.

Jason rubbed his hands together. "Are you ready?"

"For our date? Absolutely. Let me lock up." I shuffled Leo out the door, double checked GD's food and water supply, and turned out the lights.

We stepped onto the brick sidewalk, and Jason watched me lock and bolt the front door. Detectives are big on security, but I wasn't fussed about burglars. Everyone knew we live-streamed video of the museum at night. That way, people could watch for ghostly activity or just laugh at GD's antics. I swear, that cat understood what the webcams were for, because he spent hours preening in front of the cameras.

Jason checked his watch. "I think we have time to walk."

"Where are we going?"

He grimaced. "I wanted to leave the surprise for the last minute, but under the circumstances, you deserve a heads-up."

"A heads-up?" I asked, taking a step backward. "Are you taking me to the police station? This isn't another interrogation?"

He laughed shortly and looped his arm over my shoulders, pulling me close enough for me to feel his body heat mingling with my own. "That wouldn't be much of a date." Then he cocked his head as if considering the possibility of my arrest. Both of us knew it wasn't totally out of the question, not if his partner had anything to say about it. "Ah, anyway. We're going to Reign."

I stopped beside a plum tree. "The chocolate shop?" My heart skipped a beat. Jason and I had worked on paranormal research together before. Was he finally going to bring me into a real police investigation?

"Since you love chocolate so much, I booked us a chocolate-making class two months ago." He gave me an abashed look. "I figured they'd cancel the class, but it's still on. I hope your mother doesn't mind me taking you to a murder scene."

"Oh," I said, disappointed. Of course he wouldn't bring me into his police work. It was probably illegal. Certainly unethical. Teaming up had been a crazy idea. "What does my mother have to do with it? Has she been harassing you?"

His eyes glinted. "Come on. Your mother isn't the type."

"You don't know my mother," I muttered.

"I know you two are close, and that's all I meant. After what happened, I wouldn't blame you if you didn't want to go ahead with the class."

"No," I said quickly, taking his hand. "It was a great idea. I love chocolate." Good thing the molinillo wasn't nearby to rattle at the lie. I'd *loved* chocolate, past tense. Before I found Atticus's body.

Gently, Jason squeezed my shoulders, drawing me against him. My heart thumped faster. I hoped he couldn't feel it.

"Good," he said. "I admit, I'm looking forward to more time in that shop."

Ah ha! A joint investigation! "No leads?" I asked innocently.

"None I can discuss."

My heart shrank. Why did I keep coming back to us working together when I knew it could never happen? But if my boyfriend keeping his work and personal life separate was the only downside to our relationship, it was a downside I could live with. "I met India, Atticus's wife, today," I said casually. "She works at Plot 42."

"I know," he said. "She told me she grew up in the Midwest and likes being back in farm country."

"Oh? I read that her husband and Orson had lived in San Francisco."

45

"Yes, that's where India and Atticus met. And why were you reading up on Atticus and Orson?"

"For my chocolate research. Reign's my supplier for the Gallery." Okay, that was a weak excuse. I hurried on. "Did you know that cocoa was used in religious ceremonies as early as 2000 BC? The Aztecs used the seeds as currency. And Montezuma drank cups of chocolate as an aphrodisiac."

"I'm taking you to the Irish pub's next trivia night."

I was only good at country capitals and paranormal trivia. Ask me about the American Spiritualist movement or the history of tarot cards and I could write a dissertation. "As long as you can handle the pop culture questions."

He pulled me closer and I burrowed into his warmth. "I've got you covered," he said. "So, what's new at the museum?"

"Aside from the chocolate exhibit? I'm researching starting a subscription box service. You know, like those boxes you can get every month with new dog toys and supplies? But paranormal!"

"A paranormal box?"

"I thought a good name for the subscription might be the Cryptic Crate? Every month, subscribers would get a new set of themed magical items, plus a quick email course or a pamphlet from the museum."

"Sounds like a lot of work."

"Weekdays are slow at the museum. I may as well spend the time writing pamphlets or creating email courses." Though preparing shipments was my least favorite part of the job. My neck tightened. But I had to do *something*. I needed a more consistent income stream. Adding the Gallery had brought in repeat clients, and I was now selling products in addition to tickets, but I could do better. I had to increase sales if I ever wanted to move out of my aunt's garage apartment.

We passed the darkened windows of a Taqueria.

"It's still weird to me to see closed restaurants at this time of night," Jason said.

"What do you mean?"

"In New York, you can get food at all hours." He glanced at me and smiled. "But there are other advantages to small-town life."

"Aw, shucks." I laughed. "You're making this small-town girl blush."

We paused in front of Reign's glass door. Its sign said *Closed* but light streamed from the windows, making trapezoids on the sidewalk.

Jason knocked.

A few moments later, Orson, in a brown apron, jeans, and a T-shirt, opened the door. "Come on in," he said, smiling beneath his beard.

We walked inside. Three other couples stood in nervous pairs beside shelves filled with chocolates. They all wore hair nets.

Orson locked the door behind us, and I flinched. Had he murdered his partner for the money?

"We're all here," he said, "so let's get started. You two will need hairnets." He pulled two from the pocket of his apron and handed them to us. "Good thing none of you have beards." He pointed to the white net covering his chin.

Orson then led us into the kitchen. "Before we get started, I'd like to give you a brief tour of the factory and an explanation of how we make our chocolate. We won't actually have time tonight to make chocolate from the bean. But we will be pouring molds and making candy, combining Reign chocolate with locally sourced ingredients. That said, I think an understanding of the entire process is useful first." He motioned toward the glass-fronted room at the rear of the kitchen. "We'll start in here."

He opened the door to the room. Its other three walls were made of rich, dark wood. On the left, pallets stacked with burlap sacks of cocoa lined the floor. A rectangular metal table stood in the center of the room. Aside from dust, the only thing on the table was a plastic box with a large metal screen on its bottom. I guessed it was a sifter. Against the right wall stood metal racks filled with plastic bins labeled in what looked like code.

I found a spot at the base of the table, beside a garbage bin lined with dusty green plastic. The waste bin was empty except for a fast-food drink container, a straw poking from its lid. Even though garbage bins are for garbage, something about the discarded cup bugged me.

Orson set a tablet computer on the table and played a video of the cocoa harvesting process. He picked up the box sifter. "This is our storage and sorting room. We have to sort the cocoa beans by hand. During harvesting, all sorts of things get through—rocks, screws, bits of plastic, and cracked beans. If a bean is cracked, it will roast more quickly than the others in its batch, so those have to be discarded as well." He glanced toward the plastic garbage bin at the base of the table, beside Jason and me. "I like to sort late at night before going home. I can zone out then and relax."

He cleared his throat. "This room is temperature controlled, because the beans we get from overseas are raw. Once they've been sorted, we roast them." Orson opened the glass door and led us back into the kitchen, to a small orange machine with a funnel at the top. "This is where the real flavor comes in. We develop a roast profile for each batch, with a specific temperature and roasting time. We only use two ingredients in our chocolate—sugar and cocoa—so the roast profile is important."

A mousy woman raised her hand. "You sell chocolates with beans from different countries. Does it matter? Do the beans taste any different?"

He handed each of us a roasted bean to taste.

I cracked it open with my teeth. It was dry and bitter, leeching the moisture from my tongue.

Jason made a face. "The things I do for love."

Love? My heart stopped, then beat double-time. He'd said the word casually. He couldn't have meant it, because we'd only been together a few months. Was I even ready for that kind of commitment?

"Yes," Orson said. "They taste different depending on where they're from and what sort of season they've had. Cocoa beans are a lot like wine, with complex flavors that vary based on the terroir. That's the amount of rain, the weather, and the location."

He showed us three more machines—a cracker machine, a winnower, and a vibrating machine—and then stopped in front of the melangeurs. Melted chocolate swirled inside the metal vats, which were roughly the size of tall soup pots. He pointed to the line of red and white tape across the bottom of the floor beside the melangeurs. "There's expensive chocolate in these, so don't get too close." Orson explained how the melangeurs worked. "And then the vats tip." He glanced at me, and something seemed to flicker in his eyes. "So we can pour the chocolate out for the next stage, tempering."

Deep metal shelves above the melangeurs held giant bricks of chocolate in thick, clear plastic bags. "Are those what come out of the melangeurs?" I asked.

I was trying to sound like I wasn't panicking. Did Jason love me? I liked him. A *lot*. Chemistry? Oh, yeah. But the honeymoon period in a relationship wasn't to be trusted. After it ended, there were always complications.

"Yes," Orson said. "We pour the melted chocolate into this rough block form. Each brick weighs ten pounds, but it's still not finished. We've got three more steps to go."

Jason nudged me. "I know what you're thinking."

I sucked in my breath. "You do?"

"Ten pounds of chocolate. I'd bet you'd like one of those in your kitchen."

"Heh heh. Yeah. That's what I was thinking." It was a good thing Jason wasn't a mind reader.

Orson finished the tour, then paired us up at long metal tables in the kitchen. Plastic trays lined with wax paper sat on the table in front of us. Along one side of the tray were plastic cups, with small rounds of filling, in two neat columns. A medium-sized bowl covered with a red plastic lid sat beside the tray on a folded towel.

"You can take the lids off," Orson said. "Each bowl contains over two pounds of tempered chocolate, and it will stay liquid as long as you stir it occasionally. Just don't stir in any hardened chocolate at the sides or bottom." He explained about tempering and couverture chocolate, but I only caught every eighth word.

I had to stay cool and stop obsessing over what Jason had said. He hadn't meant it. *Think about something else.*

The image of Atticus's body lying beside the melangeurs swam into view. My stomach went from butterflies to roiling snakes trying to crawl up my throat. How hot had the chocolate been when it splattered across Atticus? Had it burned him? Had he felt it?

"You okay?" Jason nudged me.

"Sorry." I swallowed my bile. "I guess I'm having a hard time concentrating."

"Orson said he'd give us a recipe handout after the class," Jason whispered. "So you can relax and ponder the murder."

"I was just thinking of…" I glanced toward the melangeurs. "I hope he didn't suffer," I said in a low voice.

Jason pulled me close, and I relaxed against his broad chest. "He didn't," he murmured into my hairnet. "It's okay."

But it wasn't. I couldn't get Atticus out of my head.

His partner led us through techniques for dipping the fillings, demonstrating with his own bowl. "Of course, we don't sell nougats and creams," Orson said. "But I wanted you to get a sense of things you could do with our melted chocolate at home." He distributed plastic squeeze bottles filled with chocolate. Soon, we were squirting dollar-sized pools of chocolate onto the wax paper. We dotted the chocolate with organic almonds and dried fruit. My chocolate coins came out lopsided, but Jason managed perfect circles.

"I think my chocolate is defective," I muttered.

"It came out of the same bowl as mine," Jason said.

"I'm talking about the squeeze bottles. Why are your coins perfect?" Actually, all of his chocolates were perfect, while mine had dribs and drabs of chocolate oozing from their bottoms.

"Maybe I'm just that good." His eyes glinted suggestively.

Orson circled around the table toward us.

"Oh, look," I said. "Orson's coming."

Jason turned toward him, and I swapped our trays behind his back.

"How's it going?" Orson asked.

"Great," Jason said. "But Maddie's having a little trouble with …" He turned toward me and glanced down at the trays.

"With what?" Orson asked. "Your chocolates look perfect, Maddie."

"Nothing," I said innocently.

"I've been meaning to stop by your museum to see your Magic of Chocolate exhibit," the chocolate maker said.

"You should," I said. "We've got a haunted molinillo."

"How is it haunted?" Orson asked.

"I'm still researching that." Or, at least, I hoped Herb was. "Where's the ladies' room?"

"Down the hall and on your right," Orson said, moving on to the next couple.

"You know," Jason said, "I *am* a detective. I do notice things like swapped trays."

"Who's *just that good* now?" Grinning, I peeled off my gloves and hustled past the glass-doored storage room and down the hall.

The door to the office yawned open.

I shivered, a chill prickling my spine, and slowed to a halt. Something tugged gently at my gut, drawing me closer to the open door. If I believed in ghosts—and I was halfway there—I'd almost think the spirit of Atticus was urging me on.

My fists clenched. Who was I kidding? It wasn't Atticus calling me into that office; it was my own need to set things right. And there were detectives for that. An excellent one was waiting for me to return to the class.

I glanced over my shoulder. The class was out of sight behind the kitchen's tall rolling racks. And that meant *I* was hidden from view.

To snoop, or not to snoop? That was the question.

I shouldn't.

But there were a lot of things I shouldn't have done, and that had never stopped me before. I thought of Atticus, sprawled on the floor and dripping chocolate. My eyes briefly closed. I slipped inside the office.

The room was spartan. Plastic bins and cardboard file boxes teetered atop metal bookcases. Two simple metal desks faced each other across the linoleum floor. Nameplates proclaimed their owners—Orson Malke and Atticus Reine. A third desk sat wedged into a corner.

I sidled to Atticus's desk and tugged on the top drawer.

Locked. As were all the others.

Rats.

I glanced at the third desk. It also had a nameplate: *Tilde Otterstrom, Accountant.*

Footsteps sounded in the corridor outside. Orson's voice echoed in the hall. "I think I've got one in my office."

My heart seized. There was no way he'd believe I'd gotten lost on the way to the bathroom. I turned right, then left, searching for a place to hide. I grasped the rolling chair, thinking to hide beneath the desk.

"Hey, Orson?" Jason asked. "Have you got a minute?"

"Sure. Is this about Atticus?"

Crap, crap, crap! I edged toward the door and peeked out. Orson's back was to me. Jason's was not, and he was studiously not looking my way. But I knew he knew exactly where I was.

Smothering a curse, I slipped behind Orson and into the hallway. I backed away, into the bathroom.

I washed my hands. They'd somehow become smeared with chocolate in spite of the gloves I'd worn. I adjusted my hairnet (not a flattering look), and walked into the hall.

Jason lounged beside the bathroom door. "I can't take you anywhere," he muttered.

"How did you know I was in the office?"

"The chocolate handprint on the door."

Horrified, I swayed to a halt. I'd left prints?

"Don't worry. They're too smeared for analysis. At least tell me you found a clue that'll break open the case."

"Uh. No."

He smothered a laugh. "Next time, exercise a little restraint, okay? Or at least keep your gloves on."

My gloves had been more chocolate-covered than my hands. I sighed. What had I learned, after all? That Reign had an in-house accountant named Tilde. Which was kind of interesting. I'd have thought a business this size would use a contractor for their accounting. Or maybe Reign was a bigger enterprise than I'd imagined?

"I'm sorry," I whispered, blood pounding in my temples.

"Sorry you did it? Or sorry you got caught?"

Sorry I hadn't found anything. But I forced a smile and kept that to myself.

SIX

LEO STROLLED THROUGH THE museum's front entrance and the doorbell danced on its hook. Textbook under one arm, he stopped in front of the glass counter. His black hair flopped into his eyes. "Am I late?"

"Nope." It was ten in the morning on Friday, and business wouldn't pick up until after lunch. Our sole customers, a middle-aged couple, moved about the Fortune Telling room and exclaimed over the antiques.

"If I gave you the evil eye, it's because I'm antsy," I said. "I need to go to Reign before things get busy." Last night's investigation at the chocolate shop had been a massive fail. My snooping hadn't ruined my evening with Jason, but I was still smarting over getting caught so easily. Master detectives don't leave chocolate fingerprints. Orson would have to notice them eventually. Would he tie them to me? My stomach burned at the thought. "Can you take over? I shouldn't be gone more than thirty minutes."

GD meowed and hopped onto the counter. The ebony cat brushed against the tip jar.

Leo ruffled GD's fur. "No problem. I can handle things here."

I glanced outside. Fog pressed against the windows, coating them in a damp sheen. "Thanks." I slid off the tall chair and grabbed my thick, sand-colored vest off the wall peg by the bookshelf. Shrugging it over my Paranormal Museum hoodie, I bustled onto the brick sidewalk.

The end of the block was obscured by gray fog. I jammed my hands into my vest pockets. The wind shifted, blowing the scent of the dairy pastures into town, turning the fog acrid.

Wrinkling my nose, I strode down the walk, triple checking at corners so I wasn't surprised by a car hidden by the mist. If Orson had figured out what I was up to last night, I was in for an unpleasant welcome at Reign Chocolate. But finding Atticus's body seemed a sign—was I now believing in signs?—that I was meant to be involved in solving his murder. I knew how arrogant that sounded, and I didn't expect to *solve* it solve it. But if I could learn something that would help the police, it would be worth it.

The street seemed strangely lonely for late on Friday morning. Maybe it was the fog or my imagination that set my nerves jangling, but I caught myself shrinking in my jacket and vest, my shoulders hunching.

I passed a well-lit cafe. People lined the long table at the window, their heads bent to computers and phones, isolated even in company.

I shivered and hurried on. Reign was an easy walk, and I needed the exercise. Now that I was over chocolate, maybe I could finally lose those last ten pounds. It had been distressingly easy not to sample the chocolates we'd made last night.

A single set of footsteps echoed behind me.

I glanced over my shoulder. An iron streetlamp pierced the fog.

Tugging my hood over my head, I lengthened my strides. A gust of wind twisted a length of mist into a wraith. It coiled, tentacles of fog flinging outward, reaching for me.

Instinctively, I sheared away. The fog wraith dissipated and I laughed at myself. But the soft sound came out broken, uneasy.

Behind me, footsteps slapped wetly, like something out of a Lovecraft story.

I needed to stop reading those.

Visions of eldritch gods and tentacular horrors tickled my mind. I swallowed, my heart speeding. *Ridiculous*. It was only a shopper. There was no one better at freaking myself out over nothing than me.

I stopped and turned, waiting for the other pedestrian. I'd prove to myself I was being paranoid.

The footsteps halted.

I widened my eyes, straining to penetrate the fog.

A gust of fog billowed toward me. It curled in on itself, folding at the top as its bottom fringe flowed outward, grasping.

I stood my ground and cocked my head, listening. The damp morning had turned still and silent. For a moment I imagined the town had vanished and I was alone. Then a car rolled past, a gray, indistinct shape, and the spell broke.

"Forget this," I muttered. Mouth dry, I turned and ran.

Now all I could hear were my own footsteps, the pounding of my heart in my ears. Exercise, I needed the exercise. It wasn't as if I was afraid of a footstep. I dodged a mailbox. A van rolled past, a dark rectangle in the fog.

Running is good for you, especially when—

I glanced over my shoulder and collided with something solid.

"Hey!"

"Ooof!" I staggered sideways and pinballed off a cinderblock wall.

"Watch it!" The picketer, Sam, waved his placard at me: *UNFAIR!*

"Sorry." I brushed myself off, hoping the dim light hid the flush I felt rising to my cheeks. "Sorry. I thought someone was … I should have been looking where I was going."

We stared at each other for a full five seconds.

"Weren't you the one who found the body?" he asked.

"Yeah." If someone had been following me, were they waiting to get me alone? "Um, weren't you outside at the time?" Had Sam seen anything? He obviously fit into the disgruntled employee category. But had he been angry enough to kill? I edged away from the man and told myself not to be so paranoid. We were in public, and just because he might have motive didn't make him a killer.

"Right," he said. "*Outside.*"

"Must have been weird," I said, scanning the foggy street and seeing more fog. "You finding out your boss was dead inside Reign the whole time you were out here."

"Yeah. I had no idea. Didn't see a thing."

"How long were you here that day?" I asked and cocked my head, listening. Were those footsteps?

"Since ten that morning."

I stared past him, into the fog. "And no one went in and out the whole time? Not even any customers?"

"Sure, there were customers. I could see them through the window. Atticus was working the counter."

"Do you have any idea when you stopped seeing him behind the counter?"

Sam shrugged. "A woman went in before you. She waited at the counter five minutes and left in a huff." He glared. "I remembered her because she crossed the picket line. Like you."

I shuffled my feet. "In fairness, it's not really a line. I mean, you need more than one person ..."

His nostrils widened.

"Look," I said, "I had to go inside. I mean, I had an order."

"So?" He brandished the sign. Its wooden handle had a pointy end, ideal for staking vampires or nosy paranormal museum owners. "I had a job, and Orson fired me for no reason!"

"Orson did? Not Atticus?" So much for the picketer's motive to kill Atticus. And since we were alone on the sidewalk, I'd call that a good thing.

His face darkened and he stepped closer. "What did Atticus know about anything? He was just the marketing guy, flitting around with magazine photographers and acting like a hotshot. And he didn't do a damn thing about it when I was fired, even though he knew it was unfair."

Or maybe Sam had a motive after all. I edged away. "Why were you fired?"

"I'm telling you, there was no reason. I came to work on time. I even came to work early, I asked for more responsibility. And because of it, I got fired."

"That's strange. You'd think an employer would want someone like you, someone ambitious."

"Orson said he wanted someone happy with where they were at. Can you believe it?"

What would I do if Leo wanted to be manager? Because there just wasn't a whole lot of growth potential in a paranormal museum. "Maybe he just didn't have a position for you, and thought it would be better to let you go now rather than wait for you to quit." It wasn't fair, but I could see the rationale. Still, I'd never do that to Leo. He was like a little brother to me. Leo was also a lot less annoying than my real brother.

"You know, even if I did see who killed Atticus, I wouldn't tell the cops." Sam thrust his sign toward the chocolate shop's glowing windows. "He was weak, and he deserved what he got. If he'd had any guts, he would have stood up for what was right. But no, he did everything Orson said like a little puppy dog. If Orson said I had to go, I was going, even if it was wrong."

"I'm sorry to hear things went down like that," I said tightly. I'd never been a fan of victim-blaming. "Did you see Atticus go into the kitchen with anyone that morning?"

"Hey." Sam pointed the sign at me. "Why do you care?"

"I guess because I was the one who found him." I shifted my weight and backed toward the door.

"Wait, are you actually going in there? After everything I told you?"

"Um. Yeah. I need an invoice—"

"But they're crooks!"

I halted. "Crooks?" Was something underhanded happening at Reign?

"They fired me for no reason!"

"Oh." That made them jerks, not crooks. And I suspected there was more to the firing than Sam was saying. "You know what? I'm going to ask them about that."

"You don't need to ask them. I told you what happened."

How was I going to get out of this? "Right. Um … thanks." I turned and darted into the chocolate shop, the bell jingling in my wake. The scent of chocolate coiled, ghostlike, around me.

Orson stood behind the counter in a brown Reign T-shirt, apron, and baseball cap. His net was gone, exposing his thick brown beard. Bleary-eyed, he straightened off the cash register. "Maddie? Here for more chocolate already?"

"Here about that counter position. I talked to my mother last night. She's the president of Ladies Aid. You can expect some phone calls from people looking for work." I glanced through the front window at Sam, pacing the sidewalk and shouting.

Orson sighed. "Did he bother you?"

"No." I hesitated. "He told me you fired him for no reason."

The man bristled. "I fired him because he's aggressive and abrasive, and that's not the kind of counter help we want."

"No," I said, "I guess you wouldn't. Hey, is your accountant in? My invoice was smeared to the point of being unreadable," I lied. My fingers curled. "And since Adele and I are splitting the bill, we both need something for our files. Could I get another copy?"

"Yeah. Tilde's here. I'll—"

A young woman walked into the shop, purse over her arm. She wandered to a display of chocolate bars.

Orson tracked her movements with his gaze.

"If she's in the office, I know where it is," I suggested.

His narrow face creased with relief. "That would be great. Thanks. Just stay out of the kitchen." He pointed to his head. "No net."

I nodded, relieved he hadn't seemed to have connected me to the chocolate handprint. "Right." I walked around the counter and down the long hallway, past the open kitchen to the office.

The door was closed, the frame free of any handprints, chocolate or otherwise. So someone had seen mine and cleaned it off. Wincing, I knocked.

"Yes?" a woman called out, her voice dull.

I opened the door and leaned in. "Hi, I'm Maddie Kosloski from the Paranormal Museum. Orson told me I could find you here."

The woman looked up from her desk in the corner. She was thirty-something and slender, her brown hair knotted into an elegant bun. She tugged at a wisp of hair dangling beside her earlobe and rose from her chair. Its wheels squeaked against the linoleum floor. She adjusted her blouse, tucked inside her navy pencil skirt. A matching blazer lay slung over the back of her chair.

We clasped hands. I smothered a wince as my bones ground together. She released me.

I let my arm fall to my side, my hand flexing.

"I'm Tilde." She sniffed. Her nose was red, her face blotchy as if she'd been crying. "How can I help you?"

"It's a small thing, really, but since I was so close … Could I get another copy of our invoice? Somehow, by the time the chocolate reached me, the invoice had gotten smeared, and my accountant can't read the numbers on it." Since I was my own accountant, it was a double lie. I stuffed my hands into my vest pockets.

"That's no problem." She returned behind her desk, the red soles of her pumps flashing, and peered at the computer. "You said you were from the Paranormal Museum?"

"Yes. Though the invoice may be under the Fox and Fennel. Adele and I went in together on the order."

"To take advantage of the bulk discount, yes. I've got it." She tapped some keys and the printer beside her desk hummed.

"So you're the Reign accountant," I said, louder than I'd intended. There was something familiar about the woman, but what?

"Mmm-hmm."

"I didn't think a business this size would have its own in-house accountant. Does Reign have other shops in California?"

"Not yet," she said. "I'm only part-time with Reign, but they let me use their office."

"Oh?"

"Nepotism." Gracefully, she rose and whisked a sheet of paper from the printer. "My cousin is married—*was* married—to Atticus." The skin bunched around her eyes in a pained expression.

"You're India's cousin?" That explained the sense of familiarity. They had the same heart-shaped face, the same porcelain skin, the same light-brown eyes. She even walked like India, though her movements held a certain coiled tension. "You must have been close to Atticus. I'm so sorry for your loss."

"Thanks." She handed me the warm invoice. "But we never were that kind of family."

"At least you get to work together."

A muscle pulsed in her jaw. "I moved to California recently and thought I'd set up my own practice rather than working for someone else. Atticus thought it best if they didn't do their own bookkeeping. He was marketing. Orson is chocolate making. Neither are—*were*—big on the numbers side."

Neither was I, but I couldn't afford a bookkeeper, not even part-time. I lived for the day I could offload that chore. Payroll tax forms were the worst. "Have you got a card? I'm not looking for someone now, but I hope to hire a—er—new accountant in the future."

She plucked one off her desk and handed it to me.

"Tilde Otterstrom," I read. "Very Swedish."

"I'm from Kansas. What can I say?"

The door banged open and we both jumped.

Lola, elegant in camel slacks, walnut cable-knit sweater, and matching plaid shawl strode into the room. She stopped short on her four-inch stilettos without even a hint of a wobble, glanced up from her phone's screen, and smiled. "Oh, hello, Maddie. I didn't expect to see you here. Is everything all right?"

"She needed a fresh invoice," Tilde said.

"Mine got smeared," I said.

"Ah." Lola scanned me from my tennis shoes to my hoodie hair, and I suddenly felt underdressed. "I guess a new invoice is the least we can do after what you went through finding Atticus."

Tilde's shoulders jerked. "You were the one? Did you see anybody?"

My stomach knotted with suspicion. Funny how everyone was interested in what I'd seen. I grimaced at my rampant paranoia. Tilde's curiosity was natural. The newspapers had printed that Atticus's death had been the result of foul play.

I hesitated, unsure if I should discuss the case. But I wasn't a cop, and I hadn't seen anything but the murdered man. "No. I didn't see anyone." But I'd heard that closing door. Had it been the killer?

"It's strange, though," Lola mused.

"Someone killing Atticus is more than strange," Tilde said sharply. "It's horrible."

"Not that," Lola said, fixing me with her gaze. "That's awful. It's just that before his death, I never saw you at Reign, and now you seem to be here all the time. I heard you attended one of Orson's classes last night."

"Nothing strange about it." I tugged down the hem of my vest. "My, um, friend had ordered tickets weeks ago. And I keep coming back here because of my order."

Lola bowed her head. "Sorry. I guess I'm getting paranoid. With everything that's happened, and everything we need to do now Atticus is gone ..." She fiddled with the brown-and-white plaid shawl over her shoulders, not meeting my gaze, then turned to the accountant. "Are last month's financials done yet?"

Tilde stiffened. "Yes. I gave them to Orson last week."

"You know how my husband is." Lola's smile was wintery. "Can you forward them to my email?"

"Of course," Tilde said.

"Atticus scheduled an interview tomorrow with *Feast California*," Lola said. "I want to make sure I can quote some strong numbers, in case they ask."

"So, they'll be asking about Reign?" Tilde arched a brow.

"What else would they be interviewing me about?" Lola said sharply. "It's a food magazine." Her scarf slipped off one of her shoulders.

Tilde sniffed. "It just seems that most of your interviews are about ... you."

Meow. That seemed a little catty—and bold toward the boss's wife. But maybe as Atticus's cousin-in-law, Tilde felt she could get away with it. Uncomfortable, I shifted my weight.

Lola flushed. "I can't help it if *California Dwellings* was more interested in my home than the chocolate shop. Atticus said it was still publicity for Reign." She turned to me. "It's part of brand building. Atticus believed that we—the people involved in Reign—were the brand, so we have to publicize ourselves and not just the business. It's not something I'm entirely comfortable with, but I'm sure you understand. You're a business owner. You're part of your brand too."

Good Lord, I hoped not. What did that say about the museum's brand? Out of shape? Cheap date? Borrrrring?

"People do business with people," the accountant said as if parroting someone else. She made a face. "Not with businesses."

"That's what Atticus always said." Lola tossed the errant edge of her scarf over her shoulder. The phone in her hand pinged. She looked down and tapped something onto the screen. "I don't know how I can keep up with this social media schedule. Was there anything else we can help you with, Maddie?"

"Um, no. Thanks, Tilde. Nice seeing you, Lola." I backed out of the office and walked through the store to the sidewalk outside.

The picketer scowled at me.

I hurried down the street and into the mist.

SEVEN

PLEASANTLY EXHAUSTED FROM A busy Friday, I swept the museum. The broom shushed across the checkerboard tiles. The rocking chair creaked beneath GD's weight. The cat snuggled into a tighter ball, his head crooking toward the ceiling.

I leaned against the counter and surveyed my realm. As much as I loved a busy and profitable museum, after closing was one of my favorite times, when it was just me and the exhibits.

Something brushed against my leg, and I jumped.

Purring, GD wound around the ankles of my jeans.

"Very funny," I said. "You got me good." How'd he get from the chair to me so quickly?

The phone rang in my hoodie pocket, and I checked the number. Jason.

Grinning like a fool, I answered. "Hi."

"What's going on?"

"I'm closing the museum. You?"

"Just thinking of you."

"Tonight's girls' night, but if you just happened to stop by the microbrewery—"

"I can't. I'm at an accident on Zinfandel Road. A motorcycle and a truck full of artichokes."

My heart stopped. "Leo's—"

"Not involved. Neither is Mason."

My face warmed. Of course it couldn't have been Leo. He'd only just left and couldn't have gotten as far as Zinfandel Road. "Is anyone badly hurt?"

"Yes. Drive carefully tonight. And avoid Zinfandel Road. I've got to go. I'll talk to you tomorrow."

We said hurried goodbyes and I hung up, saying a silent prayer for the motorcyclist. And then I wondered why a roadside disaster had made Jason think of me.

GD at my heels, I turned off the lights in the Gallery and Fortune Telling rooms, then grabbed the zippered cash envelope off the counter. San Benedetto was a low-crime town, but I always got a little nervous carrying cash to the bank. I wished Leo was with me.

I turned to the bookcase to leave.

GD sprawled in front of the hidden door. He yawned, showing off his needlelike teeth.

"Really? You're resting right there, right now?"

He rolled onto his back and pawed at the air.

"Come on. Scoot." I reached down and nudged him away.

Quick as a wink, he whipped around and bit my hand.

"GD!" I rubbed my palm. The cat hadn't broken skin. He never did. And he never bit customers—only me, the hand that fed him.

He meowed and raised himself on his hind legs, his forelegs pawing their way up my jeans.

Some cats climb all over people. GD was not one of those cats.

"What's wrong with you?" Scowling, I pressed the special book spine. The bookcase snicked open, revealing Adele's darkened tea room and our shared hallway that led to the alley.

GD howled, an unearthly wail that prickled my scalp.

I shut the bookcase and double checked his food and water bowls. Both were full. "I don't get it. What's the problem?"

He hissed, and I half-turned.

In front of the bookcase, GD had gone full Halloween cat: back arched, fur standing on end.

Pulse beating erratically, I looked over my shoulder.

No apparition floated behind me.

"If it's a ghost that's sending you into a tailspin ..." I paused to enjoy my own pun. Cat. Tailspin. Heh heh. "Anyway, tell him or her to go to the light. Now I have to drive to the bank." I strode to the bookcase and gently shoved the cat aside with my foot.

He bit my ankle.

"Ow!" Hopping on one foot, I pushed open the bookcase and slipped into the tea room, gloomy in the darkness. I shut the door in front of GD, his fur bristling.

In the dark, it was impossible to see if the cat had broken my skin. I hurried down the tea room's long hallway and pushed open the heavy alley door.

My pickup waited in the fog-shrouded alley. A light slanted from above, illuminating the beads of moisture on the vintage truck's windows. I glanced at the lit windows above the motorcycle shop next door.

Mason's apartment.

Memories arose, unbidden, of the time I'd spent with him there. Guiltily I shoved them aside. I was over Mason and happy with Jason. But Mason and I had had good times. It had been that darn post-honeymoon phase that had done us in. I lifted the hem of my jeans and examined my unblemished ankle.

That, and—

A car's headlights flicked on at the end of the alley. The car rolled slowly toward me, waiting for me to cross to my truck.

Releasing my hem, I waved to the car and maneuvered around a garbage bin. I strode toward my red pickup.

The car's engine roared.

I stared, disbelieving.

The car bulleted toward me.

I gasped and dropped the cash bag. Leapt forward, one foot landing on top of my driver's-side tire. I launched myself flat onto the hood of the pickup.

A crash.

The truck lurched.

I slid sideways, halfway down the hood. I clawed frantically at the slick metal.

A screech. A bang.

Another earsplitting crash, and the car's taillights disappeared around the corner.

I half rolled, half fell off the hood and sat, panting, on the damp pavement. *Damn. Damn, damn, damn.* I rubbed my hip. It hurt. A lot.

Something metallic rattled.

A window scraped open above me. Mason leaned out, his blond hair shaggy and unbound. "What the ... Maddie? You okay?"

"I'm fine," I croaked.

But he'd closed the window before I could finish.

Grasping the cold front bumper, I levered myself to standing and retrieved the cash bag. I swayed, adrenaline clotting my system. How had the driver not seen me? I rubbed my palms, grimy and damp, on the thighs of my jeans.

A door slammed open and Mason jogged into the alley. "Maddie! What happened?"

"Someone was driving too fast," I stammered. But I'd *thought* they'd seen me. I'd assumed the person was driving slowly to let me cross to my pickup. I'd even waved to the driver. Had the person not noticed? Or had the near miss been something more sinister?

I studied my pickup. A brownish streak scuffed its side. At least old trucks are sturdy, especially versus lightweight modern cars with plastic bumpers and fiberglass sides.

Mason swore. "The guy had to know he hit your pickup." His brows slashed downward. "I saw the car. A 2016 Ford Mustang, copper colored."

"You know the year?" I laughed shakily. "Whoever it was, they picked the wrong alley for a hit-and-run."

"I couldn't read the plate," he said darkly. "But maybe Slate can help you track the guy down."

"Did you see the driver?"

"No. Too dark. Oh." He stooped and picked my rear fender off the ground. "That's gotta hurt."

I groaned. "I thought I'd gotten off easy." I'd inherited the pickup from my dad, and the sight of the vintage bumper in Mason's hands wrenched my gut.

"Looks like the dumpster didn't escape this idiot either." He examined a long scrape along its green side. "This guy was out of control. Probably drunk."

"Probably," I said faintly.

"I can put your bumper back on, if you want."

That would save me time. Mason rebuilt bikes, but he'd helped me out with my old truck before. And since we were romantically over each other, the favor wouldn't be awkward. Nope, not at all. "Um, thanks. That would be great."

"Want me to keep the bumper for now?"

"I guess so. I can't do much with it."

"All right." He braced the bumper against one brawny shoulder.

"Mason?" His girlfriend Belle leaned out the window above us, her long hair dangling.

"I'll be up in a sec," he shouted to her. He met my gaze. "Well. I'd better..."

"Yeah." I backed to the pickup. "Me too. I've got to drop off this deposit."

He hiked up the concrete steps to his apartment.

I drove to the bank and dropped the cash bag in the night deposit bin. In the bank's parking lot, I studied my phone. Jason would want to know about the hit-and-run, but it wasn't an emergency. I hadn't been hurt, and the driver was long gone. And Jason was probably still at the accident scene, dealing with real trauma. Biting my lip, I settled for sending him a text, asking him to call when he could.

I checked my appearance in the side-view mirror. My hair stuck out from my ponytail in predictable places. I smoothed it behind my ear, grabbed my purse, and strolled across the street to the Bell and Brew.

Pausing beside the hostess stand, I scanned the restaurant: the wooden tables, the red-leather booths. Light glinted off the microbrewery's metal-tiled ceiling.

Harper signaled to me from a booth opposite a pair of giant copper beer vats. Adele sat in the seat across from her.

I waved and hurried over. Ducking beneath a stained-glass lamp, I slid into their booth.

Adele glanced up, then returned to frowning over another wedding to-do list.

Harper eyed me. "What happened? Did your mother find out you were investigating? Because you look like you're on the run."

"No. What...?" I looked down. My hoodie was askew, the hood wrapped around my neck. I hadn't noticed that detail in the car mirror. Even without the hoodie issue, I looked underdressed compared to Harper in her chocolate-colored turtleneck, and Adele in a sea-green silk blouse. "Someone nearly ran me down in the alley behind the museum," I said. "I had to jump on top of my truck."

"People can be so inconsiderate." Adele thumbed through a sheaf of papers and didn't look up.

"Are you all right?" Harper asked me.

"Fine," I said. "The car scraped my pickup, took off the bumper, hit a garbage bin, and drove off."

"Unbelievable," Adele muttered.

"Mason got the make and model—"

"Mason?" Harper asked.

"He was upstairs and saw it happen from his rear window."

"Is this an Alfred Hitchcock film?" Harper asked, arch. "Why's he ogling you through his rear window?"

"Um, I don't—That's not the point. Someone nearly killed me."

"It's highway robbery!" Adele glared.

"No," I said. "It was only a hit-and-run. My cash bag wasn't stolen."

"What are you talking about?" Adele thrust a paper menu into my hands. "Put the word 'wedding' in front of the word 'party' and the prices triple!"

Harper rolled her eyes.

"I'm talking about my near-death by Ford Mustang." Jaw tight, I explained again about the hit-and-run. "The more I think about it, the more I think the driver had to have seen me. It was like he accelerated intentionally," I concluded.

"He?" Harper asked.

"Or she. I couldn't see past the headlights."

"Why would someone intentionally target you?" Adele asked.

"Because ..." I fumbled. What *had* I done to put myself in the crosshairs? "Well, there's the murder at Reign. I was the one who found Atticus."

"So?" Harper said. "You didn't see the killer, did you? And you already told everything you know to the police. Even if the killer knew you were the one who found the body, why come after you?"

Good question. Maybe the hit-and-run *had* just been a case of bad driving. A reckless, panicked teenager? I'd already imagined being followed by a phantom in the mist. Maybe my imagination was getting the better of me again?

My legs shifted, restless.

Or maybe it wasn't.

EIGHT

"Good morning." Jason leaned across the glass counter and brushed a kiss across my cheek. My skin tingled at the contact. Damn, he smelled good—of soap and Alpine forests.

Watery sunlight struggled through the museum's front windows. A sullen gray blanket of fog shrouded the low rooftops across the street. The wall heaters rattled, and a dehumidifier hummed behind the counter.

"I'm sorry I couldn't call you last night," he said. "I ended up working past midnight." He wore his usual work uniform—a navy suit and plain white shirt—and he looked sexy as all get-out.

I closed the computer window on Lola's social media accounts. She and Atticus had known how to work their online marketing. I could learn a thing or two from her. "It's fine. You were busy." Besides, Jason and I had a standing date for tonight, Saturday, when we both got to decompress. "Got any fun plans for the day?"

"Solving a murder. Shopping for a new laptop. Planting tomatoes."

"Tomatoes?" I goggled at him. "You garden?"

"I'm a homeowner. You give the weeds an inch, they'll run all over you."

"You're making me feel better about renting."

"Come on," he scoffed. "I saw you white-washing your aunt's fence last month."

"Yeah, I'm a real Tom Sawyer. Or was it Huck Finn?"

"Sawyer. And he tricked his way out of the job."

"Damn. I've given the game away. I was going to trick you into it next time."

"Just say the word and I'll be there. Men exist to do the grubby manual labor women shouldn't have to."

I laughed. "That's exactly the sort of retrograde, sexist attitude I can get behind."

Bracing my hand on his broad shoulder, I kissed him again just because I could. His cheek was rough against mine, and I smiled.

GD sprang to the counter and rubbed against Jason's suit jacket. But any hairs the cat might have been trying to mark him with were hidden by the jacket's dark navy threads.

I frowned at the cat. Last night it had seemed like he'd tried to stop me from going outside, almost as if he'd known there was danger in the alley. But that would imply GD cared about my safety, and that was about as likely as the cat having psychic powers.

I drew a breath to tell Jason about the hit-and-run driver.

"I'm sorry," he said, stroking the cat, "but I won't be able to make our date tonight."

GD purred.

"Oh." Disappointed, I straightened. "Work?"

"The Malkes have organized a candlelight vigil for Atticus. The chief wants an extra police presence."

"Orson and Lola are throwing a vigil? Does the chief think there'll be trouble?"

"Whenever a crowd gathers, there's an opportunity for problems."

"Jason, about last night—"

"I'm really sorry, but there was no way I could have gotten away. Besides, I thought girls' night was sacred."

"It is, but that's—"

"How's your haunted molinillo research?" he asked, in an artful attempt at diverting me.

"Umm ... Herb's in charge of that. He'll look into it." As the dealer, Herb was my best source. For now.

Jason relaxed against the counter. "How much did he want?"

"For the research? Nothing." I frowned. Jason was obviously relieved I'd gone along with his change of subject. It was kind of irritating. Maybe separating detective and personal life wasn't as simple for me as I'd thought.

"Be careful," he said. "You get what you pay for."

"Meaning Herb won't come through?" I pulled my phone from the pocket of my hoodie. "Want to make a bet?"

"Hmm, what do you have that I want ...?" He gazed thoughtfully at the ceiling.

"My rapier-sharp wit? My all-American good looks? My totally random knowledge of the weird and occult? Don't the police sometimes use outside advisors for stuff like that?"

Jason grinned. "Forget about it. I'm not using you as a police consultant. Besides, we don't have any occult cases."

"Phooey. I'll just have to settle for knowing I'm right about Herb."

He quirked a brow.

"Challenge accepted." I called the paranormal collector. Herb answered on the seventh ring, just as I was starting to think he was avoiding me.

"Maddie? I have that information we discussed," the paranormal collector whispered. "Have you got a pencil? I really don't have time to fiddle-faddle around. Not with—ow!"

"Um, are you all right?" I asked.

"Yes, I—Ooof! Blast it!"

Bemused, I rubbed my chin. "What's going on?"

"A simple home exorcism. The poltergeists aren't behaving the way they—Stop that!" There was a crash. "I'm on the phone!"

There was a long silence.

Jason drummed his fingers on the counter.

"Herb?" I said.

"You already have the seller's name on the receipt, but here's her phone number." He rattled off a string of digits.

"I thought the original owner was from Mexico," I said.

"The original owner, not the woman I bought it from. I'm afraid you'll have to take it from here."

"Sure, I can do that." The timing was bad, but I really did enjoy researching the objects in the museum. "But, Herb—"

"This is simply outrageous," he said in a muffled voice. "You can't have used the right ritual. I told you we shouldn't have used Latin. If we can't control a simple poltergeist—" The phone went dead.

"Trouble?" Jason said.

I hung up the Bakelite wall phone. "Um ... just a poltergeist problem, which neither of us believe in, so I guess there's no problem at all." Did I even *want* to know what was going on with Herb?

No, I did not. "Unless you really do want to start an occult police consultancy," I continued. "You've helped me often enough researching objects in the museum." Had those moments been diversions as well, keeping me from murder investigations? If so, I got it. I really did. I wasn't a cop, and there were good reasons why civilians shouldn't get involved in murders.

"I'll leave the ghost-busting to you," he said.

"You say that, and yet you keep sticking your nose into my artifact investigations."

"Sticking my nose into someone else's business? Who could I possibly have picked up that habit from?"

"Herb gave me a number for the molinillo seller," I said hastily. I pulled a three-ringed binder from beneath the old-fashioned cash register and thumbed through its pages. "Got it." I smoothed the molinillo receipt with my palm.

"You going to call the seller?" Jason asked.

I glanced around the museum. It was only nine thirty, and two lonely customers roamed the museum. "Why?" I teased. "I didn't think you were that interested in the molinillo. The way you're acting, I might think you enjoyed investigating haunted objects."

"Investigating the past makes a nice break from police work." A shadow crossed his face.

I laid a hand on his, atop the counter. "Was the accident that bad?"

He gusted a breath. "It was a motorcycle and an artichoke truck. The biker didn't make it."

My lips compressed. It was awful, but a part of me could only feel relief that Leo hadn't been involved. "Let's see what Susan Jennings can tell us." I dialed, and to my surprise, I didn't get voicemail.

"This is Susan."

I straightened off the counter. "Hi, this is Maddie Kosloski from the San Benedetto Paranormal Museum. I bought a haunted molinillo that I believe once belonged to you?"

She chuckled, her voice rich as melted caramel. "So you're the sucker who bought it."

"Sucker? You mean it's not haunted?" I asked, alarmed.

"I mean I don't believe in ghosts, and that thing *is* haunted."

Okay. I blew out my cheeks. "Do you mind if I put you on speaker so my associate can hear?"

"Go ahead."

Associate? Jason mouthed.

I set the phone on the counter and clicked the speaker button. "Why do you think the molinillo is haunted?"

"First," she said, "because the guy at that shop in Oaxaca told me so. And second, because it rattled every time my son told a lie. He's a teenager. Do you have any idea how often that thing was going off? Believe me, Rick wanted it out of the house even more than I did. It would have been funny if it wasn't so creepy."

"What exactly did the seller from Oaxaca tell you about the molinillo?" I asked.

"Only that it was haunted by a sad woman's ghost and rattled whenever a lie was told."

"Can you tell me the name of the shop?" I asked.

"I got it on a trip to Mexico two years ago. So, no. Sorry, I can't remember and didn't bother keeping a receipt. But the store was off that famous pedestrian street, with the cobblestones and the colorful buildings."

"The Andador?" Jason asked.

"That's my colleague," I said hastily.

"Yes," she said, "that's what the street was called. You've been to Oaxaca?"

"Once," he said.

"The shop was a hole-in-the-wall in this sweet little plaza near the Santo Domingo church. It sold Mexican hot chocolate tablets and tubs of mole. And now I'm getting hungry," she muttered.

"Thanks," Jason said. "That's helpful."

Was it? Because I didn't speak much Spanish and had never done an international investigation before.

"You're welcome," she said. "If I think of the shop's name, I'll let you know. But don't hold your breath." She hung up.

"Do you think a hole-in-the-wall would have a website?" I asked, glum.

GD pawed my hand. His claws were not extended, which was unusually considerate for him.

"Doesn't matter," Jason said. "I know that plaza. I'd be surprised if there's more than one shop selling chocolate there. And if there are more, we can ask them all."

"We can? Do you speak Spanish?"

"We can—"

The front door jolted open, and a woman in a scarlet Victorian-era gown with a shiny black corset on the outside staggered into the museum. She carried a large cardboard box in one arm and a coffee urn in the other. A pocket watch dangled from a hook on her corset. Her miniature top hat canted at a jaunty angle over her chestnut hair, which was pinned into a neat bun.

Jason leapt to relieve her of the box. Ceramics rattled inside.

She brushed the thick bangs from her eyes and blew out her breath. "I made it! Am I late? I'm not late, am I?"

I hadn't known my chocolate scryer would be wearing a steam-punk costume, but ... she looked fabulous. I grinned. "No, you're right on time." I hurried around the counter. "Jason, this is Ursula Morgan, our chocolate fortune-teller."

"That's my alias." She winked. "Can't have the police on my tail."

"She's joking," I said quickly. I hoped she was joking. After everything Herb had put me through over the past year, I took nothing for granted. "Jason's a detective with the San Benedetto PD. Let me get you set up."

Jason trailed us into the Gallery. We placed the coffee urn on the square table against the wall near the fortune-telling canopy.

"Do you mind if I make a few calls?" he asked.

"No," I said, adjusting the canopy. "Go ahead." Fortune-telling by hot chocolate! I might not have been able to compete with the wineries, but I was excited about this idea. I half hoped to get a reading myself. If it involved chocolate, my fortune couldn't be bad.

My stomach lurched, and I sobered. My recent history with chocolate hadn't exactly been good.

The fortune-teller rummaged in her cardboard box. She withdrew a stack of wide white mugs and a box of hot cocoa packets, then arranged the packets and mugs, along with a set of saucers, beside the urn.

"All right," she said, "here are the rules set by the state of California. I cannot pour the water, I cannot open the hot chocolate packets, I cannot stir the hot cocoa. Whoever I'll be reading for will need to do that themselves, so we don't violate any food service rules." She smoothed her skirt, touched her chestnut hair, and adjusted the angle of her hat.

"I'm glad you know the laws," I said, "because I don't." And I preferred not to get busted for serving hot chocolate without a license. Detective Laurel Hammer would be only too happy to haul me in.

We talked marketing, and Ursula promised to pitch the chocolate and tarot decks. Fortunately she had her own copy of the chocolate deck, so every time she used it for a reading, she'd be promoting sales.

I suppressed a cackle of Scrooge-like delight. Cackles aren't sexy, and Jason still leaned against the counter, talking into his phone.

Mason walked into the museum. At the sight of the detective, he stopped in his tracks and glanced my way.

Jason pocketed his phone.

I settled Ursula in the comfy chair beneath the star-spangled canopy. Two customers wandered into the Gallery. Their eyes widened at the sight of the fortune-teller.

Ursula snapped a picture of the setup and smiled. "For social media. You know how it is."

"Right." I should post some photos too. "I'll grab some shots of you telling fortunes later. And good luck," I whispered. She was charging for readings and giving me a ten percent cut. I probably could have gotten more, but I was just happy to have her in the museum.

She settled into her chair and the customers sidled toward her.

I hurried into the main room. "Hi, Mason. What—"

Jason crossed his arms, rumpling his suit jacket. "Mason was just telling me about the hit-and-run last night." A muscle pulsed in his jaw.

I stiffened, my body going hot with discomfort. Dammit, I should have told Jason right away. "He got a better look at the car than I did." I turned to my neighbor. "What brings you to the museum?"

"This wine and chocolate thing. Belle ... Maddie, you're creative. I thought I should do something too and was looking for inspiration. Got any ideas?"

There was a rattle from the Gallery, and I glanced over my shoulder. The male half of the tourist couple adjusted the bowl that held the molinillo.

"But this looks like a bad time," my ex continued. "I didn't get a license plate, Slate, but if you need anything else—"

"Not right now," Jason said, brusque. "But thanks."

Mason swiveled on his heel and strode out the door.

"Why didn't you tell me?" my boyfriend demanded.

"I'd planned to, but Mason beat me to it," I said. "Since it happened last night, it didn't seem that urgent. The emergency's over."

Jason's dark brow creased. "What happened, exactly? Give me the details."

I explained about the near-miss.

"You could have called me last night," he insisted, his firm mouth pressing into a slash.

My stomach tightened. "I wasn't hurt, and it was late, and you were at the accident scene. It didn't seem like there was much to be done. Mason caught the make and model of the car, though—a 2016 Ford Mustang, copper colored."

Jason's expression stilled. He rubbed his jaw.

"What?"

"Atticus had a 2016 Ford Mustang," he said neutrally. "A shiny brown. It was parked behind the chocolate shop when he died."

We stared at each other.

"I'm pretty sure Atticus wasn't driving last night," I said.

Unless ghosts really *did* exist. Heh heh.

NINE

MY LAST CUSTOMERS STROLLED from the museum, bags of chocolate and tarot cards in hand.

Locking the door behind them, I flipped the sign in the window to *Closed*.

Ursula emerged from the Gallery, her scarlet gown trailing on the checkerboard floor. She dropped her receipt book on the counter. "Wow. Was that the last of the customers?"

"We're clear," I said. "We just closed." Beat, I sagged against the counter and rubbed the back of my aching neck. I'd somehow wrenched it in my wild dive onto my pickup.

The bookcase swung open and Leo backed into the museum, carrying a cardboard box. Inside, the chocolate scrying bowls and plates clinked.

GD looked up from his spot on the rocking chair. His ears swiveled toward Leo.

"This batch is clean." Leo set the box on the table. He reached overhead, yawning, his black Paranormal Museum tee rising up to expose his flat stomach. "Another day of fun and profit."

"And magic!" Ursula said.

"It *was* fun." Even if it hurt to turn my head. The day had been busier than usual thanks to Wine and Chocolate Days. Maybe it was the chocolate buzz, but there'd been a whimsical energy in the air. Even GD had been mellow, letting me pet him without biting me in retaliation. "Everyone was talking about your fortunes, Ursula."

She raised her slim hand over her mouth, covering a yawn. "Good things, I hope."

"You were a hit," Leo said.

"I don't think I've ever read so many fortunes in one day," she said. "I'm exhausted."

"You're not too tired to come back tomorrow, I hope?" I asked, anxious.

She grinned. "Are you kidding? I'll be back. Business was terrific today." She handed me her receipt book.

I flipped through the pink pages and whistled. "I didn't think you'd get this much traffic. I mean, people who come into a paranormal museum are usually in the mood for stuff like this, but this is amazing."

"The chocolate scrying was more popular than the tarot cards. I think people just liked the idea of drinking hot chocolate while they got their fortunes told. And who can blame them on a day like this?" She glanced at the window. Behind it, street lamps glowed on the sidewalk, their light streaking the damp glass. The sun had set, fog deepening the twilight to the color of slate.

"Since I'm already set up," she said, "is it okay if I arrive tomorrow a little later? Say at ten?"

"That's perfect," I said. "We probably won't get busy until after eleven, but people do show up at opening. Tourists get to San Benedetto sooner than they planned, when it's too early for wine tasting. Then they find their way here to kill time."

Ursula braced her hands on her lower back and stretched. "Maybe I'll finally get a chance to explore your museum."

"You can look around now if you like," I said. "I've got to do some cleaning before we lock up."

"Brilliant!" She clapped her beringed hands together and wandered into the Fortune Telling Room.

Leo angled his head toward the broom, half-hidden behind his motorcycle jacket hanging from a wall peg. "Do you want me to ..."

"You can take off," I said. Even though I paid Leo a fair wage, I always felt a teensy bit guilty about having him work what was essentially a dead-end job. Or maybe I was just afraid he'd quit, so I never pushed too hard. Some day he would go. He was destined for more than taking tickets in a paranormal museum.

"Thanks, boss." He grabbed his jacket off the peg and hustled out the front door.

I locked it behind him and collected the remainder of the cocoa-smeared bowls and plates from the Gallery. Balancing the box of dinnerware on one hip, I pushed the hidden latch on the bookcase and it swung open.

A faint light gleamed in the closed tea room. Behind the counter, neat rows of brushed-nickel tea canisters glinted dully on the shelves.

Shadows shrouded the tables. Out of the corner of my eye, one of the tablecloths rustled, as if stirred by a spectral breeze. I whipped my head toward the movement, and pain sparked up my spine. Rubbing my neck, I watched the table.

Nothing moved. Of course. Because, paranoia!

The kitchen door, off the hallway to the alley, stood ajar. A sliver of light knifed through the opening and along the bamboo floor.

"Adele?" I called, sidestepping into the hallway. The bookcase door swung shut behind me. I shuffled deeper into the gloom, toward the kitchen. My flesh pebbled. "Hello?"

"In here!" Adele said.

Relieved, I edged the kitchen door open with my hip.

Adele stood at a long metal table in the center of the kitchen, frowning at one of her interminable wedding lists. She made a note with a pencil. "More bowls to wash?" she asked without looking up.

"Yeah. Thanks for letting us use your sink."

"I *should* complain. You're probably cutting into my business by giving out free hot chocolate."

"It's not exactly free," I said. "They have to pay for the reading." And I knew for a fact Adele's business had been booming, because I hadn't been able to find a seat or even beg for a to-go sandwich at lunch.

"I suppose you're going to the vigil at the park tonight?" she asked.

"Yes, I was planning on it." I was glad the town was coming together for the vigil, and I wanted to be a part of it. But I had a more mercenary reason as well. They say a murderer can't resist coming to his victim's funeral, and I thought the same might be true for candlelit vigils.

"I thought as much," she said. "I'm coming with you."

"You are?"

"I can hardly let you go alone after that hit-and-run." Adele's face scrunched. "The killer might be at the park. Dieter may come too. And Pug would love it. You know how he adores people. But I can't bring him. His cold has turned into a respiratory infection, and he needs to rest. My mother agreed to watch him tonight."

"Is it serious?" I asked.

She blinked rapidly. "The vet says as long as he eats well and gets lots of rest, he'll be fine. And I can't not go to the vigil. I have a policy of attending all my suppliers' funerals."

Adele had more etiquette in her little finger than I had in my entire body, but that sounded a little weird.

"Er, do many of your suppliers die?"

She looked up from her list and shot me a severe look. "Everyone dies. Atticus is the second supplier I've lost, but he's the first I've lost to murder—that I know of, at least. At any rate, funerals and vigils are for the benefit of the survivors, not the dead. Atticus's friends and widow need to know they have the support of the community." She smiled, sharklike. "And along the way, we can talk about your job managing the social coverage."

I sucked in a quick breath. "My … what?"

"Social coverage. You know, taking candid snapshots and posting them at the wedding."

Beads of sweat broke out on my forehead. I wasn't a professional photographer. Sure, I took photos for museum events and exhibits, but that was different. I was my only critic. Adele would expect perfection.

She jammed her hands on her hips. "You forgot, didn't you?"

"No, of course not!" I swear this was the first time I'd heard about having social media responsibilities for the wedding. "It's just … Why me?"

"All you need to do is remember the hashtag."

"There's a wedding hashtag?" Please, let it not be Nakakraut. Or Finkielmoto.

"I told you this! Hashtag, DAOMG."

I stared at her blankly.

"DAOMG! Dieter and Adele, OMG!"

"Right, right. DAOMG. Easy-peasy." I was never going to remember that hashtag. Escaping her glare, I bustled to the sink and got busy washing cups.

When I returned to the museum, Urusla swished from the Fortune Telling Room, a blissful smile on her face. "I never thought I'd get to sit inside an actual spirit cabinet. You have an amazing collection! And all those old tarot cards! I love the way the colors have faded and softened. Or were they originally printed that way?"

"No, they've faded."

She checked the pocket watch dangling from a hook on her corset. "I should get going. See you tomorrow at ten!"

"Till then." I let her out and finished tidying the museum.

Adele slipped through the bookcase, and together we walked through the fog to the park. We joined a trickle of people arriving in twos and threes. The trickle became a river and then a lake, people massing in the park. Sparks of light flowed through the darkness, and I realized I was seeing candles being lit, the flame passing from person to person.

My heart swelled. I'd spent most of my adult life living overseas, moving from country to country, before returning to my home town. During the process, I'd lost my sense of community. Being a part of one again made me realize how important it was to me.

I scanned the crowd, hoping to see Jason. But if he was there, he was hidden in the sea of people.

A man slipped behind the gazebo, his movements furtive.

Breath quickening, I stood on my toes for a better view, my tennis shoes sinking into the soft lawn. The man had looked like Sam, that picketer from Reign.

"What?" Adele asked.

Brow wrinkling, I stared at the gazebo. The man's figure shifted between the wooden slats. It *was* Sam. He hadn't sounded like he had much love for Atticus, but maybe he was bigger than his anger.

"What?" she repeated.

"Huh? Oh. Nothing. I didn't say anything."

"You had that *look*."

"What look?"

The sleeves of our jackets brushed other sleeves in the crush of people. Someone handed Adele and me candles. We lit them off the flames of the candles beside us.

Too close beside us.

I pulled my hair forward so that it wouldn't accidentally catch fire. For no good reason, crowds made me a little nervous. Even though this one was calm and friendly, I had to force my muscles to relax.

I scanned the park for my community-minded mother. This was just the sort of thing she'd come to, but I couldn't find her in the crowd.

Someone jostled me from behind and murmured an apology before I could turn. I did a quick hair check to verify it was not in flames and returned to people watching.

Orson and his wife, Lola, stood bundled in long coats at the top of the gazebo steps. Lola rested her hands against her husband's chest and lowered her head. The widow, India, stood a step lower, huddled in a colorful Indian blanket coat.

Adele turned her candle in quick, nervous rotations between her fingers. "There must be three hundred people here."

"At least." I adjusted the cardboard circle at the base of the candle that kept the wax from dripping on my fingers.

Reign's accountant, Tilde, stood at the base of the gazebo steps, a navy knit cap pulled over her sleek hair. She looked away, toward a set of speakers propped on a picnic table. I wondered at the relations between the four—Tilde and Lola, Tilde and her cousin India, the three women and Orson. The odds were that someone close to Atticus had killed him. I shivered. Was I looking at a killer?

"Actually," I said, "it's probably closer to five hundred people."

"I've invited five hundred to the wedding," Adele whispered. "It's so many people."

"You could always elope," I joked.

"Are you crazy?" She rocked in place. "Do you have any idea how much money we've spent? My parents would be furious. Plus, I've wanted to get married in that vineyard since I was eight. I can't elope!"

"I was kidding," I said. "You're super organized. I'm sure things will work out."

She groaned. "You make it sound like it's easy. All I do when I'm not working—and sometimes when I am—is plan this wedding."

"Harper and I can help."

"You *are* helping. You and Harper have been wonderful in spite of all my craziness. But there's only so much you can do. Dieter and I still have to make the decisions. And Harper ..." She sighed.

"What?"

"She's been distracted lately. Have you noticed?"

I clasped my hands together on the base of the tiny candle. I *had* noticed.

"Hey, beautiful." Dieter, in a lightweight blue jacket and jeans, jogged to a stop next to Adele. Grasping her around the waist with one arm, he gave her a swift kiss. In his free hand, he held a half-dozen plastic zip-ties.

Adele's shoulders relaxed and she smiled, rumpling his shaggy hair. "You made it."

"Sure," he said, his bronzed face creasing into a grin. "I wasn't going to leave my girl alone. Though it wasn't easy finding you in this crowd. Besides, they wanted my help setting up some quick fences." He brandished the zip-ties. "Check it out. One of the guys showed me how to break out of these. Tie me up."

He handed me a zip-tie and turned around, his hands behind his back. "Zip me, Mad Dog."

Uncertain, I glanced at Adele.

She sighed and nodded.

I wrapped a zip-tie around his wrists and pulled it closed.

"Tighter," Dieter said.

This could not end well. "If you say so." I tightened the plastic band.

"Watch." He bent double and raised his arms high behind him. "One, two, three." He slammed his wrists onto his lower back.

Nothing happened.

"One more time." He brought his wrists down hard on his low back again and grunted. "It worked for the other guy."

Adele and I shared a look and burst out laughing.

He straightened, his face scrunching. "What's so funny?" His shoulders pulled back and he wriggled, his neck angling one way, then another. "Maybe they're twisted the wrong way."

"Maddie?" Belle Rodale, Mason's girlfriend, appeared beside Dieter. She tossed her long auburn hair over one shoulder and placed her hand atop the head of the blond boy beside her—their son, Jordan.

"Hi, Belle." I shifted my weight. Belle and I had never had a bad relationship, but I felt awkward in her presence. Mason had been her boyfriend first, then mine, and then hers again when he'd discovered they had a son together. It had been the ultimate post-honeymoon-phase complication.

Dieter grimaced and bent over, thunking his wrists on his backside.

"What's he doing?" Jordan pointed at Dieter, who was now pretzeled in half.

"Escaping from zip-ties," Adele said, and her lips pursed.

"I've almost got it," Dieter said.

Holding three candles, Mason emerged from the crowd. "Got some." At the sight of me, his eyes widened. His gaze darted to Belle, to me, to Belle again. "Hi, Maddie. I guess I should have figured you'd be here."

Belle's brow furrowed. "Were you friends with the Reines? I'm sorry, I didn't know."

"No," I said, "not really. But Adele and I bought chocolate from Reign for our businesses. You?"

"Atticus was a rider," she said. "Mason knew him." She rubbed her arms beneath her puffy turquoise jacket. "I can't believe something like this could happen. This place is getting as dangerous as Sacramento."

Mason smiled. "Sacramento's still a safe town, and so is San Benedetto." He reached out as if to put an arm around her. But at the last minute he dropped his broad hand onto her shoulder.

"Was Atticus in your motorcycle club?" I asked him.

"No," Mason said. "He wasn't much of a joiner. He said he preferred to ride with his wife. He had a silver Harley, a classic from the sixties. It was a real beauty."

Bent double, Dieter struck his bound wrists against his butt.

"I don't suppose he said anything to you about being worried," I said, "or—"

Dieter staggered sideways, knocking me into Belle.

I jerked my candle away before it could torch her long hair, but the flame had gone out. "Sorry," I muttered, then glared at Dieter.

"Is a zip-tie the modern version of the ball and chain?" Mason joked.

Belle's eyes narrowed. "That's not funny."

"They're cutting off my circulation." Dieter panted. "They're supposed to break."

"Here." Mason unclipped a pocket knife from his belt and sliced through the plastic tie.

Rubbing his wrists, Dieter heaved a sigh. "You're a lifesaver."

Adele's lips quirked. "Promise me you won't try anything like that at our wedding."

"Thank you all for coming." Lola's voice rose above the crowd. She held an oversized cordless microphone in her hands. "We're here to honor a passionate man, a visionary, Atticus Reine. But first we'd like to thank everyone in this unique, loving community. You've helped us in so many ways over the past few days. Your thoughtful gestures, your conversation, and your hugs have kept our family at Reign strong during this time of grief."

A loud bang cracked the air.

The crowd shifted, pressing me sideways.

I looked around for the source of the noise.

Another bang, a shriek, screams.

Someone shoved me from behind, and I stumbled. And then people were running, bodies tangling.

More bangs in quick succession. People stormed past, jostling us from every angle.

My feet were swept from beneath me. I landed hard on the damp grass and gasped, the air driven from my lungs. Someone stepped on my hand. I yowled in pain.

Get up, get up. I had to get up or get trampled. Limbs shaking, I scrambled forward, rising, and got knocked flat.

Someone stepped on my calf, and I cried out again, pain blazing from my toes to my knee.

"Maddie!" Mason waded through the crowd and hauled me to my feet. "This way."

He half-carried, half-pushed me through the crowd to a cluster of oak trees by the creek. Belle, Jordan, Adele, and Dieter huddled together.

"You're hurt," Adele said, her brown eyes wide. "You're covered in mud."

My leg and hand and side ached. Mud streaked the knees of my jeans. "Just some bruises." I took a step and winced. "I think I'm okay."

"Maddie!" Jason hurried toward us. Lines of tension released in his handsome face. He grasped my shoulders and pulled me to him. "Thank God."

I pressed against the corded muscles of his chest, a sense of security descending like a warm blanket at his touch. "What's going on?"

"Some idiot set off firecrackers by the loudspeakers," he said. "It's only firecrackers," he bellowed. "Wait here," he told us. "I need to check on the injured."

The park had cleared. A few people lay moaning on the muddy lawn. Uniformed police officers hurried toward them.

"I'll help." Mason jogged after him. "I have medic training."

"Who would have done such a thing?" Adele wiped her eyes, and I realized she'd been crying. "I thought … When we couldn't find you …"

Dieter wrapped an arm over her shoulders. "It was probably just kids."

"At a vigil!" She gulped. "How stupid could they be? Someone could have been killed."

I gazed across the park, and my heart squeezed. First a murder and now this mayhem. What was happening to my home town?

TEN

Sunday passed, Ursula reading chocolate dregs and tarot cards, filling the museum to the top of its black crown molding with customers. The museum was closed on Mondays, a day I'd normally spend taking inventory or doing marketing. But I was too restless to do that kind of work today. I was still trying to make sense of the stampede at the vigil.

Sun sparkled off the Formica counters in my fifties-era kitchen as I poured over the newspaper article, looking for clues.

The firecrackers had been set off behind the picnic table where the stereo speakers had been placed. At the edge of the crowd and just above the embankment to the creek, the table and speakers had provided a good hiding spot for the prankster.

But *had* it been a prankster? I bounced my heel on the base rung of my chair. Or were the firecrackers somehow connected to Atticus's murder? Sam had been lurking by the gazebo. Maybe he hadn't been willing to let bygones be bygones after all.

I rubbed the back of my hand and smoothed the paper on the kitchen table. My hand and calf ached from getting stepped on. And my neck still hadn't recovered. But I was okay, and no one had been seriously injured at the park. It could have been so much worse.

My cell phone rang. Distracted by the streaks of black newspaper ink on my fingers, I answered without checking the caller ID. "Hello?"

"Madelyn, this is your mother. Is it true you were at the vigil Saturday night?"

"Yeah, but I'm okay." I rubbed my palms clean on the thighs of my jeans. I was a little surprised my mother hadn't been at the park herself. As president of the Ladies Aid society, she was ubiquitous at public events. But I was glad she'd passed on this one.

"And you were the one who discovered Mr. Reine's body?"

I winced. "Where did you hear that?"

"So, it's true!"

"Well, yes, but—"

"This is all my fault."

I leaned back in my kitchen chair. It wobbled alarmingly. "Your fault? Why? Do you know something about Reign Chocolate?"

"Not really. If you must know, they've been rather standoffish when it comes to community events."

"That surprises me. They advertise that they source their ingredients locally. Except for the cocoa beans."

"That's not the same as—You *are* investigating this, aren't you?"

"I wouldn't say *investigating*." I rose and set my lunch plate in the sink. "But I did find Atticus's body, and—"

"I know I've encouraged you in the past—you were so lost when you returned to California—but I was wrong. You need to leave this to Jason. He's such a lovely man. I was thinking of inviting him over to dinner. Do you think it's too soon?"

"No, it's—wait. What? You were wrong?" My mother was never wrong. Or at least she never admitted it.

"It's bad enough that your brother works in those awful countries. Every day I check the news to see if someone's tried to blow up his embassy. My heart can't take worrying about you being in jeopardy too."

I leaned one hip against the counter. "Mom—"

"No, I mean it. I realize forbidding you will only encourage you to do it anyway. I simply want you to think about the risks. I'd like to have grandchildren someday, and since your brother and sister show no sign of procreating, that leaves you. You could have been killed at that vigil."

I squirmed. "It was just some stupid kids with firecrackers." My mom had been casting long, weepy, and creepy gazes my way ever since we'd gotten into a dangerous situation last winter. I hoped she got over it soon.

"How are things going with Jason, by the way?" she asked.

My face heated. It hadn't taken long for her to cycle back from procreation to my boyfriend. "I'm not talking about my love life with you."

"I don't see why not," she said. "It's a perfectly innocent question. Now, he doesn't have any children from his prior marriage, does he?"

"Mom!" This was getting way too personal, and no, he didn't.

"What?"

I drew a deep breath and crossed my ink-stained fingers. "I'm not investigating. I'm just keeping my ear to the ground, like anyone would. I know I'm no private detective."

"You *could* be a detective, don't get me wrong. You're quite clever. I'd just prefer you to stay alive. Jason too, of course, but that's different. He's a professional, and he's armed."

I almost asked her about any gossip she'd heard on the gang at Reign, but then I remembered I wasn't investigating. "Well, I'm okay. Thanks for calling."

"Have you spoken with Harper lately?"

"Harper?" I asked, surprised. "We met for girls' night on Friday. Why?"

"Oh, no reason. Just curious. Let me know about that dinner with Jason. Bye!"

"Bye." Perplexed and a little deflated, I stared at the phone. My mother usually had her finger on the pulse of all the local gossip. Too bad I couldn't pick her brain without admitting I was investigating. What I needed was an alternate source.

I escaped to my laptop and the wide, wonderful world of social media. Lola Emerson-Malke was plastered all over the Internet. She had social accounts on every platform I knew about, and probably some I didn't.

She'd posted photos of the vigil—pre-riot—and I scanned them for clues. There were lots of artful shots of candlelit faces and close-ups of somber mourners, but none of Orson.

My mouth twisted. Leaving her husband out of the shots seemed kind of weird. If she was keeping up the social media for business purposes, Orson, as the last surviving chocolate maker, should be featured.

I scanned through several vigil pics of India, her expression bleak. If India was faking her mourning, she was a damned good actress.

Something rapped the kitchen window, and I looked up, startled. A small brown bird pecked the glass, cocked its head, and flew off. Lost in thought, I stared past the blue curtains.

I shook it off and checked the social media accounts of my other suspects. Reign Chocolate's accounts hadn't been updated since Atticus's death, and there were no clues as to his murder on the site that I could find.

For the heck of it, I checked up on my friends. Adele's accounts were filled with the usual tea and scone recipes and tasteful photos of tea sets and flowers.

Harper ... My brows lifted. Harper had gotten active lately on social media, posting pictures of clients and charity work she was involved in. I whistled. She was involved in a lot of charity work. Good for her. She'd been private in the past, for fear that her interest in Italian witchcraft would be discovered. I was a little surprised to see her stepping out online now. I bit the inside of my cheek. Had I imagined a change in her? If something was up, she'd tell me. Right?

I should post more about the museum. Maybe I should get myself online more? After all, it was only an online persona. It wasn't real.

I looked out the kitchen window again. The fog had cleared, and blue sky framed my aunt's two-story house next door. Vineyards and orchards stretched as far as the eye can see, which was pretty far. San Benedetto was so flat, you could watch your dog run away for a week.

Good thing I owned a cat then, though GD would take issue at being labeled a possession. In his opinion, I was staff.

I sighed. Enough messing around online. It wasn't getting me anywhere, and it was high time I got out of my apartment. I really needed to visit to Penny at the Wine and Visitors Bureau and find out if she had any intel on the chocolate company.

Grabbing my purse and a lightweight blue jacket, I walked downstairs to my truck and drove into town.

The Wine and Visitors Bureau was in a gabled building on the outskirts of downtown. Vines, just starting to bud, climbed its brick walls. I parked in the lot beside the educational vineyard.

Like my museum, the Visitors Bureau was closed Mondays. But I knew Penny would be in her office. I walked to the side door and gave it an experimental tug. It creaked open, and Penny plowed into me.

"Ooof!"

We bounced off each other.

"Sorry," we said in unison.

She touched her curly gray hair and brushed the ample frontage of her black cardigan. It was embroidered with tiny bunches of grapes and wine bottles. "Hello, Maddie. I hear your chocolate exhibit is not to be missed. Something about a fortune-teller?"

"I'm glad to know you heard about it." I rubbed the back of my neck. "She'll be at the museum every weekend this month."

Penny's brow furrowed. "Weekends are my busiest time, but I wonder if I can escape for a chocolate reading? And speaking of escapes, no offense, but I'm in something of a hurry." Her gaze traveled from my head to my toes, taking in my neat white blouse, jeans, and open-toed black shoes. "Unless you want to be my plus-one and come to lunch with me? I really don't enjoy these things. I'm just not the networking type."

"What things?"

"Lola Emerson-Malke is having a tea at her house. If she had any public spirit, she would have held it at the Fox and Fennel." She sniffed. "Unless Adele is catering it at Lola's and I hadn't heard?"

"I don't think so." Surely Adele would have mentioned that.

"Too bad. So, would you like to be my plus-one?"

My cheese sandwich hadn't exactly been filling... "Sure. I'd love to come."

"I'll drive."

We piled into her Honda. Cardboard boxes jammed the rear seat, forcing my passenger seat forward. I hunched, uncomfortable, my knees scraping the glove compartment.

We roared onto the road, and I hastily buckled my seat belt.

"Sorry about the boxes," Penny said. "I hope you can fit all right." She zipped out to pass an asparagus truck and I smothered a yelp.

A yellow VW bug roared toward us. Horn bleating, Penny swerved back into our lane.

I caught a glimpse of the VW's driver, Herb, shaking his fist as we flashed past.

"I'm glad you stopped by the Visitors Bureau," she said.

I gulped. "Oh?"

Her hands clenched the wheel. "It's this murder. It brings back such terrible memories."

Of a body Penny had discovered. I bit my bottom lip. I'd been there when she'd found that body. It hadn't been a good day.

Her voice quavered. "Perhaps I'm being silly in my old age. San Benedetto always seemed like such a safe and quiet place. Now... I'm not so sure. This has to stop, Maddie."

Guilt twisted inside me. But I wasn't responsible for what had happened at Reign. So why was my heart pounding, sweat beading my hairline? Was it remorse, or fear of becoming road kill?

"You heard I discovered Atticus's body?" I asked.

"I had not heard that. Does your mother know you're looking into this?"

"Who says I am?"

Penny shot me a look. "Because you're always in the thick of it, aren't you?"

I slumped in my seat. "I'd rather she didn't know. She'll just worry."

"You can't blame her for that."

"No." I sighed. "I guess I can't."

"But I confess, I'm glad you're taking an interest. You were so decisive when …" She swallowed.

When she'd found that body. I'd felt more panicked than decisive that day, but I was glad she thought so.

Penny cleared her throat. "Of course, we have a wonderful police force."

"Of course," I said quickly.

"But there's nothing like small town gossip, is there? So let's see if I can clear anything up." She tapped her chin with one pudgy finger. "Some people think our new chocolatiers are a little too chic for San Benedetto, but I'm thrilled they're here. As much as I love our, shall we say, natural farm atmosphere, we can use a little modernization."

"I've heard the grumbles too," I admitted. "Mainly about how expensive their chocolate is. But I don't think it makes a motive for murder."

"Certainly not!" The Honda drifted left and Penny bumped along the yellow median. "But those chocolate makers …" She crimped her lips together.

My hand tightened on the car's grab bar. "What about them?" I squeaked.

"Oh, it's probably nothing."

"Penny…"

"I did hear they were tardy with some of their payments to one of the farmers," she said rapidly. "He's a bit of a crank, though. Frankly, I'm only surprised he didn't demand payment up front."

I studied her profile. Why did I get the feeling that this wasn't what she'd initially been about to say? "Which farmer?" I asked.

"Oh, I can't remember. Not a vintner."

"You remembered he was a crank."

She turned down a long driveway. "He's eighty-five. Trust me, he's no killer."

"Maybe not, but you should tell the police."

"Hmph."

Trellised grapevines lined the yard in front of a two-story Victorian. The house gleamed white, its red-tile roof a counterpoint to the cloudless sky. A timber-frame extension with a vaulted ceiling and lots of windows had been added to the front of the house. The extension's double doors were thrown open to reveal a dining area. Women mingled inside, and also in the small vineyard.

Penny parked behind a row of cars, and we crunched down the gravel path to the gathering.

Lola, in black leggings, knee-high suede boots, and a loose camel-colored turtleneck, emerged from the dining area. She snapped a picture of a trio of women with her phone, then glanced toward us and waved. "Penny, hello!"

"Hello, Lola. Maddie is my plus-one," Penny replied, motioning to me. "She runs the Paranormal Museum."

"Of course, we know each other." Lola smiled warmly. "I'm glad you came. I should have thought to invite you, since you're an associate member of the Visitors Bureau, like us. Here." She squeezed between Penny and me and snapped a selfie. She glanced at the screen. "Cute!"

"I'm very sorry for your loss," Penny said stiffly. "What happened at the vigil was inexcusable."

"Ah." Lola released us. "I guess this event seems a little disrespectful, all things considered. But Atticus and I had planned this networking tea for weeks."

"You and Atticus?" I asked.

"I helped him with marketing," she said. "Well, I have to support Orson any way I can. So it didn't seem right to cancel today's event. And since we're going forward..." She brandished her phone. "What's the point of having an event if you don't post photos, right?"

"That's an extension, isn't it?" I nodded toward the dining area jutting from the front of the Victorian.

"It is." Lola beamed. "We wanted more space, especially for the kitchen and dining room, but we wanted to keep the Victorian feel. The renovation was featured in *California Dwellings*."

"How did your interview go with *Feast California*?" I asked.

She sighed. "It was fun, in spite of the circumstances. They brought a photographer, and I think we may go on the cover." She leaned closer. "That's another reason I planned this tea for today. We had to rake the gravel before the magazine photo shoot, and I thought I'd take advantage of how nice everything looks."

Penny edged toward the open doors to the dining area and the rough wooden dining table inside.

"Do the police have any idea who set off the firecrackers?" I asked Lola in a low voice.

"None. Or if they do, they're not telling me." Lola's expression darkened. "I told them who to look at, but I don't think they believed me."

My breath hitched. "You know who was responsible?"

Lola glanced around at the milling women. None were close enough to overhear. "You probably noticed the other day how oddly Tilde was behaving."

"You think Tilde set off the firecrackers?"

"She walked away from the gazebo right before the firecrackers went off. I was taking pictures." She scanned through her photos. "Look." She handed me the phone. On its screen was a blurry shot of Tilde, walking past the picnic table with its sound equipment.

"Would you email me that?" I asked. That photo was going straight to Jason.

"Sure. What's your addy?"

I gave her the museum's address, and she typed it in with her thumbs.

"But why would Tilde disrupt the vigil?" I asked.

"She was practically stalking Atticus," Lola said, not looking up from her phone. "Tilde's horribly jealous of whatever her cousin India has—including her husband."

Now that was interesting. Could Atticus's murder have been a crime of passion? "Can I use your bathroom?" I asked.

"Of course." She gave me directions to the downstairs bath.

Careful to wipe my feet on the mat, I walked inside the Victorian. Lola and Orson must have knocked out some of the interior walls too, because the living room was open and spacious. I found the guest bathroom easily, beside the stairs.

No one was around, the soft chatter coming from the dining area now hidden around a corner. Lola and Orson were suspects. I might not get this chance again. Heart pounding, I tiptoed up the stairs to a long hallway and tried a door.

Locked.

Rats. My gaze darted up and down the hallway.

I wasn't sure what I was looking for, but I tried another door. It opened onto the master bedroom. White walls. A gray carpet. Antique furniture painted in pinks, deep blues, and grays.

A door stood open in the opposite wall. It was probably the master bath and not the office I'd hoped for, but I tiptoed toward it anyway, glancing at the bureau as I passed. I didn't see any incriminating evidence.

A board creaked in the hallway.

I froze, breath stopped in my chest.

I stood like that, taking shallow, quiet breaths for I don't know how long. But I must have imagined the noise. It didn't repeat itself, and no one strode inside shouting *j'accuse!*

The door did indeed lead to a bathroom, and I paused in the entry. There was a fireplace besides the giant claw-foot bathtub. Stifling a sigh of envy, I went to the mirrored medicine cabinets and opened them. They were filled with expensive-looking indigo bottles of organic tinctures and lotions. I plucked an orange plastic pill bottle from a shelf. Lola had a prescription for Valium.

Ugh. Now I felt like the worst kind of snoop.

Pulse racing, I returned downstairs without being spotted and rejoined the garden party.

"Find it all right?" Lola asked.

"Maddie?" My mother stood before us, the sunlight glinting off the silver threads in her hair. She wore crisp white slacks and a blue denim shirt tucked beneath a belt studded with turquoise. Her jaw hung open. It snapped shut.

I flinched.

"How unexpected," my mother said in a strangled voice. "I was hoping to talk to you, dear. Hello, Lola. Would you excuse us for a moment?" She grasped my elbow and steered me toward a peach tree. "What are you doing here?" she hissed, her blue eyes snapping with annoyance.

My spine stiffened. "Penny invited me."

"I'll just bet she did." My mother's face pinched. "You have no business investigating that man's murder."

"We were just talking—"

"You were interrogating."

"Actually, Lola was doing most of the talking."

She angled her head, her squash-blossom earrings dancing. "You said you wouldn't."

"I said I *wasn't*." And I hadn't been, at the time. "Honestly, we were just talking."

"There's no *just talking* with you when murder's involved."

"Lola told me that Tilde, India's cousin, was obsessed with Atticus. Do you think it could be true?"

My mother's eyes narrowed. "Don't even try to make me an accessory to whatever it is you're doing."

"Hi, Fran." Penny, holding a plate full of finger sandwiches, waddled up to us. "What's new at Ladies Aid?"

My mother rattled off their latest list of fundraisers. "Can I count on you?" she asked Penny, but she stared hard at me.

"All excellent causes," Penny said. "Of course I'm in. Maddie? What about you?"

"I'm in too," I said, my stomach sinking. If I knew my mother, I was in up to my neck. I edged away. "Well, I'll see you later."

"Oh, no, Maddie." My mother's smile didn't touch her eyes. "I'm not done with you yet."

ELEVEN

I sat behind the museum counter and checked our online sales. Outside, the street lamps flickered on in anticipation of the coming darkness. Twilight had fallen, the sky turning the color of a bruise. After my mom's chewing out, I felt a little bruised. The woman was giving me mental whiplash.

When I'd first started sticking my nose into other people's murders, she'd warned me off. Then she'd gone all in, urging me on. Now she was warning me off again? I wished she would make up her mind.

I examined a fresh bandage around my thumb—a casualty of packaging ghost-hunting equipment for shipment. Cardboard paper cuts were the worst. Maybe starting up a subscription box service *wasn't* the best idea. It would mean more packing and mailing.

GD hopped onto the glass counter. He stretched gracefully across it, his ebony tail lashing the keyboard.

"The joke's on you," I said. "I'm not using the computer."

I was still wrestling with the need to make more money. Lola had a gorgeous house. I had a rented garage apartment. Harper was making money hand over fist as a financial advisor. And Adele's tea room had to be more profitable than my museum.

GD lightly bit my hand.

I scowled at the cat. "Stop that."

Sure, the museum was over-the-top fun, but I was a grown woman. How was I ever going to retire at this rate? Another idea for bringing in income had occurred to me: maybe I should offer an online class on ghost hunting. I could partner up with the ghost hunters who staked out my museum every month ... Or I could get going on that subscription service, though I didn't really want to. I taped the last of the packages. My problem was I had too many ideas.

Take the murder. Orson could have killed Atticus for the buy-sell insurance. Of course, the insurance money would enable Orson to buy India's share of the business. That half million paid to India, in turn, gave her motive.

My mouth pressed flat. And what was up with the tension between Tilde and Lola? Tilde was India's cousin. If Tilde wanted to keep her job, it didn't pay to give attitude to the owner's wife. And if Orson was going to buy India out, Tilde's nepotism angle would vanish.

And then there was Sam, the employee they'd fired. Revenge was an incentive for murder, and he'd been nearby when Atticus had died and also when those firecrackers had gone off. But I was pretty sure he'd been outside the chocolate shop when I'd heard the door close, and that sound had to have been the killer leaving, right? Which meant Sam hadn't killed Atticus. And he might be willing to share gossip about his ex-employers.

I needed to talk to Sam.

Unfortunately, I didn't know his last name or where to find him. "Maybe he's at the chocolate shop," I told GD.

The cat sneezed.

"It doesn't hurt to look," I said, defensive. Besides, I could use the exercise. I'd eaten a little too well at Lola's lunchtime tea, and my jeans felt snugger than usual.

I locked the cat inside the museum and pocketed the key.

GD stared sullenly through the window, as if peeved I'd abandoned him. It's not as if he enjoyed my company. To GD, I was merely a kibble delivery system.

Someone shrieked behind me.

I whipped around, heart thudding.

A crow shot from a denuded plum tree and into the darkening sky.

I swore, pressing my hand to my thumping heart, and looked up and down the street. A bird. It had only been a bird, and my face heated with embarrassment. At least no one had seen my mini freak-out. The wide street was deserted. The few lit shop windows only served to highlight all the blackened windows up and down the street.

My low heels clacked on the brick sidewalk and I shrugged out of my jacket. The sun was a dying hint upon the horizon, and there was something oppressive about the evening air.

Footsteps pattered behind me. Tensing, I glanced over my shoulder. A woman with a toddler clasped to her chest hurried past.

I blew out my breath. *Calm down.* Nothing bad was going to happen walking down Main Street.

Unless I'd just jinxed myself by thinking that.

Lights flowed from the windows of Reign, and I hurried toward them. Sam wasn't pacing the sidewalk, and I almost felt relieved. But it meant I'd have to track him down some other way.

The chocolate shop was still open. I figured I might as well check out what was happening inside, even if the smell of cocoa now made my stomach queasy.

I pushed open the door and nearly bumped a customer standing in line. I edged inside. Customers milled in front of the polished driftwood displays of chocolate. They lined up at the counters, nibbled from sample trays.

Behind the counter, Tilde and Orson worked two cash registers.

The accountant looked flustered. A brown apron hung askew over her business-like blouse. Strands of dark hair escaped her bun.

Orson's smile seemed harried but genuine beneath his beard. Behind the register, he was beard-net free.

Tilde turned too quickly, bumping into him.

He grinned, steadying her, then turned to chat with a customer.

Scowling, Tilde banged out an order on her cash register and handed a brown bag to a waiting customer.

I grabbed a chocolate bar off the shelf and got in line. They were doing amazing business for a Monday evening. I guessed from Tilde's presence that they hadn't hired new counter help yet. Working the cash register couldn't be a part of her job description, but she was doing it anyway. She might be grumpy, but she was willing to pitch in. It made me like her more.

"Maddie?"

I turned.

Belle stood in line behind me.

"Oh," I said, "hi! Satisfying a chocolate craving?" Belle was tall and slender. I had none of those attributes, and jealousy pinged through me. I needed to either get over my insecurities or get off my duff and lose weight.

"Something like that." She shifted, crossing her arms over her denim blouse. "Even after moving to Sacramento, I still have a few clients here in San Benedetto. The salon lets me rent a chair."

"Great." *Great, great, great.* The salon had to be closed by now. She was obviously in town to spend time with Mason, as usual. Which was normal, given their relationship. Why not admit it?

"Have you seen Mason?" she asked.

I started. "Not today. Why?"

She opened her mouth as if to speak, then closed it. Her pale brow furrowed. "No reason. So how are things with you and the detective?"

"Great. He took me on a date to a chocolate class." I motioned toward the counter.

She blinked. "Before or after the murder?"

"Um. After."

"Tell me he wasn't ..." She lowered her voice. "Detecting on a date."

I grimaced. I'd been the guilty party on that score. "He booked the class six weeks ago. It was just one of those things."

"And you?" Belle asked beneath the murmur of the crowd. "Is your being here now just one of those things?"

"Not entirely," I admitted.

"If you're here to interrogate someone, I don't think you'll have much luck. They look way too busy to talk."

Tilde passed a paper bag over the wooden counter to a customer, and the line edged forward.

"I'm sure you're right," I said. "But here I am. I don't suppose you've heard any murder gossip at the salon?"

"Do you really think all hair stylists gossip with their customers?" she asked shortly.

"No, I—uh—" Why was I always sticking my foot in my mouth around Mason's girlfriend?

"Well, they don't. Just me." Belle broke into a grin. "I did hear that Tilde has a shoe habit, if it matters."

My shoulders relaxed. "Shoes?"

"Manolo Blahnik, Miu Miu, Louboutin, Jimmy Choo … I guess you haven't been looking at her feet."

We edged closer to the counter.

"No," I said. "And I figured you for more of a hair person."

"Hair's a professional interest. Shoes are for fun." She hitched up the hem of her jeans to display a sequined pump. "I can only dream of the shoes she wears."

We moved forward in line.

"I did notice she was wearing those pumps with the red soles." I wasn't a total fashion ignoramus, even if I did tend to wear Paranormal Museum T-shirts a lot. But that was advertising.

Belle sighed. "Christian Louboutin. Elegant and sexy all at the same time."

"How expensive are those heels?"

"It depends on the style. Six hundred, two thousand, more?"

Two thousand dollars for a pair of shoes? I lowered my head, studying Tilde behind the register. How could a self-employed accountant afford that? Maybe I *had* gone into the wrong business.

The person at the counter took their bag and left.

Excusing myself to Belle, I stepped up to Tilde's register and handed her the chocolate bar. "Hi, Tilde. Nice to see you again."

"That will be eight dollars."

I bit back a grimace and fumbled with my wallet.

"Things have gotten busy at Reign." I thumbed through my bills in search of something larger than a one.

Her brows slashed downward. "Ghouls. It must be true that no publicity is bad publicity, because since Atticus's murder made the national news—"

"National?" I blurted.

"He's a name." Tilde said the last word as if it tasted bitter on her tongue. "Lola probably sent out a press release."

"Tilde!" Orson bustled over to us. "Are you doing okay here?" He shot me a glance.

"Fine," she said.

"Because we're a little short-staffed tonight," he said.

"No luck on finding a new counter person?" I asked.

"Actually," he said, "thanks to your mother, we did find someone. But she can't start until tomorrow. Are you just getting the chocolate bar?" He snatched it up and walked to his register. "Eight dollars."

I handed him the bills. "Have the police—"

"No. And I really can't talk about it now."

My face warmed. Belle was right. This was a terrible environment for an interrogation.

I bought the bar. Looking for Belle, I hustled from the shop. When we weren't being stiff with each other, she was fun to talk to. Maybe I could invite her to lunch, or at least exchange numbers.

But I didn't see her on the sidewalk, and I felt ... relieved.

TWELVE

"Hola!" Twisting the cord around my finger, I pressed the wall phone's receiver tighter to my ear. "*Me llamo... Habla inglés?*"

"A traditional Japanese wedding, can you believe it?" Adele paced, her pink heels silent on the museum's checkerboard tiles, an elegant white mug in her hand. Beneath her Fox and Fennel apron, she wore a slim pink pencil skirt and white blouse.

Oblivious to GD's glares from the haunted rocking chair, Pug whuffed in his bed beside the counter. Adele hadn't wanted to leave him at home, but she couldn't bring a sick dog into her tea room. The museum was now the designated kennel.

A man's voice crackled over the phone line. "Yes, yes! How can I help you?"

I relaxed. Jason had come through with the name of the shop owner at the right chocolate shop in Oaxaca. I'd been planning to spend my day on this, since the museum was closed on Tuesdays, but Adele had other ideas.

"Have you seen the hats they wear?" Adele picked up the bronze skull and set it back on its pedestal. "Can you imagine wearing one of those in the June heat?"

"Hi, I'm Maddie Kosloski from the San Benedetto ..." I hesitated. If I said I was from a paranormal museum, the man might think I was a crackpot. "San Benedetto. I'm trying to reach Mr. Moreno."

GD dropped from the chair and stalked toward the pug.

"Yes, this is Pablo Moreno."

Adele rubbed a pink lipstick stain from the mug. "My mother says I need to be more accommodating, but she's just afraid of *her* mother. And it's my wedding, isn't it?"

"I recently purchased a haunted molinillo," I said. "The seller told me she bought it at your shop, and I wondered if I could ask you a few questions about it?"

"The Santa Muerte molinillo?" he asked.

"Santa ... Saint Death?" My voice cracked on the final word.

GD leapt onto the counter, his ears pricked with interest. For the cat, murder apparently took precedence over dogs. Pug, expression plaintive, looked up at him.

"What does Santa Muerte have to do with the molinillo?" I asked.

"The woman who owned it was a devotee of the Saint."

Great. A devotee to Saint Death, whoever that was. But you never knew. Saint Death could be totally innocent and have absolutely nothing to do with necromancy. Nothing at all. "I don't know much about Santa Muerte," I said cautiously. "What does being a devotee to her mean?"

"In that lady's case, it means she was in trouble and needed the Saint's protection. But the Saint could not help her. She died of a broken heart."

Romantic, but vague. "I'm sorry to hear of her passing. Was the lady a friend of yours?"

"I knew her sister. She gave me the molinillo after the funeral. She said it was bad luck."

"And those stiff robes," Adele said, brandishing her mug and managing to spill not a drop. "They're totally unflattering to my figure."

"What was her name?" I asked Mr. Moreno. "The owner of the molinillo, I mean. Not her sister."

"Felicitas Ocasio."

I made a note on a yellow notepad. "And the molinillo became haunted after she died?"

"That is what her sister told me." He coughed. "The molinillo was very—how do you say? Annoying."

"It's enough to make anyone crazy," Adele said. "I can't make *everyone* happy."

"Why annoying?" I asked.

"Wouldn't *you* be annoyed?" Adele slammed the mug on the counter.

The cat started, green eyes wide, fur bristling. Pug sneezed.

"I have a busy shop," Mr. Moreno said. "The molinillo would not stop shaking. Customers thought we were having an earthquake."

"So you had it on display?" I frowned at Adele, but she'd turned to the window and was pondering the morning fog.

"I have many molinillos," the chocolate shop owner replied, "but a haunted molinillo was something new, and it is an antique. Special. I thought displaying it would be charming. But when that American woman asked to buy it, I was glad to see it go. I do not believe in ghosts, you understand, but that molinillo is haunted."

I smiled, wry, at the echo of Susan's words. She hadn't believed in ghosts either, and yet... "Is there anything else you can tell me about Felicitas? Was she a professional chocolate maker?"

He barked a laugh. "Her? No. She used the molinillo like everyone does, for making our famous chocolate drink. She was young. She was beautiful. And she loved the wrong man."

"Why wrong?"

"Because he broke her heart," he repeated.

"When you say she died of a broken heart, do you mean—?"

"A broken heart," he said firmly. "And that is all."

I winced, feeling rebuked. "Is there anything else you can tell me about the molinillo?"

"It shakes when someone lies. But I think you already know this."

"So, if this story of the haunted molinillo is true—"

"It is."

"Maybe I can include fake cherry blossom bouquets." Adele adjusted the *Closed* sign in the window. "Maybe that will satisfy her."

"Then how does the lying fit into it?" I stuffed my finger in one ear. "Did Felicitas's boyfriend lie to her?"

He sighed. "He lied to everyone. I am sorry, I must go. I have a customer."

"Thank you, Mr. Moreno. You've been a big help."

But he'd already hung up.

Thoughtful, I set the old phone on its wall receiver.

At least I had a name. What had really happened between Felicitas and her boyfriend?

GD sniffed the dangling cord, his whiskers twitching, then got bored and hopped to the ground, landing beside Pug in his dog bed.

Pug got to his feet. GD shoved him aside with a well-placed bodyslam and dropped to a lounging position. The dog whuffed and snuggled in beside him.

I didn't think I could bring myself to track down her sister and ask. Most of my exhibits were connected to people decades dead. But the people who'd known Felicitas were still alive. Her tragedy was recent, and must still be painful for those involved.

I glanced at the notepad on the counter and sighed. Sometimes I wondered if taking over this museum had set cosmic forces in motion. Was Herb right? Was it more than coincidence that I was involved in *two* chocolate-themed cases—murder and molinillo.

"So," I said to Adele, "what are you going to do?"

Adele turned from the window. "I love my grandmother, but I can't turn my wedding plans upside down for her. Can I?" Her expression turned pleading. "She's threatened to curse me."

"Cursing?" I blinked. "Is that a Japanese thing?"

"Don't stereotype. People throw curses around all over the world. It's universal. You own a paranormal museum! You should know this."

"Okay, okay." I raised my hands in a defensive gesture. "Sorry."

"No." Adele blew out her breath. "*I'm* sorry. It's all gotten so complicated. Dieter just wants to have a fun party, but this is our wedding!" She bit her lip. "I love Dieter, but we're so different."

"Different in important ways?" I asked, knowing the answer.

"No. We agree on money and family and the critical things. And when I'm with him, it's as if … I'm lighter."

I nodded. Adele and Dieter might have had a whirlwind romance, but they'd known each other forever, and Adele was level-headed.

This wasn't a post-honeymoon-phase complication. It was pre-wedding stress.

And I wasn't going to be blindsided by a romantic complication with Jason once the scales of desire fell from my eyes. I wasn't sure where things were going with us, but I didn't expect any unpleasant surprises. Jason was an open book. My stomach squirmed. At least, I hoped he was.

"I've known him for so long—I *know* him," Adele said. "He's a good man. I love him."

"And wedding planning is stressful."

"Sometimes I feel like I'm having an out-of-body experience. Some days everything is awful. I look at myself and wonder, how did this happen? And then other days ... When Dieter and I came together, it was all so easy. How did I get so lucky with him?"

"Because you and Dieter deserve to be happy."

"And I was so caught up in my problems," Adele said, "I wasn't even listening to your advice. What do you think about the Japanese wedding?"

Oh, jeez. Did I have advice? I fumbled. "I think that everyone involved in your wedding is coming from a place of love."

Adele stared at me. "That's ... exactly right. How did you ...?"

"I might have read it in a magazine," I admitted.

She laughed. "All right. You've listened to my rant. You've even taken in my poor dog." She bent to ruffle his tawny fur and pulled a bone-shaped treat from her pocket.

Pug eagerly gobbled it down. The cat sniffed and stalked into the Fortune Telling Room. He and Pug generally got along, so I wasn't worried about keeping an eye on them. But GD did not like watching others eat if he wasn't getting a piece of the action.

"Now what's bothering you?" Adele asked.

"Aside from my molinillo research?" I motioned to the yellow pad on the counter. "Nothing."

"Don't lie to me, Maddie. I saw the look on your face a few minutes ago."

I peered at the computer, open to an invoice. Why was I hiding my relationship worries from Adele? She knew the worst of me, and she was one of my best friends. "I was just wondering—"

Someone rapped on the door. Mason's broad frame filled its window.

Adele looked a question at me, and I nodded.

She unlocked and opened the door. "Hi, Mason. How are things?"

"Hi, Adele, Maddie." A blue T-shirt stretched across his chest. His thick blond hair was tied back in its usual ponytail.

I swayed on my tall chair, and hopped off before I fell off. "What brings you to the museum?"

"Um … Wine and Chocolate Days." He jammed his fingers in the front pockets of his faded jeans.

A semi drove past, rattling the objects on their shelves.

Adele quirked a brow. "Don't tell me you're thinking of getting involved this late in the game. Besides, I wouldn't think motorcycles would have much to do with wine or chocolate."

"Yeah," he said. "They don't. That's the problem. And I don't have Maddie's creative brain."

"Chocolate wrapped in foil to match the chrome?" I suggested. "Chocolate shaped like motorcycles? I dunno. Search the Internet for motorcycles and chocolate. Maybe you'll find something." That advice was even less helpful than what I'd given Adele.

He glanced at Adele. "Thanks. That's exactly what I was looking for."

Something rattled in the Gallery, and I looked out the window. Herb's VW Bug drifted past outside.

A chill rippled up my spine. I leaned across the counter and peered into the Gallery. Still and silent, the molinillo sat angled in its ceramic bowl.

"Something wrong?" Mason asked.

"No," I said, uneasy. "I'm fine."

In the Gallery, the molinillo rattled.

THIRTEEN

Wednesday dawned rainy and cold, customers trailing muddy footprints across the museum's black-and-white floors. The heater steamed the windows, fog muffling the museum in a sullen gray blanket.

But at least we had customers—more than usual for a Wednesday thanks to Wine and Chocolate Days. Guests studied the framed photos of murderers on the glossy white walls. Milled between shelves lined with haunted objects. Wandered in and out of the Fortune Telling Room. Told silly lies over the molinillo in the Gallery and laughed, sharing nervous glances.

Leo had left for his statistics class, and I sat alone behind the counter. I handed a middle-aged couple their tickets and brochure, and they wandered into the Gallery.

Shifting on my tall chair, I half-heartedly studied a web page on how to start a subscription box business. I bit my bottom lip. Did I have the bandwidth to stuff boxes every month? And why had my mom asked the other day whether I'd spoken with Harper? The latter was a small mystery and easily solved. All I had to do was call Harper and find out what was going on.

As if summoned by my thoughts, Harper strolled into the museum. The collar of her long cinnamon-colored coat was turned up against the chill. She tugged her dark hair free from the thick matching scarf wrapped around her neck. "Is Adele here?"

"No. She's probably in the tea room."

Harper's shoulders relaxed. "Thank God."

"Uh oh. What's happened?"

"You know that wedding checklist of hers?"

I groaned. "How could I forget? Did you know she made me her social media manager?"

Harper burst into laughter. "Oh boy. Hold on." She walked behind the counter and nudged me away from my computer. She opened an Internet site. "You need to read this."

Q: *Who should I assign to manage social media coverage during the wedding so I don't have to?*

A: *Taking candid snapshots is a great job for that awkward friend, who'll either end up a wallflower or fall into the wedding cake if they're not kept busy.*

I sputtered. "That's—I am not awkward!"

Harper raised her hands, palms out. "Hey, don't shoot the messenger."

"There's got to be another reason she asked me to take charge of her social media." I blew out a breath. Adele's wedding wasn't about me. I needed to get a grip. "So, what's on your mind?"

"I was supposed to send out the event schedule to the vendors, so they'll have time to give us feedback."

"You didn't forget!?"

"No." She glanced at the bookcase, toward the tea room hidden behind it. "But I couldn't get in touch with the baker, the woman who was supposed to make the wedding cake."

My scalp prickled. "*Supposed* to?"

"So, I drove to Sacramento yesterday, where the bakery's located."

"And?"

"It's out of business," Harper whispered.

My stomach lurched. "Okay. Okay. Let's not panic. We have three months until the wedding. This isn't a disaster."

"Only two and a half months." She clawed a hand through her hair. "Don't you remember Adele complaining? All the good bakeries need five or six months lead time."

I swallowed, bracing my elbows on the counter. "Adele must have had a runner-up on her bakery selection. I'm sure if she explains the emergency, she'll be able to find someone to make the wedding cake."

"I know it will all work out in the end," Harper said. "But how are we going to keep her from having a major freakout now?"

The bookcase slid open and Adele strolled into the museum. "You wouldn't believe the caterer. I felt like I was on a bad date. He almost laughed at my budget, and acted like my request for a vegan, gluten-free alternative was crazy! But the good news is, I think Pug's getting better. He was coughing much less last night."

Harper and I glanced at each other.

"What's wrong?" Adele braced her hands on her hips, rumpling her Fox and Fennel apron.

Harper shot me a helpless look.

Tell her, I mouthed. Best to get this over with.

Harper bit her bottom lip. "Um, you know that baker in Sacramento you chose for your wedding cake?"

"How could I forget?" Adele said. "They were the only cake samples Dieter really loved. And her designs are gorgeous. Why?"

"I went there this morning," Harper said, "to deliver the event schedule."

"Is there a problem? That's why I wanted the vendors to see the schedule now, so we could work any issues out in advance."

"The bakery's out of business," Harper blurted.

Adele blanched. "What?"

"They're gone," she said. "The building's vacant."

"But ..." Her arms dropped to her sides. "They can't be out of business. Maybe they moved," she said, voice reedy.

"I talked to one of her neighbors," Harper said in a rush, "and he told me that they'd gone out of business and sold their equipment. I checked their website, and it still says they're at their old address. There's nothing online about, well, anything. The phone number's not working. I guess it's been disconnected. And no one responds to my emails."

The wall phone rang, and I jerked on my tall chair. "Sorry," I muttered. "I should ..." I lunged for the receiver. "Hello, this is Maddie at the Paranormal Museum."

No one answered.

"But I gave her a deposit," Adele whispered.

"Hello?" I asked again, impatient.

Adele, pale and wide-eyed, stared at Harper. Harper knitted her lip.

I didn't know whether to drop the phone and hug them or duck beneath the counter.

"There's a bomb," a mechanical voice rasped.

"Fantastic," I said, and blinked, an icicle piercing my core. "Wait. What?"

The voice was electronic, as if run through one of those voice changing machines. "There's a bomb in your museum."

My mind blanked, unwilling to process the information. But my body got the message, and a cool shiver stiffened my spine. "Who is—"

A dial tone buzzed.

Breathless, I took two tries to hang up the phone. It had to be a crank call. But was it possible? I scanned the museum, the customers milling about.

"What's wrong?" Harper asked.

People had been in and out all day. Someone could have tucked a bomb anywhere. "You need to get out," I blurted. "Now!"

Adele blinked. "Well, that's not very nice. Just because my wedding is blowing up in my face—"

"That was a bomb threat." I hurried around the counter. "Harper, call the police. But make the call outside. Adele, you might want to—"

But she was already moving toward the hidden door. She slipped into the tea room and pushed the bookcase shut.

Harper hurried outside, her cell phone pressed to one ear.

"Excuse me," I said loudly.

On the haunted rocking chair, GD pricked up his ears.

Guests turned and stared.

"There's been a bomb threat," I said, in what I hoped was a calm and commanding voice. "So, everyone please make your way outside and away from the building."

A cluster of guests turned to each other, consternation on their faces. I hustled past them and into the Fortune Telling Room. Half a dozen people were examining the aged tarot decks, the spirit cabinet, and the vintage spirit table with its crystal ball.

"Hi," I said. "I'm sorry, but there's been a bomb threat. Please walk outside and away from the building."

I rushed back into the main room, where the same guests were still standing around like bumps on logs, waiting to see what would happen next. My neck stiffened. "I'm not kidding, it's a real bomb threat. The police are on their way." I hoped the last bit was true. But they'd take Harper seriously. They had to.

Through the window, I could see people milling on the sidewalk outside. I guessed they were from the Fox and Fennel, because no one was budging from the museum.

I trotted into the Gallery. Four people examined the chocolate bars on the black shelves. I clawed my hair. "Excuse me…"

A portly, middle-aged woman brandished a bar of Reign chocolate from Peru. "I'd like to buy this, please."

I struggled for patience. "I'm sorry, but there's been a bomb threat at the museum. Everyone needs to go outside and move away from the building as quickly as possible."

"But what about the chocolate?" she asked.

"Your ticket is good all day," I ground out. "I'd love it if you came back, and you can buy it then."

A cell phone rang in someone's pocket, and I started.

"I can't come back if the museum's been exploded," she said.

"It's probably just a prank," I said, my voice taut. "But for safety's sake, we all need to move outside."

A woman poked her head inside the Gallery. "I'd like to buy a deck of those chocolate tarot cards."

Seriously? Bomb threat! Odds were it was a fake, but it wasn't the sort of risk worth taking. "Look, if it's a fake threat, then nothing will happen. But if it's real, it's a problem." *Talk about understatement.* "So there's no point to sticking around. We all need to leave.

You can buy the same chocolate bars at Reign, just down the street." I grabbed a box of Tarot cards off the shelf. "And I can sell this to you outside."

"Then why can't you sell me the chocolate outside?" the first woman asked.

My hand clenched on the tarot deck. "Fine. Let's go!"

Adele strode into the Gallery, her heels clacking. "What are you people doing in here? Don't you know there's been a bomb threat?" She clapped her hands. "Out. Everyone out now, please."

The rooms cleared.

"Really, Maddie," my friend scolded as she scooped up GD. "It's probably a hoax, but you need to take these things more seriously. I mean, what were you doing in there? Waiting to see if you got blown up?"

Augh! "I was—forget it." I hustled her out the front door, then returned inside to double check the Fortune Telling Room—empty. I hurried onto the sidewalk. Sirens wailed, growing louder.

"The police are on their way," Harper said, pocketing her phone. "They said to get everyone out and wait across the road."

My reflection wavered in the window of the motorcycle shop next door. "Mason! I've got to tell him about the threat. I'll meet you across the street."

Heart thudding, I darted into the motorcycle shop.

A burly man ran his hand over the polished seat of a sleek bike.

Mason and Belle stood in one corner, tension vibrating through their bodies. She stabbed a finger at his broad chest. Mason hung his head and said something in a low voice.

She shook her head, her loose auburn hair flowing over the shoulders of her motorcycle T-shirt. Her lips pressed into a tight line.

"Mason! Belle!"

They jerked apart, their faces flushing.

"Someone called in a bomb threat to the museum," I said. "The police are on their way. But since you're next door—"

"Got it. We're closed," Mason shouted to his customer. "Bomb threat."

The burly man nodded and shuffled out the door.

Mason grasped both our arms. "Come on. Outside, you two."

"The police said to wait across the street," I said, breathless, as we exited onto the drizzly sidewalk.

Laurel's blue muscle car screeched to a halt beside us. A squad car parked behind hers. As Mason and Belle crossed the road, I felt my muscles release. At least they were safe.

The detective stepped from the sports car and motioned to the two cops emerging from their black-and-white. "You two, set up barricades. You know the drill." She glared at me. "If your cat's in there, it's on its own." She looked as if she enjoyed the idea.

"He's across the street," I said, wiping the damp from my forehead. "With Adele." GD's relationship with Detective Laurel Hammer was as fraught as my own. The detective detested us both.

Laurel shot a startled look at the opposite sidewalk, her hand drifting to her holster. Her mouth compressed and she relaxed her arm. "What happened?" she asked.

"Someone called the museum and said there was a bomb inside," I said.

"Did you recognize the voice?" She stared, lips curling, at the museum.

Across the road, Adele's waitresses poured tea into white cups for the crowd huddled beneath shop awnings.

"No," I said. "They used one of those mechanical synthesizer things."

The detective snorted. "They have apps to change voices nowadays. Yeow!" She rocketed into the air and pointed at a nearby plum tree. "You said that cat was across the street."

GD prowled toward us, his head low.

I scooped him up before he could get to Laurel. The cat howled, thrashing in my arms.

"Anyway," I said quickly, "the museum's been cleared, and so have the Fox and Fennel and the motorcycle shop."

She eyed the struggling cat. "Who wants to blow up your museum?"

GD nipped my hand and growled.

"Ow!" I scowled at him. "No one! I mean, I don't know. It's gotta be a hoax, right?"

"Knowing my luck," she mumbled beneath her breath.

"What?"

"Yeah, it's likely a prank. But don't even try to tell me this was random. It's always *your* museum. Arson. Murder. Stampedes. I should have it shut down as a threat to public health."

"It's not—You can't do that, can you?" I hugged GD tighter and he quieted, black ears flicking.

She stepped closer, looked at GD, and retreated a step. "Do you know what happens to bars with customers that always cause trouble?"

Gulp. "No."

From the corner of my eye, I watched cops herd passing pedestrians to the other side of the road. Why were Laurel and I still standing dangerously close to a museum that might explode?

"Have you heard of nuisance laws, Kosloski?"

"We're not a nuisance," I said, shrill. "It's not my fault. I didn't ask for this."

GD meowed an agreement.

A blue Prius swerved into a parking spot on the street. Mike, a wiry young reporter from the *San Benedetto Times*, leapt from the car. He snapped a picture of Laurel and me with his cell phone. "What's going on? Bomb threat?" His Adam's apple bobbed above his thin blue tie.

The detective's steely eyes narrowed. She turned to me. "You called the press? What is this, a publicity stunt?"

I edged sideways. "I didn't call the press. Tell her, Mike."

"Nah," he said, "it was an anonymous tip. The person used one of those voice-changing apps."

Laurel glared at me. "What's that saying of yours? No publicity is bad publicity?"

"It's not my saying." Anxious, my gaze flicked to the brick museum. "I didn't invent it. Look, this is a real bomb threat."

The detective's nostrils flared. "That horror show of yours is a menace to life and limb."

"It's not," I said weakly.

The bomb threat had to be a random prank. Right? My stomach flipped. Or had someone targeted me, my customers, my friends?

FOURTEEN

So, there was no bomb.

But the museum was shut down for the rest of the day while the police and fire departments poked around looking for one. The ticket refunds were a dagger to my shriveled heart, though most of the customers seemed cheerful enough about having a bomb-threat story to tell.

The authorities finally let Jason and me inside at closing time.

"Oh, Maddie." Hands on his hips, Jason surveyed the museum. Books and curios lay tumbled from shelves and scattered across the checkerboard floor. "I don't like this." Muscles rippled beneath the shoulders of his navy suit jacket and quickened my pulse.

I tore my gaze from him and swallowed. "Me neither. Couldn't your officers have been a *little* neater?" I picked up the bronze skull, which had rolled beneath the antique rocking chair. My forehead scrunched with annoyance. Bronze skulls aren't cheap! Fortunately, it seemed undamaged.

Imperious, GD perched on the counter, his tail wound around his paws.

"I'm talking about the bomb threat," Jason said.

"I know. It's a lot like what happened in the park, isn't it?"

He stared at me.

"A prank that isn't funny," I explained. "It might have been only firecrackers at the vigil, but the stampede caused real harm." I jammed my hands into the pockets of my hoodie. Today's bomb threat might have had the identical effect if people had panicked. Was the same mind at work? And what did it have to do with Atticus's murder, if anything?

"You think the two incidents are connected," he said slowly.

"Well... maybe." Were they? Having an overactive imagination was both blessing and curse. My imagination was great for marketing the museum. But it also led me down dark rabbit holes of imagined future ruin and an impoverished old age. I pushed my hands deeper into my pockets, stretching the black fabric. Was I imagining a connection between the disaster at the vigil and the bomb threat?

Jason rubbed his chin.

"You think I'm crazy," I said.

"No. No, I don't. But we don't have any evidence the firecrackers at the vigil were anything more than a prank. I can't make a case built on speculation. But I don't know why kids would target your museum. The local kids *like* your museum."

We were a special favorite among Goths and teenage boys. "I don't know why someone would do this either, unless it's also somehow connected to the murder. The timing is suspicious."

His brows lowered. "Why would someone threaten your museum over a chocolate maker's murder?"

"Because I was the one who found the body? Maybe the killer thinks I saw something I shouldn't have?"

"Which you didn't."

"No, of course not." My cheeks seemed to tingle. "I told you everything I saw and heard." I hesitated. "But I do have sort of a reputation for, um, getting involved. And since Atticus's death, I've been, well, seeing more of the suspects than usual."

"Seeing." His gold-flecked eyes narrowed.

Uh oh. "Penny invited me to be her plus-one at Lola's tea on Monday." And I'd forgotten to send him Lola's photo of Tilde at the vigil. My stomach sank.

He grunted. "Don't those sorts of things usually happen on weekends?"

I relaxed a bit. He wasn't going to bust me for interfering, which, let's face it, I just might have deserved. "Not in San Benedetto. Not when most of our business happens on weekends. Monday is a local business owner's only real day off."

"Anything unusual happen at the tea?"

"Not really. Lola told me that Tilde—the accountant—was obsessed with Atticus, who happens to be her cousin-in-law. I think the phrase Lola used was 'practically stalking.' Oh, and my mom wanted to ask if you were free for dinner."

"Hmm. Did India know about her cousin and husband?"

"I'm not sure if there was anything to know. Lola said Tilde was obsessed, not that she and Atticus had an affair. She thought Tilde might have set off the firecrackers. She sent me a picture. Here." I grabbed my cell phone and forwarded him the photo.

His phone pinged. He ignored it. "Lola Emerson-Malke said that?"

"Yes."

"But why tell you? You were snooping, and she knew it, didn't she?"

"It's not like I was searching her closets." I hadn't gotten farther than the master bathroom. "I mean, sure, we were talking about Atticus. I found the man's body. He was her husband's business partner. His death is front of mind."

Jason glanced toward the wreckage in the Gallery. My neat pyramids of chocolate bars and tarot decks lay in untidy heaps.

"What about the molinillo?" he asked. "Were you able to get in touch with that shop owner in Oaxaca?"

And the subject was changed. I felt an instant's squeezing disappointment, then shrugged it off.

"Yes," I said casually, "he was a big help. He told me the original owner was a woman named Felicitas Ocasio. She died of a broken heart over some guy. Her sister inherited the molinillo, but the rattling freaked her out. So she sold it to his chocolate shop."

Jason lounged against a freestanding shelf and propped his chin on his broad hand. "A broken heart? You mean a heart attack?"

"I don't think so. If it had been, he would have told me straight out, wouldn't he?" I frowned. Unless Mr. Moreno's command of English wasn't as good as I'd thought. "When I pressed him, he just repeated himself. I don't think he had a high opinion of Felicitas's boyfriend."

"Interesting. Felicitas Ocasio ..." Jason grinned, and I felt my worries melting. "I've got a friend on the Oaxaca police. We can ask if he knows anything about her death." He shrugged out of his suit jacket and dropped it on the counter beside GD. The cat sniffed its navy sleeve.

"Really?" I asked. "That's fantastic! Thank you!"

"So where do I start?" he asked.

"What?"

He rolled up his sleeves. "With the cleanup. You'll be here all night if you're on your own, and since I don't see Leo anywhere, I'm guessing you are."

"I didn't want to call him in for this. He's studying for an exam."

"Which leaves me. Where do you want me?" He waggled his brows, and I laughed at the double entendre.

I stepped closer and rested my hands on his broad chest. "Right here."

———

Leo sold a ticket to a woman draped in a scarlet caftan and thick scarves. He handed her a brochure and a tarot card. "Your card of the day."

She glanced at it and smiled. "The Star. My lucky card. Thank you."

Ears twitching, GD watched the transaction from his perch on the counter.

"If you have any questions about the exhibits," I said, "just ask." I leaned on my broom. Jason and I had straightened everything up last night, but I'd saved the real cleaning for this morning.

"Thank you." She wafted past me. "But my spirit guides usually tell me all I need to know." The woman vanished into the Fortune Telling Room.

Leo groaned. "A bomb? I miss all the good stuff. Why didn't you call me yesterday?"

The cat meowed an agreement.

"You were in class," I said. "And there's not much you can do for a bomb threat except leave."

"I wasn't in class all day," he grumped.

"Sorry." *Not sorry.* Why would I bring Leo into a potentially dangerous situation? I adjusted a creepy doll on its pedestal and brushed off my hands on the hips of my jeans. "You could help me with a new project."

He cocked his dark head. "Oh?"

The paranormal box-of-the-month service seemed too big for me and Leo, but I had another promotional idea. "What do you think about the museum doing a podcast? You know, we could talk about objects in the museum, weird paranormal stories, take some callers..."

His brown eyes lit. "Are you kidding? Podcasts are hot right now!"

"The thing is, I'm not sure about the technical side—"

"Hey, I got this. We can do it right here in the museum after hours, when it's quiet. I've got equipment we can use."

The bookcase swung inward and Adele backed into the museum. She carried a box of Reign chocolate bars. "Can you do me a favor?"

I tugged at the collar of my T-shirt. I owed her about a million for the Fox and Fennel being shut down yesterday. She'd soothed all my guests with free Earl Grey on the sidewalk and hadn't complained about her own loss of business. "Thanks, Leo. Let's talk more about this later." I turned to Adele. "Sure. What's up?"

She set the box on the glass counter. "My parents think they're going to be short on chocolate, and I've got extra bars. Can you take these to Plot 42?"

"When?"

She winced. "Now? I'd go myself, but—"

"It's fine," I said quickly and took the box. The bomb threat had lost me some business, sure. But at least my guests had bought tickets in advance (and I'd promised the tickets were good for a return visit). Adele had to be out a lot more. How many of her guests had left without having had a chance to pay? Plus, her staff earned hourly wages whether she sold tea or not.

I checked my watch. It was nearing noon. "Leo, do you want me to get you a burrito on the way back?"

"Do you have to ask?" He quirked a brow. "Super beef burrito, hot salsa, refried beans."

"Got it. Adele?"

She backed toward the open bookcase. "No thanks. I prefer to keep my stomach lining."

"I'll be back in an hour," I told Leo and hurried to my vintage pickup.

As much as I loved our fifties-era downtown, my muscles relaxed as I escaped through the adobe arch. Rows of twisted vines fanned past the truck windows, the first hints of green sprouts appearing on the vines. Yellow mustard flowers blazed between the rows. Puddles from yesterday's rain glistened in the sunlight.

Cranking down my window, I inhaled the scent of damp earth. I wouldn't want to be a farmer—the work and hours were too hard. But I loved living around farms, cow smell and all.

I turned down the gravel road to Plot 42 and parked behind the weeping willow.

Grabbing the box off the seat, I slid from my pickup and ambled toward the open barn door. Droplets glistened on the orange and yellow mums along the path.

I passed the chalkboard *Open* sign and walked inside the tasting room. Hanging metal lamps blazed cheerfully from the barn's rafters.

The tasting bar was empty. But it was still early for wine tasting, and only a Thursday.

Voices floated from behind the steel wine barrel racks on my left. Adele, Harper, and I had played in this barn, so I didn't think twice about walking behind the wall of barrels. Then I recognized one of the voices—Orson Malke—and stopped short of the narrow corridor.

"… knows about … affair …" The word sputtered on the damp air.

"This is awful," India said. "Atticus—"

Her words were lost, too low for me to hear.

I edged closer to the wall of barrels. My foot brushed something metal and it clattered on the concrete floor. I winced.

"Hello?" India asked.

Cursing silently, I backed into the tasting room proper. "Is anyone here?" I called. "Chocolate delivery!"

India hurried around the stacked barrels. "Oh, hi Maddie."

"Adele asked me to bring this chocolate." I shifted the box in my arms. "But I thought I heard Orson here?" I angled my head toward the steel barrels. "Was there a miscommunication? Did he already bring you the chocolate you need? Because if he did, I'll return this to the Fox and Fennel."

Orson emerged from behind the wall of barrels. "No miscommunication." He combed his fingers through his beard. "I was here to check on India. I didn't realize there was a chocolate deficit."

India toyed with her braid, her fingers twitching nervously. "You heard us?"

"Ah … not really." I walked to the tasting bar and set the box on top.

When I turned, India and Orson faced me. They formed a barricade, their arms crossed over their chests.

I stepped backward and bumped against the bar.

Beneath India's tank, her muscles were taut as barbed wire. "It's not what you think," she blurted.

"India!" Orson half turned, arm outstretched as if to grab her. "We don't know—"

"Orson and I dated before I met Atticus," India said. "But we all parted amicably. We were all okay. They never stopped being best friends. And then Lola..."

"Found out about the affair?" Wow, I was getting pushy.

India flushed. "There was no affair. Well, I mean—"

"She misspoke," Orson said. "When India and I were first dating, I was dating Lola as well. Lola and I weren't exclusive, but I never told her about India. It wasn't technically an affair, even though it might have felt like one."

"There's no sense telling Lola now." India bit her lip. "Nothing happened between us after we were each married. There's nothing between Orson and me now but friendship."

"And there never will be," Orson said stiffly.

Color me suspicious, but if that were true, why had they been discussing it? "Sorry. It's none of my business."

"You don't believe us," India said, her light brown eyes earnest.

"Look," I said, "this is between you two and Lola. And from what you say, it was no big deal. Besides, I can only imagine what you're both going through right now."

She tugged on her braids. "You have no idea. Someone killed my husband, and all I can think is that they're still out there, watching. It's made me paranoid. I even accused—" She glanced at Orson, and he laid a broad hand on her shoulder.

"It's all right," he said. "Lately I feel like I'm being crushed in a melangeur myself."

"It's not all right. It wasn't fair of me." India shivered. "I must be going crazy. I even feel like I'm being watched sometimes, watched by someone who—" She swallowed.

"You felt like someone was watching you?" I asked. "When was this?" Maybe I hadn't been paranoid about those phantom footsteps after all.

She laughed harshly. "All the time. Crazy, right? And then I kept thinking of what Atticus said before he died."

Orson made a sound in his throat.

"He was worried about the books," she continued, "but of course they're fine. Tilde said they were fine. She does the books, and Atticus was never a financial guy. Oh, he was great at making deals, but when it came to day-to-day budgeting…" She smiled wanly at Orson. "You know how he was."

"But the books worried him?" I asked. "How?"

She gestured with one hand. "I don't know. He never said."

Cousin Tilde did the books. Cousin Tilde was in love with Atticus. Cousin Tilde had conveniently disappeared before the firecrackers went off at the vigil. My insides quivered. Was cousin Tilde a killer?

FIFTEEN

YAWNING, LEO SLOUCHED TOWARD the museum's front door. He shrugged into his black motorcycle jacket. "You sure you don't need me for anything?"

"I'm good here. Thanks for everything today." I slid that day's cash into the zip bag and locked it in the small safe beneath the counter. I was getting excited about the podcast, and Leo had given me some good ideas. We were going to do a test run on Tuesday night.

"Then see ya tomorrow." He sketched a casual wave and vanished onto the darkened sidewalk.

"See you," I called.

The door banged shut. The *Closed* sign slipped sideways in the window.

I adjusted the sign and surveyed my museum.

GD stalked an invisible mouse in the main room. The bronze skull gleamed on its pedestal. Even the creepy dolls looked prim, their singed skirts arranged neatly about their legs.

I'd spent most of the day tidying up, so there wasn't much left to do now. Even better, I'd sold an abundance of chocolate and tarot cards. *Thank you, Wine and Visitors Bureau, for all the tourist promotions.*

The Bakelite wall phone jangled and I nearly jumped out of my shoes. Bomb threats rattling in my skull, I gingerly plucked the receiver from its metal hook. "Hello?"

"Maddie Kosloski?" a woman whispered.

"This is Maddie. How can I help you?"

"It's Tilde, from Reign. Can you come here?"

"To the chocolate shop?" I stilled on the outside, but on the inside, my pulse giddy-upped. "Why? Is something wrong?"

"It's about your invoice," the accountant said. "There was a small problem."

"A problem? Do we owe you more—"

"No, no, nothing like that. Just, please come. As soon as you can." She hung up.

Puzzled, I stared at the receiver, then glanced out the window. The iron street lamps flickered on. No way was I going to that chocolate shop alone.

I hung up and dialed Jason.

"Hello?" His voice was low and rumbly, and heat spread from my chest.

"Hi. It's Maddie. I'm calling from the museum phone."

"Is your cell phone not working?"

"No, it's fine. I was just near this one."

"Can't stay away from me, can you?"

My cheeks warmed. "No, that's ... Well, yes, but that's not why I'm calling."

"Let me guess, the killer tied you up and you just escaped."

"Um, is that sarcasm?" I grinned. I couldn't help myself. "Because if it is, you're not very good at it."

He chuckled. "I'm only giving you a hard time. What's going on?"

"I just got a strange call from Tilde." I wrapped the cord around one finger. "She asked me to come to Reign. Something about an invoice, but she wouldn't explain what. It seemed ... weird."

"I'll meet you there in ten minutes."

"Thanks," I said, grateful I didn't have to explain my fears. We said quick goodbyes and hung up.

I checked GD's food and water, then grabbed my purse and strode out the door, locking it behind me.

San Benedetto pretty much rolled up its sidewalks when the sun went down. Aside from a few lit restaurants and bars, the road seemed eerily deserted. Hunching my shoulders, I hurried down the sidewalk.

I didn't trust Tilde. Not after everything I'd learned. But at this point, I wasn't sure what information I *could* trust. Just because Lola told me that Tilde had been stalking Atticus, it didn't make it true. I thought back to the vigil. Had Tilde stepped away from the gazebo so she could set off the firecrackers? And if she had, why?

My breath plumed before me. Ribbons of black cloud blotted out the stars. A gibbous moon rose above the squat brick-and-stucco buildings on Main Street.

India and Orson told me their romantic relationship was long over. But was it? And if Lola had found out that they were still an item ...

No. If Lola found out, it wouldn't have been a motive for her to murder Atticus.

But if India and Orson were having an affair, they had reason to kill. A crummy reason, but reason enough.

Someone jerked me backward by the collar.

I gasped, spinning around and raising my fists. Pain lashed my cheek and I gave a low cry.

And stared at a plum tree.

I glared at the swaying branch, low and whip-thin, that had snagged my hoodie. "For Pete's sake." Annoyed and a little embarrassed, I unhooked myself, smoothed the hood over my thick down vest, and continued on.

Atticus's death *could* have been unintentional. People didn't realize how deadly a hard shove could be. What if there'd been a quarrel, Atticus was pushed, and he fell and cracked his skull?

On that soft rubber mat? No way.

I approached another plum tree and gave it a wide berth.

Okay, he'd hit his head on something else.

On the melangeur? That would explain why the vat had tipped, but not the position of Atticus's body.

Or, someone had whacked him in the head with something, and then he'd fallen, grabbing the melangeur on the way down ...

A black Mercedes cruised by. It slowed, and my scalp prickled.

I must be going crazy. That was what India had said, and that she'd felt like she was being watched. So did I. Were we both paranoid? Or was it only me?

I picked up the pace and arrived at the chocolate shop as Jason's black SUV parked beside the sidewalk.

He stepped from the car. His muscular shoulders filled his navy suit jacket and my heartbeat quickened. This was the way it was supposed to be—the two of us, working together.

He kissed me lightly on the cheek, then more firmly on the mouth. In spite of my anxiety, I melted into his embrace.

A car honked, roaring past.

We broke apart, breathless.

"What have you gotten yourself into now?" he asked.

"Nothing, I hope. That's why I called you."

"And I appreciate that." He eyed Reign's windows, his brows pulling together. "Tilde asked you to meet her here? The shop is closed."

"No, it's—" I turned. The lights were on inside, illuminating the mercury cinderblock walls, the counters, the chocolate displays. But a *Closed* sign hung in the front door. "That's strange. I thought Reign closed an hour after the museum on Thursdays." Maybe Tilde wanted to have a private conversation?

Or maybe she was one of those female serial killers and I was her next victim.

Good thing I'd brought someone armed and dangerous. I cut a glance to his hip. Yep. He was armed.

I knocked on the glass door.

No one came to unlock it.

"The office is in the rear of the building," I said uncertainly. "Maybe Tilde can't hear me knocking?"

"Wait here. I'll check the back door." He strode around the corner.

I peered through the glass. Kitchen lights streamed through the narrow window in the cinderblock wall behind the register.

One hand braced on the door's elegant handle, I leaned closer, nose nearly touching the glass.

The hallway lights were on too.

Weird. A chill rippled my spine.

I pressed closer, straining to see deeper into the shop. Tilde was probably in the bathroom.

The door jolted open.

I squeaked and staggered inside, stumbling into a chic display table. The pyramids of chocolate bars shuddered at the impact but didn't fall.

The door had been unlocked this whole time? Wildly, I looked around. "Jas—"

The door clicked shut behind me and I jumped. I worked to slow my breathing and rubbed my damp palms on the thighs of my jeans.

"Jason?"

No response.

Of course he couldn't hear me. He must be at the back door by now.

"Hello?" I called, uneasy. "Tilde?"

The secondhand on the clock above the kitchen window ticked. "Tilde?"

I strained my ears.

Something creaked.

I started, whirled.

Chocolate bars sat stacked on their shelves. A spiky air plant clung to a bit of driftwood dotted with wrapped chocolate squares.

I blew out my breath. The sound had probably been the building settling.

Yeah, that was it.

"Hello?" I called.

A car drove past outside.

This was ridiculous. I strode down the hallway, pausing to stick my head inside the kitchen. It was empty, the metal racks and counters gleaming. I hurried to the rear door and pushed it open.

Jason stood there, hand raised. He dropped his arm to his side. "How'd you get inside?"

"Turned out the front door was open."

He cursed softly.

"I don't think anyone's here," I said, stepping aside.

He prowled past me, pushed the office door open, and vanished into the room.

Feeling suddenly vulnerable, I hurried after him.

He stood behind Tilde's desk, staring at the floor.

My heart clenched. *No. Oh no.* "Is she—?"

"Go outside," he said sharply.

But he was too late. I couldn't unsee Tilde, lying beside her desk, blood pooling around a square block of wood centered over her heart.

SIXTEEN

Jason knelt beside the fallen woman and took her pulse. But her eyes were open and dull.

Tilde was dead.

My insides wrenched, and I pressed my hand to my mouth.

One of Tilde's arms was outflung, her hand curled against the wall, pink fingernails pressing into her palm. I stared at the strange square block pinned to her chest. Pinned...

I gasped, reeling into the hallway. She'd been stabbed with a receipt holder. And suddenly, the image of Tilde seemed to merge with that of Atticus's body. *Wrong, wrong, wrong.*

I rubbed my eyes, and the strange double-vision vanished.

Jason pulled his cell phone from his jacket pocket and called it in. He ended the call and looked up at me, still standing horror-stricken in the open doorway. "You should wait outside," he said.

Right. I should because it was a crime scene, and my presence risked messing it up. It was a logical request, and no doubt police procedure, but my throat tightened. I nodded and left the building, to shiver on the front sidewalk.

A gray Mercedes rolled past, the light from its headlamps flattening the street in tones of gray and yellow. It flicked its high beams, temporarily blinding me.

When I'd rubbed the spots from my eyes, a man, his fists jammed into the pockets of his windbreaker, strode toward me.

My breathing grew uneven. I edged against the wall of the chocolate shop to make way.

He passed, head lowered, without acknowledging my presence.

A siren sounded in the distance, and I pressed myself closer to the wall. First Atticus, now Tilde. The accountant must have known something, seen something...

But why had I seen Atticus when I'd looked at Tilde's corpse? There must be some connection, something more than the coincidence—no, it couldn't be coincidence—that both were killed at Reign.

I straightened off the wall. I had to return to the chocolate shop and figure this out.

Turning, I reached for the door handle.

A blue sports car screeched to a stop behind me and my shoulders tightened.

"Kosloski!" Laurel slammed the muscle car's door. "Where's Slate?"

"He's inside, in the office. But—"

"Stay here."

She stormed into the chocolate shop.

Folding my arms, I cooled my heels on the sidewalk, and more law enforcement personnel arrived. One cop tried to shoo me off, but I explained I was with Jason, and he let me stay.

All right. I'd just figure out what was bothering me about the murder scene—aside from the murder—without going inside. I shuddered, remembering Tilde's supine form. Come to think of it, I would *rather* stay outside.

The gibbous moon rose higher above Main Street's single-story buildings. I hugged my arms tighter and leaned against the wall, trying to make myself inconspicuous.

The phone in my pocket rang, and I jerked away from the cold brick. I fumbled the phone and saw it was Harper.

"Harper! Thank God you called."

"Why? What's wrong?"

I slithered away from the door, away from the cops flowing in and out of the shop, away from the corpse cooling in the building behind me. "There's been another murder," I said in a low voice. "Tilde. But don't tell anyone. It's just happened. No one at Reign knows yet." *Except for the killer.*

"What happened? Where are you?"

"At the chocolate shop."

Harper groaned. "Tell me you didn't discover the body. You know how the police feel about that."

"I was with Jason. I probably shouldn't be telling you anything right now, but ..." But I was standing on a dark and lonely street and my adrenaline was ebbing, leaving me shaky.

"Do you want me to come over there?"

"No," I said quickly. Jason definitely wouldn't appreciate bystanders. "I only ..." I cleared my throat. "It's good to hear a friendly voice. Why were you calling?"

"What? Oh. I just wanted to see what you were up to."

"Standing on a sidewalk, hoping this doesn't mean another interrogation at the police station," I said. But something in Harper's voice had rung false.

"Surely that won't happen, since you and Jason found the body together?"

"I guess," I said uncertainly. "I hope so."

Jason and Laurel walked outside. He scanned the sidewalk.

I raised a hand and caught his eye. "I need to go. I'll talk to you later."

"Sure. Call me if you can."

We hung up and I pocketed my phone, hurrying over. "Jason—"

Laurel's lips peeled back in a snarl. "I'll take her statement."

Jason nodded, expression impassive. "Sure. Maddie, we'll talk later." He returned inside the chocolate shop.

The glass door banged shut.

"Is everything all right?" I asked Laurel.

"A woman's been killed, nitwit. Of course it's not all right. Now tell me what happened."

I ran her through our discovery of the body. She kept returning to the moments when Jason and I had been separated—him at the rear of the building, me inside Reign.

Finally, exasperated, I said, "You can't think I killed her while Jason was outside?"

"I think you've made a real problem for him," she snapped. "As usual."

"What does that mean?"

Her jaw clenched. "You shouldn't have gone inside that damn shop alone. What the hell is wrong with you?"

"The door was open," I said weakly.

156

"Did you even think about what this might mean for his career?"

"His career?" I asked.

She rolled her eyes. "Question answered. Now get out of here before I decide to arrest you."

"But—"

"Get!"

I scuttled down the sidewalk. Had I caused problems for Jason? It had seemed simpler to go through inside and let him in at the rear. Or was that just a neat excuse? Had my urge to snoop gotten Jason into trouble?

I paused outside an Irish pub and called him.

It went to voicemail, and my midsection tightened.

Guilt-stricken, I left a message for him to call and hurried to the alley behind the museum, where my pickup waited.

Light streamed from the windows above Mason's motorcycle shop. I was swamped by an urge to run up those concrete steps, knock on his apartment door.

I didn't want to be alone.

Ridiculous. I was a grown woman and a paranormal museum owner, not some damsel in distress.

I climbed into my pickup and drove home.

In my driveway, I sat for a moment in the cab and listened to the ticking of the metal cooling. The bare branches of a nearby oak rubbed against each other, clicking like bones.

I drew deeper into the seat, zipping my hoodie to the top. My aunt's house was dark, her driveway empty. Dark fields stretched around me, and I realized how isolated I was in my little garage apartment.

The gibbous moon vanished behind a cloud, plunging the scene into blackness.

Swallowing, I stepped from my pickup and shut the door.

Two slim shadows detached themselves from my front porch.

My fist clenched on my keys. Had Laurel changed her mind? Was I going to be arrested? Did the killer have an accomplice?

"Maddie?" Harper called.

Smiling with relief, I trotted up the stairs. "What are you two doing here?"

"Harper told me what happened." Adele unbuttoned her long coat, exposing an ice-blue dress dotted with white flowers. "We thought you might need some support." With one hand, she brandished a wine bottle from her parent's vineyard. The other held a brown-paper gift bag.

"I know I wasn't supposed to tell anyone." Harper combed her fingers through her dark hair. "But it's Adele. And … wine!"

I let them inside my apartment and flipped on the lights. While they shed their coats and uncorked the bottle in my kitchen, I conducted a quick, secretive search, pulling open the closets, checking beneath my queen-sized bed. No one hid beneath it.

Self-conscious, I smoothed my T-shirt and returned to my small, nautical-themed living area.

Harper and Adele lounged on the gray-blue couch, glasses of red wine in their hands. Someone (I guessed Adele) had shoved aside a stack of paranormal-themed magazines and set out a cheese platter.

I dropped into the matching lounge chair. "Who brought the Gorgonzola?" I felt the urge to say *something*, to fill the room with noise and humanity. I wasn't hungry but leaned forward and snagged a crumbly green-veined wedge.

"I did," Adele said. "I thought it would make a nice break from wine and chocolate pairings."

"I always get a little tired of chocolate this time of year," Harper agreed, one leg tucked beneath her jeans. A crumb of cheese garnished the chest of her coffee-colored turtleneck sweater. She grinned. "But I get over it fast."

"What happened?" Adele adjusted her dress around her legs.

I drew a shuddering breath. "I got a call from Tilde to meet her at Reign," I said. "It sounded weird, so I called Jason. He met me there, but there was a *Closed* sign in the window, and no one answered our knocks. So he went around the back. It turned out, the front door was unlocked, so I went inside and let him in through the back door. Then we found her. It was just like Atticus."

"She was covered in chocolate?" Harper asked.

"No." I rubbed my hands on my jeans. "No, she was stabbed." *Pinned like a butterfly.* The cheese turned to lead in my stomach.

"You mean, it was like Atticus because you found the body in the same chocolate shop?" Adele asked. "Of course it reminded you of his murder."

"No," I said slowly. "It was more than that."

"More than what?" Harper asked.

Unseeing, I moved my arm, imitating the position of Tilde's, sprawled on the floor.

"Is that sign language for give me a drink?" Adele asked. "Is a wine glass supposed to magically appear in your hand? Because I put your glass on the table right next to you."

"No, it's just ... Her arm." I straightened, eyes widening. "It was her arm. We assumed Atticus had knocked over the chocolate when he fell. But there wasn't any chocolate on his arm nearest the melangeur. If he'd grabbed the vat and tipped it over, there would have been chocolate on his hand or arm, wouldn't there?"

Adele wrinkled her forehead. "I guess."

"Think about it," I said. "The melangeurs tip forward so workers can pour out the chocolate. If Atticus had grabbed one and fallen beneath it, there would have been chocolate on his sleeve."

"So you think someone put Atticus there and tipped the chocolate on top of him?" Adele shuddered. "That's sick."

"Or someone was trying to send a message about the victim." Harper sipped her wine.

"But don't you see?" I asked. "It means it's all connected. Everything. The murders. The firecrackers at the vigil. The bomb threat at my museum."

"I don't get it." Adele set her wine glass on the coffee table and propped her elbows on her knees.

"It's the same mind," I said, leaning forward in my chair. "They're all dark pranks. Maybe Atticus fell near the melangeurs, maybe he was dragged there. I don't know. But someone dumped that chocolate on him *after* he was dead or unconscious. And using a receipt holder to stab their accountant—"

Harper choked on her wine. "A receipt holder? One of those metal pointy ones?"

"Yeah," I said. "And it was …"

"Awful." Adele paled.

"Wrong." Harper shook her head, her glossy black hair cascading around her shoulders.

"Both," I said. "I mean, sure, Atticus makes chocolate, so maybe it pointed to chocolate making being the reason behind his murder. But why would a murderer leave hints about the motive?"

"Because he's crazy?" Adele asked.

"Obviously, the killer's disturbed," I said. "But I think it's more than that."

"If the killer wasn't leaving a message, then why dump the chocolate?" Harper asked. "And why the other pranks?"

I sank back in the soft chair. "I don't know." I plucked a glass of wine from the nearby end table and sipped absently. "I should have figured it out sooner. But Jason banished me to the sidewalk—"

"What?" Adele asked, outraged.

"And then Laurel interviewed me—"

"Laurel?" Adele asked. "Not Jason?"

"Laurel." An uncomfortable flush of heat rolled through me. "I guess it would have been weird for him to interview me, since we're dating." I bit my lower lip. *Had* my actions gotten him into trouble? I'd been so set on helping him find the killer, I hadn't thought through the ramifications for Jason.

"But why did Tilde call you to Reign?" Adele asked. "Not to find her body."

"She said something about an invoice, but I'm not sure I believe her."

"She must have known something about Atticus's murder," Adele said. "Why else would someone kill her? But if she saw or knew who killed Atticus, why not tell the police?"

"Could she have been blackmailing someone?" Harper asked.

"Or maybe she was unsure of what she'd seen," Adele said.

"Maybe someone overheard her call you and decided she knew too much?" Harper asked.

My stomach turned, the wine souring in my mouth. If Harper was right, that would make me partly responsible for her death.

"Okay," Adele said, "let's assume you're correct and the bomb threat is connected to the murders. Why target you and your museum?"

"I don't know," I said. "Except I found Atticus, and I thought I heard something when I was alone with him."

"Heard something?" Harper cocked her head. "You mean, you might not have been alone? The killer could have still been there?"

"Maybe," I said. "But at this point, they must know I'm no threat."

"Unless the killer thinks you know something that you haven't told the police," Harper said.

My mouth went dry.

A bomb threat.

A near hit-and-run.

They were right. I'd become a target.

SEVENTEEN

THERE ARE PEOPLE WHO visit the Paranormal Museum for a laugh, or because they're stuck drying out between wine tastings. But a surprising number are genuinely interested in the strange and supernatural. Maybe something happened to them they can't quite explain. Maybe they grew up on a diet of Tolkien or Harry Potter and have loved the mystical ever since. More rarely, the visitors are true believers in the supernatural. But most have a story to tell. I love hearing those stories.

Usually.

"I don't believe in ghosts," the middle-aged blonde assured me. She twisted the bangles on her wrist. "But I just can't explain what happened in that apartment." She shuddered. "The weird shadows. That creepy hand…"

"Uh-huh," I said. The line at the counter was six deep. Something crashed from the Fortune Telling Room, and I winced.

Leo, in a Paranormal Museum tee and torn jeans, handed out tickets and brochures, bagged tarot cards and chocolate.

I worked the register, and I was wearing the exact same tee. Maybe it *was* time for a fashion upgrade.

"Trust me." I keyed in the blonde's chocolate bars. "I get it. It's hard to trust your senses. And it's smart to ask if there are alternate explanations for the phenomena. Not every bump in the night is a ghost."

"I know. But what do you believe?" she asked. "I mean, is the museum really haunted?"

"Not the museum itself," I hedged. This was always a tricky question. I wasn't sure what I believed, but I couldn't exactly advertise my agnosticism. "The way these things work, it's the objects inside that are haunted. My experts say ghosts or psychic energy attach to items that have meaning for the prior owner. Like the molinillo." I nodded to the Gallery.

I handed her the change and Leo passed her bag across the counter. "Have a great rest of your day." I beamed.

The blonde winked. "The wineries are next on our list. How could the day be bad?" She swaggered outside with her boyfriend.

The bell above the door jingled in her wake.

Jason caught the open door with one hand and walked inside. My favorite detective took in the crowds. "Bad timing?"

"Uh ..." I rang up a T-shirt.

"I got a hot lead on the molinillo," he said. "I'll come back later." He ducked out the door.

"Wait. What—?"

The door jangled shut.

What lead? With the sleeve of my hoodie, I wiped a handprint off the glass counter. I was more interested in leads on the murders than on the molinillo. But violent crime was his business, the molinillo mine.

"Do you know anything about, um, shadows?" a gangly twenty-something at the counter asked.

"What kind of shadows?" Leo asked briskly, wrapping a T-shirt.

"I've been seeing shadows moving up and down my apartment stairs." He scratched his narrow chin. "And there's no reason for them. I've checked everything. Reflections, window angles ... But they're just ... there."

"Shadow people," Leo said. "No one knows what they are, but most think they're not ghosts."

"Are they dangerous?" he asked.

Leo reached beneath the counter for a dented metal recipe box and pulled out a business card. "Do a search for shadow people on the Internet. If you think you need to do something about them, you might want to call this woman." He handed the customer the card and bagged the T-shirt.

"Thanks." The young man pocketed the card and left, bag in hand.

"We should talk about shadow people on our podcast," Leo said to me.

"Maybe," I said, sweating, and handed a woman a box of chocolate Tarot cards.

We worked through the line. Finally, around lunchtime, the crowd eased, in quest of food more substantial than chocolate.

I slipped into the Fortune Telling Room to check for damage. A clear glass bottle lay shattered on the floor.

Cursing beneath my breath, I retrieved the whisk broom from a low cabinet and swept up the pieces. I plucked its placard from the shelf:

Mrs. Antoinette Matteson was born Antoinette Wealthy in 1847. This Buffalo, New Jersey, Spiritualist and psychic healer, or "clairvoyant doctress," grew into her mediumistic powers after the death of her husband, when she became the sole support for her family.

This bottle once contained one of her custom herbal remedies, compounded from recipes Antoinette discovered during trance states. In her book, The Occult Family Physician, *she wrote: "During the twenty years of my mediumistic experience, many hundreds, in fact I may say thousands, of remarkable cures have been made through the aid of my spirit guides." She died in 1913.*

I grimaced. I'd liked that bottle, a relic of America's Spiritualist movement, and from a time when women had to get creative if they wanted a career. Options for women working outside the home during the nineteenth century had been limited. In a way, I was following in Antoinette's footsteps with the museum.

Returning to the main room, I dumped the shards in the waste bin. I sagged against the glass counter, my elbow nudging GD's tip jar. "Wow."

"Wine and Chocolate Friday," Leo agreed. "Lunch?"

"It's your turn to make the run. What are you thinking?"

He scrunched up his forehead. "Burrito?"

"Fine by me." The day Mexican food gave me heartburn was the day I was packing it all in. I handed him cash.

He pulled on his motorcycle jacket and sauntered out the door.

I grabbed my cell phone from beneath the counter and called Jason.

"Maddie?" His deep-timbered voice rumbled through me. "How are you doing? I'm sorry I didn't get a chance to talk to you after ..."

"Tilde," I said heavily.

"I'm sorry you had to see that."

"Me too. And I'm sorry ... Did I make things worse for you?"

"No," he said, his voice firm.

"Jason, Laurel suggested—"

"I know what she suggested," he said in a neutral voice. "Laurel is protective of her partner, just like I'm protective of her."

But had Laurel been wrong? I had a sick feeling she hadn't.

"You can't plan for finding a body," he said. "Well, you can plan for it," he corrected, "but things happen. You stayed calm and you gave a clear statement. You did good."

I wasn't convinced, but I let it drop. "So, what do you mean you have a lead on the molinillo?"

He chuckled. "I thought that would get your attention. My friend in Oaxaca said he'd look at the files. I'm supposed to call him today."

"Oh," I said, weirdly disappointed. I was glad Jason was taking an interest, but I'd hoped to talk to the Mexican detective myself.

"What if I come to the museum and we call him together?"

I brightened. "I'd love that!"

"When's a good time?"

"Any time this afternoon should work."

"How about now?" He strolled into the museum.

Grinning, I leaned across the counter and kissed him. His cheek was rough against mine, and I had to restrain myself from throwing my arms around him. We weren't alone, and I'm not a big PDA fan.

GD sneered, whiskers twitching, from his perch on the haunted rocking chair.

"Do you think your friend in Oaxaca learned anything?" I asked.

Jason pulled his phone from the pocket of his navy suit jacket. "Let's find out."

The bookcase swiveled open and Adele stalked into the museum on skin-toned sling-backs. She wore a matching pencil skirt and white blouse beneath her Fox and Fennel apron. Strands of inky hair escaped her chignon. She moaned, "This is a disaster."

"What's wrong?" I smothered my frustration. I loved Adele, but Oaxaca! Detective! Molinillo!

"The wedding cake. My second, third, and fourth choices don't have enough time to make it now."

Jason frowned. "The wedding's not until June. What's the problem?"

She braced her elbows on the counter, her head in her hands. "You explain."

"Wedding cakes need to be booked four to six months in advance," I said. "We're just past the window."

"It's only a cake," Jason said. "How tough can it be?"

Adele raised her head and glared. "Only a cake?! The cake is the focus of the entire wedding!"

"I thought the happy couple was." His mouth quirked.

"You don't understand," she said. "What am I going to do?"

"There must be a solution," I said. "Maybe we could simplify. Maybe there's an amazing cake decorator at Ladies Aid—"

She made a squeak of horror.

"Take it from someone who knows," Jason said. "The wedding is the least important part of the marriage. And it doesn't predict future success."

"I know you're right." Adele gripped the hair close to her scalp. "But there's knowing, and there's *knowing*. No matter how logical I try to be about it, it's my wedding!"

"We'll figure something out," I said, soothing. "I'll call my mother. She's been to tons of weddings. Maybe she'll have an idea."

"Fine. Call her." Shoulders slumped, Adele trooped through the open bookcase into her tea room. It snicked shut behind her.

Jason smiled grimly. "Want to call your mom?"

"No! I want to call your buddy in Oaxaca." I also really liked saying *Oaxaca*. I wanted to visit the place because of the name alone.

Jason's smile broadened. "Then let's do it." He made the call and put the phone on speaker.

"*Bueno?*" A man's voice floated, tinny and broken, from the phone.

"Alejandro, it's Jason."

"Jason! I have what you were looking for."

"I've put you on speaker," Jason said. "My friend Maddie is with me."

Friend? I made a face at him. "Hi, Alejandro," I said.

"Ah, the lady with the haunted museum. *Encantada.*"

"What did you find?" Jason asked.

"The Miss Ocasio case is officially a suicide."

"Officially?" Jason's face tightened.

The man laughed shortly. "*Officially.* I spoke with the lead detective, however, and unofficially, he liked her bastardo boyfriend for her death."

"Why?" Jason asked.

"The boyfriend dealt in narcotics. And people had a habit of disappearing around him."

"What was his motive for killing Felicitas?" I asked.

"She was pregnant."

"Oh," I said softly. How awful. "How exactly did she—?"

The man swore. "*Lo siento.* I must go. An emergency. Call me later." He hung up.

Jason pocketed the phone. "It's stories like this that made me leave the big city."

"You're not getting much of a break from murder and mayhem in San Benedetto."

"At least the public doesn't see me as the enemy. What did you think of Alejandro's story?"

"I wonder if there's more to it, since we got cut off. Do you think Felicitas knew her boyfriend was dealing drugs?"

"Why wouldn't she? They were together. She'd have to know."

I shot him a look. Yeah, in a perfect world, there'd be no secrets. I squirmed, thinking of the recent investigations I'd been keeping secret from my mother. "If the molinillo legend is rooted in fact, and rattles when lies are told, that would imply her boyfriend was keeping things secret."

"Lying to her about his drug dealing?"

The front door jingled and swung open.

"At least we don't have any dark secrets from each other." Jason smiled, wry.

Mason walked inside, stopped short. A flush of red swept from the collar of his black T-shirt to the roots of his hair. "Dark secrets?"

I straightened off the counter. "The case of the haunted molinillo."

"Are you sure about that?" The muscles beneath Mason's motorcycle tee tensed.

Confused, I shifted my weight. "Well, yeah, I'm ..." I trailed off, realizing that Mason thought we were talking about his situation— the son he hadn't known about. But that wasn't his fault. Belle had given birth to their son while he was overseas in the military, and she hadn't told him until recently. And he and Belle had never married.

"Why would she lie?" Jason asked, his arms loose at his sides. "It's a haunted molinillo."

Mason turned to me and his hands unclenched. "You don't have to protect me, Maddie. I get it. The situation with Belle wasn't kind to you."

"It's fine." My cheeks warmed. "It was no one's fault." Well, maybe Belle's, but ... whatever.

"You wanted something?" Jason asked him.

He hesitated. "Someone's been using my dumpster. I thought it might be Dieter. I'd ask him myself, but I haven't seen him since the vigil, and he doesn't answer his phone."

"He screens his calls," I said. It was super irritating. "But I don't know why he'd use your dumpster. He hasn't been doing any construction work here—not that it would be an excuse if he had," I added quickly. I hoped we weren't in for another bout of dumpster wars. It was amazing how touchy people could get over dumpster use and positioning. Though I'd thought Mason and I were past that.

"Have you seen anyone else around?" Mason asked.

"No," I said, "and Adele certainly wouldn't abuse your dumpster. I know I haven't." Heh heh. Dumpster abuse. Maybe San Benedetto needed a dumpster protective services division.

Mason glanced at Jason.

The detective raised his hands, palms out. "Hey, I'm not getting involved."

Mason grunted, turned on his bootheel, and strode out.

"That went well," I muttered. When I'd first met Mason, he'd been on a tear about dumpster issues as well. Was our relationship regressing?

I glanced at Jason, who was watching the slowly closing door. The two men had completely different temperaments. As fun and exciting as Mason was, I preferred Jason's easygoing demeanor. And it was time I told him my theory about the murders. I drew a breath.

"Has he been coming around much?" Jason asked.

My head jerked back. "Who? Mason? No more than usual."

"What's usual?"

"We're neighbors. Jason, have you noticed—"

"—that Mason came here to tell you something, and he backed off when he saw me here? Yeah, I noticed."

"What?" I adjusted the hem of my T-shirt. "No. He left because he was embarrassed. He thought 'dark secrets' meant his situation with Belle."

Jason eyed me skeptically. "Yeah, but he came here for a reason. He's been hanging around your museum a lot lately. Is everything okay between him and Belle?"

Heat, made of mingled embarrassment and annoyance, flushed my face. "I don't know. Why would I? Mason and I are over."

"I know that." Jason's eyes darkened with annoyance. "But I'm not sure he does."

"What's that supposed to mean?" I asked sharply. Mason and I had broken up. He was with someone else. And I wasn't a cheater.

"I mean—"

The door opened and Leo clomped in. "Hi, Jason. Here's your burrito, Mad. Grilled veggies with refried beans and hot salsa." He set a small paper bag on the counter.

"Thanks," I said. "Jason, about—"

He leaned across the counter and kissed me lightly. "I know. You haven't done anything wrong, and I'm not jealous. But for his sake, you need to shut this down."

Shut it down? I hadn't started anything! "But—"

"You know I'm right."

"Right about what?" Leo asked.

"Nothing," I muttered, looking away.

Jason slid a tattered business card across the counter. "Here's Alejandro's number. Feel free to call him again."

"Thanks. I will." I watched him leave.

"Who's Alejandro?" Leo asked.

"A detective in Oaxaca," I said. "He may have more information on the molinillo."

Leo grinned. "Cool."

I flopped against the counter. I hadn't had a chance to tell Jason my theory—or profile—on the killer. It was a day of bad timing.

"What's wrong?" Leo asked.

"Nothing. Something I forgot. It's not important." But I felt a chasm of things unsaid growing between myself and Jason. And I wasn't sure how to fix it.

EIGHTEEN

"A FAKE CAKE!" ADELE paced in front of my counter. "What does that even mean?"

My gaze darted to the computer screen. "Um, are you sure that's what my mom said?" It was the end of that long day, and I'd settled in to do online research on Atticus and Orson. I'd just found a magazine profile about the two when Adele walked into the museum.

"A fake cake and then a sheet cake to serve the guests," Adele said. "She said it would save the baker time."

I set down my pen, resigned to doing no research until Adele got the cake business off her chest. "Why didn't any of the bakers suggest that?"

"Maybe because they knew I'd say no? I can't have a fake cake! It's bad karma. What does that say about the marriage? That it's a fake too?"

"Why would it say anything about your marriage?" I asked, trying for a reasonable tone.

She shooed GD off the haunted rocking chair and dropped onto the seat. "I don't know."

"And when did you care about karma? Isn't that more Harper's bag?"

"I've always cared about karma. I just didn't call it that."

GD leapt into Adele's lap and coiled into a silky black ball.

Distractedly, she stroked his fur. "Maybe I'll see that fortune-teller of yours tomorrow for advice."

Now I knew something was seriously wrong. Adele thought anything to do with the paranormal was a waste of time. "Adele, this seems like it's about more than a cake. What's really bothering you?"

She stared at the ceiling. "Do you have any idea how many people have told me recently that opposites attract?"

"No-o."

"They keep reminding me how different Dieter and I are. When we're together … we always seem like a good thing. He's so relaxed, and I'm …"

"Not."

"Right." She leaned forward. "But we agree on the most important things, like family and money and morals. I didn't think these personality issues would bother me. But … this wedding! It feels like everything's on my shoulders. I wish he'd get more involved. Dieter doesn't even seem to care!"

"I'm sure that's not true. Have you talked to him about it?"

"Of course I have. And he's offered to do more work, but …"

"But what?"

She winced. "I'm not sure I trust him with the job."

"Adele …"

"I know!" Her fists clenched in GD's fur. "But a wedding is so important, and he's just so casual about everything. All he wants is to get married. He doesn't care how."

"And that's a bad thing?"

"It is when you're trying to please two extended families full of demanding people."

"Maybe Dieter has the right idea. If you can't please everybody, why try?"

She glared at me. "Honestly, Maddie, you're as bad as Dieter. And you're in customer service!"

"Huh?"

Adele set GD on the linoleum floor and stalked to the bookcase. "I'll figure this out somehow." She slipped into the tea room and shut the bookcase behind her.

I half rose from my seat to go after her, but I sat back down. This was something Adele and Dieter needed to work out on their own. Besides, murder research was calling.

I read the profile.

"There's something highly suspicious about someone who doesn't like chocolate." Atticus Reine, in his San Benedetto chocolate factory/store, grins beneath his impressive beard.

Five years ago, Atticus and his best friend, Orson Malke, began experimenting with chocolate in their San Francisco apartment. They crushed cocoa beans to make their chocolate from scratch, and added nothing but pure cane sugar. Their simple brown wrappers stood out in a sea of chic graphics. But it's the chocolate—the alchemy of heat, cocoa beans, and sugar—that has taken the chocolate world by storm.

"I won't say that we make the best chocolate in the world," Orson says. "But if we don't, then who does?"

Orson's wife, Lola, insists on a tasting in their updated Victorian home. We sit in their elegant dining area, the French windows open to their organic garden. The tasting is complemented with local cheeses and central California wines. Lola talks about the chocolate as if it were a fine wine, complete with forward flavors, complexity, and balance.

Many purists prefer their plain chocolate bars, which are identified by country. But I confess I'm partial to the bars enhanced with local ingredients. Sea salt from the Pacific. Lavender. Dried, locally grown citrus and nuts.

"We keep it simple," Orson says. "The ingredients should enhance the experience of the chocolate, rather than be the experience. Because in the end, it's all about the chocolate."

But evaluating chocolate—like wine—is subjective. Expert Donald Warner insists Reign chocolate is prized more for its clever marketing than the quality of the chocolate itself. "Not a single bar is perfect," Warner complains. "There are always defects."

"The bars are made by hand," Orson insists. "And the imperfections are part of their beauty, and, frankly, of the organic process. What's important is taste, and Reign chocolate is among the top in the world."

I drummed my fingers on the glass counter. Orson was right. People expected glossy perfection when they bought things. We were used to standardized items made in factories. But that wasn't reality in the world of handmade products.

GD leapt onto the counter, his tail lashing the screen.

Annoyed, I brushed it aside. Returning to the search page, I clicked on the next article, this one a profile of Lola and Orson and Reign:

While others sampled wine in quaint farmhouses, I sat with chocolate maker Orson Malke and his wife, molecular biologist Lola Emerson-Malke. We tasted chocolate…

I frowned. Atticus had barely been mentioned in the articles I'd turned up. There should have been a *bit* more about Atticus, shouldn't there? Had Atticus been that modest? Or had he kept a low profile for a different reason?

I needed to learn more about him, and the Internet wasn't cutting it. On impulse, I called the chocolate shop.

"Hello, this is Reign," Lola said.

"Oh, hi," I said, surprised to hear her answer the phone. "This is Maddie from the Paranormal Museum."

"Hello, Maddie. What can I help you with?"

"You're working at Reign now?"

She laughed shortly. "God, no. But whenever a phone rings, I can't stop myself from answering. If you want to speak to Orson, I'm afraid he's busy training the new assistant."

"Oh. It's about my chocolate display here at the museum. I wanted to put something up about Atticus, to honor him." I winced. It was a lie, but honoring him wasn't a bad idea. I should have thought of it sooner.

Something rattled in the Gallery. Brow furrowed, I leaned across the counter. That wasn't … the molinillo? Or could someone be in there? The hair rose on my arms. I'd thought all my guests had left.

"You mean like a eulogy?" Lola asked.

I rose and walked around the counter for a better view of the Gallery. "Something like that, but I didn't want to bother India. I was thinking a small placard, with something about his life and work with Reign. I've been searching online, but most of the articles are about you and Orson." I edged to the open doorway and peered around the corner into the Gallery.

No one was there.

The molinillo sat at an innocent angle in its tall ceramic bowl.

"That was all Atticus's idea. He thought the chocolate maker made for a more compelling story than the marketer."

Then how did Lola end up in so many of the press pieces? "That makes sense," I said. "I wish I could have talked to him about his marketing strategies, and how he put you and Orson front and center."

"I wouldn't say front and center, but you've seen our home ... You know, I was just leaving for the day. Why don't you stop by my place? I'm sure we have something at the house you can use."

"At your house? Not the chocolate shop?"

"The office was the domain of Atticus and Tilde." Lola paused. "Orson does most of his paperwork from home. He won't be coming home until late tonight, so I'd love it if you could join me. As much as I enjoy our place, it can get lonely at night."

My lips pursed. "May I bring a friend?" Because I was definitely not going to meet a murder suspect alone.

"The more the merrier," Lola said. "Can you meet me there in an hour?"

"Sure. Thanks."

We hung up.

I glanced at the bookcase that led to the tea room. Adele could use a break. But I had a feeling she'd view an impromptu invitation to Lola's as an annoyance.

I called Harper, and she agreed to meet me at the Malkes' home.

When I arrived, Harper's BMW was parked in the long gravel driveway. Light glowed from the two-story Victorian, transforming it into a fairy-tale confection. Behind its floor-to-ceiling windows, Harper and Lola gestured animatedly inside the home's extension.

Parking behind the BMW, I stepped from my pickup. Rows of barren grapevines cast long, twisted shadows in the front yard. They shifted in the moonlight, stretching their long fingers toward me.

I pulled my hooded jacket tighter. The night had grown cold, the stars above dimmed by the lights from nearby Sacramento.

Something rustled in the nearby hydrangeas.

I stilled. If Lola and Harper were in the house, then who—?

A striped gray-and-black tail whisked across the drive. My muscles relaxed. A raccoon.

Annoyed by my jumpiness, I crunched loudly down the driveway and up the steps to the peak-roofed extension. I noticed an old-fashioned bell pull beside the French doors and reached to tug the rope.

Lola met my gaze through the glass and moved toward me. My hand dropped to my side.

She opened one of the French doors. A gust of wind billowed her long blond hair, tangling strands across her cable-knit sweater. Her jeans were narrow, tapering into suede knee-high boots, and once again, I felt underdressed in my schlumpy Paranormal Museum tee.

"Maddie! Thanks for coming," she said. "And thanks for inviting Harper."

Harper raised a glass of red wine in my direction. Its rich color almost exactly matched her turtleneck. "Maddie's thoughtful that way." She winked. Harper knew exactly why I'd invited her.

A cheese platter sat on the rustic wooden table alongside a bottle of zinfandel and a bouquet of white flowers. A folded sheet of paper lay beside the sky-blue vase. Benches ran along the long sides of the table. On one wall stood a tall, white, glassed-in sideboard. Magazines lay artfully scattered atop it, open to pages with photos of Lola and Orson and their home. Opposite the sideboard hung a framed, oversized magazine cover featuring the Victorian.

"Would you like a glass of wine?" Lola asked.

"Thanks," I said.

She poured from a bottle of a local zinfandel and handed the goblet to me. "To Atticus."

"And to Tilde." An ache speared the back of my throat. If I hadn't stopped to call Jason, or if we'd figured out that the door was open sooner, would she still be alive?

Lola blinked. "Of course. And to Tilde." She took a sip. "I still can't believe what happened."

"What did happen?" Harper asked.

"I'm not sure," Lola said. "I only know what I read in the papers." She shivered. "I'm not sure I want to know more. How are things at that museum of yours, Maddie? I heard someone called in a bomb threat."

"Ah. That." I turned the wine goblet in my hands. So far the bomb threat hadn't affected foot traffic in the museum. "I think something like a paranormal museum tends to attract pranksters." I really hoped that was all it had been. But the timing was too coincidental, and a prickle of fear raced up my spine.

"That's the problem with boring, small-town life," Harper said. "The kids need to get creative to have fun."

Lola smiled. "And we can't have that."

"In spite of our small-town atmosphere, I never had the chance to get to know Atticus," I said. "What was he like?"

Lola sobered, staring into her wine goblet. "He was funny. Charming. Clever."

"Honest," Harper said.

Lola looked up from her wine.

"I knew him and India," Harper explained.

Lola nodded. "My husband likes to think it was their chocolate that put Reign on the map. But Atticus was as important to the company's success as Orson. Maybe more so. I don't know what we'll do without his marketing skills. I've been trying to fill in, as you know, but I'm an amateur."

"Why is the company called *Reign*?" I asked.

"It was named after Atticus," she explained. "Well, not *after* him, but the idea came from his last name, and then the crown imprint on the wrappers from that."

"And the plain brown wrappers?" Harper asked.

"Atticus felt the contrast of something simple and the crown had an impact," she said. "He was a genius."

"How is India holding up?" Harper plucked a piece of cheese from the white ceramic tray on the wooden table.

"As well as can be expected, after losing her husband and then her cousin in such an awful way," Lola said. "Maybe I should have invited her tonight, to get her mind off this double tragedy." She rubbed the rim of the wine glass against her bottom lip. "It's hard to know what to do when someone is grieving."

"Were she and Tilde close?" I asked.

"Close enough for Tilde to follow her to California, I guess," Lola said. "I assumed..." She adjusted the cheese platter on the table. "I guess I assumed a lot of things," she said in a subdued voice.

"Do the police have any idea why someone would have killed both her and Atticus?" I asked.

Lola rubbed her arms, rumpling the sleeves of her thick sweater. "It must be some sort of grudge against Reign, don't you think? I've asked Orson to come away with me, take a vacation. But he won't. And now he's insisting that he can do Tilde's job and manage the accounts too. He's going to give himself a heart attack."

"Who might have a grudge against Reign?" I asked.

"Sam Reynolds." Lola's delicate face pinched. "I've noticed he hasn't returned with his picket sign lately. He was harassing us all and our customers. I heard he bothered you one day," she said to me.

I nodded. "He let me know he was upset with Reign's management."

Lola's mouth compressed. "Tilde told me he was lurking at the back door when she left one night and followed her all the way to her car, cursing and making threats."

"Why was he fired?" I asked, curious if the story would change.

"He ..." Lola blew out her breath. "It just wasn't a good fit. Atticus should have fired him long ago, for all our sakes, Sam's included. Retail isn't easy, and the work's not for everyone."

"Is Sam from around here?" I asked, dissatisfied.

"He's a local," Lola said.

That would make it easier for me—er, the police—to track him down. I cleared my throat. "Atticus's death has affected so many people." I hesitated. "There seemed to be some tension between you and Tilde at the chocolate shop."

Harper shot me a warning look.

Lola flushed, her words coming more rapidly. "She thought because she was India's cousin she could slack off. But Tilde was making mistakes. Or at least, that's what Orson told me. Of course, it's horrible that she's dead. But that doesn't negate her poor performance."

"No," I said. "I guess not."

"But you said you wanted to talk about Atticus." Lola's gaze narrowed. "Not our accountant."

"You're right," I said. "I suppose in my mind, the two will always be linked now that they're both dead."

The three of us stood silently for a long moment. Outside, a wind chime tinkled, faint and musical.

Harper shook herself. "I love what you've done with your home. This extension really updates this old Victorian."

"Thanks," Lola said. "We worked hard on it, and we used reclaimed materials wherever we could."

Seemingly mollified, Lola regaled us with tales of the remodel and restoration—the horrors of outdated plumbing, wonky electrical wires, and tiny rooms.

I tried to look interested, nodding and mm-hmming at appropriate moments.

After we'd discussed Harper's business, the weather, and my museum's next exhibit—arty photographs of ghosts—I finally got to the supposed reason for my visit. "About that tribute to Atticus—"

"I found the eulogy that Orson's been working on." Lola lifted a folded sheet of paper off the table and handed it to me. "Maybe you can develop something for your museum from that."

I folded the page into quarters and slid it into the back pocket of my faded jeans. "Thanks."

After hashing over the weather some more, Harper and I said our goodbyes and escaped. We walked down the curved driveway, the gravel rattling beneath our shoes.

"Did you get what you wanted?" Harper asked.

"I'm not sure. I feel like…"

"Like what?"

"Like everyone's lying, or keeping things back." And Lola had said something that had left my nerves jangling.

Now all I needed to do was figure out what.

NINETEEN

Outside the museum, iron street lamps flickered on in the Sunday night gloom. Inside the museum, GD slept, his head and paws dangling off the edge of the haunted rocking chair.

I handed a bag of chocolate-covered almonds across the counter. "Have a good night," I said to my final customer.

She clasped the bag to her ample chest. "Thanks!"

Relieved, I followed her to the door and flipped the sign to *Closed*. Tonight was officially the end of Wine and Chocolate Days. I rubbed my aching neck. As much as I'd enjoyed the chocolate inspiration, I'd already moved on to thinking about future project ideas. An exhibit of faerie art. Experimenting with the paranormal museum podcast. Solving a murder.

Ursula, the buckles on her scarlet corset clinking, peeked from the Gallery. Wisps of brown hair escaped from beneath her steampunk hat. "Is it over?" she squeaked.

"Yep, we're closed," I said. "Rough crowd?"

She smiled. "Not at all. I made six hundred dollars today, and that's after what I owe you. If you ever want to do this again, let me know."

"There's always the Wine and Chocolate Days next spring." I would need to figure out a new twist for my chocolate exhibit. But I had twelve months to figure it out.

She pressed her hands into the small of her back and stretched. "I've got one packet of chocolate left. How would you like a reading?"

I *definitely* wanted a reading, but she had to be exhausted. "Are you sure you're up for it?"

"Come into my parlor," she intoned.

I followed her into the Gallery. The black shelves were denuded, great gaps where tarot cards and chocolate bars used to stand. The Wine and Chocolate Days promo might have been over, but my *Magic of Chocolate* exhibit would run through the end of the month. I needed to restock.

She motioned to the canopied table. "You know the drill. You'll have to make your own drink."

I made myself a cup of cocoa and stirred, while Ursula wrote a receipt and counted the museum's share of her take.

"Where's Leo today?" she asked.

I smothered a yawn. "He had a big exam to study for, so I gave him the afternoon off." I sipped my drink, warmth cascading through my veins, and leaned back in the chair. "Ah. I needed this." The chocolate didn't make my stomach lurch, so at least I was getting over my cocoa trauma.

"I could see how busy you were, but don't tell me about your day. It might taint the reading."

"How does this work?" I asked, and took another gulp.

She raised a wide, empty cup. "Chocolate dregs left along the rim refer to something immediate. The middle of the cup represents the near future, and the bottom is the key to your situation. I look for symbols within the dregs and use my intuition to interpret them." She peered into my cup. "Leave a teensy bit of liquid, maybe a tablespoon, in the bottom."

I finished the hot chocolate and hoped she'd tell me something good. Not that I believed in fortune-telling, but I didn't exactly disbelieve either. Not after all the odd things I'd seen in the museum.

"Swirl your cup three times in a clockwise motion," she said.

I swirled and handed her the white cup.

She clapped a saucer on top and flipped the cup over. "I need to drain the liquid, and that creates the pattern." Careful not to spill, Ursula removed the cup, turning it right-side up and setting the saucer on the table.

She studied the dregs. "There's conflict swirling about you now. You'll have a difficult time seeing your way through, but you'll get there, so persevere. And..." Her face scrunched.

A shiver of apprehension rippled through me, and I leaned closer. "And what?"

"See this stain here, shaped like a knife?"

"Yes," I said. Once she'd pointed it out, the chocolate shape *did* look like a dagger, complete with blood dripping from the blade. An image of Tilde flashed into my head and I shuddered.

"Usually, that means danger. Real and immediate." She shivered. "Sorry, I don't usually have such dark readings."

I frowned. I'd gotten feedback from all her customers, and none had left frightened or disturbed. They'd all been delighted with their readings.

Her face cleared. "Of course. It's the museum, all these objects that you're connected to, the photos of murders and haunted things. Are you researching anything in the museum now?"

"Yes," I said, embarrassingly relieved. "As a matter of fact I am."

"That's likely what this is about then." She tilted the cup and studied the dregs. "The object you're researching is connected to someone who died violently, correct?"

"It looks that way, but I'm not sure. My research isn't finished."

She nodded. "There was violence in that death. Trust the chocolate. And it looks like murder. And here…" She pointed to a splotch of chocolate shaped like a dog. "This means the support of friends. A friend of yours will need your help in the near future, within the next four weeks, I think. It will be a big ask, but you'll both feel good about it in the end."

Adele. It didn't take a Nostradamus to predict more wedding insanity in my future.

"You're in a relationship now," she said, "but it's complicated. Both parties have shields up because of other attachments from the past."

"*Both* parties?" What was Jason shielding?

And hold on. Did *I* have shields up? What if I hadn't completely gotten past my breakup with Mason? Maybe Jason was right, and I needed to cut things off more cleanly. After all, why *was* Mason hanging around the museum so much?

"Remember," the fortune-teller said, "honesty really is the best policy… And this closed book." She pointed to a smudge of chocolate. "There are still mysteries to be revealed." She angled the cup. "Strange," she muttered. "There's a key at the bottom."

I rubbed the back of my neck. "What does that mean?"

"Mmm? Oh. The bottom of the cup is where I find the key to unlocking the story. It's the element or personality trait that will help you to move forward, or figure things out, or be successful. And I see a key at the bottom of your cup."

"I don't understand."

"A key symbolizes a secret that will unlock the mystery, so basically it's saying the key is the key. Sorry. Whatever the secret is, it's still hidden." She sighed. "This was my worst reading of the day."

I straightened, alarmed. "What?"

She reached across the table and touched the back of my hand. "I didn't mean the worst fortune, just my worst telling. I guess I'm more tired than I thought."

"No, no. I enjoyed the reading. And I'd love to have you back for future events." But anxiety jittered my insides. I didn't believe in fortune-telling. Or at least I didn't *believe* believe. So why was I getting so worked up?

"I read wine dregs too."

I laughed. "I'm keeping your number on speed dial."

She paid me the museum's cut and I helped her pack her things into cardboard boxes. After seeing her to the door, I locked it behind her.

A hidden mystery was the key. Well, there was *one* mystery I might be able to unlock. I found the phone number for the detective in Oaxaca and called.

"*Bueno?*" he asked.

"Hi, Alejandro? This is Maddie Kosloski from California."

"Oh, hello, Miss Maddie. How are you this evening?" Something clattered in the background.

"Fine. Is this a good time to continue our conversation about Felicitas Ocasio's death?"

He sighed. "Why not?"

"You said officially her death had been ruled a suicide. But your friend suspected Felicitas's boyfriend might have had something to do with it." There was a loud noise on his end, like a truck rumbling past, and I raised my voice. "How exactly did she die?"

"What?"

I repeated myself.

"Drug overdose," he shouted. "Everyone said she was not a user, that she'd never taken drugs before, and my friend believed it. Felicitas was a good woman, a good Catholic, and suicide is a mortal sin. She worked hard, took care of her parents, was top of her class. More importantly, she only had one needle mark, the one that took her life. Perhaps it was her first time and she made a mistake. But there were bruises on her neck, as if someone had held her down."

One of the fluorescent lamps flickered above me, and I glanced up. Photos of convicted murderers stared down at me from the museum walls. "And your friend thought someone had injected her against her will?"

A horn blared in the background.

"What?" he shouted.

"As if someone had injected her against her will?"

"Yes, yes." He erupted in a stream of Spanish. I picked out a curse.

I swallowed, sickened. "Then why was it ruled a suicide?" I asked over the street noise.

"What?"

"Why a suicide?"

"Because the bruises were inconclusive," Alejandro said. "And witnesses said she had been distraught the day before her death. Her family did everything they could to get the finding changed to murder, but ..." I could almost hear the shrug over the phone. "Politics."

"But it sounded like there was clear evidence of foul play. How could politics—"

"You have politics in America too, I think," he said shortly.

"Yes, of course," I said. I would like to think it didn't influence criminal investigations here, but that was naive. Still, it was strange politics that would cover up a drug murder. "Maybe she was distraught because she learned her boyfriend dealt in drugs?"

"Her relatives said he told her he worked as a driver for a cocoa company. It turned out he was delivering a different kind of coca."

"You mean, cocaine? Was that what killed her?"

"Yes. Injecting is a much more dangerous method of using the drug, but it causes the most intense effects, so fools take the risk. Now you see why it was easy to call her overdose an accident."

I gnawed my bottom lip. This was getting worse by the second, but I couldn't stop. "What happened to the boyfriend?"

"He disappeared after her death."

That sounded suspicious.

GD hopped onto the counter and brushed against the tip jar.

"We found his body a week later," the detective continued. "He'd been beaten to death, we guessed by one of his colleagues. He was in trouble, and he knew it and ran."

"Do you know how long he'd been dead before his body was found?"

A long pause. "I thought you wanted to know about Felicitas."

I hesitated. Had I imagined the edge to his voice? "I do, but if her boyfriend was the killer, that's part of the story. Isn't it?"

"Is it?" He coughed.

I waited, hoping I hadn't offended Jason's friend.

"He was dead roughly a week," he finally said.

So, the boyfriend had died not long after Felicitas. "I see. Thank you for telling me about the murders."

"I hope it is helpful." He cursed in Spanish. "I must go. Good luck with your museum." He disconnected.

Feeling drained, I sat back in my chair. What a brutal story, ugly and cruel. Poor Felicitas.

I looked toward the Gallery, and the molinillo in its ceramic bowl. Felicitas probably hadn't known the truth about her boy-friend's drug dealing until it was too late. Was that the key to the molinillo's mysterious rattling—a lie that had killed Felicitas? Or perhaps the lie was that her boyfriend had ever loved her?

I massaged the heel of my palm against my chest. I'd write out the story for the molinillo display, but I'd leave Felicitas's name out. She'd been betrayed in the worst way, and she deserved privacy.

Heavyhearted, I called Jason.

"Maddie," he said, his voice warm. "Is everything okay?"

I laughed shortly. "I hope I don't only call when I've got a problem."

"Of course not. It's just …" He cleared his throat. "I don't like the way we left things the other day."

"Me neither." I leaned one hip against the glass counter. "You're right. Mason has been hanging around the museum more than usual. I thought he was trying to get back to being friends, and it was awkward, so I avoided asking him what was going on. But I will, next time I see him. And if it isn't clear to everyone already, Mason and I are over. For good."

"I know. I trust you. One of the things I love about you is your honesty. Though you tend to bend things a bit when it comes to murder investigations."

There was that L-word again. And I wasn't sure if I was ready for it. "That's not fair. Whenever I learn something, I tell you right away."

"I know, I know. I just wish you wouldn't *accidentally* come across so much relevant information. But people are more willing to gossip to civilians than cops. And you seem to have a knack for … whatever it is you do." '

Lightly, I bit my bottom lip. "So, are we good?"

His voice lowered to a rumble. "We're good."

Relief slumped my shoulders, because I didn't want to fight, and I didn't want to give up what I was doing either. I coughed. "I've been thinking about the murders—"

"Maddie …" he began, in a voice reinforced with rebar.

"You've probably already considered this," I said quickly, "but hear me out. Don't both these murders seem like they were done by the same sort of … *mind* as the bomb threat at the museum and the firecrackers at the vigil?"

A cautious pause. Then, "Go on."

"Stabbing an accountant with her own receipt holder. Death by chocolate for a chocolate maker—"

"He was bludgeoned," Jason said. "The chocolate didn't kill him."

"Even so, dumping chocolate on him after he'd fallen—"

"You think someone dumped it on him because his sleeve was chocolate-free?"

I deflated. "Um. Yeah. Am I wrong?"

"No. I'd come to the same conclusion."

GD meowed. Tail high, he brushed against my arm.

Okay, maybe my detecting brain wasn't exactly unique. "Right, but doesn't it seem almost childish, as childish as—"

"A bomb threat and firecrackers. I agree."

"You do?" So, he *had* thought of the connection. I didn't know whether to feel disappointed I wasn't dazzling him with my brilliance or relieved my idea wasn't crazy.

"Here's the thing. When we catch the killer, the defense will have a field day if the lead detective had a relationship with a material witness."

My heart sank. "Material... Are you saying I'm a material witness?"

"You discovered the body," Jason said. "You were with me when the second body was discovered. And if the bomb threat is connected to the murders, you took the call. You're the only person who can testify to what you heard."

"Oh." My throat tightened. Where was all this going? "Have I made things harder for you? I haven't wrecked the case or anything, have—?"

"No," he said. "You haven't done anything wrong. But from now on, if you get any brainstorms, talk to Detective Hammer."

"To Laurel?" Was he nuts? She *hated* me. She'd never listen to anything I had to say. My stomach spun. "Are you saying they pulled you off the case?"

"I've never been on it. Not since you discovered Atticus's body."

"But I thought—Why didn't you tell me?"

Silence.

"What?" I asked. And I swear I could *hear* the look Jason was giving me over the phone, which, yes, I know is technically impossible.

"Are you actually complaining that I don't keep you in the loop about police investigations?"

"Ah..." Yeah. That probably wasn't realistic.

"I didn't think so. Don't sound so glum. Me being yanked is just bad luck. You were the first on the scene at a murder. And it didn't help that you were covered in chocolate."

"From the CPR!"

"Don't worry. We have a tape of the 911 call. We know what happened."

"The police don't really think I'm a suspect, do they?"

"Why would you be a suspect?"

"No reason," I said quickly. "I just wish you hadn't brought up my murdery chocolate coating."

"Mmm," he said in a velvet-edged voice. "That has possibilities."

We weren't talking murder anymore, and my pulse sped.

"Damn, I have to go," he said. "Sorry, I'll call you later."

"You'd better." Because I was starting to get over my chocolate phobia.

TWENTY

A GRAY WALL OF fog pressed against the Gallery's windows Tuesday morning. I stooped to refill GD's food and water bowls. Licking his chops, the cat nudged me aside and got busy crunching kibble.

I rolled up the sleeves of my fitted blouse—white with tiny blue flowers that matched the color of my jeans. "You're welcome." *Cats.*

In the Gallery, I surveyed the black shelves. They were delightfully empty. I made notes on my inventory list, then retrieved boxes of chocolate and tarot cards from Adele's storeroom.

GD came to supervise as I constructed pyramids of chocolate bars. He leapt to the top of my alchemy display and wound sinuously between fake cocoa pods and grinding stones.

I adjusted a stack of chocolate-themed oracle decks. Wine and Chocolate Days had been a good promotion. I needed to thank Penny at the Visitors Bureau for organizing the event.

Penny, who knew all the wine-related business gossip. Penny, who I suspected had been holding back when she'd taken me to Lola's tea. Penny, who like me was obsessed with her work and would no doubt be locked away inside the Wine and Visitors Bureau, which, like my museum, was closed today.

Oh yes, a thank you call was definitely in order. Purring with satisfaction, I ruffled GD's fur.

The cat hissed with surprise.

"See ya!" Grabbing my blue faux-leather jacket off its peg, I sauntered out the front door. I had to jump to sidestep Mason on the brick sidewalk.

"Oh, hey." He stuffed his fingers into the front pockets of his worn black jeans. "Going somewhere?"

"To …" *Shut it down.* If only I knew how, or even what I was shutting down. "Uh-huh."

"How's the haunted milano you've been promoting?"

"The molinillo?" I asked, surprised. "Good. I mean, it's an inanimate object, so it doesn't have an emotional state, but I think I have most of its story." With both Felicitas and her boyfriend dead, it was unlikely I'd learn more. But that was life. Not every mystery was completely resolved. Sometimes you had to rely on guesswork and intuition.

He crossed his bulging arms over his chest. "What's the story?"

"It looks like Felicitas—the woman who owned the molinillo—was murdered, likely by her boyfriend."

"So why does it rattle when someone lies?"

I was starting to hate this story. "Because her boyfriend lied to her. He kept it secret that he was a drug dealer. But the real betrayal was that he lied about loving her. You don't murder someone you love because they get pregnant." I shivered in the fog. Poor Felicitas.

I couldn't even imagine the pain she must have felt. Her lover's hands around her throat, the breathless agony...

Okay, maybe I could imagine it a little *too* well. "If only he'd just let her go."

Mason smiled faintly. "Like you let me go."

"That wasn't the same," I said, feeling myself color. "I—" I'd had real feelings for Mason. But had I been in love? Letting him go hadn't been easy, but maybe it should have been harder. "Anyway," I said, brusque, "honesty is better than the death-by-a-thousand-cuts of little relationship dishonesties." Or in Felicitas's case, it was better than actual death.

His gaze shifted to the brick sidewalk. "Right. Hey, there's something—"

The door to the motorcycle shop opened and Belle leaned out, her hair swinging past her shoulder. "Mason, a customer has a question I can't answer."

He nodded to her. "Right. I'll be right there." He turned to me, a question in his eyes.

"Mason..." *Get it over with. Ask him what's going on.*

He glanced over his shoulder toward the motorcycle shop. "Yeah?"

I chickened out. "I've got to go. Good luck with the customer." I hurried to my pickup and drove off.

At the Wine and Visitors Bureau, I walked through the twisting fog to the brick building's side door. I tested the latch. The metal door creaked open, a melancholy whine that raised the hair on my arms.

"Hasn't anybody in this town heard of oil?" I muttered.

I leaned inside the long hallway. Cardboard wine boxes sat stacked along its walls. "Penny? It's Maddie." My voice echoed off the tile floor.

I walked inside. "Hello?"

Above me, a fluorescent lamp flickered and pinged. Penny's office was at the far end of the hall, which was lined with closed doors.

"Penny?" I called more softly.

I crept down the hallway. Penny's office door stood open. Inside—a desk overflowing with papers. Stacks of boxes. A purple cardigan slung over the back of her rolling chair.

But no Penny.

Maybe she was in the restroom.

I edged from the office and toward the opening to the tasting area. My thigh struck a box, rattling the bottles inside. I cursed, rubbing the muscle, and limped forward.

The overhead light flickered, and I glanced up.

Motion blurred at the edge of my vision. A woman shrieked.

I gasped and stumbled backward, shielding my face. "No!" When I didn't get clobbered, I peeked through my fingers.

Penny lowered a near-black wine bottle and clutched one hand to her heaving chest. "I thought you were a burglar!"

I straightened out of my crouch. "I called out. Didn't you hear me?"

"I was in the ladies' room." She placed the bottle on a nearby box. "What are you doing here?"

"Looking for you." I eyed her. Penny's long-sleeved black tee read: *Wine Rack*. The sentiment seemed racy for grandmotherly Penny. But she took her duties at the Wine and Visitors Bureau seriously.

"Did you need something?" she asked.

"Sort of. I felt like there was something you wanted to tell me last week about Reign, but that you were being polite."

"Ah." She tugged down the front of her tee. "Come into my office."

I followed her inside.

She shifted a stack of manila folders off a chair, then settled herself behind the desk. Primly, she folded her hands. "What did you want to know?"

"What didn't you want to tell me at Lola's?"

"I probably told you too much," she fretted. "I never should have been talked into joining that wine tasting beforehand, but they were old college friends of mine. It seemed wrong to refuse. I always gab too much after a glass or three."

"Would you like one now?" I half-joked. Maybe it would unstick her tongue.

She stared over her cat-eye glasses. "No, young lady, I would not."

"Look, if you don't want to tell me, then tell the police. Two people are dead, and someone phoned a bomb threat in to my museum."

"You think the bomb threat is connected to the murders?"

"I'm not certain, but … yes, I do."

She frowned. "But you're an associate member of the Wine and Visitors Bureau!"

"Ye-es."

"That's outrageous! An attack on one member is an attack on all. We're like NATO."

Whoa. Maybe Penny took her duties a little *too* seriously. I hoped I hadn't unknowingly signed on to any containment pacts. "So, will you help me?"

She leaned back in her chair. It creaked beneath her bulk. "I wish I could."

Oh, come on. "Penny, please. NATO!"

"It's not that I don't want to. I just don't think I'll be much help. I told you about the late payments from Reign to that farmer?"

"Yes."

"Well, as you know, I've been working with the wineries to help them organize the wine and chocolate tastings."

I nodded, encouraging.

"And since Reign is such a big name, getting their shop on board seemed like a huge coup. I mean, they've been in national newspapers and magazines."

"Sure." I nodded encouragingly.

"But Orson could be difficult to work with."

"Orson?" I asked. "Not Atticus? I thought he'd be the liaison with the Visitors Bureau."

"Atticus was our point man, and he was a dream, but he wasn't always available. They're still a small shop, you know."

So small they were artisanal. "And Orson?"

"I suppose he was so busy with the chocolate-making, having to deal with the sales side was frustrating."

"Hmm." Disappointed, I studied my tennis shoes. She was right. This didn't exactly illuminate the crimes.

"And then there was that argument."

My spine snapped into alignment. That sounded more promising. "What argument?"

"I stopped by Reign one morning. It was early. They'd just opened for the day, and they weren't expecting me. But I needed their approval on some flyers."

"Yes?" I asked, bracing my forearms on the knees of my jeans.

"I mean, I couldn't print it without approval. What if something was wrong? We couldn't afford to reprint. Do you have any idea how much color printing costs?"

"Roughly a dollar a page." I'd become a fixture at the local copy shop with my flyers promoting Gallery exhibits.

"Exactly! It's crazy! But I can't use our printer." She motioned toward a corner of the office and a printer buried beneath a Vesuvius of paper. "The colors always get strange."

I crossed one leg over the other and jiggled my foot. "Penny, what was the argument about?"

"Orson and Atticus were shouting. Atticus said something about being compromised. And then they noticed I was there and clammed up. Orson told me some of the cocoa beans had been ruined—that's what had been compromised. Apparently, cocoa beans are even more expensive than color printing."

"You're sure it was Atticus who said they were compromised?"

"I might be getting older, but I can still tell who's who." She glared over her glasses.

"I just meant..." I sucked in my cheeks. "It seems a little strange Atticus was complaining about cocoa prices and bad beans. He was marketing, not chocolate-making."

"They were business partners. A financial loss would affect them both." Penny twisted in her chair and plucked the purple cardigan from its back.

"Hmm..." It was my go-to noise of dissatisfaction. Something wasn't right.

"I attended one of their chocolate-tasting workshops." She shrugged into her cardigan. "Honestly, I couldn't tell the difference between one bar and another. I thought I had a good palate—I used to be a sommelier, you know."

"I didn't know that," I said, impressed. Becoming a sommelier wasn't easy.

"But my favorite chocolate is still See's."

It was mine too, and we paused, silent, lost in misty recollections of those white chocolate boxes.

"Butter creams." I sighed.

"Summer berries."

"Cranberry truffles."

"And wine," we said in unison, and laughed.

"I don't suppose that gives you any better idea of who killed Atticus and that poor woman," she said.

"Not really. Have you told the police about any of this?"

"Do you think I should? The argument I heard seemed so minor. Maybe you could tell that boyfriend of yours. If he thinks it's important, he can call me."

"Actually, Detective Hammer is in charge of the case."

"Oh." A look of consternation crossed Penny's broad face. "Maybe I'll call the police hotline then."

"Call the police about what?" my mother asked from behind me.

I started guiltily in my chair.

In the doorway, my mother gazed down with a forbidding expression. She folded her arms over her pale blue wool coat.

"Something odd I overheard at the chocolate shop," Penny said. "Maddie was giving me some advice."

My mother's brows pinched. "Was she now?"

I shrank in my seat. *Eeek!*

"Because I was under the distinct impression," my mother continued, "that she had promised to stay out of the Reign murders."

"Had I?" I squeaked.

"You had."

My chin dipped to my chest. "I don't actually remember that," I mumbled.

"I do. Quite clearly."

Penny cleared her throat. "Well. What brings you to the Wine and Visitors Bureau, Fran?"

"Ladies Aid."

"Ah, yes," Penny said. "The charity event." The two began rattling off statistics on ticket sales and table costs.

I lifted myself from my chair and attempted to make like a ninja and slink past unnoticed. But that was impossible in a room this small, especially with my mother blocking the door.

"Just one moment, Madelyn." She raised her index finger. "Are you free for lunch today?"

"Um—"

"Good."

I waited awkwardly beside a tottering pile of boxes. Honestly, I was an adult. It's not like I needed my mother's permission to talk to Penny about the murders.

Finally she and Penny wrapped up their conversation, and I followed my mother into the mist-shrouded parking lot.

She stopped beside her Lincoln SUV. "I hope you know why I asked you to lunch."

To yell at me some more? "I have no idea."

Her brow lowered. "Madelyn, we need to talk."

TWENTY-ONE

LUNCH WITH MY MOTHER. Normally, I enjoyed spending time with her. All the other Kosloskis were off doing exciting things in amazing places, and now that I'd given up the wild international life (*ha*), I figured the remainders had to stick together.

But lunch today was frosty. I sat at the table in the breakfast nook in her kitchen, poking my chicken Caesar salad with a fork.

Outside the paned windows, the front yard was gray, a low mist dampening the hood of her new SUV. Her old Lincoln had been blown up last December. That had sort of been my fault, so in fairness, she had reason to be annoyed.

I cleared my throat. "Have you heard from Shane yet?" I could usually distract my mother with gossip about one of my siblings.

"You're changing the subject," she said.

Usually distract. Not always. "Well …" At a loss, I turned the fork between my fingers. "I guess I am. Mom, I don't understand what's going on here. You practically dragged me into two murder investigations last year. You said I was good at it."

"You are. You're good at everything you do. Well, nearly everything. Those piano lessons were a disaster."

"I never wanted to take—" I clamped my jaw shut. *Never mind.* "So, what's different now?"

"What's different is, last year I saw someone aim a compound bow at you. You were shot!"

"Only grazed."

"*And* we were both nearly blown up. Just because you have a talent for something doesn't mean you have to do it." Her shoulders hunched. "No, it isn't that. I was arrogant. This town …" She motioned toward the SUV. "I thought nothing really bad could happen to us here. But that was ridiculous. Places change, and so do people. I thought I was in control of things." She laughed hollowly. "What a rude awakening last winter was."

I swallowed, my throat dry. My normally unstoppable mother had hit a wall. "But you were right about getting involved then. Things worked out."

"Shane's being transferred to Afghanistan."

Stunned, I flopped back in my chair. "What?" Our embassy there was still a frequent target of attacks. Shane might be annoyingly perfect, but he was my brother, and my stomach burned with worry.

"As you can imagine, there aren't many volunteers to go to that embassy. Your brother said he doesn't have a choice in the matter, and …" Her voice hitched. "He wants to go."

"I'm sure he'll be safe," I lied. "They have lots of protection at the embassy, plus Marine guards." *Afghanistan. Good God.* It had been a year since I'd last seen my brother.

I stared out the window at the oak by my mother's SUV. Mist twined in its bare limbs. As kids, we would gather mistletoe from that oak, build precarious tree houses in its branches. My throat thickened.

"I'm *not* sure about his safety." She knit her fingers together on the table. "But we all must do our duty. You, however, have no duty to insert yourself into these murders. In fact, as a good citizen, you should let the police do their jobs."

I could have argued it was my duty to make sure the police had all the facts. But that seemed churlish. My mother couldn't make sure Shane was safe, so she was going to make sure I was. Dammit.

"I don't want to have to worry about you both," she continued.

"Mom, I'm not going to do anything crazy," I hedged. What would I do if she demanded I promise to drop things?

She rose and took our plates to the sink. "No, I suppose you won't. You've always been more risk-averse than Shane and Melanie."

My mouth flattened. More risk-averse? I owned my own business, a paranormal museum. That was risky! But I wasn't going to argue.

Silent, I cleared the table and washed the dishes in the kitchen sink. Fortunately, my mother didn't press her point. I helped her clean the kitchen, and we talked about next month's ghost photography exhibit.

I grabbed my jacket. "Well, thanks."

"Wait. Take this."

She forced a frozen chicken Alfredo casserole on me, and I escaped with it to my waiting pickup. My mom hadn't made me promise to stay out of the murder investigation, and that was good. I didn't want to worry her, and I sensed I was getting close to the answer. I couldn't give up now.

Drawing a deep, guilty breath, I glanced at the foil-wrapped baking dish on the seat beside me. My mother knew I didn't like chicken Alfredo. What was I going to do with this huge casserole?

Give it to someone who could use it.

Someone like ... India.

I called Adele's father.

"Maddie? What's going on?" he asked.

"I have a casserole for India. Is she working today?" I glanced at the dashboard clock. It was just past one o'clock. The wineries would be getting busy.

"No, she's at home as far as I know."

"Great, thanks. If she's not, I'll leave the casserole on her porch," I said. "Can you give me her address?"

"Sure. Let me dig it out." After a minute, he rattled off her address and phone number, and I scribbled it into my notepad.

"Thanks. Er, how's the wedding planning going?"

He chuckled. "Fantastic, since I've been banned from helping."

"I hear you," I said, wistful. I was glad to be assisting Adele with her big day. But there was an awful lot to do. "I'll talk to you later."

We rang off, and I drove slowly down the fog-bound roads. Wraiths of twisted grapevines stood like sentinels along the roadside.

Would my brother be in danger? You didn't hear much about Afghanistan in the news anymore, but we still had troops there. I wasn't sure if no news was good news, or if we'd just grown indifferent, uninterested. My stomach twisted. I wasn't indifferent any longer.

India lived in a sprawling ranch house in a neighborhood tucked between vineyards.

I parked on the sidewalk beside her emerald lawn. The circular driveway was empty, which didn't bode well for finding her at home. But I walked up the concrete drive, past a barren dogwood tree and to the front door. A wreath of dried grapevines knotted with twinkle lights encircled the brass knocker.

Casserole balanced on one hip, I rang the bell. Its solemn tone echoed through the house.

I waited a few minutes. Finally, I dug into my purse and retrieved a pen and notepad. Setting the casserole on the low bench beside the door, I scribbled a note and tucked it beneath the baking dish.

I waited another minute or two, then slowly walked down the drive. A gust of damp wind tossed my hair, and something banged behind me.

My neck tensed. I looked over my shoulder.

A tall redwood gate at the side of the house drifted open, banged shut.

My mouth pursed.

It would only be neighborly if I made sure the gate was shut fast. What if India kept a dog in the back yard? It might escape, run into the street, and get hit by a car.

Deliberately, I walked to the tall gate. It creaked open, horror-movie-inviting. A narrow concrete path threaded between the house and a high wooden fence. A dust-covered barbecue leaned against the stucco wall.

"India?" I called.

My heartbeat sped. Paranoia had become an old friend, but I'd stumbled across two too many dead bodies recently. What I felt now wasn't paranoia. It was rational fear. I *really* didn't want to find a third corpse.

"Hello?" I whispered and crept down the path. The hem of my jeans brushed the yellow mustard flowers growing between the concrete and the fence.

I rounded the corner of the house. Neatly swept wooden deck. Wood-beam awning. Elegant outdoor chairs. Beside the kidney-shaped pool, near the diving board, was a single large cardboard box. The grounds seemed recently landscaped, with a low-water selection of lavender bushes and not a leaf out of place.

But the cardboard box was a sour note in the immaculate yard, and I walked toward the pool. *Affaire* was printed on the side of the box.

There was a soft noise behind me. I started to turn.

Something struck the center of my back, knocking the wind from my lungs. I pitched forward, arms windmilling helplessly, and plunged into the pool.

The water was cold as knives. I came up sputtering, eyes blurred and stinging with mascara.

A strong hand grabbed the top of my head and forced me beneath the surface.

I clawed at the sides of the pool. My fingers scraped cold concrete. My legs kicked, useless.

My hands scraped across the rim of the pool. Heart exploding in my chest, I grasped at it, straining to pull myself up. But I didn't move, didn't break the surface. I hadn't taken a breath when I'd gone in, and didn't know how long I could last without air. *Breathe. I had to breathe.*

Stars sparked in front of my eyes. *If not up, then down?* I pushed away from the side of the pool.

But whoever held me had a firm grasp of my hair. A chill wracked my body.

I flailed beneath the water.

My lungs burned, the demand for air unbearable, overwhelming. This couldn't be happening. Shane was going to Afghanistan, and I was going to die in a California swimming pool. And it hurt, hurt, hurt, an agony of cold and fire in my chest. Black flames flickered at the edge of my sight.

I gasped, sucking in water. Then I really knew agony. My lungs seemed to tear, slashed by rough blades. Distantly, I felt my limbs writhing. My vision telescoped.

My final thought was that my mother was going to be furious.

Then the darkness closed in, complete.

TWENTY-TWO

I AWOKE IN WATER, my arms pinned to my sides. I jerked away, coughing, lungs aching, and vomited water into the pool.

India let go like I was radioactive, and she floundered backward in the water, splashing. "It's okay. You're all right."

I found my feet and stood, hip deep in the pool. Coughing, I scraped my wet hair from my face. "What the hell?"

She raised her hands in a warding gesture. Her green-and-blue yoga outfit was soaked to the collar, her ponytail plastered to her neck. Water beaded her delicate face. "I found you in the pool. What were you doing in my pool?"

Shivering, I sloshed toward the pool steps. My legs collapsed after the first one, and I crawled up the remainder and onto the wooden deck.

"What were you doing in my pool?" India repeated more sharply.

I rolled off the deck onto the pavement and sat, staring at the gray sky. Someone had tried to kill me. I shuddered. They'd come too close to succeeding.

India trudged out of the pool and stood over me, dripping. "You haven't answered my question. What are you doing here?"

I coughed. "The gate was open. You weren't answering your door. I thought..." My lungs ached, and I rubbed my chest.

"What did you think?"

Cold seeped from the concrete into my bones, and a deeper chill settled into my heart. Someone had tried to kill me.

Violently. Hands-on.

I began to shake, my trembling having nothing to do with the cold air on my wet clothes. I rolled onto my side and sat up. "I guess I thought you might be dead."

Her legs folded beneath her and she sat hard on a deck chair. She clasped her arms. "Oh."

My teeth chattered. "With everything that's been happening—"

"I get it."

We said nothing for a long time.

"How did you get in my pool?"

"I was looking at the box. Over there." I pointed, hand wavering, to the diving board. The box had vanished.

"What box?" she asked.

"There was a cardboard box," I rasped, my throat raw. "It seemed out of place. The rest of your yard is so neat."

"Thanks," she said dully.

So where was the box now?

"Someone pushed me into the pool and held me under."

She quirked a skeptical brow. "So, you trespassed in my back yard, examined a box which isn't there, and then someone tried to drown you?"

A bout of coughing wracked me and I pressed my hands to the cold cement, bracing myself. When I looked up, her expression hadn't changed.

"Someone killed your cousin and husband." I sucked in a deep breath, working to calm myself, and started hacking up a lung instead. "I'm not lying. Something's going on," I said more quietly, "and it's connected to your family."

She rose. "Come inside. I'll get you a towel."

Thoughts jumbling, I trailed after her. My feet squelched in their sneakers. At least she trusted me enough to let me into her house.

The interior was a disappointment of unmatched furniture and movie posters. I'd thought India would have more flare, like Lola, but maybe I was holding her to unfair standards.

She opened a closet door and tossed me a beige towel. "I'm not sure if I should call the police."

"Neither am I." I peeled off my sodden jacket and grimaced. Faux-leather probably liked water about as much as real leather. I rubbed my arms with the rough towel. India hadn't trusted my story. But I was in her house, so she hadn't completely disbelieved me either. "How did you find me?" I asked.

"I came home and saw that the gate was open. I thought I heard a noise, so I called out and walked into the back yard. You were face-down in the pool." A quick gust of air escaped her, half laugh, half sob. "You weren't faking being nearly drowned."

"Do you have any idea who's behind this, India?"

"No." Turning away, she grabbed another towel from the closet and wrapped it around herself like a cloak. "I don't know."

"Someone was here, at your house—"

"The only person who I know for sure was here is you."

"Then who took the box?" I asked.

"What box?!"

"The box that …" Hell. What was the point? "I left a casserole on your doorstep," I finished weakly.

She walked to the front door, opened it, stooped. She returned inside with the foil-wrapped casserole. "Thanks."

"It's chicken alfredo. Let it defrost, then reheat for thirty minutes at 350. Now, putting aside how weird it looked that I was floating in your pool, why would someone be lurking in your back yard?"

"Aside from you?"

I repressed a scowl, icy fear replaced by hot, welcome anger, though not toward her. Someone had tried to snuff me out of existence, as if I didn't matter. It was insulting. "Aside from me."

She pulled her hair free from her hairband and rubbed her head with the towel, obscuring her face. "Sam's been here." Even muffled by the towel, I could hear the strain in her voice.

"Sam?" I asked. "You mean the guy Atticus fired?"

"Orson fired him, not Atticus."

"Then what did he want?"

She emerged from beneath the towel and clutched it to her chest. Her slim shoulders hunched. "Justification," she whispered. "His job back. I'm not sure. He was …" She swallowed. "He was angry. Unbalanced."

"Unbalanced?" I squeaked. Was he unbalanced enough to push someone into a pool and hold them under? But if so, what did he have against me?

India smiled, wry. "Let's just say I didn't let *him* inside the house."

I guessed she didn't think I was crazy. "Did you tell the police?"

"It didn't seem worth it." She shook her head. Droplets from her hair struck the closed closet door. "Should we call 911?"

"That's for emergencies. This one is kind of over. But you should call them about Sam." I looked around. "My purse."

"Is at the bottom of the pool."

I groaned. *Dammit.* I doubted my phone had survived underwater. And I really didn't want to go for another swim. In all the excitement, I *might* have peed in the pool.

"We can fish it out with the net," she said. "Come on."

Towel draped around my shoulders, I followed her outside. My purse lay at the bottom of the deep end. Beside it on the pale blue pool floor was my phone. A pen and candy wrapper floated on the water's surface. My face heated. How long had *that* been in my purse?

India was adept with the pool net, and after a few attempts she retrieved all my things, including the wrapper. I stuffed it into my ruined purse.

"Let it dry out before you turn it on," India advised, nodding to the phone.

"I will." How long would that take? "Do you know where I can find Sam?"

"I'm not sure finding him is such a good idea."

I was too angry to care. "I need to know if he was here earlier."

"You should call the police about today."

My heart sank. Laurel wouldn't believe me. In her mind, any disaster was always my fault. But I couldn't *not* report the attack. "I'll call when I get home. But do you know where Sam might be?"

She angled her head. "His address is in Atticus's office files. Wait here." She went back through the sliding glass door into the house.

So, she trusted me in the house, but not in her husband's office. I could hardly blame her under the circumstances. Rubbing my chest, I studied the pool. I couldn't have been unconscious in the water long, or I wouldn't have...

... survived.

I'd been lucky. My limbs trembled, and I slowed my breathing. I was alive. Now wasn't the time for the hysterics I sensed shrieking at the edge of my awareness.

I scanned the yard. Where had my attacker gone?

India must have gotten to me fast. She said she'd come through the same open gate I had, but she hadn't seen the person who'd been holding me under.

The yard was surrounded by a six-foot redwood fence—not impossible to get over, but not easy either. I walked around the other corner of the house to a side yard with a decrepit swing set and tetherball pole. At its end stood another gate. My would-be killer could have heard India coming down the walk and escaped that way.

Five minutes later, she emerged with a slip of paper in hand. "Here." She held it out to me.

Composed, or at least pretending to be, I took the paper.

She didn't loosen her grip.

"You *are* calling the police, aren't you?" she asked.

"Of course. You should too. About Sam, I mean."

"About Sam." She nodded, her brandy-colored eyes serious, and she released the slip of paper.

"In case you forget, the directions for heating the casserole are on the note I left."

"Right. Let me know if you find anything, will you?"

"Sure. Thank you for saving my life."

"You're welcome." Her face crumpled. "I only wish you could have…" She pressed a hand to her mouth and fled into the house.

I looked down at the concrete stained with pool water dripping from my jeans. I wished I'd been able to save Atticus too.

Feeling sick, I got into my pickup, tossed my ruined jacket on the passenger seat, and turned on the heater. My clothes stuck to my flesh. Inside my sneakers, my feet would soon start to itch. I should go home and change, but I couldn't, not yet. There was something I needed to find out first.

I drove to the address India had given me—a bungalow on the wrong side of the tracks. The yard was knee-high with weeds. A Honda faded to a sullen pink squatted in the driveway. Squelching over to the Honda, I laid my palm on its hood. The metal was cold. If Sam had been at India's drowning me, he hadn't taken this car.

I peered through its window. Wrappers from Reign, crumpled fast food cups and boxes, and flyers protesting the chocolate shop lay scattered on the passenger seat and floor. Yup. This was Sam's car. So he probably hadn't tried to drown me, and since I was here…

I walked to the house and pressed the cracked plastic doorbell. It buzzed, setting my teeth on edge. I studied the paint peeling off the front door.

A curtain flicked sideways.

Sam opened the door. He was barefoot and bare-chested, a paunch riding over the hips of his faded jeans. His gaze traveled from my toes to the top of my head. "What happened to you?"

"Uh." I looked down at myself. My blouse had gone sheer, my blue bra visible beneath it. I crossed my arms over my chest. "I fell into a pool."

"Fell?" He sagged against the door frame.

Maybe honesty was the best policy. "Someone pushed me in and tried to drown me. At India Reine's house."

He quirked a brow. "India pushed you in?"

"I don't think so. She was the one who pulled me out." She'd saved my life. Had I even said thank you? I couldn't remember.

"So, she's a hero." He sneered and crossed his arms, mirroring me. "What do you want?"

"Where have you been for the last hour?"

"Here." His soft jaw jutted forward. "Why? Do you think I pushed you in?"

That tracked with the cold car, but I took an involuntary step backward. "Atticus and Tilde are dead. Someone called in a bomb threat at my museum and then tried to drown me."

"And India didn't notice someone trying to drown you in her own pool?" His eyes rolled.

"She wasn't—it's a long story. But something's going on with that chocolate shop, and you're the only one who might be impartial enough to tell me what." Because sometimes flattery is the best policy.

He straightened. "Damn right I'm impartial."

I waited. "So?"

"So, what?"

A new ache spread up my neck and behind my eyeballs. "You said your firing was unfair. Why don't we start with that? What happened, exactly?"

He shrugged. "Beats me. All I was trying to do was learn the roaster. I was in the storage room, grabbing a few beans from one of the plastic bins. Orson walked in and pitched a fit."

"Why?"

"Probably because the beans looked moldy. I figure he panicked—those beans are expensive—and took it out on me."

Moldy? Were they the ruined cocoa beans Penny had mentioned? "Did he know you were practicing with the roaster?"

Sam licked his lips. "No one else was using it. You'd think he'd be happy I was trying to work things out, become a better employee. But he was totally possessive of the whole chocolate-making process. I'd signed a nondisclosure agreement. It's not like I was trying to steal any chocolate-making secrets."

In other words, Orson didn't know Sam had been playing around with his equipment.

"I figured he'd cool off by the next day," Sam continued. "But when I got to work, he handed me my paycheck and told me to get out. Just like that. I told you it wasn't fair."

"That does seem a little extreme," I admitted and rubbed my jaw. "Did anything else happen?"

He stiffened. "You think I'm lying?"

"No." My mouth went dry. "I'm only trying to understand what happened."

"I *told* you what happened."

"What about Tilde, the accountant?"

Sam slouched against the door frame and his stomach bulged forward, his spine folding. "What about her?"

"Did she have any enemies? Were there any conflicts?"

He snorted. "Orson didn't like her. I heard him tell Atticus she was nosing around where she didn't belong."

"Nosing around where?"

"How should I know? You think Orson was ever in the mood for my questions? Besides, that accountant was a blackmailing snake."

"Blackmail?" I asked, startled. This was the first I'd heard of that.

A dog barked from a nearby yard.

"Tilde caught me coming in late once. It was only a few minutes, so of course I wrote on my timesheet that I came in on time. I mean, I'd practically forgotten about the whole thing by the time it came to submit timesheets. She threatened to tell Orson I was cheating unless I gassed up her car."

"Did you?"

"I wanted to keep my job, didn't I? I put three hours of pay into her gas tank." He spat a curse.

"And Lola?"

"The rich wife? I only saw her in the chocolate shop when she was swanning around getting her picture taken."

"I mean, did she ever have any problems with Tilde?"

"Not that I heard."

"Did you see India around the shop much?"

His expression turned wistful. "India would come by to bring Atticus lunch. Always had a smile for everyone. I'm sorry for her. She didn't deserve to lose her husband that way, even if he was a jerk."

"She didn't only lose her husband. Tilde, the accountant, was her cousin."

Sam's expression smoothed. "Was she?"

He'd known. Why was he lying about something so trivial? "Were you at the vigil for Atticus?"

He snorted. "Why would I be? I like India, but that only goes so far."

Now I *knew* Sam was lying. I'd seen him at the vigil. What else was he lying about? "Tilde said you followed her to her car one night when she left work and threatened her."

"*Tilde* said? Tilde's dead. Doesn't much matter what she said." He stepped backward into the squat house and slammed the door.

TWENTY-THREE

I STARED AT THE computer in the museum's dim light. Friday evening stragglers drifted through the main room. Clutching chocolate bars, they muttered over the creepy dolls, examined the placards beneath the exhibits.

I was so in trouble.

The week had passed, blessedly uneventful. No one was murdered. My *Magic of Chocolate* exhibit had gotten a mention in a Sacramento paper, and the museum had been packed all week. I felt kind of guilty about not telling Jason of my near-drowning. But he'd made it clear that this sort of info was for the officer in charge, Laurel Hammer.

Unfortunately, I hadn't talked to Laurel either. Or at least not directly.

When I'd returned, still damp and with a drowned cell phone, to my garage apartment three days earlier, I'd discovered that my wall phone was out of order. So I went next door to my aunt's. She admitted she'd disconnected the phone since I never used it. Then my aunt drafted me into cleaning out her garage. When she'd finally lent me her cell phone, she watched me dial, and I ended up leaving Laurel a vague message. My aunt would have told my mom about my near-death experience in a New York minute.

The next day, from the museum, I'd left another, more detailed message for the detective about my near-drowning. Then I went to buy a new cell phone, which ended up being with a new provider to save money. Museum ownership had turned me into a penny-pincher.

Thursday, when Laurel didn't call, I phoned the desk sergeant from my new cell phone. He told me she was off work that day.

I braced my head on my fist and scanned the Affaire website for the fifth time. The box with that name on it had to be important somehow, or the person who'd tried to drown me in India's pool wouldn't have removed it. Affaire was a chocolate-making company in the San Francisco Bay Area. It sold wholesale blocks of chocolate to bakeries. Had Atticus been researching the competition? But Reign was artisanal—they wouldn't be competing with wholesalers. And could I believe that India hadn't know anything about the box? The weather hadn't been great that week, so it was possible she hadn't been in her back yard. But it seemed weird.

"Hi, can I buy this?" a woman asked.

My head jerked up from my phone, where I'd been programming my mother's number. A sale! "Sure!" I sold her the tarot deck and shuffled the last happy customers out the door.

The bookcase swung open. Adele leaned against the door frame. "You need a break. Instead of the microbrewery, why don't we go to the wine club pickup party at Plot 42?"

I flipped the sign in the window to *Closed* and eyed her. Wisps of jet black hair had come free of her chignon, and her face looked worn. "Rough day?"

"Oh, you know. Friday."

"Friday," I agreed. Though unlike most people I had to look way ahead, to Monday and Tuesday, for my time to run errands and relax.

Dammit. And I needed to call Laurel again.

"So?" Adele asked. "Will you come?"

"Are you kidding?" I dropped a pen on the counter. I couldn't wait to thrash over what I'd learned about Reign with my friends. "I've got so much to tell you."

"Great! You can bring Jason."

I eyed her. "Bring Jason to girls' night?"

She blushed. "Dieter's coming."

I'd suspected girls' night might not survive Adele's wedding. But all good things must come to an end. "All right. I will."

She straightened off the door frame and her shoulders relaxed. "Perfect. Harper will meet us there."

Promising myself I'd clean the museum in the morning, I re-filled GD's food and water bowls, double-checked the locks, and called Laurel. At this point I had her number memorized. It was only one digit off from Jason's. Maybe the police had a special deal for partners.

"This is Detective Hammer. Leave a message. If this is an emergency, call 911."

"Um, hi. This is Maddie. Listen, I've left a few messages. I guess I'll just tell you again in case you didn't get them … Someone pushed me into India Reine's pool and tried to drown me on Tuesday. I didn't see who—"

Beep!

I pressed the phone to my forehead and breathed deeply. Okay. Forget Laurel. She *must* have gotten at least one of my messages by now. I debated programming her number into my new phone—at least that way I could screen her calls. Instead, I called Jason.

"Maddie," his voice purred. "I was just thinking of you."

My insides warmed. "Good things, I hope?"

"The best. What's going on?"

"I'm headed to Plot 42. Their wine club pickup party is today. Do you want to come?"

"I've got to finish a report, but I'll meet you there."

I grinned. "Great. See you then."

We hung up, and I strolled through the shared hallway to the alley and my pickup.

Two shadows moved behind the blinds in Mason's upstairs apartment. Annoyed with myself, I looked away. Would there ever be a day I didn't glance up when I left my museum?

Adele emerged from the building. She rattled the heavy metal door behind her, making sure it was locked, then stepped inside her Mercedes.

We caravaned down fog-bound streets, beneath the San Benedetto arch and out into farm country.

Tires crunching, I trailed Adele's taillights down the gravel drive to Plot 42. Light gleamed from the converted barn. Cars packed the lot, but I followed the Mercedes into the private family lot behind the barn.

I hopped from my pickup and stretched, inhaling the scent of damp earth.

Adele joined me and stretched too. "I'm glad we can just relax here."

Raucous music flowed from the barn.

I pointed to her chest. "You might want to take that off."

Adele looked down at her Fox and Fennel apron and her cheeks darkened. "You should have told me earlier." She whipped the apron over her head and tossed it on the seat of the Mercedes.

"I've learned some interesting things about Reign," I said.

"Oh?"

We strolled into the barn, and I flinched at the blaring music. At the far end, a local cover band played "Rhiannon." Twinkle lights swagged the rafters. People jammed shoulder-to-shoulder at the tasting bar. Clusters of tall chairs surrounded wine-barrel tables.

Adele scanned the crowd for Dieter.

Harper waved, alone at one of the small tables, and we joined her.

"I wasn't sure I'd be able to hold your chairs," she shouted over the music, and I promptly claimed one. "This place is a madhouse," she finished.

"I'll get the wine." Adele disappeared into the crowd.

Harper pointed at her full wine glass beside a bowl of chocolate. "I've already got..." She sagged in the chair. "Never mind. Long day?"

"The museum was pretty busy."

"I remember when you complained about just the opposite when your museum was floundering." She smiled.

I raised my hands. "Hey, I'm not complaining. I'm just ready for a break."

On the low makeshift stage, the musicians paused between songs and conferred.

Lola and India strolled past. India offered a tray of chocolates to passersby and looked miserable. Lola walked arm-in-arm with San Benedetto's mayor and with Mike, our intrepid local reporter.

"Try that dark chocolate from Tanzania with the cab," Lola was saying, pointing to India's tray. "Notice how it brings out the fruit flavor in the chocolate? It's eighty percent."

The mayor nodded enthusiastically.

I braced my elbow on the table and shielded my face. "Tell me when Mike's out of sight," I muttered.

"The reporter?" Harper's gaze tracked Lola and the mayor's progress. "I thought no publicity was bad publicity."

"He keeps asking me about the bomb threat. That's not the sort of publicity I want."

"Uh-huh," she said doubtfully.

Lola released the mayor's arm to snap a photo of him, glass raised to his lips.

Mike scribbled in a leather-bound notebook. "Eighty percent...?"

"Cocoa," Lola said.

India shifted her weight and glanced toward a table surrounded by middle-aged couples.

The mayor leaned close and muttered something in Lola's ear.

"Don't worry." Lola laughed. "If you don't take a picture, it didn't happen."

"Not exactly in mourning, is she?" Harper asked.

"It wasn't Lola's husband or cousin who died," I said.

Frowning, Adele materialized at our table cradling three wine goblets filled with ruby liquid. "The estate cabernet." She frowned at Harper's glass. "Why didn't you tell me you already had a glass? Oh well, someone will drink it."

"Dieter can have it," I said.

"He's more of a beer person," Adele replied.

"Dieter?" Harper raised her brows. "I thought this was girls' night."

"Oh, you know," Adele said vaguely, watching the open barn door.

"Whatever." Harper leaned left, watching Lola and the mayor vanish into the throng.

"I thought Wine and Chocolate Days were over," I said. "I know, my exhibit's still up, but what's with these chocolate tastings at your parents' wine club pickup party?" I nodded toward India.

"We had some Reign chocolate left over," Adele said, "and Lola offered to play chocolate sommelier."

"What did you decide about the wedding cake?" I asked her.

Adele's face crumpled. "Sheet cake and a fake tiered cake. I had no choice. I just hope some kid doesn't decide to try to eat the fake one. He'll end up with a mouthful of Styrofoam."

"I thought the reception was adults-only?" Harper asked.

"It was," she said, "until Dieter told me about all the kids on his side of the family. We'll hire some nannies and set up a separate play area for the children on the other side of the house."

"I've been thinking about the murders," I said. "Sam said Tilde was into petty blackmail. I wonder if she was killed because she knew too much? But if so, what did she know? Did she witness Atticus's murder, or did she somehow suspect who was behind it?"

"What's the mayor doing talking to Lola?" Harper's brow wrinkled.

"Who cares?" Adele replied. "I've got bigger fish to fry. Do you know any good babysitters?"

"No," I said, impatient. "Now, about the murders—"

"I thought you'd decided to drop that business," Adele said.

This is what came from not telling them about my near drowning. But the only way to make sure it didn't get back to my mother was to keep it to myself, India, and Laurel—if I ever managed to track down the detective.

I squirmed on my chair. "Not *drop*, not entirely. But I heard there was some conflict between Orson and Tilde. Orson told Atticus she was snooping. And if he told Atticus, he may have told others, like the killer." Assuming Orson himself wasn't the killer. I hadn't forgotten the insurance policy that resulted in him benefitting from Atticus's death.

"What are they telling that reporter?" Harper toyed with her wine glass.

I frowned. What was wrong with Harper? I understood Adele's obsession with her wedding, but Atticus had been one of Harper's clients. I thought she would've cared more about his murder.

"Lola's a publicity hound," Adele said. "Of course she's talking to a reporter. She doesn't have Atticus around anymore to manage her promotions."

"It sounds like you know Lola better than I do," I said.

"You can't avoid knowing Lola." Adele sipped her cabernet. "She's made sure of it by inserting herself into every single article connected to Reign. *And* everything else to do with this town."

"Is she a wine club member?" I asked.

"Yep," Adele said, white lines appearing at the corners of her lips. "And look how she's taken over the party. India works for my father, not for Lola."

"I'll be right back." Harper rose and plunged into the crowd.

"What is *with* her?" Adele asked. "You'd think she didn't care about my wedding."

"Well, we do talk about it an awful lot."

The band segued to David Bowie.

Adele glared. "Of course we do. How do you think you plan a wedding? You manage events at the museum. You know what sort of planning is required."

"Yes, but—"

"And those events are nothing compared to a wedding. It's only the most important day of my life." She gulped her wine.

I winced. "I know, I know. Sorry."

Adele set down the glass and hung her head. "No, I'm sorry. I shouldn't have blown up at you like that. This wedding is making me lose my mind."

"Your wedding's going to be fabulous. I mean—a vineyard! It will be gorgeous! And in the end, all anyone cares about is you and Dieter."

"And the cake." She moaned.

"Ply everyone with enough wine and they'll forget the cake."

"I don't want a bunch of slobbering drunks at my wedding. What will the children think?"

There *was* that. Thoughtful, I snagged a piece of chocolate from the bowl on the table and popped it into my mouth. It stuck in my throat and I washed it down with wine. Maybe I hadn't completely gotten over my recent aversion to chocolate.

"I could organize a petting zoo," Adele mused.

"Sure. Kids love petting zoos." There had to be a way to get her to stop obsessing over the wedding and start obsessing over my murders. Okay, that might have been a *tad* selfish.

I cleared my throat. "I'm sorry, I keep thinking about the murders. You're my best friend. I should be giving your wedding more attention, but I haven't been able to get these deaths out of my head."

Adele laid a hand on mine. "Of course you can't. You found the bodies! And all I can think about is myself. Enough. How can I help?"

"Is there anything else you know about Lola that you haven't told me?"

"For starters, I don't know why Harper is so obsessed with Lola and the mayor tonight. It's like my wedding isn't even happening."

Agh! Enough with the wedding. "Someone tried to drown me in India's pool on Tuesday," I blurted. It was the only thing I could think of to get her attention. And if I couldn't trust Adele and Harper to keep their mouths shut, who could I trust?

Adele blinked. "What?"

"What?" Jason asked from behind me.

I winced. Turned. "Oh … hey, you made it."

In his blue suit and tie, Jason glowered. "What's this about someone trying to drown you at India's?"

"Why didn't you tell me?" Adele asked.

"I wasn't hurt," I said weakly. "I was waiting until I told Laurel."

"You mean you haven't told her either?" Jason's nostrils flared. "Unbelievable. You didn't think to report an attempted murder at the home of a material witness?"

"I tried!"

He scowled. "Not hard enough. We could have gotten the alibis of everyone involved. Now days have gone by."

I'd left four messages for Laurel! How could he think I'd blow something like this off? "I already checked alibis," I ground out. "India could have pushed me in, but she's also the one who pulled me out. Sam doesn't seem likely—his car engine was cold when I drove to his house right after the incident. And Orson and Lola were at the chocolate shop." I'd gone there after leaving Sam's on Tuesday afternoon, and Lola had said they'd both been there all day.

"You checked? I could have you arrested for interfering in an investigation," Jason fumed.

"But—"

"You withheld evidence. When Laurel finds out, she'd be within her rights to arrest you."

"But I left her messages!"

"Messages." Adele angled her head. "I'll bet they were vague, or she would have gotten back to you. Honestly, Maddie. What were you thinking?"

"I was detailed!" This was so unfair. Maybe I *could* have asked Jason to pass the message on to Laurel. But I hadn't, because it seemed like tattling on Laurel, plus … I hadn't wanted him to tell me to stay out of the murders. Annoyance and reason warred inside me. "Fine," I finally said. "I'll call her again tonight."

"Now would be good," Jason said.

I slid from my chair. "I'll go outside to do it." *And leave another message, no doubt.*

"I'll come with you," he said grimly.

He didn't trust me to follow through? *Ouch.* Just for that, I wouldn't program his number into my new phone.

Harper appeared at my elbow. "So much for girls' night. No offense, Jason."

"None taken," he said.

"What did I miss?" she asked.

"Maddie's about to be arrested for withholding evidence," Adele said tartly.

"Huh?"

"Long story." I trudged from the noisy barn.

Jason followed.

"I did leave messages, you know, and I *did* say someone tried to drown me in India's pool."

He didn't respond.

I dialed. "You know, the reason I have her number memorized is because I've called it so often. Also, it's only one digit off from yours, which I only realized after—"

"This is Detective Hammer."

Laurel didn't sound happy to hear from me. But ordering me to the station seemed to lift her spirits.

I pocketed the phone. "I'm going to the station."

"I heard," he said.

"I'm sorry," I said stiffly. Jason seemed to be having a hard time believing me. "I should have told you right away."

"Why didn't you?"

"You told me to tell Laurel this stuff first, but she never got back to me."

He just looked at me.

"I left her four messages."

"She should have called you back for something like this."

"Well, she didn't. Jason, Laurel really—" *Hates me.* I exhaled slowly. If I complained yet again about how his partner had messed with me, it would look like I was the one with the problem. But he was a cop. Shouldn't he be able to tell who was being honest?

He shook his head. "Is that all that's going on?"

I screwed up my face. "My mom would flip out if she heard about the attack. Especially if it made the papers."

"You're a grown woman, and you're still afraid of your mother?"

"My brother's being sent to Afghanistan," I snapped. "She's worried. And yes, I know that's no excuse. But I left—"

"Messages," Jason said, stone-faced. "Got it. You said India saved you. What happened, exactly?"

Did he get it? I had my doubts, but I explained about the casserole, the open gate, the pool.

"Why didn't India call the police?" he asked.

"I don't know." And I *had* sort of been trespassing in her yard. But if India had tried to kill me, why then had she revived me? Had she had second thoughts? No, it couldn't have been India.

"Well." I scuffed the gravel drive with my toe. "I should probably go to the station."

"I'll follow you in my car."

My heart bottomed. He didn't trust me to do that either. Swallowing the angry lump in my throat, I nodded.

Jason walked me to my pickup and watched while I slithered inside and locked the doors. His sedan followed me all the way to the squat brick police station.

I met him on the front steps. Silently, he perp-walked me inside the sickly green reception area.

Laurel stood beside the reception window chatting with a beefy uniformed policeman. A shark-like smile spread across her face. "Well, well, well. Kosloski. Let's have a chat about withholding evidence in a police investigation."

TWENTY-FOUR

ADELE WINCED AND ROTATED the white tea cup between her hands. "Laurel kept you overnight?" Her hair was done up in a prim chignon, and she wore an ice-blue silk blouse beneath her Fox and Fennel apron.

Slouched across from her in the booth at the tea room, I examined the white teeth marks GD had left in my palm that morning. "No, only for a few hours. And she didn't charge me with interfering in an investigation after all." Thankfully, Laurel seemed to conclude that the attempted-murder-by-drowning was connected to the Reign murders.

I'd clung to that bright spot all weekend. Jason and I still hadn't spoken, and my mouth twisted. I wasn't sure if I should apologize or break up with him for not believing me. My ego told me to break up. But the thought squeezed my neck and chest, brought despairing tears to my eyes. I looked past the gauzy curtains to the sidewalk outside and blinked away the heat. Jason was usually so … sensible. I wanted to give him a chance to make things right. "I can't believe Jason didn't believe me." My grip tightened on my cup.

"I'm sorry I didn't either, but I was …" Adele briefly closed her eyes. "As self-obsessed as Lola. Jason will come around. Everyone knows Laurel is totally irrational when it comes to you and GD. I wouldn't be surprised if she deleted your messages."

"Thank you!"

"Did she give you any excuse?"

"She played innocent and told me she didn't get the messages. When I asked how that was possible, she didn't take it well." I hadn't believed Laurel, but I'd backed off. In the moment, getting out of the cop shop before sunrise was more important than getting her to admit she'd ignored my calls.

"Give Jason a chance. It's got to be complicated for him. She's his partner, and if she did ignore your report of a crime—that's serious."

"Yeah," I said heavily. I'd wasted so much time agonizing about whether Jason and I were in love or not. Perversely, now I was certain I did love the man. And just as certain that if he didn't trust me, I had to end it.

"But why didn't you tell Harper and me about the attack at India's?" Adele asked.

Swallowing, I fiddled with the cuff of my olive blouse. "I wanted to tell Laurel first, like I said. But first she was off work, and then she didn't answer, and then one thing led to another …"

"Why didn't India call the police?" Adele folded her arms.

"I'm sure Laurel will ask her that." I checked my watch. "What time did you say our appointment with the caterer was?" I'd officially rededicated myself to Adele's wedding. Detecting was only getting me into trouble, and since it was finally my day off, I had the time.

"In fifteen minutes, and don't change the subject."

I scooted from the booth, my jeans squeaking on the faux-leather. "Then we should get moving. Do you want me to drive?"

Adele shuddered. "In that old jalopy? No thanks. We can take my Mercedes."

"My truck's not old," I said loftily. "It's vintage." But my shoulders relaxed, relieved the subject had been changed. I gulped the last of my mint tea and followed my friend's clicking heels to her Mercedes. In the foggy alley, I did *not* glance up at Mason's windows. At least that was progress.

The caterer's business was located in an industrial park on the outskirts of San Benedetto. Thick mist hugged the low, corrugated metal building sandwiched between a wine tasting room and a sign shop.

"Don't say it." Adele eyed the door beside the retractable garage door and smoothing her tulip skirt. "This caterer really is the best in fifty miles."

"I believe you." Adele was choosy when it came to pretty much everything. It was one of the reasons she was so successful.

She walked inside without knocking, and I followed her into a small room. Oversized framed photographs of successful catering events lined the rear wall. Good smells—bacon and cheese and something sweet—floated from a back room. A small round table covered in an elegant white cloth sat in one corner. High-backed wooden chairs with inviting cushions surrounded the table. On its top stood a cut-crystal vase filled with multicolored ranunculus flowers.

A door behind the counter opened and a plump, middle-aged woman in a black apron hurried from the back room. "Ms. Naka-moto?" She smiled.

Adele stuck her hand across the counter. "That's me. This is my friend Maddie Kosloski. She's helping me plan the wedding."

"Moral support is important," the woman said, grinning, "but we'll try to keep things painless." She grasped my hand. "Nice to meet you. I'm Margaret."

"Hi, Margaret," I said, smothering a wince. Margaret had a grip.

From beneath the counter she pulled a slim binder, its spine labeled *Nakamoto-Finkielkraut*. "Are you ready to finalize the menu?" She motioned us to the table.

The three of us sat, and I eased back against the cushions.

Adele and the caterer finalized the menu and the head count, occasionally looking to me for confirmation. This part of the job was easy—I agreed with everything Adele wanted.

"What about wedding favors?" the caterer asked. "Have you decided if you'd like us to provide them?"

Adele glanced at me, and I nodded. We'd already hashed this out and agreed to let someone else do the work. "Yes," she said. "But we want to keep the costs low. What do you recommend?"

"Candied almonds are traditional for many weddings," Margaret said. "The bittersweet taste represents life. The sweet coating is a wish for the newlyweds to experience more sweet than bitter. Our almonds are organic and locally sourced. But we're doing a new twist—coating almonds in Reign chocolate." She winked. "You may not know this, but chocolate is considered an aphrodisiac."

Oh, I knew. I canted my head. "Reign is providing you with bulk chocolate?" I asked, intrigued. "I thought they only sold retail." If

239

Reign was going into the wholesale business, maybe Affaire was a competitor after all.

Adele shot me a warning look.

I shrugged. I wasn't investigating, just curious. "Since one of the owners is, um, gone," I said to Adele, "we want to make sure they'll be able to fulfill their future orders. Who knows what'll happen to Reign by the time your wedding rolls around?"

"Mr. Malke has assured me Reign won't experience any disruptions," Margaret said. "After all, it's Orson Malke who makes the chocolate. Poor Mr. Reine was responsible for the marketing."

"How long has Reign been supplying you with bulk chocolate?" I asked.

Adele cleared her throat.

"Only two months," the caterer said. "We've never had a problem with the orders, and I don't expect any in the future."

"I'm sure it will be fine," Adele said, "but—"

"Is Reign selling their chocolate in bulk to anyone else?" I asked.

Margaret's face pinked. "No. We're exclusive. So exclusive that … Well …" She leaned forward, her gaze darting toward the industrial door. "We got lucky. Orson made the deal with us, and we didn't think anything of it."

I nodded, encouraging.

"Apparently," the caterer continued, "Atticus didn't know about it until after it was done. He wasn't happy about the arrangement. He thought Reign should stay purely retail to maintain the brand. But we'd already signed a contract. So we're the first caterer to use their chocolate." Her brow creased. "Of course, now that Orson is on his own, he may decide to sell to other restaurants or bakeries."

Reign was a small operation. Wholesaling chocolate seemed like a big shift. No wonder Atticus had been upset that the decision had been made without him. Did the shop even have the facilities to produce the quantities needed for wholesaling?

"The chocolate coating would go well with the wine we'll be serving," Adele said. "But June gets awfully hot. Although the reception won't be until evening, when it's cooler, you'll be setting up the tables earlier. Won't the chocolates melt?"

"We can put the favors out last, and usually we pack them in Reign's boxes—"

"Reign has boxes sized for wedding favors?" I asked. They must have been serious about wholesaling.

Adele kicked me beneath the table and I sucked in a gasp of pain.

"Oh, yes," Margaret said blithely, "Orson was quite proud of those boxes. We have to pay for them, of course."

"Of course." I rubbed my shin and silently cursed Adele's penchant for pointy-toed shoes.

"What sort of cost are we talking about?" Adele asked.

The two talked price points, and Adele shook her head. "I know Reign chocolate is popular, but this is a little outside our budget."

"We could drop the price by putting them in net bags," Margaret suggested.

"And making them more susceptible to melting in someone's pocket," Adele said. "What about the more traditional candied almonds?"

"We can, of course, do that too," Margaret said smoothly. She flipped a page in the binder to a photo of candied almonds in net bags and named a price.

Adele's smile faltered. "I'll need to discuss this with Dieter. Can I call you in a few days with a decision on the favors?"

"Of course! I'll be right back with a final menu printout for you to sign." Margaret escaped into the back room.

"Are you seriously interrogating my caterer?" Adele hissed at me.

"I'm sure it all has nothing to do with the murders," I said quickly. But why had Orson been making deals behind Atticus's back? "I didn't know Reign was selling wholesale. Did you?"

"That's not the point. You promised your mother you wouldn't investigate."

"I doubt the caterer is involved in the murders." And I hadn't promised. Not exactly.

"Of course she isn't!"

I grimaced. "So, there's no harm. This is only background information. Like researching the history of my haunted molinillo." Why couldn't I seem to stop myself from turning things into an investigation? This was Adele's time, not mine.

Margaret returned with the menu, and Adele signed it. Then Adele and I drove to town in silence and she dropped me at my closed museum.

GD lifted his head from his spot on the rocking chair. He gave me a hard stare, then tucked his head beneath a paw and resumed snoozing.

"Nice to see you too." I dug out my water-stained notepad, pulled out my new cell phone, and called India.

"Hello?" she asked, caution dampening her voice.

"Hi, India, this is Maddie."

"Oh," she said. "I just got back from the police station."

Uh oh.

"The detective wanted to know why I didn't report your near-drowning," she said.

I covered my face with one hand. "What did you tell her?"

"That I didn't witness what happened, and you said you'd call the cops. Why didn't you?"

"I did, but ... it's a long story. I'm sorry if I caused you problems." I wasn't actually sorry, but I didn't think telling her that would get me what I wanted to know.

India blew out a shaky breath. "My husband was murdered. And then my cousin. There's nothing anyone can do to make things worse."

"I'm sorry," I said quietly, and this time I was sincere. Outside the museum's window, cars drifted past in the mist. "Is there anything I can do *for* you?"

"If I could think of something, I'd ask. Why did you call?"

"Does Reign have any other production facilities beside the one in their San Benedetto shop?"

"No. That's the whole point of artisan chocolate. Reign is small, and everything's made by Orson. Why?"

"I was just curious. Thanks." I paused. "How are things going?"

Her laugh was mirthless. "They released my husband's body."

"Oh. I'm serious about that offer of help. Just let me know what you need."

"The mortuary's taking care of nearly everything."

"That's good." I remembered my father's funeral. There had been so many decisions to make, and though none of them had been earth-shattering, they'd seemed that way through my haze of grief. A remembered ache pinched my heart. "Let me know if—"

"Sure." India hung up.

Thoughtful, I pocketed the phone. Reign wholesaling. Did it mean anything?

My pulse quickened.

I thought it might.

TWENTY-FIVE

THE MICROBREWERY WAS QUIET Monday night. A few older couples staked out booths, their conversations echoing softly off the dark tile floors, the pressed-tin ceiling, the giant copper vats.

I slid into the red booth beside Harper. Her dark hair cascaded over the shoulders of her coffee-colored turtleneck.

Adele's heels clicked across the tile floor. "As much as I love girl time, I hope this is important, Maddie. I've still got tons of wedding planning to do." She neatly swiveled into the booth, her pale blue tulip skirt flaring around her knees.

"How did it go at the caterers?" Harper asked.

Adele slewed her gaze in my direction. "*Someone* turned it into an interrogation."

Harper's full lips quivered. "Did she?"

"The caterer is buying chocolate wholesale from Reign," I said. "I was surprised, that's all. I thought Reign only sold retail."

They stared at me.

"Okay, yes, I may be obsessing," I admitted. But the wholesaling *meant* something. I needed to talk to Orson. Or Jason. My heart pinched. But there was always Laurel. I really didn't want to talk to Laurel, but for the first time, that prospect was more appealing than facing Jason.

Harper sighed. "Denial ain't just a river in Egypt, Maddie."

"What's that supposed to mean?" I asked, indignant. I'd already admitted I was obsessing.

"It means—"

A waiter materialized at Harper's elbow. "Hi, I'm Paul. Can I get you started with drinks?"

"The Hefeweizen," Harper said.

"The IPA," Adele said.

"Hefeweizen," I said.

"And beer-battered artichokes," Harper added.

Impatient, I shifted in the booth. I wasn't in denial.

"Anything else?" the waiter asked.

"What are your specials today?" Adele asked.

He checked his notepad and rattled off the list.

"We'll need a few minutes, I think," Adele said. "Thanks."

The waiter strode away.

"What do you mean, denial?" I asked.

Adele pressed her index finger onto the wooden table. "You're turning into your mother."

"My—what?" I sucked in a breath. *No. No way.* "That's a bridge too far."

"Is it?" Adele asked.

"Explain," I said, crossing my arms.

My friends shared a look.

"Oh, come on," Harper said. "You must have noticed."

"Noticed what?" I asked.

Another long look.

Harper turned to me. "Your mother has her finger in every pie in San Benedetto. And you manage to get yourself involved in every murder, which puts you in the intriguing position of knowing everything that's going on."

"I found two bodies!"

The waiter returned with the beers and deep-fried artichokes. "Are you ready to order?"

"I think so," Adele said.

I sat, heels bouncing, while the others ordered.

"Blue cheese burger and garlic fries," I rapped out when the waiter got to me. "Medium rare." I was so not my mother. I jammed an artichoke into the ceramic bowl filled with ranch dressing and popped it in my mouth. The damn thing was scalding and I gulped my beer, feeling blisters rise on the roof of my mouth.

"Careful," the waiter said. "They're hot."

"Mmph!" No kidding.

He ambled toward the kitchen.

I brandished an artichoke heart. "And I'm not my mother." That was just crazy.

"Your mother is San Benedetto's unofficial queen bee," Harper said. "No offense. I like your mother. She gets things done. In fact, when I run for town council, I'm going to ask for her support. But let's face it, she's involved in town business in a way that isn't normal."

I stared, thunderstruck. "You're running for town council?"

"That's amazing!" Adele shrieked. "You're going to be perfect for the job! Who's in charge of your campaign? Can I be in charge of your campaign?"

Harper's cheeks turned dusky rose. "Yeah, I'm running. I've been thinking about it for a while now."

"But why didn't you tell us?" Adele asked.

She lifted her shoulders, dropped them. "You've been busy with the wedding. Maddie's been busy dealing with dead bodies. The time never seemed right. But something's changed in San Benedetto, don't you feel it?"

"Change is inevitable," Adele said.

"No," Harper said, "it's more than that. Our crime rate has gone up. People are on edge. We need to find the money to hire more police, put up more street lamps."

"We're going to get you elected," Adele said. "It's about time there was new blood on the town council."

"I'll help too," I said. "You're going to be great. You know the town. You understand what it's like for small business owners. And you're smart and organized and honest."

Harper turned her beer mug on the table. "Thanks. But I'm not on the council yet."

"You will be," Adele said confidently. "First, though, we need to get my wedding out of the way and deal with Maddie's little problem."

I scowled. "I don't have a little problem."

"It's bigger than you think," Adele said.

"Fine," I grumped. "Tell me what my problem is."

"You *want* to investigate these murders," she said. "You want it so badly that you're sneaking behind the backs of the people who care about you the most."

I slumped. Maybe they weren't crazy. I had been making a lot of friends and family mad lately. "All right. I get the point. Laurel's in charge, and I'm no Nancy Drew." But that didn't let Jason off the hook for not believing me about those phone messages, and misery tore at my heart.

They glanced at each other.

Harper's brow furrowed. "That isn't what we're saying at all."

"You need to figure out a way to be true to yourself," Adele said. "You *are* like your mother in a way. Both of you are good at helping people solve problems. Sure, you're great at the museum. I'm almost not embarrassed anymore about having my tea room next door to it. But if you can't figure out a way to get involved in the things you care about *and* be honest with the people around you, you're never going to be happy."

They were right. I'd been dancing around my mother like a nervous colt. And the fact that Jason had taken Laurel's side over mine really hurt. The beer glass blurred, and I swiped at my eyes with the back of my hand. If he didn't believe me, we didn't have a relationship to lose. I needed to face him.

The waiter stopped beside us, a tray on his shoulder. He whisked our plates onto the table. "Can I get you anything else?" The tray dropped to his side. "More beer?"

"No thanks," I said, lifting my half-full mug.

"Not right now," Harper said.

"Okay. Enjoy." He bustled away.

"I need to talk to Jason," I said slowly. "And to my mother."

"Not if you're eating those garlic fries," Adele said, pointing at my plate.

Right. I needed to lose a few pounds anyway. Appetite gone, I shoved the basket away and sipped my beer. "Any suggestions?" I asked.

"Blunt honesty," Harper said.

Adele nodded. "If he still doesn't believe you, he isn't right for you."

I stared at my hands, wrapped around the cool mug. "I don't get it," I said. "Four messages, and she ignored them. And I'm frankly … so pissed off he took her side." Sure, they were partners, but I was his girlfriend.

Adele's brows drew together. "Are you sure she ignored them? I mean, I believe you left the messages. I just wonder if there could have been some mistake. Laurel's never liked you, but I always thought she was a good cop."

"I even left a message with the desk sergeant!"

"But that's …" Harper's face creased with worry. "I know you and Laurel have issues, but that's dereliction of duty. If she ignored your messages about a crime, this whole town has a problem."

And Jason had a partner he couldn't rely on. Suddenly, I found it hard to swallow. I was going to lay it on the line with him about my relationship with Laurel and why she'd ignored my messages. And if he didn't want to hear it, I needed to know that now.

Our conversation shifted to lighter things: Adele's wedding, Harper's plot to rule San Benedetto, the museum's upcoming ghost photos exhibit. Finally, crumbs scattered across the table, we paid the bill and emerged on the dark sidewalk. The fog had lifted, stars faint above the glow of the iron lampposts and the low buildings.

We lingered on the brick walk in front of the Bell and Brew, and I leaned one hip on the wrought-iron fence that marked off the restaurant's outdoor tables. I wasn't looking forward to my conversation with Jason. But now that I'd decided to have it, a weight seemed to have lifted from my shoulders.

Tackling my mother wouldn't be easy either, but—

"Maddie?" Penny from the Visitors Bureau waddled up to our group.

I straightened off the fence and smiled at the older woman, her thick parka buttoned to her chin. "Hi, Penny. Where are you headed?"

Expression strained, she canted her head toward the microbrewery. "It's good to see a friendly face. I'm picking up takeout for myself and a friend."

"A friendly face? Is something wrong?" I glanced down the darkened street.

Her gaze followed mine. "These murders have made me paranoid." She laughed uneasily. "For a moment I thought I was being followed. I almost got back in my car and drove home, but it was just Mr. Sanderson with his beagle."

"The murders have unnerved everyone," Adele said. "It's no fun thinking a killer is out there, someone we might even know."

"That's an understatement," Penny said. "This afternoon I got it into my head that someone had snuck into the Wine and Visitors Bureau after it closed, and I was there alone." She looked over her cat-eye glasses at me. "I've taken to locking the side door."

I laughed. "Noted." No more sneaking into the Center and giving Penny a potential heart attack.

A Mazda drifted down the road toward us.

Penny's grip tightened on her oversized purse. "Have you learned anything—"

A bang. A flash on the opposite side of the street.

Penny and Adele shrieked. Harper leapt backward, stumbling against the low iron fence.

The Mazda swerved toward us, brakes squealing. The car screeched to a halt six inches from the sidewalk. Behind the wheel, the elderly driver's eyes bulged.

Two dark figures ran down the street.

"Call the police!" Unthinking, I raced across the road after them.

Adele shouted something. But all I could make out were the pounding of my feet on the pavement, the gust of my breath, the roar of blood in my ears.

The figures turned a corner.

I lengthened my strides, my anger giving way to anxiety. But I kept on anyway, rounding the building.

A teenager, hands on his knees, leaned against the wall of the bank. A second laughed and punched his friend on the shoulder.

"What did you two do?" I snarled.

They straightened, whirling.

I knew these two, and I got mad all over again. They were regulars in the museum—Gary Matthews and Walter Wiggins.

"A firecracker. You two idiots set off a firecracker," I said, realization dawning.

Gary paled, his freckles going gray in the amber light. "It was only a joke."

My teeth ground together. "You nearly caused a car accident. What if someone got hurt? It wouldn't have been so funny then."

Walter's narrow shoulders curled inward. "A car accident?"

"Mr. Thorenson was driving down the road when your firecracker went off. He nearly plowed into us on the sidewalk."

"We didn't mean for anyone to get hurt," Gary said. "It was only a firecracker. He wasn't hurt, was he?"

"No," I admitted, my fury fading. "He looked okay. Did you set off those firecrackers in the park a few weeks ago?"

"What?" Walter looked at his friend. "You mean, at the vigil?"

I nodded.

"I wasn't anywhere near the vigil," Walter said. "I wanted to go, but my dad made me stay home and do homework. He even helped me with history."

"Gary?"

"It wasn't me," Gary said. "I was grounded for cow tipping."

"Cow tipping?" Kids still did that? "Look, I know it can get a little boring out here, but think, will you?"

"Are you going to tell our moms?" Walter asked.

I was tempted. But as pranks went, theirs hadn't been that awful. I was angry mostly because it had scared *me*. "I'll try to keep your names out of it. But if I catch you or hear about you doing anything else, all bets are off."

"Thanks." They raced down the street and vanished around a corner.

Frowning, I trudged back to Main Street. Mr. Thorenson's Mazda was parked at an angle on the road, its headlights illuminating the sidewalk. People had spilled from the brewery and stood in a grim circle.

I ran toward the crowd, my view blocked by the heavily clothed backs. I tapped our waiter on the shoulder. "What's going on?"

He looked over his shoulder. "Looks like a heart attack. I called 911."

"A heart…" Suddenly, I found it hard to breathe. Not Mr. Thorenson. He'd looked fine! I pushed past the waiter.

Penny sat slumped against the wrought-iron fence. She clutched her chest. Her face was gray, her breathing shallow, her eyes closed.

Adele crouched beside her. She looked up at me. "An ambulance is on the way."

"Not Penny," I whispered. Was fear about to claim another victim?

TWENTY-SIX

GRAY DAWN LIGHT FILTERED through the hospital windows. Yawning, I stretched in the waiting room's thin-cushioned chair and tried to work the kink out of my neck.

My mother strode through the sliding glass doors. "How is she?"

Even at five a.m., my mom's jeans were perfectly pressed, the razor-sharp collar of her blouse positioned with millimeter precision over the lapels of her corduroy jacket. But the fragile skin beneath her eyes was the color of a bruise.

Relieved, I stood. I hadn't known whom to contact on Penny's behalf besides my mother, so I'd left a message last night. For once I was glad my mom was an early riser. "The doctors said she had an anxiety attack but they're keeping her for observation," I explained. "They're moving her from Emergency into a room. I'm just waiting to check in on her once she's moved."

My mother's shoulders slumped. "What a relief. What happened?"

I explained. "Penny told me she was anxious about the murders," I finished. "On the way to the microbrewery, she even thought someone was following her."

"Someone's imagination running away with them?" my mother asked dryly and folded her arms. "Hard to believe."

My cheeks warmed. My mom knew me too well. I had a tendency to imagine the worst too. "She must have thought the firecracker was a gunshot or bomb and panicked." The scene had been awful, Penny gasping for breath, her face purpling. It was hard to believe fear could cause that much pain.

My mom shook her head, her squash-blossom earrings swinging. "Penny's not the only one who's tense. You should hear the talk at Ladies Aid. All of San Benedetto is jumpy. This murderer needs to be caught." Her mouth pinched. "But that doesn't mean you have to do it."

"Mom, I'm sorry I've worried you. But if I have a chance to learn something, I'm going to."

"Madelyn—"

"It's important. People tell me things they wouldn't tell the police. All I'll do is pass it on to Jason. Or Laurel."

She raised a skeptical brow. "You're actually going to help Laurel?"

"Of course, because ..." Because if Jason thought I was a liar, we were breaking up. "I have to. And I like investigating. The fact is, as much as I love the museum—and I do love it—there's more to life than work."

"Have you thought of joining a gym?"

"I swear I haven't gained any weight—"

"Your weight is fine. I meant there are other productive hobbies you could enjoy aside from sticking your nose into murder investigations. You could join Ladies Aid."

I shuddered. *No, no, a thousand times no.* "But sticking my nose into murder investigations is what I *do*."

She stared at me, then pressed her hand to her mouth. Her shoulders quaked. "Oh, Madelyn, you really are your father's daughter," she gasped, laughing. Then she straightened. "All right. I didn't tell your brother not to go to Afghanistan. I don't suppose it's fair of me to tell you to stop … whatever it is you're doing. But that doesn't mean I have to like it."

I hugged her. "I know, Mom. Thanks."

"Now go home," she said gently. "You're exhausted. I'll stay and see if there's anything Penny needs."

I yawned again, my eyes gritty from lack of sleep. "Thanks. Tell her I'm thinking of her."

I left the hospital, stopping at the museum to check on GD's food and water. Startled by my early morning appearance, he scowled from his perch on the haunted rocking chair. Then the ebony cat tucked his paw beneath his head and resumed napping.

I drove home, kibble duty done. Stumbling upstairs to my apartment, I kicked off my tennis shoes, tugged off my clothes, and tumbled into bed.

———

I startled awake, blinking, confused.

My front door thundered beneath someone's fist.

Outside my bedroom window, sun and blue sky had broken through the earlier gloom. Puffy cartoon clouds floated above my aunt's house.

Someone knocked on the door again.

I staggered from bed and tugged on a cotton robe. "Keep your pants on!" Annoyed, I jerked my belt tight and scraped a hand through my hair. I stormed into my nautical-themed living room, smothered a yawn, and yanked open the door.

Jason stood on the steps in faded blue slacks and a white shirt open at the collar. "Thank God."

"What's wrong? Has something happened?" I stepped aside and he strode past me.

"I heard you were at the scene last night. And then you weren't answering your phone this morning. I thought—" He drew me into a hug.

"I might have done something crazy?" My words were muffled against his muscular chest. Pulling away, I dropped onto the soft, blue-gray couch. "And what do you mean, 'at the scene'? I told the officers it was just some kids with a firecracker. I saw them running away. I told them it was Gary Matthews and Walter Wiggins. And the boys told me they had alibis for the vigil, by the way. Gary was doing homework with his dad and Walter was grounded for cow tipping. Or maybe Gary was grounded. I can't remember."

Jason lifted a single brow. "So that's really all that happened?"

"Of course. I wouldn't lie about it."

Jason dropped onto the couch beside me. "I know. I talked to the desk sergeant. He told me you left a message for Laurel last week about the attack at the pool."

"Oh."

"I don't know what happened. He left the message on her desk."

"I left other messages too, you know," I said pointedly. "On her voicemail."

"She told me she's been having problems with her phone."

Sure she was. I lowered my head. "I don't trust Laurel."

"I know you don't," he said. "But she's a good cop. I believe her." He flushed. "I checked her phone records, okay? And if you tell her that... don't tell her that. The point is, I'm sorry. I shouldn't have jumped on you like I did."

"You didn't believe me."

"That's not true. I did believe you left the messages."

I opened my mouth to argue.

"The *detailed* messages," he amended. "But I can't... not believe Laurel without evidence. We're partners. That means something."

"I thought we meant something too," I said quietly.

"We do. Which is why I took time to sort this out before reacting."

Before reacting? He'd—I thought back to the evening at Plot 42. Jason had been upset I'd been interrogating potential murderers. He'd been annoyed I hadn't told him about the near-drowning, and... I realized that he'd never accused me of lying. He'd been pissed but he'd been thoughtful, too, trying to sort things out, waiting to gather evidence before reacting.

Like a good cop.

I liked that he was a good cop.

"So why did you follow me outside the barn, like you didn't trust that I would call Laurel or find my way to the police station on my own?"

"You'd told me someone had tried to kill you. I wasn't going to leave you alone."

Well, that was just... reasonable, dammit. "But you've definitely been avoiding me this past week."

"Can you blame me? I could see you were furious. I thought we both needed some time to calm down. And I needed to figure out what was going on with Laurel. From what I can tell, she actually didn't get your messages."

"Well," I replied grudging, "Laurel and I aren't exactly besties, and I tend to assume the worst about her motives. I should have asked you to deliver a message to her when it was obvious mine weren't getting through."

"Maybe. But I get why you didn't. And I shouldn't have gone into cop mode that night at the winery. You're my girlfriend, not my suspect." His brows furrowed. "Sometimes it's hard to turn it off. But you've never lied to me. I do trust you."

So, he wasn't perfect. He hadn't reacted exactly the way I'd have liked him to that night. But I wasn't flawless either. I just needed to make sure we could both live with each other's imperfections. I rose and walked around the coffee table. "There's something else. I know you're not happy in general about me collecting town gossip and talking to murder suspects."

"True."

I paused beside his chair. "But ..." I drew a breath. "San Benedetto is my home, and people tell me things, and I'm not going to pretend I'm not interested if I can help."

"So you're not backing off," he said flatly and stood.

"No." I grimaced.

"Okay."

I blinked. "What?"

One corner of his mouth quirked upward. "I said, okay. We're not going to change each other, Maddie. Well, I like to think you bring out the best in me, but it's still me. And I wouldn't want to change you. I love your curiosity and stubbornness and inventiveness, even if it does make me crazy sometimes. And as long as you don't cross the line into interfering with an investigation or with-holding evidence, we're good."

"Oh." I rubbed my jaw. Stale makeup sloughed off beneath my palm. I thought I'd brushed after last night's blue cheese burger, but my teeth felt furry. What did I smell like? "Well, good. I wouldn't want to change you either."

Jason's strong arm encircled my waist and he pulled me closer. "Good? Is that all you have to say?"

I clapped a hand over my mouth. "I need to brush my teeth."

It turned out Jason didn't care about my dental hygiene. The heady sensation of his mouth, hard against mine, sent shivers of desire racing through my body. Blood coursed through my veins like a river in the spring.

After we broke apart, panting, he didn't release his grip around my waist. He cleared his throat. "Are we still going slow?"

"I think it's best," I said weakly. "Obviously, we're still figuring some things out in our relationship."

"Right," he said. His forehead crinkled with concern. "I heard you were at the hospital most of the night. How's Penny?"

"I think she'll be okay," I said. "But if you knew I was at the hos-pital, why were you so panicked when you came here?"

"It's two o'clock. Usually you're at the museum by now checking inventory or investigating a haunting." Humor glinted in his tawny eyes.

My stomach rumbled. "It's two already? That explains why I'm so hungry."

He grinned. "I'm off duty. Want to grab lunch?"

"Yes." I wriggled from his grasp and escaped into the bathroom. Ugh, my mascara was smeared beneath my eyes. It must be love since Jason hadn't burst into laughter when he'd walked through my door. I stilled. *Love*. I did love Jason. But I'd just had that week of thinking about ending things, so clearly my feelings weren't to be trusted. I scrubbed violently at the dark makeup. I'd table the love issue for later.

At record speed, I cleaned myself up and changed into a pair of khaki slacks and a white blouse.

He drove me to my favorite taqueria, because good boyfriends know where you like to get your Mexican food. We sat outside, enjoying the unseasonably warm weather.

I took a careful bite of my veggie burrito, and for once, beans didn't cascade down the front of my blouse. "Will Laurel follow up with the boys from last night?"

Tiny black birds, eager for crumbs, hopped beside our red plastic table.

"She'll have to, if she's going to keep up with my high standards." Jason grinned.

"Tell me you two aren't competing."

"We're not, because I'm clearly the better cop."

I choked down a laugh, and, I think, a bean. "Don't make me do something I'll regret."

"Like what?"

"Like defend Laurel."

"A sure sign of the coming zombie apocalypse. Seriously, though, Laurel's good." He aimed a nacho at me. "You can trust her."

"Then she's going to check the boys' alibis for the night of the vigil?"

"Of course."

Rats. "Their parents are going to kill them."

"Maybe that's not such a bad thing."

I peeled back a strip of foil and dunked one corner of my burrito into a plastic cup of green sauce. "Did you know that Reign Chocolate is wholesaling to Adele's caterer?"

"Who is Adele's caterer?"

I gave him Margaret's name.

Jason shook his head. "I hadn't heard about it. But I'm surprised an operation that size—one that makes everything by hand—has the bandwidth to wholesale."

A warming glow flowed through me. It felt good to talk this over with him. I should have pushed the issue sooner. "It surprised me too. And I was thinking of that box I saw in India's yard, the one that disappeared after the pool incident."

"Incident?" He grimaced. "Is that what we're calling it now?"

"That's what I'm calling it. The box was from a chocolate company in the Bay Area called Affaire."

Jason frowned. "Was Atticus checking out the competition?"

"I don't know. Affaire is strictly a wholesaler, selling to restaurants and bakeries and other candy companies. If Reign's getting into the wholesaling business, maybe that's all it was. But that wouldn't explain why whoever pushed me into the pool took the box."

"No," he said. "It wouldn't."

"Personally, I never thought Reign's chocolate tasted that spectacular, but I'm not a chocolate connoisseur." I shifted my basket of tortilla chips and leaned closer. "But there's another reason that box might have been there, and why someone might have wanted to cover it up."

"Oh?"

"Do you think Reign could have been cheating? Passing off Affaire chocolate as their own instead of making it themselves from the bean? That would explain how such a small shop could have jumped into wholesaling to a caterer like Margaret."

"That's a leap. Reign may have another production center."

"They don't," I said. "I asked India. And remember the table in the storage room, where they sort the cocoa beans by hand?"

"Yes," he said cautiously. He reached across the table and wiped the corner of my mouth with his thumb.

"Whoops." Because sour cream dribbling down my chin was always a good date look, I flushed and grabbed a napkin. "Moving on—"

"Do we have to? Because you've got another little bit there ..." He leaned closer. Slowly he brushed his thumb across my upper lip.

I scrubbed at my mouth and glanced at the napkin. It was pristine white. "There was nothing on my—" I sputtered. "You're a laugh riot."

"Made you look."

"Moving *on*," I said more loudly. "The plastic that lined the garbage bin at the end of the table was dusty, like it had been there a while. But there were no bad cocoa beans or bits of leaves or rocks inside the bin—which is what they were sorting for, remember? There was only a paper cup from a fast food restaurant."

Jason nodded. "As if they weren't sorting cocoa beans at all. Orson is the chocolate maker. If Atticus had found out—"

"It might have been a motive for murder. Orson would want to stop Atticus from blowing the whistle. It might also explain why Sam was fired after he tried to figure out how to roast beans on his own. He told me the beans in the temperature-controlled room looked moldy. What if they were moldy because they'd been lying around for a while? What if those sacks of cocoa beans are just for show?"

"It's possible," Jason said, noncommittal.

Possible?! My theory was solid. "Tilde, the accountant, would have known whether payments were going to Affaire or to buy cocoa beans from overseas."

Jason raised a single dark brow. "And you think Orson killed her because of it?"

"He seems the obvious candidate. But wait, there's more."

"A set of Ginsu steak knives?"

"Ha ha. I overheard Orson and India talking about an affair. I assumed they were talking about an *actual* affair. India and Orson admitted they used to be together, and suggested it was the affair they'd been talking about. But what if Orson and India were arguing about Affaire chocolate? Maybe Atticus brought the box home from the shop for some reason—maybe he needed it to move some junk—and then he became suspicious, or realized what it meant?"

Jason popped a nacho into his mouth. "But if India knew about the chocolate scam—let's assume Atticus told her what he'd learned— why wouldn't she have come forward?"

I gnawed the inside of my cheek. Good question. If India knew the truth, she was in danger.

Unless she was in on the con.

Unless *she'd* been the one who held me under in the pool. Then when I'd lost consciousness, she'd somehow ditched the box— maybe threw it over the neighbor's fence. And then she'd decided a corpse floating in her pool would be too difficult to explain away and revived me. Uneasy, I shifted on the scarlet fiberglass bench.

"It's speculation," Jason said. "We examined Reign's books and didn't find anything unusual."

"But were you looking for regular payments to an outside chocolate company?"

"Our forensic accountant looked at the accounts, and she looked again after Tilde's murder. Trust me, she would have found something like this."

"Oh," I said, disappointed. Of course the police would have looked into it. A dollop of beans and rice dropped onto the side of my palm. I wiped it off with a napkin.

"But there could be a second set of account books." Jason pulled out his phone. "I'll call Laurel."

I smiled, relieved. Maybe my theory wasn't crazy after all.

TWENTY-SEVEN

JASON HAD BEEN RIGHT about my work schedule. I normally did
put in an hour or two at the museum on Tuesdays. So after my very
late lunch, I zipped over.

I filled GD's bowls. The cat sniffed my ankles, considered his
line of attack, and then seemed to decide against it. He sneezed and
hopped onto the glass counter.

Feeling reckless, I ruffled his fur. There might be less than two
weeks left on my *Magic of Chocolate* exhibit, but I could still update
the information on the molinillo. I booted up my computer.

While the computer whirred and pinged, I straightened a pyramid of chocolate bars on the counter. Did I really want to write out
Felicitas's story? It seemed too tragic, too recent, too real.

I shook myself. Truth was a good thing, even if it was sometimes painful. "It isn't right for her death to be written off as a suicide or an accidental overdose," I told GD.

The cat's tail twitched. He stared at an empty spot three feet to the left of the counter.

A wave of cold air flowed through the museum, and goose bumps stippled my arms. I glanced out the window. The sun was still shining. I fiddled with the heater dial on the wall above the register.

With a shiver only partly due to the cold, I reached for a museum hoodie on the shelf behind me.

The cat howled.

"I just fed you. What more do you want?"

GD batted my hand with his paw.

"Whatever." I typed up a new placard for the molinillo—the suspected murder of Felicitas, her boyfriend's lies, and his murder after her death. If I was an eye-for-an-eye type of person, I'd say justice had been done. But something didn't feel right.

Fingers stiff with cold, I printed out the new sign and laid it on the counter to check for typos. "What do you think?" I rubbed my hands together and blew into them.

GD sat on the paper and sneezed.

"Thanks," I said dryly and shooed him off the page.

I laminated the sign and brought it into the Gallery, GD trailing behind me. My breath misted the air. What was going on with the heater today?

The heater rattled and GD started, his green eyes widening.

I hooked the sign onto the hanger pin on the side of the pedestal. Cocking my head, I listened for … I didn't know what I was listening for. They say ghosts suck the warmth out of rooms, but my museum was in an old building, and there probably wasn't any such thing as ghosts.

Cold fingers crawled up my spine. Uneasy, I slipped my hands into the pockets of my hoodie. "I don't care if a ghost *has* dropped by for a chat," I told GD. "I'm working."

Someone banged on the front door and I jumped, missing the cat's tail by a millimeter. GD yowled and streaked into the main room.

The new molinillo sign popped off its hook and slipped to the checkerboard floor. I scooped it up and hurried to the front door.

Orson Malke peered through the glass.

I hesitated, then unlocked the door and peered out, my foot wedged against it in case Orson tried anything funny. No, I wasn't paranoid. Not at all. "Hi, Orson. I'm sorry, but the museum's closed today."

The chocolate maker colored and rubbed his neat beard. "That's not actually . . . I wanted to see you, not the museum. Though I hear it's a great museum," he added quickly. "Can I come in?"

Could the man at the top of my murder suspect list join me inside a lonely museum?

Um. No.

"Things are kind of a mess in here," I said. "Why don't we go to the Fox and Fennel?" Where a horde of tea-sipping little old ladies were ready to deliver a beatdown with their handbags if he tried anything.

He wavered, then nodded. "Sure."

Grabbing my purse from the counter, I walked outside and locked the door behind me. I followed him into the tea room.

The Fox and Fennel was packed. Women braced their elbows on crisp white tablecloths and lounged on soft ivory couches. Customers lined up beside the tiled mint-green counter and waited patiently to pay for a brushed-nickel tea tin from the wooden shelves.

A harried-looking Adele hurried up to us. "I hope you're not here to eat. I don't have a single table free."

"That's okay," I said slowly. "Orson and I can talk in the museum." I still didn't like the idea, but I didn't think Orson was crazy enough to try anything now that Adele was a witness to him being with me.

"I'll send your order over." She gave me a significant look—*message received*—and handed us paper menus.

We ordered tea. I pressed the spine on the bookcase, and Orson's eyes widened when it swung outward. "No way. You've got a secret passage? Cool!"

"It was Adele's idea. But yeah, it is cool."

He followed me into the museum.

I arranged Leo's tall chair in front of the counter and sat in my own chair on the opposite side. "So, how can I help you?"

Orson frowned. "I heard you had an accident at India's house."

I hung my purse on the back of my chair. "I wouldn't call it an accident. Someone pushed me into the pool and held me under until I passed out."

GD hopped onto the counter.

Orson stroked the cat and didn't meet my gaze. "What were you doing at India's?"

Now that was an interesting reaction—no curiosity about the attempted murder, just my trespassing.

"Looking for India," I said.

"In her back yard?"

"The gate was open. With everything that's been going on …" I shrugged. "I guess I was paranoid." Though clearly I hadn't been paranoid enough.

He shifted on his chair. "Did you … see anything?"

I raised a brow. "See anything?"

"Was anyone else there?"

"No."

His expression relaxed.

"All I saw was a box from Affaire Chocolate."

He blanched.

I plunged in, heart pounding. "Given the size of the box, the fact that you're wholesaling to caterers in spite of your small facility, and the argument I overheard between you and India about an 'affair,' I'm guessing you and Atticus were using Affaire chocolate and pawning it off as Reign's original chocolate."

GD purred. His tail lashed the tip jar.

Orson shook his head. "No. You have no proof."

The lament of someone who really *was* guilty. "Not yet," I said in a steady voice. "But the deception would explain Tilde's death. As the accountant, she would know where the money was going."

His shoulders collapsed. "Using Affaire chocolate was only temporary. But I didn't kill Atticus. Or Tilde."

"So you were passing off Affaire chocolate as your own?"

"You don't understand," he said miserably.

"Fraud?" I asked, darting a glance at the closed bookcase. "I think I can understand that. You killed Atticus and Tilde. Now that India knows, do you plan to kill her too?"

Orson's eyes widened. "What? No! I would never hurt India!"

"Because she was in on it with you?"

"Because I'm not a killer. And … I love her." He crumpled on his chair. "That argument you heard—it wasn't about the chocolate."

Whoa. What? "You mean—"

The bookcase creaked open. A waiter shuffled inside carrying a tray with two small pots of tea. He set it on the counter between us. "Will there be anything else?"

"No thanks," I said.

The waiter departed, leaving the bookcase ajar.

I leaned across the glass counter and dropped my voice. "Do you mean you two were having an actual affair?" I'd been right the first time? How often did *that* happen?

He nodded.

Well, damn. "That doesn't really help your case. An affair with Atticus's wife is an even stronger motive for murder."

"No, you don't understand. I was with India when Atticus was killed."

I arched a brow. "The woman you were having an affair with is your alibi?" That just meant they could have done it together, or India was covering for him. On the other hand, he could be covering for India.

Orson groaned. "I know how it sounds. And it's only a matter of time before the police find out."

Sooner than he thought. I'd have to tell Laurel.

"Call India. Call her now," he urged. "Ask her about the alibi."

Twisting on my seat, I excavated my phone from my purse. "Are you sure about this?"

"I'm sure. Call her."

"Sorry, what's her number?"

He told me, and I made the call.

"Hello?"

"Hi, India. It's Maddie."

"Yes?"

"I'm in the museum with Orson." I coughed lightly. Asking Orson about the Affaire chocolate was awkward enough. Asking the two of them about a real affair was a whole other level of uncomfortable. "He asked me to call you. He said the two of you were together at the time of your husband's death."

A long silence. "He did?"

"Is it true?" I asked.

"He asked you to call me? Why?" A faintly hysterical note tinged India's voice.

"I think he wants you to confirm his alibi. And yours."

Over the phone, her breath came soft and quick.

I waited. When she didn't respond, I continued, "He said you two were romantically involved."

"No," she said wildly. "No! It isn't true! I loved Atticus. Why is he doing this to me?" she sobbed.

"India—Orson needs an alibi."

"No, he doesn't. Orson didn't do anything. It was Sam, don't you see? Losing his job the way he did sent him over the edge. He keeps coming around the house harassing me, and Lola, and he bothered Tilde too. Why do you think my gate was open that day? Sam must have opened it. He must have been inside. He's after us all."

I straightened in my chair. I'd nearly forgotten about Sam. "Have you told the police Sam's been bothering you, like I suggested?"

"Of course I told them. Do you know how easy it is to get a restraining order?" She gulped. "Not at all. You offered to help me. Can you help me with that?"

I didn't miss the sarcasm. But maybe I could help. "I could talk to—"

She hung up.

Or not. I set the phone on the counter.

"Well?" Orson asked.

"She said you weren't having an affair."

"She's lying!"

GD's head swiveled toward him. The cat growled, a menacing sound that raised the hair on my arms.

Slowly, Orson exhaled and set down his cup. "She's lying." His tone was low, urgent. "She feels guilty now that Atticus is dead, don't you see?"

I saw that *someone* was lying.

Somebody pounded on the front door, and I jumped in my seat. GD flowed like quicksilver off the counter.

Detective Laurel Hammer and two uniformed officers glared through the window. "Open up," Laurel shouted.

"Um," I said, "I'd better." I rounded the counter and unlocked the door.

The cops marched inside.

"Orson Malke?" Laurel asked. "You need to come to the station with us."

Above his beard, his face turned the color of cement. "What? Why?"

"We've got more questions."

"Am I under arrest?"

Laurel flashed a counterfeit smile. "Not yet. But if you don't co-operate, you will be."

He rose, his limbs shaking. "All right. All right. It's fine. I'll come."

Laurel stared down at me. "Well?"

"Uh," I said, "do you want me to come to the station too?" *Say no. Say no!*

"Don't you want to know how we found him here?" she asked.

Did I? "Okay, how did you find us?"

"I asked at the chocolate shop," the detective said. "The assistant said Mr. Malke had gone to see you at the museum."

Which meant he hadn't come to kill me. Murderers generally prefer not to advertise.

Her eyes narrowed. "Now why would Orson want to talk to you so badly that he'd leave his work in the middle of the day?"

"We were just ..." I floundered.

"Interfering with an investigation?" she asked.

Had I been? But this wasn't fair! Orson had come to me. "I wasn't interfering," I said.

Her lip curled. "We'll see."

"Wow," a man said behind us. "This cat is really friendly."

The color drained from Laurel's face. "The cat ..."

We turned.

GD sat perched on one of the uniformed officer's shoulders. The cat's green eyes gleamed, malicious. He hunched, his shoulder muscles flexing, his paws kneading the cop's shirt.

"GD, no!" I shouted.

The black cat launched himself at Laurel.

She shrieked, ducked, and covered.

I lurched sideways, trying to catch GD mid-air. The cat passed harmlessly through my outstretched fingers. I overbalanced and tripped over Laurel.

The detective and I collapsed in a tangle of arms and legs and slammed against the counter.

Chocolate bars cascaded from above. They pelted us, sprawled on the checkerboard floor.

"Got him," Orson said.

Laurel and I glared up at GD, smirking in Orson's arms.

The cat purred.

A muscle pulsed in Laurel's jaw. "That. *Cat*." She said the word like a curse.

I scrambled to my feet and slipped on a chocolate bar. I grabbed the antique cash register for balance, then snatched GD from Orson. "Bad cat!" Did he really hate Laurel, or was he just trying to get me in trouble? Or was it a sort of two-for-one deal?

"He's possessed," Laurel rasped, struggling to her feet. "A menace!"

"He's only a cat," I squeaked.

GD squirmed, and I clutched him tighter.

Orson cleared his throat. "So. Police station?"

I shot him a grateful look. Murder suspect or not, he'd stopped GD from assaulting a police officer. If the cat had succeeded, I was sure Laurel could have found a crime to charge me with if she'd tried hard enough.

Laurel's nostrils flared. "Stop gawking," she said to the cops. "Let's move!"

With the uniformed officers flanking Orson, they marched him out the door.

The bookcase creaked open and Adele peeked inside. "Are you all right? What happened?" She sidled into the museum.

"GD tried to kill Laurel again, and I think Orson's about to be arrested." One-handed, I gathered the chocolate bars off the floor.

"Oh, GD." She took him from me and the cat snuggled against her Fox and Fennel apron. Twin lines appeared between her brows. "I hope the police have got it right. I really thought India had done it."

"Atticus's wife?" I asked, surprised.

"The spouse is usually the killer. Isn't that what they always say? It's got to be someone close to the victims. I've got two cousins I wouldn't mind murdering right now. One is demanding a gluten-free menu at my wedding. Another wants to bring guests I don't even know. And I just got half a dozen RSVPs from distant relatives even though they knew darn good and well the deadline was three weeks ago! It's almost as if they think because we're family, they can act like divas. Now I have to go back to the caterer and change the headcount."

"Ouch." Absently, I poured tea into my cup and stirred, my spoon clanking on the side. "I'm sorry people are being such pains."

"I should be used to it by now," she said. "So, what did Orson want? Or did you call that little meeting?"

"He did. India said the ex-employee, Sam, was harassing her and Lola," I said, evasive. I wasn't sure if Orson's story of an affair was real, and even though I knew Adele wouldn't blab, I wasn't comfortable sharing it. "Sam was also bothering Tilde."

"Hmm. I thought you decided Sam couldn't have pushed you into India's swimming pool because his car engine was cold."

"Well, I did." But I still didn't like what I was hearing about the man. Could I have been wrong?

I straightened my blouse, which had gotten twisted in the scrimmage. India had said this time that she'd reported Sam to the police. The investigation was Jason and Laurel's job. I would tell Laurel what Orson and India had each told me. I'd done my part.

For now.

TWENTY-EIGHT

In the Fortune Telling Room, GD and I eyed the round table loaded with electronic equipment. The table wasn't quite an antique, built in the groovy sixties with a circular Ouija board painted on the wood. But it was vintage, and I didn't want it scratched.

"Maybe I should get a tablecloth," I said, anxious.

Beside the spirit cabinet, GD lashed his tail and growled. The cabinet's tall doors stood slightly ajar. I edged them open, making sure Herb wasn't inside.

GD sneezed, derisive.

"And I do *not* want to hear your opinion," I told him.

"Uh." Leo looked up from fiddling with the computer and eyed me askance. "Are you talking to me or the cat?"

"GD."

"Okay. Then everything's set up for the podcast."

The bell over the front door jangled, and I frowned. I thought I'd locked it after Leo arrived.

"Maddie?" Mason called out.

I hurried into the main room. "Hi. Is something wrong?"

My neighbor jammed his fingers in the front pockets of his jeans. "No. Why would anything be wrong?"

"Because …" I glanced at the open entry to the Fortune Telling Room. "Let's go outside."

Mason followed me onto the sidewalk. The moon was full, the light from the street lamps reflecting like mini-moons in the shop windows. I rubbed my arms in the evening chill.

"What's up?" he asked.

"I could ask you the same thing. You keep coming around and acting weird. What *is* it?"

He opened his mouth to speak and I raised my hand, palm out, to stop him.

"No," I said. "On second thought, I don't need to know."

"But I'm—"

"You're a good guy, Mason. But whatever's going on is none of my business. And you need to stop coming around and giving me the skunk eye."

He blinked. "The what?"

"You know what I'm talking about. I mean, you're not a skunk, but … I'm with Jason, and I'm happy with him." My heart warmed. And Jason was happy with me, even if I still thought his partner was a jerkface. So I wasn't going to overanalyze what we had. For now.

"I can't get drawn into whatever's going on between you and Belle," I continued. "You and I need to spend less time together, even if I do like and respect you. So, unless you've got information about the murders—"

My cell phone rang and I dug it from my pocket, recognizing a familiar number. *Jason.*

"If you know something about the murders," I said, "tell Detective Laurel Hammer. Sorry, but I need to take this." I turned away from him and put the phone to my ear. "Hi, Jason. What's going on?"

A sixties-era van drifted past.

"Orson Malke's been released."

"Really?"

"Lack of evidence."

"You mean you didn't find a second set of books?" I asked, dismayed.

"Lack of evidence," he repeated evenly. "We did put a tail on him, but he's slipped it."

"What?" Slipped it? But that made him look totally guilty! Was he?

"Look, I can't get over there right now, but I've got a bad feeling. Are you alone?"

I glanced at Mason. "No."

"Good. Try to keep it that way. Are you still at the museum?"

"Yes. Leo and I are doing our test podcast tonight."

"All right. Call me when you leave."

"Why?" I asked. "If they released Orson, it must mean there was good reason. Is something else going on?"

"India Reine has disappeared too."

"What do you mean, disappeared?" I yelped.

"Just what I said. Look, I can't talk about this right now. Just stay with Leo, okay?"

"I will." We said our goodbyes, and I hung up.

"Problem?" Mason asked.

"Um, no." Mason might be ex-military and twice Leo's size, but I couldn't ask him to stay, not after what I'd just told him.

"Belle and I aren't having problems," he said.

"Oh." Self-conscious, I shuffled my feet on the cold sidewalk. "That's good." Then why had he kept coming around looking like a lost puppy?

"We're getting married."

"Oh!" Oh wow. Married? That was quick. No, it wasn't. They had a history, a son. And I was happy for them. "Congratulations!"

"I wanted to tell you how grateful I am to you for ending things between us the way you did and letting Belle and I rebuild our relationship." He scratched his temple. "But I guess I felt kind of guilty. I mean, what kind of guy has a kid and doesn't know about him? And I realize finding out the way you did hurt you."

My face heated. "It was fine," I said. "It all worked out. For everyone."

"I know. But it might not have if you hadn't cut me loose. Anyway, Belle's been itching for me to tell you we're engaged, but it never seemed like the right time. That's why I was giving you the, uh, skunk eye. And that business about the dumpster... It didn't happen. Sorry, but it just felt like the wrong time to tell you and I couldn't think of what else to say."

I laughed. "Since I didn't follow up with Dieter, you're forgiven. But I am happy for you both. This is wonderful news."

He backed down the sidewalk. "Well. Thanks. I'll be seeing you. But not too often."

"Right!"

He turned and strode down the street.

Married! There must be something in the air. First Adele and Dieter, and now Mason and his girlfriend.

Feeling lighter, I returned inside the museum and locked the door carefully behind me.

GD sat waiting at the counter. He slipped to the checkerboard floor and followed me into the Fortune Telling Room.

I rubbed my hands together. "So?"

Leo checked his phone. "Right on time. You ready?"

"Wait. We're going to start *now*?"

"I posted on social media that we'd be starting at seven. It's six fifty-eight."

"You posted on social media?" I bleated. "I thought this was only a test run!"

"It is, so we can test the caller system. Don't worry, I doubt we'll get many callers on our test night."

Great. I pulled out the folding chair and sat down, checked my podcasting notes, zipped up my hoodie. It was even colder inside the museum than outside.

"Don't look so worried," Leo said, dropping onto the metal chair beside me. "It's only a beta test. It's not supposed to be perfect."

"Right." A beta test. How bad could it be?

———

Maddie: Welcome to—Is this on?

Leo: It's on.

Maddie: Welcome to our beta test of the Paranormal Museum Podcast, live from the San Benedetto Paranormal Museum. I'm your curator, Maddie Kosloski.

Leo: And I'm Leo.

Maddie: Aren't you going to use your last name?

Leo: Then people would know who I am.

[PAUSE]

Maddie: [Clears throat] Right. Well, San Benedetto's Wine and Chocolate Days are over, but our Magic of Chocolate Exhibit will continue through the end of the month. So be sure to stop on by. We're giving away a free tarot card to each guest.

Leo: And we've got a caller.

Maddie: What do you mean, we've—

Leo: Hi, you're live on the Paranormal Museum Podcast.

Male Caller: I'm calling about the cursed molinillo.

Maddie: [Laughs uneasily] Cursed? It's not cursed. It's only haunted. For people who aren't familiar with the term, a molinillo is a kitchen instrument used to whisk Mexican hot chocolate. The molinillo in our exhibit was once owned by a woman in Oaxaca who died tragically. It's haunted.

Male Caller: Then why have there been two chocolate-related deaths since you've put it on display?

Maddie: Wait a minute, is this Herb?

Herb: No names! The cops may be listening.

Maddie: Herb, as you well know, the molinillo rattles when someone nearby tells a significant lie. That's not a curse, that's a haunting. The prior owner was murdered by her boyfriend after she learned he was dealing drugs and he learned she was pregnant with his child. He was killed not long after ... [PAUSE]

Leo: Is something wrong?

Maddie: I think ... my story might be. Her boyfriend was killed almost immediately after she was. What if her boyfriend didn't kill her? What if she threatened to expose his secret, that he was dealing drugs, and in turn expose his fellow criminals? What if his partners killed them both?

Herb: Does it make a difference? The molinillo's still cursed.

Maddie: It's haunted, not cursed! Her death was ruled a suicide in spite of the evidence that she'd been murdered. I was told that was a political decision, but I think it was really a cover-up. She didn't commit suicide. Maybe that's what the molinillo was trying to tell us. Maybe that's why it rattles when a lie is told. The public story about her death is a lie.

Herb: But it *could* be cursed.

Maddie: *Goodbye* Herb. [Whispered] Leo, end the call.

Leo: Thanks, Herb, for calling in.

Maddie: Is he off the line?'

Leo: Yes, when the red light goes off, it means he's off the line.

Maddie: If he starts another curse scare—

Leo: We're still live.

Maddie: [Hurriedly] Okay, so let's talk chocolate. *Cocoa* means, "food of the gods."

Leo: We have another caller.

Maddie: What? I thought you said hardly any—

Leo: Hello, you're on the Paranormal Museum Podcast.

Female Caller: I want to talk about lies.

Maddie: Um, this is the Paranormal Museum Podcast. Tonight, we're talking about the magic of chocolate.

Female Caller: [Laughs] There's no magic to murder.

Maddie: No, I suppose there's nothing magical about what happened to the molinillo owner. I'm sorry, I shouldn't—

Female Caller: I'm not talking about that. [STATIC] I'm talking about Atticus and Tilde.

Maddie: Who is this?

Female Caller: I saved your life. Don't you recognize me? [STATIC]

Maddie: India?

India: They say if you save someone's life, you're responsible for them forever.

Maddie: India, are you all right? You sound, um, distraught.

Leo: She sounds drunk.

Maddie: Shhh! India, where are you?

India: The two people I loved best died because of a lie. Maybe that molinillo of yours really is cursed, because history is repeating itself.

Maddie: India, why don't you call me on my cell phone? We can talk privately.

India: You … know. You saw.

Maddie: I know what? India, call my cell.

India: You know it all. I told you. [BREAKING GLASS]

Maddie: India? Are you okay? Look, I'll call—

[LOUD ELECTRONIC NOISE]

Maddie: GD! Get off the keyboard!

Leo: We lost the connection. Sorry.

Maddie: Okay, I think we're going to have to cut this podcast short.

Leo: We've got a caller. Hi, you're on the Paranormal Museum Podcast.

Maddie: India?

Detective Laurel Hammer: Kosloski!

Maddie: Cut the podcast. Cut the podcast!

———

"What have I told you about interfering with an investigation?" Laurel's voice crackled over Leo's computer.

I leaned toward the microphone. "It's not my fault India called. At least you know she's still alive." I frowned. "Why were you listening to my podcast?"

"Why do you think? Whatever you do, mayhem follows. India Reine said you knew everything. What do you know?"

"Nothing! I don't know what she was talking about."

"What did she mean about history repeating itself?"

Sweating, I unzipped my hoodie. "I'm not sure. She was saying something about a lie? We know Orson was lying about the chocolate."

"Tell her we can give her the audio file," Leo whispered.

"We can give you the audio file," I said.

"Email it." She hung up.

Leo and I stared at each other.

GD meowed.

"At least we know your social media promotion worked," I said weakly.

"I'm not so sure," he said. "Herb is basically stalking the museum. Hammer's probably got our phones tapped—she really hates you. And India … Okay, I don't know why she was listening."

I stilled. Was India tracking me too? "She sounded off, didn't she?" I asked, worried. I also didn't like the way that call had ended. "Like she'd been drinking."

"Or on drugs."

My scalp prickled. That was how Felicitas had died. History couldn't be repeating itself, could it? And the molinillo … Was Herb right? Was it really cursed? I shrugged out of my hoodie. *No such thing as curses. No such thing as curses!* "Has it gotten hot in here?"

"Yeah," Leo said. "It happened during the podcast. I guess the heater finally started working."

"It's always been working," I said grumpily.

On the spirit table, Leo's cell phone rang. He answered. "Yeah? Where ... yeah ... I'll be right there." He hung up. "Sorry, I gotta go."

"Is something wrong?"

"A friend of mine's car broke down. She's stuck on the side of the road."

"She?" In spite of my anxiety, my ears pricked. Leo had never mentioned a girlfriend.

He blushed. "I can't leave her there."

So, she *was* a love interest! "No, of course not. Go." *And then bring her to the museum so I can interrogate her.*

"I'll come in early tomorrow to put this stuff away." He motioned to the equipment on the table.

"I'll put it away. Don't worry about it."

"Thanks." Leo ducked his head and hurried from the Fortune Telling Room.

I shut down the computer and unplugged the cables. Careful not to damage the vintage table, I removed the equipment and hid it under the counter in the main room.

Beneath GD's critical gaze, I fanned out the tarot deck atop the painted spirit table and returned the crystal ball to its place.

Houdini seemed to wink at me from his vintage poster. The room seemed brighter, somehow, almost as if a spell had been broken ...

I chuckled softly. *Broken spells? No way.* I was starting to buy my own ghost stories. If Felicitas Ocasio was at peace, it wasn't because I'd publicized the truth of her murder. I wasn't even sure I had the truth.

Returning to my own computer, I rewrote the molinillo sign with a new story—that both Felicitas and her boyfriend had been killed by drug dealers and the story swept under the carpet due to local "politics." It was just guesswork, but it felt right.

I laminated the paper, punched a hole in the top, and strolled into the Gallery. The molinillo sign I'd put up that afternoon had fallen again to the checkerboard floor. Brow pinching, I whisked it up and hooked the new sign onto the pedestal.

I stared hard at the hook in the pedestal. How had the old sign fallen off? There were no tears or breaks in the laminated sign. It *could* have been knocked off by a passerby, but the museum had been closed today. Only Leo and I had been inside the Gallery.

Unless Felicitas hadn't liked my first version of her story, and had…

Hair prickled my scalp.

Nah.

I thunked my palm on my forehead. Jason had asked me to stick with Leo tonight, and in the excitement of getting raked over the coals by Laurel, I'd forgotten.

Digging in my purse, I found my phone and called Jason.

"This is Detective Slate. Leave a message at the tone. If this is an emergency, call 911." *Beep.*

That was a new greeting. Jason and Laurel now even had matching messages. "Hi, Jason, it's Maddie. Look, something came up, and Leo had to go. I'm leaving the museum now and heading home. Call me when you can."

GD howled.

"All right, all right." I refreshed the cat's food and water, double-checked the locks on the front door, and exited through the bookcase.

The hallway I shared with the tea room was pitch black. I felt my way to the heavy metal door and shoved it open.

The dim silhouettes of garbage bins and my pickup faded into the gloom. I glanced up at Mason's windows. They were dark, and I smiled. He was probably at Belle's, telling her he'd finally broken the news about their wedding.

The metal door clanged shut behind me. "Gagh!" My shoulders twitched. *Calm down, Maddie.*

In the alley, something metallic rattled.

I flattened myself against the cool brick wall and strained my eyes.

A fat shape waddled down the alley. The animal's striped tail waved lazily.

I blew out my breath. Another raccoon.

I hurried, head down, to my pickup. I'd just go home and—

A shape reared up on my left.

I yelped, began to turn. Pain blazed in my skull. The world telescoped to a pinprick and went dark.

TWENTY-NINE

CHOCOLATE.

Its rich, bittersweet scent thickened the air.

A jackhammer banged in my skull. Groggy, I rolled onto my side and promptly threw up.

My arms were pinned behind me. Something hard bit into my wrists. Dazed, I looked around the chocolate storage room. I lay between the sorting table and a pallet laden with canvas bags of cocoa beans. Fake cocoa beans? Through the glass wall, the kitchen gleamed.

I wiped my chin on the shoulder of my hoodie and edged sideways. My butt thumped something soft.

I turned my head, gulping down my breath to stay quiet and not vomit again.

Sam lay sprawled on the wooden floor, his arms outflung, his face slack, his eyes slitted. He wore a zipped-up windbreaker and jeans.

"Hey," I said, hoarse, and nudged him with my knee. "Sam."

He gurgled.

"Wake up." My voice cracked. Fearful, I glanced into the kitchen but could see no one past metal cabinets and work stations.

Sam hadn't knocked me over the head and brought me here. He looked drugged.

So, who had brought me to Reign and why? In spite of what India apparently thought, I didn't have any secret knowledge about the killer.

I rolled to sitting. My wrists burned, the muscles in my arms aching. Gasping, I wriggled experimentally. Whatever pinioned my wrists was hard and sharp. Not metal. Plastic. Zip-ties?

I studied Sam's unbound, unmarked arms. Of the two of us, he had to be the more dangerous. The only reason someone would have left his arms unbound ...

My mouth went dry.

The only reason was to frame him for killing me. If he'd had marks on his wrists like I surely did, it would be clear we both were victims.

The disgruntled ex-employee made a perfect patsy. He had stalked India, picketed the store, been loud about his dislike for anyone and everyone associated with Reign.

I'd known he hadn't dunked me in the pool, and I'd told Jason. But the killer wouldn't know I'd cleared Sam, or that I'd told the cops about it.

I swayed, dizzy.

So why kill *me*? I thought, plaintive.

Cautiously, I raised myself onto my knees and peered through the window, past the metal workstations.

The kitchen was still empty.

I shivered in the chill room. Atticus had done a good job keeping up the facade, spending money to air-condition this room even though there were no real cocoa beans—or no usable ones—inside. But in spite of the cool air, sweat slicked my back.

Keeping low, I staggered to my feet and banged into the sorting table. My hoodie's zipper pinged against the metal edge. I froze at the noise.

When no one came, I rested my foot on Sam's shoulder and shook him lightly.

He groaned but didn't open his eyes.

I shuffled to the door and fumbled behind my back for the knob. My hands slipped on the metal. Finally, I caught it between my fingers and turned it.

Locked.

I muffled a curse. Of course it was locked. Whoever had brought us here wasn't going to make it easy to escape.

A low desk piled with plastic boxes of cocoa beans stood on the opposite side of the sorting table. I hurried to it and awkwardly pulled out the drawers. Maybe there was a knife or pair of scissors or *something*. But all I found were pens and scraps of paper.

No weapon. My hands bound. I was completely helpless. Swallowing my terror, I closed my eyes and took a breath. *Think!*

Dieter had demonstrated an unsuccessful zip-tie escape at the vigil. What had he done?

I closed my eyes, imagining the scene. Adele glowering at Dieter. Mason making awkward conversation. Lola on the gazebo steps holding a cordless mic, and Dieter bent double, beating his wrists against his low back.

I bent and raised my arms as high as I could behind me. Slammed them down.

Pain sparked through my wrists, and I gasped.

The ties remained clasped together.

What had Dieter been doing?

I closed my eyes. Think. *Think.* He'd said something about the ties facing the wrong way. I wriggled them around. Gritting my teeth, I tried again. Failed.

I blinked back tears of mingled pain and frustration. Dieter hadn't managed to free himself either.

I paced the small room, avoiding Sam's limp form.

Dieter had bent over.

I bowed again.

Lola had had a cordless mic at the vigil.

I slammed my wrists onto my lower back.

The firecrackers had gone off by the sound equipment. And then there was the stampede.

I turned the zip-ties so the plastic tab faced toward me. Slammed my wrists onto my low back again.

The ties broke, my arms flying free.

"Oh!" Arms trembling, I sagged against the table and rubbed my reddened wrists.

Where had Lola gotten the cordless mic from? She hadn't been holding it earlier. She must have got it from somewhere, and the logical place was from where all the sound equipment was stacked on that picnic table—where the firecrackers had gone off moments later.

Lola.

Lola who'd pushed me into believing Tilde was a crazed stalker, and then told me Sam was just as bad after Tilde had died.

I frowned. But India had also told me Sam was hanging around too much. India hadn't lied about Sam. But she could have gotten her news from Lola.

I rattled the doorknob again. And ... it was still locked.

But why would Lola kill Atticus? Orson had a better motive for murder—to protect the business. But Lola had the same motive, didn't she? She'd certainly been enjoying the celebrity that came with being married to a star chocolate maker. And the money.

My certainty grew.

Keeping my back toward the wall, I knelt beside Sam and pressed my fingers to his neck. His pulse was weak. Or maybe I was just terrible at checking pulses. But his chest rose and fell, even if his skin was grayish.

There had to be *something* that could get me out of here. I rummaged through the desk drawers a second time. Shifted plastic bins. Looked for a screwdriver. A hammer to break the thick glass. Anything. But I found nothing.

Doubtful, I stared at the glass. Could I jump through it? If it was safety glass, I'd be okay. If it wasn't ...

Tilde had been stabbed through the heart. Lola was a molecular biologist; she would have known exactly where to jam that receipt spike into Tilde's chest. It wasn't conclusive evidence. I could probably find someone's heart. I just didn't think I'd be able to do it quite as efficiently.

If only I had my phone! I patted my pockets, confirming it was gone.

Sam muttered.

"Sam?"

He didn't respond.

Kneeling beside him, I felt the pockets of his windbreaker. They were empty.

Lola had told me she'd been with her husband at Reign when someone had been trying to drown me. But Orson had just asked me some odd questions about that day, as if he suspected … that Lola had lied? Had Orson figured it out? That might explain why he'd gone missing. Either Lola had gotten rid of him too, or he was heading for the hills with India.

Desperation growing, I patted the pockets of Sam's jeans, ran my hands up his chest.

And felt a lump.

I unzipped the windbreaker. An inside pocket!

Hands shaking, I reached inside and pulled out a phone. "Thank God," I whispered.

Crouching low, my hair falling in a wild tangle like a mad woman's, I called Jason.

"This is Detective Hammer," Laurel said, her voice cautious.

"Laurel? I meant to—" Never mind! "It's Maddie," I whispered. "I'm at the chocolate shop."

The glass door rattled behind me, opened.

"Don't move," Lola said.

THIRTY

PRAYING SHE HADN'T SEEN the phone beneath my hair, I slid my hand around the front of my neck. I dropped the phone down my blouse and raised my shaky hands. "You don't have to do this, Lola," I said loudly.

Like Laurel would even care if she could hear me. She'd probably think this was a crank call.

"I'm sorry you got caught up in this," Lola said. "But I've gone too far to stop now. Stand up."

Unsteady, I got to my feet. Sam lay unmoving on the storage room's wooden floor.

"Turn around," she said.

I turned and gulped.

Camel slacks. Ivory turtleneck. A pearl-handled gun. She'd managed to match the weapon to her outfit, I thought hysterically.

"What I still don't understand," I croaked, "is why? Was it the money?" I edged away, my heel scraping the edge of the pallet. *Come on, Laurel. Hear me. Believe this.*

"I couldn't let Atticus ruin our image."

"Your image." My voice quavered.

"Image is everything. Atticus and his stupid principles. If people found out what Orson was doing to the chocolate, it would have ruined us all."

"You mean … the Affaire chocolate? You killed two people to protect your brand?" I asked, incredulous. Good God. Lola really was crazy. There was no way I was talking her out of anything. My fists clenched, my knuckles whitening.

"Do you know how much work I've put into curating my image? You can't outsource authenticity. And if people thought Orson and Atticus weren't authentic artisan chocolate makers, my image would have been ruined. Not to mention all the money it provided."

"Curating …? I thought Atticus was the marketing guy. I thought you were overwhelmed with the job after he died."

"I've always been responsible for our social media."

"Our?" I asked, stalling. Laurel knew where I was. But would she come?

"Orson and me. After all, what's the use of being a happy couple if you don't post photos online?"

"You don't know," I said.

"Don't know what?"

"That Orson and India were having an affair."

She blanched. "What?"

"An affair. I thought for a while that it was why someone killed Atticus, but—"

"You're lying," she hissed, her hazel eyes narrowing.

"No." I shook my head and pain sparked from my neck to my scalp. "I overheard them talking about it. Later I assumed they were talking about Affaire, the chocolate company, but it was one of those Occam's Razor situations. The simplest answer was correct. They admitted it to me."

"No." Lola tossed her blond hair. "You're saying this to throw me off my game. You think I'll kill them instead."

I tasted something sour at the back of my tongue. Had I just made targets of two more people? "Of course not," I said. "It's too late for that. Besides, Orson already suspects you were the one who pushed me into the pool and tried to drown me." He'd seemed so relieved that I hadn't seen anyone at the pool. He must have been glad not to have his suspicions confirmed. "If India dies, he'll know the truth, and I don't think he's as concerned with image as you are."

Her eyes narrowed.

"Were you afraid I'd see the Affaire box and figure out your husband was peddling another company's chocolate as his own?" I continued. "Or did you think that when the police found my body in India's pool, they'd blame her?"

"I knew you'd seen the box, and drowning you seemed too good an opportunity. If the police found you floating in her pool, they'd peg her for Atticus's death." Lola's mouth twisted. "The spouse is always the most likely suspect." She stepped away from the glass door and waggled the gun in my direction. "Now move. Into the kitchen."

Come on, Laurel. Do the right thing!

Feet leaden, I walked through the open door. "It was you who tried to run me down in the alley last week. How did you get Atticus's car?"

"It was parked behind Reign," she said. "The keys were in his desk."

"Were you following me on foot too?"

She grinned. "Once. For fun. You were so funny, creeping around like a cartoon coyote." Her smile faded. "Now head to the melangeurs."

"But why come after me?"

"Are you joking? Do you have any idea how many times people told me about your past adventures in crime solving?"

"They did?" I said faintly.

"And sure enough, there you were, sticking your nose where it didn't belong. So I watched you. It was obvious you wouldn't figure out what I'd done. But when I overheard Tilde calling you, I knew I had to kill her."

Dread weighted my gut. She was going to kill me in front of the melangeurs and dump chocolate on me, like she'd done to Atticus. "But if you thought I was no threat, why bring me here now?"

"Because the entire town assumes you know something. Killing you provides the perfect setup. It will look like Sam killed you because you were onto him. I'll tell the police you were asking about him, and they'll believe you did something stupid. Sam makes an excellent killer, and he could have made a spare key to Reign. I'll leave one in his pocket."

I paused beside the roaster. "Sam will never admit to killing me."

"He won't have to. He'll kill himself, a murder-suicide."

"You've thought of everything," I said heavily. I was running out of stall tactics, and it might not matter anyway. How badly did Laurel hate me? "How did Tilde figure out you killed Atticus?"

Lola pressed the gun into the small of my back. "Tilde knew where the money was really being spent. She was the one who told Atticus about Affaire."

Laurel wasn't coming. A wave of nausea swamped me. "And then what?" I looked around the kitchen for a weapon, a diversion, anything. No handy butcher knives lay on the counters. No pots of boiling water sat heating. "Did she try to blackmail you?"

Lola poked me with the gun. "She wanted to ruin me!"

"I told the police that Sam couldn't have attacked me at India's house."

"You couldn't have. You didn't see who pushed you in, or you would have reported me."

She jammed the gun into my back, hard, and I stumbled forward, my shoes squeaking on the black fatigue mat.

"I drove to Sam's house right after it happened," I said. "He was at home."

"Alone, I'm sure. Not much of an alibi." Her voice dripped with derision. She shoved me forward, closer to the melangeurs. They hummed, melted cocoa swirling inside.

"And his car engine was cold," I said. "I told the police that too."

Another nudge. Another step. I stood beside the melangeurs now. Above them, uneven bricks of chocolate, two inches thick, lined the shelves in thick plastic bags. The metal counter opposite was clear. What kitchen doesn't have a single damn weapon in it?

"India saved me." My voice shook. "She pulled me from the pool and resuscitated me. She wouldn't have had time to save me *and* get rid of the box. The police know that too. That leaves you and Orson. And I don't think Orson's willing to go to jail to protect you. Not when he's in love with India. He always has been in love with her, you know. Atticus may have married her, but she was with Orson first, and he never forgot—"

"Stop it!"

Motion whispered behind me. Instinctively, I jerked away. Something hard struck my shoulder. I grabbed for the shelves above the melangeurs to steady myself. My fingers touched thick plastic.

Gripping a bag, I swung blindly. The heavy chocolate brick connected solidly with Lola's head.

She grunted and collapsed in a tangle of blond hair.

The momentum of the ten-pound brick whirled me around. I staggered into a melangeur. The chocolate brick flew from my hands. The melangeur tipped. Chocolate cascaded to the black mat, splashed across Lola's still form, the gun.

The gun!

I kicked it away. It bounced off a low metal cabinet, skittered across the mat, and came to a halt in front of Laurel's cowgirl boots.

The detective lowered her gun, the muscles in her arms relaxing. "That cat better not be in here."

I pointed at Lola. "She's, uh ... I hit her."

"Yeah. I saw." Laurel holstered her gun beneath her fringed leather jacket. She hurried to Lola, pressed two fingers to her neck.

"You came. I didn't think you'd come."

"Did you think I'd let you die?"

"Those messages—"

"As I told Jason, my damn phone was on the fritz and I didn't know it." She patted Lola down, carefully not meeting my gaze. "What the hell do you want from me? A signed affidavit?"

"No. Thanks. For coming, I mean."

She glared. Then a slow smile spread across her face.

"What?" I asked. "What's wrong?"

My feet heated. Wet. Gooey.

I looked down. I stood in an inch of chocolate. It was seeping into my canvas shoes.

"Nothing," she said, grinning. "Nothing at all."

THIRTY-ONE

"YOUR MOM IS SO going to kill you." Adele curled in my gray-blue wing chair, her stockinged feet resting on a pile of magazines atop the coffee table. Pug snoozed in her lap, his breathing steady and clear.

My mother had been pretty mad. Relieved, but mad when she'd materialized at the chocolate shop in the middle of all those cops. If Jason hadn't agreed to come to dinner next week, I don't know what would have happened.

"Who would have thought chocolate could be so dangerous?" Harper agreed.

"It *was* a ten-pound block," I said.

"Who would have thought you could hit someone with a ten-pound block of chocolate?" Harper asked.

I made a face and reached for a slice of pizza. "I'm not that out of shape. I can lift ten pounds."

"This is the second killer you've disabled with food." Adele stroked her dog and he sighed. "Honestly, it must mean something."

Harper turned her laugh into a cough. "So, what happened to India and Orson?" she asked between mouthfuls.

"The police found them in Vegas."

Adele's feet clunked to the floor and Pug's eyes snapped open. "It's all right, baby," she cooed to him. "Are you telling us they ran off together?"

"According to Jason, India ran off. Orson was worried she might do something crazy, so in a fit of chivalry, he went after her."

Harper snorted. "Right. Chivalry."

"How'd the police find them so fast?" Adele asked. Pug's head dropped to his paws and he closed his eyes, settling in.

"Orson took a picture of his meal at a Vegas hotel and posted it online," I said. "It was location tagged." Which just went to prove that social media was the devil's cocaine. I'd keep using it to promote the museum, but if my face never appeared online, it would be too soon. I pointed at Adele. "And speaking of incriminating photos, why did you really ask me to be your wedding's social media manager?"

"Because I can count on you," Adele said simply. "Formal photographs are great, but people open up to you. I want you to be taking pictures. Unless you'd rather not?"

How could I say no to that? I supposed social media had its good points. "I'd love to."

"What else has Jason told you?" Harper asked.

"Just that Lola's got a great lawyer and is still trying to blame everything on Sam. Sam doesn't remember anything from that night. And certainly not Lola injecting him with propofol."

"Where did she get propofol?" Harper asked.

"Lola studied molecular biology. Apparently she still had access to some chem lab in Sacramento. Her knowledge of biology also made it easier for her to kill Tilde." As I'd suspected, she'd stabbed the accountant in exactly the right spot.

Three times.

I shuddered.

"I thought you said Laurel recorded your conversation with Lola?" Adele asked. "How can she get out of this?"

I shifted in my chair. "No idea. And the police have Lola's cell phone. She snapped a picture of a hugging couple on her way to the picnic table the night of the vigil. It's time-stamped and puts her at the table in time to light the firecrackers and get back to the gazebo for her speech. There were other photos, too, that put her near the scenes of Atticus and Tilde's murders." She'd been so obsessed with curating a perfect online life, she'd ruined her own.

"Tell me about the molinillo," Adele said, changing the subject.

I did. What I knew. What I guessed. But I didn't tell them about the shift in temperature in the museum, the new feeling of lightness in the Gallery. It was the sort of thing I should write up on the museum blog. But some experiences were just too personal.

Harper sighed. "Maybe the truth will set Felicitas free."

"Then I'll have an unhaunted molinillo," I groused. What good was that to the museum?

"But you'll have a great story," Adele said. "It's terrible the damage secrets can cause."

"Right," I said. "Are there any more I should know about?"

"Well…" Adele toed the magazines on the table. "There was one more thing I was hoping you could do at our wedding."

"Oh?" I asked, wary.

"I wondered if you would lead the blessing at the reception. I'd ask Harper, but you know what a pagan she is."

"I am not," Harper laughed. "Mostly."

"I'm kidding," Adele said. "Well? Will you?"

Beads of sweat broke out on my forehead. All my friends, everyone I knew in San Benedetto, would be there, watching.

My community. Offline, in person, and in real life—a life that had nearly been cut short, and that I knew was getting better. The town was healing. Mason and Belle were rebuilding their family. My relationships with Jason, with Adele and Harper, and even with my mom were stronger. Deliver the blessing? I was already blessed, and my heart expanded. "I'll do it."

THE END

ABOUT THE AUTHOR

Kirsten Weiss writes paranormal mysteries, blending her experiences and imagination to create a vivid world of magic and mayhem. She is also the author of the Riga Hayworth series. Follow her on her website at kirstenweiss.com.